MY LIFE FRΩM HΣLL

TELULAH DARLING

TE DA MEDIA / VANCOUVER

Published by Te Da Media, 2014

Library and Archives Canada Cataloguing in Publication

Darling, Tellulah, 1970-, author
    My life from hell / Tellulah Darling.

(The blooming goddess trilogy ; bk. 3)
Issued in print and electronic formats.
ISBN 978-0-9880540-9-7 (pbk.).--ISBN 978-0-9920709-0-8 (epub).--ISBN 978-0-9920709-1-5 (kindle)

    I. Title. II. Series: Darling, Tellulah, 1970-, Blooming goddess trilogy ; bk. 3.

PS8607.A74M93 2014   jC813'.6   C2014-900301-3
                                      C2014-900302-1

Front Cover Design: www.ebooklaunch.com

Sophie's Top Ten List

of

Final Showdown Terrors

10) <u>Getting Stabbed</u>: As a crazed junkie jonsing for magic and blaming me for no longer having her amped up popularity and hotness, Bethany Russo-Hill will once again manage to gut me like a fish. This time with something that causes my accelerated healing powers to fail me, and so this attack will be fatal. Instead of merely bloody, exceedingly painful, and *almost fatal*, like the last one.

9) <u>The premature death of my friends</u>: Unable to break through the wards at the apartment of Hephaestus, God of Fire, Volcanos, and Technology (where I am currently staying) in order to kill me, Zeus and Hades will find a way past the wards at my old school and kill all my friends instead.

8) <u>New deadly foes</u>: Some other wackjob Greek god, who I have not yet met, will decide to show up and wreak havoc and/or try to kill me before the equinox.

7) <u>Old deadly foes</u>: Since it wasn't enough payback that my real mother, Demeter, pretended to be my drunk, adoptive, love-withholding parent Felicia for my entire life, she will make a deal with one of my enemies to somehow screw me over; thus hastening my downfall and death.

6) <u>Not being up to the job</u>: Even though my higher superior goddess power makes me capable of taking out the minions of Hades and Zeus, those gods have an inexhaustible supply of minions. When Zeus and Hades set them full force against me, which they're sure to do in the final battle, I'll be exhausted (and thus dead) before they've really tapped into their stockpile.

5) <u>Kai being an idiot</u>: Kai *won't* show up to perform the love ritual with me on the equinox, thus assuring Zeus and Hades emerge victorious, with more expendable human casualties in their ongoing war. It's totally unfair of Kai to be mad at *me*, Sophie, just because before my human self was even born, my goddess self chose to betray him. Stupidly, I still love that idiot.

4) <u>Kai being a different kind of idiot</u>: Kai *will* show up to perform the love ritual with me on the equinox. But because the stuff that happened with Persephone still hurts him, the ritual won't work, thus assuring Zeus and Hades emerge victorious, with more expendable human casualties in their ongoing war. Insert another Persephone rant here. And some choice words for Kai in the bargain.

3) <u>Me self-destructing</u>: This constant anger I feel since learning that Persephone betrayed both my mother and Kai, my mother pulling me out of Hope Park, and being stabbed and left to die will get the better of me. I'll spontaneously combust in a giant bomb of rage, spewing destruction across a massive blast zone, and ensuring Zeus and Hades emerge victorious etc etc.

2) <u>Fear-of-aftermath affecting my game</u>: Even if I win, what will my future hold? Can I put "saved world" on a college application? If I fulfill my destiny next week, where do I go from there? A *Where Are They Now* pity piece in some Greek god trash rag?

1) <u>Me getting it all so wrong</u>: The prophecy about me being the savior of humanity will be totally off-base and the one about me being an instrument of destruction will nail it. Come spring equinox, I, Sophie Bloom, will personally destroy the Earth and everyone on it. Probably including myself.

Good times.

One

Of all the Prince of Darkness' powers, his best were his bone-melting super-kisses. Which is why, when my boyfriend Kai, (formally known as Kyrillos, son of Hades, Lord of the Underworld) pushed me up against my bedroom wall with a liplock of mind whacking proportions, I didn't do much other than grip his shoulders, try to stay in an upright position, and willingly participate.

But as right as it felt, I also knew that it was very very wrong.

"We have to talk," I gasped as I came up for air.

"Overrated," Kai murmured, nudging his hips up against mine. Instead of talking, he opted for Plan B, which was pretty much a new and improved version of Plan A. His hand clasped the back of my head to pull me closer.

If I pressed myself any harder against him, I'd be behind him.

Maybe that would be a good thing. Then I wouldn't be distracted by things like the way his stupidly gorgeous-lashed eyes fixated on me, their normal espresso brown darkened and full of heat.

Kai shook his head, flinging a wayward lock of dark hair out of his eyes. That just made me want to sink my hands into his hair. And like the most pathetic Pavlovian conditioning, one of my hands snaked up to twine my fingers into the curled ends just below his ears.

His breath caught at my caress.

Kai leaned forward and gave me the most fleeting, teasing kiss, his lips brushing mine. My stomach fluttered at hummingbird speed during that split second of connection.

Kissing, touching; our chemistry was off the scale.

Sadly, so was the weight of our baggage.

Despite the bubbly sensation his kisses gave me, my chest felt heart attack victim tight and I wanted to smack him if only to get him talking. One of us had to be the grown up and put an end to the whole messed up romance.

As much as I knew that intellectually, my body wasn't prepared to agree. My treacherous fingers gripped the front of Kai's blue sweater like a baby with a security blanket, refusing to break contact.

Kai brushed his knuckles along my side. "I miss your curves," he murmured, his lips at my throat.

Over the past few months, I had become a lean, mean fighting machine. My best friend Theo, a.k.a. Prometheus, had me on a crazy training regimen to build up my stamina and strength in preparation for my final showdown with Zeus and Hades.

Which was next Thursday.

Exactly one week from today.

And speaking of said battle …

The fate of the world rested on Kai's and my shoulders, and right now, that was a very unstable place to be. "We can't keep doing …" My voice rose an octave as he nipped at my happy spot in the hollow of my neck. "… this."

I pushed him away, placing my hand on his chest to keep him at arm's length.

Kai shot me a look of pure sorrow. "I know," he said, his voice full of misery. There was a brief pause during which neither of us moved. A pause which would have been the perfect moment to finally—after all the kissing, avoidance, and waaay more kissing—talk about the Persephone-shaped elephant of betrayal in the room.

"Honey, I'm home."

My friend Hephaestus, better known as Festos had returned. His cheerful voice drifted into the guest bedroom of his apartment located in the industrial area in Seattle, where I'd been living for the past couple months. After Bethany had left me stabbed and bleeding on the ground in my school parking lot on that awful night, when Festos had kindly taken me in to heal.

And then kept me because I had nowhere else to go. I couldn't return to school, and not because of Bethany. No, my adoptive, drunk, socialite mother Felicia—a.k.a. Demeter—had made sure to burn that bridge for me but good. She'd wanted me out from under the safety of the wards at the school and back in her clutches.

Guess she'd planned on "convincing" me to honor the original deal between her and Persephone which would let Demeter rule Olympus, after Persephone and Kai took down their fathers on the spring equinox.

Persephone had reneged on that deal. Demeter had murdered her. *Our* relationship was only marginally better. I wasn't giving Mommy Dearest squat. Besides, if she'd been willing to kill Persephone, who she loved, there was no way I was letting her get her hands on *me*, her giant disappointment of a daughter.

"Soph?" Festos was getting closer.

Kai tensed against me. I knew what was coming and grabbed at him, but he was faster than I was. He disappeared.

I screamed in frustration, picked up my desk chair, and threw it across the room. It landed on the plush brown rug with an unsatisfyingly muted thud. I stomped around, swearing with every step. I was madder than a court ordered participant in an anger management course.

Seventeen years ago, the dying spirit of Persephone, Goddess of Spring, was magicked into my newborn Sophie body. A fact of which I'd remained blissfully unaware until last Halloween. That's when a prank I'd pulled on my "frenemy minus the 'fr'", Bethany Russo-Hill, had resulted in a kiss from a bad boy (two guesses who *that* was). The kiss had awakened my goddess identity, and given me a whopper of a responsibility as the Savior of Humanity in the ongoing war between Zeus and Hades here on Earth.

Although I'd gotten Persephone's powers, for the longest time, I didn't get her memories back.

Until that glorious day when I did, in all their Technicolor vividness. That magnificent day when Kai also declared his love for me, and, for a whole freaking hour, I'd felt on top of the world.

Reality is such a bitch.

Later that night we'd learned that, back when Persephone and Kai had been voted "the couple most likely to nauseate everyone with their happy bliss," she had actually been planning to use and betray him.

Kai had walked away from me at that point. And while he hadn't been able to stay away from me, hence the on-going locking of lips, he had refused to talk about it. Just a lot of bottled anger and making out.

Which made me feel both happy and crappy.

Lately though, I seemed stuck in the latter gear.

Festos popped my door open, leaned against the doorframe, and crossed his arms. His left foot was permanently turned inward, and he held the sleek black cane he used in one hand. Although his hair was now bright blue, his jeans were saucily skinny, and his trademark fedora was at as rakish an angle as ever, the blurriness in his eyes belied the sparkiness of his look.

Festos pointed his cane at me accusingly. "Do not *e-ven* tell me that a certain spawn of the Underworld was in your bedroom again, doing lip things that were not talking."

I opened my mouth to lie and deny, but he cut me off, whipping one hand up. "One week, honeybunch.

Do you remember what happens in one week if you and Kyrillos don't sort yourselves out?"

Hot anger rose up inside me and I scratched furiously at the familiar itch on my arms. "Yes!" I snapped. "Our love ritual doesn't work. Hades and Zeus win and humanity bites it. I get it. I'm trying Fee, but—"

"But what? Hmm? His lips are laced with a paralytic that make you unable to converse? You promised me you'd speak to him."

I stared stubbornly at a spot on the opposite wall as my eyes got hot. No way was I going to cry over this.

Again.

I took a deep breath and forced myself to speak to Festos calmly. "Kai won't talk to me. When I push him, he disappears. When I follow him, he blocks me out with wards around his place. What am I supposed to do?"

Festos scowled and banged his cane on the ground. "I don't care but do *something*. Because Prometheus thinks you and Kyrillos have worked things out. And I won't keep being an accomplice in a lie to my boyfriend any longer." With a final glower, he stomped away.

Suitably chastened, I shuffled to my bed and sat down on my heavenly blue comforter. With the exception of a better mattress, I'd furnished Festos' guest room with all of the stuff that I'd had back at my boarding school, Hope Park Progressive.

Festos and Theo had even painted it the same raspberry color that my other best friend Hannah and I had used for our dorm room. I missed being back at Hope Park with her so much. Sometimes I could convince myself that my room here was my room *there*.

If I squinted really hard.

And it was dark.

And Hannah had come to visit.

Thinking of Hannah and that life I could never go back to just made my heart hurt. Like burning razor-blades were systematically and quite thoroughly shredding it apart.

Turn the misery to rage. Use it.

"No," I snapped, "and shut up. We are going to get through this peacefully." Yes, I had become the crazy person talking to the voices in my head.

Okay, one voice. Persephone's.

Ever since I'd gotten her memories back and my life had turned to a massive pile of suck, I'd heard her egging me on. Urging me to wrap my fury around me like a blanket and do unto others with a heap of goddess retribution whoop ass.

I did my best to ignore her. Mostly by obsessing about how hearing her voice meant I was probably going bat-crap crazy. Which was why I hadn't told anyone about it either.

Rationally, I understood that it wasn't literally Persephone talking to me. It was me, channelling my insecurities or neuroses or deep dark fears, and projecting them in her voice.

Didn't make it any less weird though.

I flung out a hand and smacked the button on the CD player docking stand on my bedside table. It was black, thin, and oozing with priciness. Festos loved his tech toys.

Soothing water sounds flowed out of the speakers. I crossed my legs, closed my eyes, and breathed in and out to the sound of waves lapping at the shore. Low flute music accompanied the water.

So relaxing.

So ... blech.

I hated this stuff. I massaged my temples, feeling the beginning of another headache. They'd become pretty constant companions of mine, along with hot itchy arms.

Brilliant.

I breathed through my tension, doing my best to relax my body one muscle at a time from my toes to my scalp; a technique I'd used a lot since I'd learned how Persephone betrayed Kai.

I forced myself to unlock my jaw.

The gentle waves began to crackle. Opening my eyes, I turned my head and hit the side of the speaker with my open palm. The crackling only got louder.

I rocked back and forth. *Oh no. Not again.*

There was a loud *whoosh*.

I scrambled off the bed. Fumbling for the cord, I yanked it out of the wall, unplugging the CD player. Maybe I could stop the vision before it hit me full on.

But it was too late.

I was outside. Ash and smoke blinded me. The burn in the air scratched the back of my throat. I coughed, trying to yell out for help but the fire roared too loudly. Besides, who would hear me?

My stomach clenched hard, practically doubling me over with cold fear and the queasy knowledge that I was all alone on Earth.

I balled my fists, tense against the mocking laughter that I knew was coming. That I was helpless to prevent.

My fault.

I'd failed.

SMACK! "Sophie!" Festos had my shoulders in a death grip; his face inches from mine.

Dazed, the despair of my vision still clinging to me, I touched a hand to my jaw. I felt the blood rushing to warm the spot that Festos had bashed.

"Thanks," I said, my voice cracking. I cleared my throat. "Thanks."

"What the Holy Hell just happened?" he asked. "I walked past and found you standing blank-eyed and shaking in the middle of your room."

I opened my mouth to tell him but the words wouldn't come out. I hadn't told anyone about this disjointed vision I'd been having. I was terrified that saying anything out loud would make it come true. "I think I'm losing it," I told him.

Festos rubbed his index finger over his bottom lip as he studied me.

I tried not to feel like a zoo animal as I stood there fidgeting.

"Talk to me," he said gently.

"I'm having … visions," I muttered, wrapping my arms around myself, utterly self-conscious.

"Visions, huh?" Festos pushed my arms away. He snatched the hem of my black waffle knit shirt and tugged it up to just under my boobs, ignoring my protests.

I glowered at him as he traced the white puckered scar running vertically along the right side of my gut.

"Sometimes extreme trauma can cause a disconnect," he said.

This had been extreme, all right. Despite all the supernatural attacks, the one with the most lasting damage had come from a human. My classmate and long-time nemesis, Bethany, had freaked out when I destroyed the magic tattoo that gave her enhanced popularity. She'd been using it to try to attain global celebrity and push her vapid, dangerous ideas about social status.

I'd stopped her.

She'd stabbed me.

I hadn't died.

Moving on.

I swatted Festos' hand away. "Leave it. What does that have to do with anything?" I pulled my shirt back down to cover the ugly slash.

He slung an arm around me. "How do you feel about tattoos, honeybunch?"

I blinked and thought about it. I'd never considered a tattoo. But I'd always believed that with the right design, there was something empowering about them. Maybe the first step in my straightening out this giant mess involved doing something small to reclaim my body. To feel right within myself again, instead of the slightly off-kilter grossness that had dogged me for the past couple of months. Maybe it was time to turn my pain to power. I nodded. "Tell me more."

He did.

***

Which is how I found myself, an hour later, warily stepping clear of the pine tree that served as my entry point into this stretch of Oregon forest.

I glanced up at the gray, drizzly sky. No evil minions sent courtesy of Zeus or Hades yet, but they were coming. Thus, I hugged the tree trunks as much as possible, hoping my green and brown camo clothing would buy me some cover.

I tucked my egg-shaped sapphire pendant safely back under my puffy winter vest. I didn't *need* to hold onto it, squeezing in rapid pulses when I stepped through trees to travel from point A to point B, but it made me feel better. You try walking into a tree without worrying that you're either going to get a mouthful of bark, a trunk rash makeover or, worse yet, end up all Han Solo-like embedded in wood. Then come back and mock my superstitious rituals around the magic talisman that made the traveling possible.

I stepped over a gnarled root jutting up from the dirt, and began my trek southwest to the tattoo-parlor-in-a-cabin that Festos had sent me to find. He had assured me that getting a tattoo from the Goddess Aglaia, one of the three Greek Graces, had a way of providing clarity in difficult situations. I'd thought it was worth enough of a shot to check it out.

It was slow going. There was no nice path. I hopscotched my way around ferns and rocks and over half-rotted logs. My black boots scuffed along through carpets of fallen pine needles, garnering the occasional mud splatter.

An old compass and sheer determination kept me from getting lost. I would have preferred to come out right in front of the cabin, but Festos had pressed upon me that Aglaia could be touchy. The bigger heads-up I gave her on approach, the better my chances of getting her co-operation.

I wove my way through the sea of trees. Towering Hemlocks, whose spindly branches started dozens of feet above me. Fat, needly, blue-green Cedars. Vine Maples with moss-encrusted branches trailing to the ground in long, lazy arches, tall enough for me to walk under.

The misty light filtering down to me was depressing and gray, and my breath puffed tiny bursts of white in the cold. All in all, it was a fairly classic January day.

Which pissed me off because it was mid-March. Not that you'd know by looking around.

There were no signs of spring. No tiny shoots of tough-leaved Oregon Iris, growing in preparation for its bloom of purple. No rhodos or foxgloves. No buds waiting to unfurl into thick, leathery Madrone leaves.

Nada.

I had a horrible, gut churning suspicion that somehow I was to blame. That this life sucking limbo of our world stemmed directly from how I felt. And I had no idea how to stop it. Thinking happy thoughts hadn't worked. Meditating hadn't worked. A month of plastering my room with photos of the cutest kittens the Net had to offer definitely hadn't worked.

Humanity's savior indeed.

Shouldn't a savior feel more ... capable? I scrambled around an eight-foot-high tangle of moss, fallen trunks, and winding roots, my worries causing the pain in my temples to spike.

I tugged my knit cap down more snugly over my ears, tucking a wayward strand of my dark brown hair back up inside it. Not so much for warmth, since the constant simmer of rage that I couldn't seem to shake off kept me feeling nice and toasty all the time.

More because the low pressure system that didn't seem to want to leave Earth's atmosphere these days felt like it had ground zero'd in my brain. My headache was in full swing. My teeth throbbed; my skull felt like someone had shoved it in a vice and was squeezing slowly. Wearing the fleece-lined cap seemed to help, if only psychologically.

I rested one hand against an oak tree, willing it to bud. "Come on, baby," I coaxed, channelling spring goddess thoughts its way. But its stems remained barren.

My anger at this steadfast lack of spring cranked itself to eleven. My arms started to prickle.

Destroy ... A ribbon of moss green light shot out of each of my palms.

I gritted my teeth and willed my viney brightness inside myself.

With every day, I found it harder to fight the urge to just give in and give 'er. Especially since I had no nice opposite angel voice to steer me the other way.

I took a couple of deep calming breaths, then checked the compass. If I was right, then my destination was very close. This was good because the light was starting to fade and I didn't particularly want to be out here in the dark.

Just up ahead, the trees thinned out and I was able to see more light. Like from a clearing. If there was a cabin, then this is where I'd find it. And most likely any evil minion ambush, too. Viney light powers at the ready, I stepped free of the trees into a large grassy field. Everything was still.

Too still.

Even the cabin—though I was relieved to find that it actually existed—looked tightly shut up, if well-kept. There was no birdsong, no rustle of squirrels running through the grass. Just a lot more gray limbo.

And a rush of wind as the sky above me filled with beings.

Evil minions here to party. Just my luck.

Two

Even though nowadays Zeus and Hades hated me enough to trump their loathing for each other, their cooperation was tentative at best. As evidenced by how the two minion clumps now kept to their own halves of the sky.

I surveyed them with a grim smile.

Olympian Photokia filled the right half. Seven-foot-tall, muscly dudes, they had gold thunderbolt tattoos that snaked over their bald heads. Super cool, yet bad news for me, were their freaky gold glowing eyes that shot lightning.

You know the thing about lightning strikes? You don't build up immunity. Get hit a million times and that million and first is still going to hurt like a mother. I speak from experience.

These Gold Crushers, as I called them, currently shared the sky with Pyrosim. These Underworld Infernorators resembled the guy from that painting "The Scream" except covered in flame, floating off the ground, and with arms that extended into long tentacles to shoot fire.

My anger blanketed me in an itchy warmth. "Kill you now or kill you on the equinox," I called out to them, rubbing the back of my neck to relieve the irritation. "Same same."

I felt Persephone smirk at me. Yeah, that's right. My goddess essence smirked at me and I could feel it. No wonder I was a tad concerned for my mental well-being?

Where's your peace and love now? she taunted.

I hated her. So. Much. Which was probably why I'd turned her into my inner monologue of negativity. I squeezed my eyes tight and shook my head, hoping to clear it. All that did was give the minions some kind of cue to rush me en masse.

Most families yelled at their kids when they got mad. Mine sent hit squads. Greek gods: putting the "diss" in dysfunctional.

Lightening struck. Fire flew. The world around me turned to gold and red. This had become a startlingly normal scenario over the past few months. Amazing what a girl can get used to.

I knocked away a Gold Crusher and an Infernorator with a one-two thwack of my light vines. Very grateful that my light packed a punch.

Most of the Pyrosim were content to focus their attention on the trees around me, transforming them into a river of flaming torches. Each arboreal destruction hit me in the gut like a fist. I was Goddess of Spring, and that made the trees kinda like my babies.

I knew that taking the minions out one-on-one wasn't enough. More trees were burning and a small squadron of Photokia had landed on the ground with a hard *thud* to ring me in. I had to amp up my power level to deal with this attack.

Firing single blasts from my eyes and palms wouldn't put a dent in this mob, so stage three goddess power it was. I shot a full-body shockwave of green light that took out all the minions at once. I hated doing that unless absolutely necessary because it severely depleted me. I'd need large doses of sunlight to recharge and, well, I hadn't really seen the sun in a while.

Minions gone, I surveyed the carnage around me in the fading light. I scratched at my smoking arms, staring at the blazing devastation and feeling more queasy guilt about the impact my existence had on Earth.

I couldn't put out the flames. But I could warn the goddess in the cabin to get out.

As I spun to raise the alarm, something doused me in water. Feeling like one of the animals Noah rejected, I panicked and tried to swim my way through the deluge.

Just as suddenly as the flow had started, it stopped. My cap gone, I flung my wet ringlets out of my face, wiped my eyes uselessly with my soaked sleeve, and did a double-take.

Standing before me was a vision of 1950s pin-up beauty. She was maybe 5'6", looked about my age, with round cheeks, full lips, and straight dark brown hair that fell to her waist.

She sported a large yellow rose over her left ear, the color brilliant against her light brown skin. The rose's blood red tips matched the large garnet ring she wore on her right middle finger. Her short sleeved, button-down shirt of the same red was tucked into her black pencil skirt. Her legs, about a million miles long in her red knee-high boots, were completely tattooed, as were her arms, which right now held some kind of thick, black fire hose aimed directly at me.

I raised my hands as if in surrender. "Normally, I make a better first impression."

She arched an eyebrow. Doubt flickered in her large dark eyes.

"A not-quite-as-bad one?" I amended.

She huffed in annoyance as, with a flutter of her fingers, the hose promptly rolled itself up into a neat coil and nestled against the base of a quaint well, set off to the side of her cabin.

The goddess turned and strode back to her home, heels clicking on the green flagstones that led up to her front door. Her hips sashayed according to their own special laws of gravity.

Careful you don't dislocate something, honey. With a quick look around to make sure the fire was truly out, I hurried after her like a wet dog. "Love your place," I said, trying to redeem myself.

I really did. It was the cutest, gingerbread-colored log cabin imaginable. Like if I was a wicked witch who ate kids and wanted to sucker them in, this would be my impossibly adorable HQ.

The logs were thick and smooth. The roof pitched steeply down the sides, tiled in a light red metal. Red shutters framed the four windows—two upstairs, two down—along the front of the house. To the right of the windows, ten wide-planked steps led up to a red front door, with a circular window inset in the top.

Pin-up chick ignored my compliment, stepped through her front door, and shut it firmly behind her.

Festos was right. The goddess *was* a tad touchy. If there was some kind of *Yelp* page for goddesses, I was so slamming her customer service.

I stomped up the porch and banged on the front door, thinking that Festos better be correct about her tattoos providing clarity, otherwise this was just a giant waste of time.

I pounded on the door again, fully expecting arrows to shoot out and impale me. Surprisingly, the goddess opened it.

"Enough, already." With a wave of her hand, she motioned me inside.

The inside of the cabin felt much larger than the outside. Very TARDISy. I stood in an airy foyer. Knotty planks of dark wood connected this space to the large living room and open kitchen off to one side. The furniture was all 1950s retro, with appliances in that special shade of mint green.

Her entire home smelled of coffee and chocolate. Two scents I could get behind. I liked her a bit more for it.

There was a lot of red and chrome furniture. From the "marbled" laminate table and matching vinyl chairs, to the curved, sectional sofa flanking a matching love seat. Awesome black and white portrait photos hung on the cream-colored walls in dark frames. I recognized Frank Sinatra and Ella Fitzgerald but the old-timey dude with a mustache was a mystery.

"Nikola Tesla," she said, following my gaze. "He's—"

I tore my eyes from the excellent decor to face my hostess. "A scientist guy. Yeah." Props to years of listening to Hannah. "Please tell me you're Aglaia, Goddess of Adornment, Splendor, and Beauty." I was careful to stay on her welcome mat, since I was still filthy.

She scowled. "Who saddles a child with that name? I mean really. There's not even a good nickname. Aggie?" She snorted. "I go by Jennifer."

"As in Lopez?"

"As in a name no one can mispronounce constantly. You know how tiresome that gets?"

O-kay. I held out a hand. "I'm—"

"I know who you are, Hurricane Sophie." She bent down to unzip her boots.

I scratched at my arms and tried not to go with my first impulse to mouth off to her. That didn't tend to go well in terms of getting goddesses on my side. I discounted my second impulse to blast her as well since, you know, same outcome.

This visit had been a gongshow so far. But I needed her help. Maybe the way to salvage things was to match her in cool factor. "Yeah, well, I'm here to get ink done." I said casually.

Jennifer kicked off her boots, then lined them up neatly against the wall. "You're zero for two now, camper. One more strike and you're out." Her eyes narrowed as they swung between me and her front door. "Literally."

Seriously? Now I was mad. As well as smoky, dirty, bleeding, and exhausted. "First off," I said, counting off one index finger against the other, "I'm not the one who started the fire. And given the way you had the fire hose handy, I'm not the only client to bring trouble. Second of all ..." I replayed the last minute, trying to see how I'd offended her. I shook my head. "I got nothing."

Her expression hardened. "You're here to get a tattoo. Not get ink or have a tat done. So you can skip your wannabe urban slang."

Her condescension grated on me. I fixed her with a stare. "I guess a tramp stamp is out of the question?"

Jennifer laughed. Like the action surprised her. "Use the correct terminology next time," she said. "And don't ask me if I sling ink or use a gun either. Treat me and my art with respect. Capisce?"

I nodded. "Capisce. And sorry. I didn't mean any offense." I really didn't. Also, antagonizing the one with the magic needle was never a good game plan.

The goddess eyed me up and down. "You'll need to take a shower first. I've got some of my sister's clothes. They should fit you. Follow me."

I unlaced my boots, slipped out of them, and left them on the mat.

She led me through the living room and down a corridor floored in the same dark wood.

I tried to think clean thoughts and not feel like Pigpen with my cloud of dirt.

Jennifer stopped and flung a door open to reveal a bathroom that could have held its own in a four-star spa.

The walls were a soft, muted green. Gray slate tile covered the floor. The round sink, painted with tiny vines and flowers was cool but the shower was spectacular.

"Whoa," I breathed.

She preened. "I know." She motioned to the tiny stones of green, black and white embedded in the floor and wall of the shower stall. "Hand collected."

It was a wide stall, with no door. You simply stepped onto the rocks and turned to face the six shower heads jutting out from the sleek chrome fixture. I ran my hand over the stones on the wall. "I'm amazed you ever leave."

Jennifer smiled. "Sometimes it's tough. Get clean. I'll bring you some clothes, and when you're done just head right up the stairs." She left.

I peeled off my stinky outfit, turned the jets to full blast hot, and stepped under the spray. Magnificent as the shower was, it didn't stop me feeling jittery with nerves as I made my way up to Jennifer a few minutes later.

I tried to think reassuring thoughts as I climbed the stairs. All was not yet lost. I had until spring equinox and my final showdown against Zeus and Hades to sort all this out. Kai and I were prophesied to defeat them with a love ritual that would combine our powers and allow us to seize control of their minions. *One above one below alive awake a key it is no more it is no more.*

At the moment it was the last bit of that prophecy that concerned me the most. Hopefully, this was the time to find out, once and for all, if Earth and everyone on it would gone by this time next week.

All because of me.

I squinted as I stepped into bright sunshine in Jennifer's upstairs studio. The retro vibe continued up here but instead of portraits, beautiful tattoo designs covered the walls. A massage table and small workstation sat off to one side next to a vintage wooden cabinet painted light yellow. Its two shelves held rows of ink bottles in a rainbow of colors. Below the shelves were a row of drawers, and then two large cupboard doors on the bottom. All with chrome pulls.

Jennifer motioned me over to the massage table. "Are you interested in any of my flash work or are you here for a custom piece?" She waved a hand toward her framed artwork.

"Definitely custom." I wriggled onto the table and lifted the long, soft, green sweater she'd left for me to wear along with a pair of jeans.

She raised her eyebrows. "Nice scar."

"Hoping I could transform it with a bouquet of black roses." I paused. "With really sharp thorns."

"That's not very springlike." The goddess pulled a piece of paper and a black colored pencil from her cabinet drawer. She nudged the drawer shut with her hip.

I let the hem of my sweater fall back down. "It's spring with an edge," I replied, watching her fingers fly as she sketched the flowers. "Like me."

Jennifer made a little moue of distaste. "Well, I'd like the spring who could make my crocuses bloom, not this endlessly depressing nonsense." She nibbled on the end of the pencil before adding a final detail to the drawing. "Think you could get on that?"

I bit my lip.

"Ah." She gave a flicker of a smile. "Which brings us to the real reason you're here. Beyond my fabulous artistic abilities." She held up the picture and I nodded. A simple line drawing of black roses gathered together, thorns turned out, it managed to pulsate with energy.

And project badassery, which worked for me.

At least I hoped it would work for me because, right now, I only projected wussery. I swallowed the bile that rose in my throat at the thought of discussing my visions. "I ..." I shifted my weight on the table. "I'm having these disjointed visions. I'm scared of what they mean, and Festos told me your tattoos offer ... clarity."

"Easy camper," Jennifer soothed. She rose and crossed over to a small table with what looked like a fax machine on it. "Thermal copier," she explained at my confused look. "To make the stencil." She lifted a piece of carbon paper from a pile next to the machine and inserted it carbon side down into the back of the copier. Then she placed the paper with the original drawing face down into the front slot.

"Technically," she continued, "it's not the tattoos themselves that bring clarity. It's the process of being tattooed." She pressed a couple of buttons and with a beep, the copier buzzed to life, pulling the drawing paper and the stencil slowly though. She cocked her head to one side and looked at me. "How do you know it's not just bad dreams from nerves?" she asked, keeping one eye on the copier.

"Because I'm not necessarily asleep when they happen. It's like ..." I tapped my index finger against my lip, as much to get the courage to relive the experience as to figure out how to describe it. "One minute I'm doing whatever. The next I'm not. I'm still here on Earth. But there is no one else. I mean, no one. Anywhere."

Not even Kai. Which was part of what worried me. We were in this together, so why was I flying solo in this vision? I shivered, reliving the hopelessness this vision always brought on. Seeing myself as the only one left. Knowing I must have failed somehow but not being sure of the exact fates of my friends and loved ones.

The beeping of the thermal copier startled me out of my reverie. I raised bleak eyes to Jennifer. "I want to see more. I need to see more. I need to see what happens, exactly. And how to stop it?" *Or stop myself from causing it?*

Jennifer pulled the stencil paper out of the copier and tore the carbon away from the white. She looked at the resulting drawing with a critical eye, then nodded. "Clarity can be a nebulous term. It may only make the situation clearer in a universal kind of way that you won't understand until it's too late. Meantime, it can mess with your head."

"What doesn't these days?"

She gave me a sympathetic smile. "You're sure you want to know more? Because regardless of what you learn, you need to face Zeus and Hades next week."

It no longer surprised me that Greek gods and goddesses I'd never met before knew all about me. I'd hit the Pantheon's radar the second Kai's kiss restored my true identity. Too bad most of them just stayed neutral in all this.

I'd resigned myself to the lack of active assistance. So long as their activities on Earth didn't *harm* humans, we'd just stay out of each other's business and I'd do what I had to.

"If there is any chance that this tattoo helps me avoid fatal mistakes? Absolutely." I rubbed my finger over the leather covering the massage table and blurted out, "Spring isn't coming. I'm terrified that I'm the reason. Because I can't stop feeling so angry and out of control all the time. And maybe it's just one small step between me throwing the world into this weird seasonal limbo and me destroying it altogether."

"I'm supposed to do a love ritual with a guy who is still very, *very* angry at me. Though that doesn't stop him from kissing me all the time. It's a total head trip. Not to mention that various family members want me dead and my goddess self is a constant critical voice in my head." My voice trembled.

Jennifer crossed the room and seized my wrists in her hands. I hadn't even realized I'd been scratching again. "Breathe." The air filled with the calming scent of vanilla. She tilted my face up to look at her. "Forget all that right now. Empty your mind, lie down, and focus on one breath at a time."

I nodded and did as I was told, stretching out on the massage table with a wiggle of my toes. I breathed deep until my heart slowed from foot-stomping-temper-tantrum pounding to impatient-UPS-guy knocking.

Now wearing tight-fitting black latex gloves, Jennifer lifted my shirt. She picked up a spray bottle and the sharp tang of alcohol hit my nose as she misted a paper towel and thoroughly rubbed my skin. She poured some lotion from a pale blue bottle into her palm and applied that. "Stencil Stuff. To help fix the stencil," Jennifer explained.

I squirmed, ticklish.

"Stay still," Jennifer murmured. She placed the drawing against my side, gave it one firm press, and then peeled the stencil paper off, revealing the design outlined in purple against my skin. "Let it dry."

"How big is the needle?" I tracked her movements anxiously as she picked up what looked like a metal pen tube attached to a small steampunkish horseshoe with spools inside it.

"It's not the size, honey, it's what you do with it," Jennifer drawled, fitting a needle into the tube. "Whatever you do, don't hold your breath." She sat down on a stool beside me. A tiny plastic cup filled with black liquid sat on her workstation. "Fainting would be bad."

"I won't pass out. Fall spasming into a vision, possible. But faint? Nah."

"Then allons-y." Jennifer pressed down on a foot pedal. There was a buzz and she touched the needle to my skin.

Three

Fire arced across my body. I stiffened and opened my mouth in a full-on scream. The vision was back, but this time I was able to remind myself that I was safe with Jennifer in her studio. That was something.

Even though I'd never done more than stand still in the vision, this time, I felt compelled to move.

I stepped forward and recoiled as my boot heel hit a toffee-like substance. But broiling. I jerked my foot back and looked down.

The ground was an ocean of molten lava. I stood on the safety of a low, flat rock surrounded by roiling land. I watched in morbid fascination as the surface of the lava cooled slightly, hardened, then broke apart again.

The twin smells of sulphur and burning wood assaulted my nostrils. I threw an arm over my nose to block it out.

As I lifted my eyes from the lava, I realized that the smoke had cleared. For the first time ever, I saw that I was in a garden. Although it wasn't winning any awards. Everything was dead.

Blackened. Twisted.

The ground bubbled ominously in fiery swirls, its dull crackling roar the only sound in this eerie place.

Off to one side was the only living thing. And by living, I mean barely.

It was a pomegranate tree.

Seeing the sickly tree, its branches drooping, leaves scattering to the ground, fruit shriveling and leeched of color, made me wonder. Was the reason that I was all alone not because everyone on Earth had died?

But that I had?

There was the sound of mocking laughter. Deep and rumbling, it rolled across the land like thunder. I wanted to plead with whoever it was to stop but could see no one. Then, as suddenly as it had started, the laughter stopped. A dim chant grew louder and louder until I could make out the words. "Instrument of our destruction. Instrument of our destruction."

Terror clawed at my throat. I spun, desperate to run, desperate to get away, but lava pressed in on all sides.

It was just a vision. It couldn't hurt me. I clung to this thought.

A blare of trumpets drowned out the chanting. Impossibly, I heard John Lennon start to croon that all I needed was love.

Nice thought, but I still wanted out.

I tried to wrench my feet free. But I was stuck fast.

The laughter was back, and it now drowned out the singing as the lava grew in force and rage to lick around my feet.

I realized there was nowhere to go.

I bolted up, disoriented by the light, until Jennifer's wide-eyed stare, and the buzz of the tattoo machine in her hand reminded me where I was.

My skin was flushed and prickly. I had to get out of there. I scrambled off the table and ran, easily outdistancing the sound of her footsteps coming after me.

"Sophie? Hey! Hold up!"

I ignored her. I flew out her front door, leapt off the porch and, clutching my pendent before me like a cross before a vampire, ran straight into the nearest tree, thinking of Festos' place back in Seattle.

I stumbled onto his street with my next step. Racing across the dark road, I ignored the cold damp air that seeped into the borrowed sweater and jeans I still wore. While the area was lively enough during the day, all the businesses in neighboring warehouses were now closed for the night. Alone out here, my imagination zoomed into nightmare overdrive. Fog seemed to press in on me, held at bay only by a couple of not-bright-enough-for-my-liking street lamps.

Although my hands shook like mini-earthquakes, I managed to unbolt the locks on the building's front door and hurry inside. I slammed the door behind me, slumping back against it in relief. Adrenaline still flooded my system. My chest heaved, and I stuffed my hands into my armpits to quell the trembling.

Goosebumps covered my entire body even though the building temperature was warm. It wasn't so much hearing the "instrument of our destruction" chant that was getting to me right now. My friend Cassie, who was a descendent of the original Oracle Cassandra had prophesied that months ago.

I'd chosen to ignore the prophecy. Since they were not guarantees and my alternative was to give up before I'd begun, it had seemed like the right decision. Plus, all the gods I'd met believed Kai and I were the ones who could take on Zeus and Hades, and have a chance of winning.

But after that vision?

I'd just been faced with, at the very least, my own death. More likely, I'd been stranded out there with a pretty solid confirmation that everyone else was also going to die, without me knowing how to stop it. Maybe I was naive or just plain stupid but, until now, I had firmly believed that Kai and I would win. That Hades and Zeus would be defeated, taking Demeter along with them, and leaving humans—me included—to live out long, happy, lives.

A sharp splinter of doom lodged itself in my heart. No matter how I looked at things, I couldn't see a happily-ever-after in all this.

I. Was. Freaked.

I got myself under control as best I could. Got ready to face Theo and Festos. I opened the bronze gate that served as a door for the old cage elevator, squeezed myself in, and pressed four.

The elevator began its slow, grinding ascent with a hum, bumping to a none-too-gentle stop when it reached its destination on the top floor.

Festos had the only apartment on the fourth. In fact, he had the only apartment in the building, keeping the rest of it, which he owned, empty of other tenants—supposedly for safety's sake in the event of unwelcome beings. But I figured it was just an excuse since he tended to irritate easily. Also he wanted as much room as possible to spread out his various metalworking and technological experiments.

I creaked the cage open, stepped out into a small concrete foyer, and opened the door to Festos' place. My home sweet home these days. Much as I'd complained about being shipped off to Hope Park as a child, I couldn't believe how much I missed the place now. Even going to class. I'd been keeping up my coursework through online correspondence but that meant me being 100% self-motivated. And I'd learned I was more the "have teachers ride my butt with deadlines" kind of student.

Also, it was sort of hard to care about high school classes when the fate of the world was on the line.

My body drooped in listless sorrow thinking about how I'd kill to be getting ready for bed check with Hannah and not running back like a scared puppy after I'd experienced a crazy, scalding vision of the end of the world.

Nothing I could do about it. It was what it was. And I was grateful to Festos for taking me in. He was loyal as they came, once you proved yourself. I had, back on a mission to stop Hermes, now a multi-media mogul, from making Bethany famous. Being the best friend of the god he'd been in love with for ages hadn't hurt either.

I saw just how much Festos loved Theo as I slipped through the apartment door and found Fee washing windows. Festos had a lot of areas of expertise as a god.

Housekeeping was not one of them. He'd actually had a cleaning service until about a month ago, when Theo had turned the living room into our war council. Since humans couldn't be made aware of gods and their battles, the service had been cancelled.

Festos had sucked it up with remarkably good grace and only three tantrums as the cool furniture in his hipster pad got shoved aside to make way for a giant conference table, where Theo now sat, sharing space with a large 3D relief map of the final battle site in Eleusis, Greece. The map was marked up with various entry and exit points, and a huge pile of books teetered precariously off the edge of the table next to it.

Large aerial photos of Eleusis were tacked up along the walls, next to whiteboards containing the ritual words, and various possible battle strategies. The room was in total disarray.

As I silently pulled off my dirty socks—I hadn't grabbed my boots in my bat-out-of-hell flight from Jennifer's cabin—I watched Festos clean the floor-to-ceiling windows at the far end, his back to both me and Theo. "You like how zee manservant, keep zee charming view so crystal clear?" Festos asked Theo in a horrible French accent.

At Fee's words, Theo shot his boyfriend a fond smile before returning to whatever dusty tome he was studying. "You're cleaning windows at night. You're an idiot."

Theo was combing through all kinds of ancient texts looking for anything that might give us the edge in this battle. I knew this because I recognized his hunched-over pose. All he'd been doing for the past few weeks was sitting and researching. Yeah, he lived here too now. Which made it very cosy. Theo had been a student with me at Hope Park since grade two—intending to keep an eye on me until I was eighteen and the memory spell around my goddessness lifted. But since Kai's kiss had jumpstarted my powers and Felicia had removed me from school, Theo left as well, in order to stick by my side.

His faith in me was touching.

And upsetting after what I'd seen. Which was why I didn't draw any attention to myself as I came in and saw them.

The incredible normality of the scene helped calm me down and push my fears away.

A bit.

Theo's usual garb of black, long-sleeved T, and baggy skater pants looked more rumpled than usual. He propped his head on one hand, his fingers crushing some of the tiny spikes in his shock of dark hair.

Festos rose up onto his tiptoes to wipe at a spot. "Oui, bien sur. I am an idiot of love, n'est-ce pas? And I clean for zee pleasure of your—Oh, hello, young Sophie." Festos grinned, catching sight of me as he turned to face Theo.

Theo looked over at me and scowled. Not an uncommon occurrence. "Sit." He pointed at the chair beside him, then pushed his black, thick-framed glasses back up his nose in a familiar gesture.

I couldn't face him. Not tonight.

"Magoo," he sighed, reverting to his nickname for me, "now is not the time to be keeping stuff from me."

He was right. Theo was my friend, and my mentor. He absolutely deserved me coming clean.

And I would. I just needed to sort out everything I'd seen in my own head first. "Tomorrow," I promised. I'd tell him everything then.

I walked through the open concept living space toward my bedroom. All I wanted was to curl up and obsess until I finally got so tired that I crashed. Out of the corner of my eye, I saw Theo stand up and I also saw the head shake Festos gave him.

"Tomorrow," Festos murmured.

I went to my room and shut the door.

My first order of business was to see how much of me had actually been tattooed. I pulled up the sweater and glanced down at my side. The answer was none. All I could see was the purple outline of the drawing. No black ink on me anywhere.

Which meant that Jennifer had literally just touched the needle to my skin, and my entire vision had occurred in a split second. Or, more likely, she'd never had a chance to do anything because I really had been convulsing.

Either way, I was untouched.

I wasn't totally disappointed.

I kicked off the jeans. Since the sweater was long enough and soft enough, plus I hadn't done laundry, I crawled into bed wearing it and my underwear. I tucked the comforter around me and hoped that the sun would come out tomorrow. Maybe I'd wake up and all would be glorious warmth with the arrival of spring heralding our good fortune to come.

But I wasn't counting on it.

Which left a whole bunch of hours to think through what I'd seen. I closed my eyes to mentally review the vision. To start, that pomegranate tree better not have been some kind of obvious symbolism about *her*. Because what exactly was the big message then? That Persephone was dying? Gawd, even my visions featured her.

Well, guess what Universe? That chick was history. And maybe whoever or whatever was causing these visions should be more concerned with my mortal Sophie self that was alive and kicking and planning to stay that way.

Except, what if it wasn't the universe or whoever sending this vision to me?

Since prophecies were common to the not-so-mythological Greeks I was descended from, I'd figured that these visions were too. Which is why I'd assumed that these images had been sent to me.

But what if I was generating them myself? From my insecurities and fears, in the same way I'd installed Persephone's voice in my head. Maybe I was trying to give myself a giant wake up call—that I had to put all my issues with Persephone aside, once and for all.

Kai and I *both* did. That could be why he hadn't figured in any of it. I mean, he had that pomegranate tattoo on his back, right? Maybe the tree in my vision was symbolic of him.

Of us.

Maybe the point of all these freaky hallucinations was to press the urgency of Kai and I working things out so that we remained a winning team, instead of two distinct parts that would lose.

Zeus and Hades had been warring against each other on Earth for thousands of years. They caused a lot of destruction and death, usually managing to blame it all on natural disasters. If Kai and I failed to stop them, their attacks on each other might amp up, thereby taking out more humans. Or worse, if they might just decide to harm humans for the spiteful fun of it.

Either way, we needed to defeat them.

I rolled over, mushing my pillow up to a better fluffiness level and resettling myself. I didn't really believe that Kai wouldn't show up to the big battle. He had such a horrible history with his father, Hades, that I knew Kai would do anything to take him down.

I even knew that he still loved me. But Kai's anger might dilute his intentions enough to cause the ritual to fail. And if I continued to enable him by not forcing us to hash this out, well, that would make me just as complicit in our eventual loss.

The thing that really killed me was that I didn't blame Kai for feeling gutted at Persephone's intention to use and betray him. I just didn't think it was fair that I was the one who had to deal with the fallout of his anger toward her. He believed that she was a part of me and technically, he was right.

Still …

Kai was just so damn stubborn.

Two months with both of us being mad, and still unable to keep our hands off each other. If that wasn't messed up, I didn't know what was.

I loved Kai back. Fiercely. I'd just been so scared of losing him that I'd gone along with this pattern, even though it didn't sit right with me. To be honest, I'm not sure who I was more mad at—Kai or myself.

I sighed. Come tomorrow morning, I had to confront Kai. I'd make him yell at me if he needed to. Whatever I had to do to make this wound stop festering.

My eye twitched at the brain—exploding sensation of all this overthinking. Okay, it was the pulsing of my low grade headache. But despite the throbbing, I felt filled with a sense of peace, and the courage to finally confront Kai and sort things out.

Seeing Jennifer *had* given me clarity. With new hope, and a game plan in hand, I fell asleep. Like, passed out cold.

I would have slept in even longer on Friday morning, but a particularly despised sound woke me up. A sound that struck dread into the marrow of my bones. The sound of someone singing, "Happy Birthday."

I squeezed my eyes tighter, flung the covers over my head and rolled over with my back to the door. None of which deterred Festos from tromping in, still singing the damn song.

"We talked about this," I said, my voice muffled.

He waited until he'd ended the final "to you" in a rousing falsetto before he answered me. "You talked. I ignored."

"I hate you," I said. Although it probably came out muted by the covers.

"I have cake."

Hmph. That was tempting.

Somewhat.

I poked my head out from the comforter but didn't look at him. "What flavor?"

"I don't understand the question," he replied. "Is there another flavor besides chocolate?"

"Yes," I heard Theo say. "I like pie."

I rolled over and opened my eyes in time to see Festos shoot Theo a pitying glance. "Well, *you* would. But fun people like cake." He winked at me.

Theo waved him off. "Cake is obvious. Pie is for people with depth."

Festos' idea of a deep response was to stick his tongue out.

Theo grinned. "Way to make my point."

I loved my bickering boys.

"Enough." I motioned Festos closer. "Bring me the frosted confection."

He scooted in, cake outstretched to me like an offering to a god. Smart boy.

It was really fabulous. One of those super sugary chocolate sheet cakes with red icing flowers that hurt my teeth to even think about eating. I grinned in anticipation.

"Make a wish already and blow these puppies out," Festos said, tilting his head at the eighteen lit candles blazing away on top. "The heat is opening my pores and that is *not* a good look for me."

Sitting here, with these two guys who so totally had my back, who so completely loved me, gave me the strength to keep going. No matter what went down when I finally faced Zeus and Hades, I was going to bring my A-game and not let anything get in my way.

I closed my eyes, wished for victory, and blew.

Every single candle went out. The seventeen for my birthday *and* the one for good luck. I took it as a sign. Today was going to be a damn fine day.

I flung off the covers.

Festos winced. "There's only one reason to ever be wearing last night's clothes, honeybunch, and you are far too young to be doing the walk of shame."

Theo winced. "Can we not ever put that image in my head?"

I scrambled into a pair of clean leggings. "Festos, bring cake. Theo, it's time for you to know everything."

"Hallelujah," Theo muttered.

I padded out to the living room, moved the books onto the floor and motioned for Festos to set the cake down. "Get three forks," I instructed.

Theo looked appalled.

I patted his arm. "Consider getting to eat directly from the cake my birthday present from you. I've never gotten to do that. Combined with the fact that I will also be spared Felicia's birthday call of thinly veiled contempt and disappointment, this year I'm the luckiest girl ever."

Well, not really. Which is why I got serious and started talking.

I brought Theo up to date. Where things were with Kai, the visions, the visit to Jennifer, everything that I'd been keeping bottled up inside me. By the time I was finished, it was afternoon. Surprisingly, and more than a tad sickeningly, there wasn't much cake left.

I was exhausted at the end of my tale. Physically, psychologically, psychically—you name it, it had tired me out. Plus I felt slightly queasy from all the fat, sugar, and lack of actual nutrients.

Anxious for Theo's reaction, I nudged his leg under the table with my foot. "Say something."

"Yeah," Festos echoed. Theo hadn't been happy to find out that Festos had known about things between me and Kai.

Theo shook his head at Festos. "You. Don't keep stuff from me," he said with a swat to his boyfriend's shoulder. He turned back to me. "With the exception of you and asshat needing to get past, well, the past, I don't see that we're in any worse a place than we've been since you became a goddess again. In fact, even with all this, we're still better off."

I startled. Didn't expect that. "How so?"

Theo carved off a sliver of dessert and popped it in his mouth, proving that even he wasn't immune to cake. "First, you have all of Persephone's memories back now." He pointed toward the whiteboard containing the words of the ritual. "Second, we know what the ritual is."

He was right about that. Loosely translated, I would say the first line: "I am above." Kai would take the next: "I am below." Except in the Ancient Greek that we had to speak it in, it was more like "I go down," referring to me as the heavenly Persephone descending from Olympus. Kai's line was reversed: "I go up." Then we would link hands and together we would say, "Through our love, are we power. Through our love, are we strength." As if strength came into being because of our love. That kind of thing.

It sounded *much* better in Ancient Greek. And was fraught with all kinds of meaning.

katabaino / anabaino / di'erota, sthenos gignetai / di'erota, menos gignetai

The language part wasn't even a big deal. Theo, Festos, and Kai all spoke Ancient Greek. Even I had gotten that knowledge once I'd regained Persephone's memories. Sadly, I couldn't trot it out much. It's a good thing that I'd remembered what the ritual entailed, though, because with Kai not in a sharing mood, the details of the ceremony certainly hadn't come from him.

Theo continued. "Third, we know that you have to speak it on the spring equinox. Which this year happens this Thursday, March twentieth at 6:57PM Athens time. Six days from now."

I picked up the fat blue mug in front of me and took a sip of English Breakfast tea, heavy milk, heavy sugar. It had gone cold but I drank it anyway. "We also know that Zeus and Hades are going to throw all their minions at us. Seeing how their supply is inexhaustible and we're not, that means timing our arrival on the location in Eleusis to within seconds of having to perform the ritual." I didn't want to have to hold off the minions a millisecond longer than I had to.

Theo shook his head. "Not quite." He patted a slim volume that remained on the table. "There's a bit of a snag. Because of the wards."

A few months ago, Zeus had kidnapped me and held me as his hostage up in Olympus. He drugged me with truth serum and tried to learn the location of the ritual in order to destroy the place. Luckily, I didn't have Persephone's memories back at that point and couldn't tell him anything.

Not that I would have, but he had ways of making me talk.

I'd managed to escape with Kai's help, triggering the start of the Hermes mission—that did actually resulted in said memory return.

To be on the safe side, as we waited the two months for the equinox to come, Theo and Festos had used our blood—mine and Kai's—to ward up the ritual location and keep it out of the big gods' clutches.

"What snag?" A worrisome thought hit me. "Did the wards fail? Can Pops and Hades get to the spot?"

Theo looked at me like he wasn't even going to dignify such a stupid idea with a response.

"You can't just show up, pop behind the wards, and do the ritual," Festos said. His attention was on Theo. There seemed to be some kind of wordless communication between them. Were I to guess, the gist of it would be something like: Festos was mad and Theo was telling him to get over it.

I guess Festos decided he wasn't going to. "The wards have to be down before you two can perform the ritual." He threw an extra glower at Theo, who rolled his eyes. "The spot also has to be cleansed with a brief ceremony to purify it in preparation. Which means at least two minutes of holding off every single minion in existence."

"Eep!" I squeaked out my shock and then glared at Theo. "So I wasn't the only one holding out and not sharing around here."

"First off, I only learned this last night. When you didn't want to talk," he added pointedly.

I crossed my arms. "Yes, well."

"Besides, it won't even be two minutes. Maybe one. One and a half tops. You and Kai will be fine. And I know you'll protect me. I'll take down the wards, cleanse the spot, and you're good to go."

"Theo!" I jumped to my feet. My hands clenched into "throttle him" formation. "There's blind faith and then there's 'did you walk into a bus and suffer brain damages' faith!"

Theo was his usual, matter-of-fact self. "You are destined to be humanity's savior. I staked everything on it. If I can believe it, you will too."

At that, I deflated. Theo *had* staked everything on it. Putting Persephone into my body had cost him his Titan powers. And no one had seen the crone who'd taken them since.

I sat back down and thought this through. I'd really been hoping not to have to take on the minions en masse, but since that was not an option I'd come up with a plan. "Kai can hold his own, but the only way *I* can is if I use my full body shockwave as they come at me. Repeatedly. Which leaves us with two problems. Well, probably only one. If my shockwave didn't take out Zeus, chances are it won't affect Kai."

"Too bad," Theo muttered.

"So sad," Festos agreed. There was zero love lost between those three.

I ignored them and stood up. "Our problem is that I can only fire a single kapow before I need to recharge.

Even if it is a hot sunny day which, if I wanted to bet, I say is 'highly unlikely', even in the sun I'd still need recoup time. So how do I repeatedly use that level of power?" I gathered up the cake, the forks, and my mug, and headed into Festos' open-concept kitchen. All white hi-gloss cabinets and stainless steel counters. I dumped the cake, rinsed everything off, and stuffed it all in the dishwasher.

"Uh, slightly bigger problem," Festos said. "Maximum detonate while Theo is around and you'll kill him. He's human now."

"And capable of taking care of himself," Theo said.

My mouth fell open. "Yikes. I hadn't thought of that."

"Apparently not," Festos snarked. He sighed. "Which is why I will perform the cleansing ritual to purify the area for you."

Theo began to protest, but Festos slapped a hand over his boyfriend's mouth. "Not one word, Thesi. This is non-negotiable."

Theo pulled Festos' hand away.

Commence silent scowling showdown.

I stood in the kitchen, frozen. It was actually kind of scary watching them.

Theo's fingers twitched toward the solid metal chain that was looped from his belt to his wallet. As if he might snap it off and use it to slice through his boyfriend like butter. It was actually the same magic chain that had been used to bind him to a rock after he, still Prometheus, had given mankind fire.

An eagle had come every day to eat his liver as punishment. Yeah, Zeus came up with some real doozies when he got pissed off. My lovely father had also forced Festos to both make the chain and bind Theo with it. That had been quite the setback to Festos getting a second date with Theo.

"Try it," Festos said, uncurling his right hand from his cane. "I made that chain and I will unmake it. And kill you myself if it keeps you safe." Since Festos could unleash a torrent of flame and lava with the flick of a finger, I knew this was no idle threat.

Theo's jaw tightened. "Fine. I won't go."

Festos relaxed. "Good."

Theo leaned over and kissed Festos hard. "If you die, I'll reanimate you and then kill you myself."

Festos batted his lashes, coyly. "I love you too, sweets."

I was so over cute boys and their constant PDA. Okay, not really. But it was my birthday so unless I was the recipient of affection like that, it was time to focus. I let out the breath I'd been holding. "Okey dokey. Now that we've solved the matter of Theo's survival, let's do the same about mine." I picked up a rag and ran it under the tap.

There was silence for a few moments as we all mulled over the problem.

I wiped the counter down as I thought. "Why haven't Zeus and Hades sent all the minions after me at once before now? I would have been exhausted, out of power, and pretty easily killed. Happy them." I leaned my hip against one of the kitchen counters, damp rag in hand as I glanced over at the boys still seated at the table.

Theo shook his head. "Doubt even Zeus and Hades know how much it would deplete them to do that.

They've never done such a thing. What if it weakened one more than the other? What if other gods decided to step in at that point and stage a coup? It wasn't worth the risk for them."

"So they're saving it all up for the big battle," I said. "Makes sense."

"It's also not as much of a risk on the equinox," Theo said, bending over to pick up the books I'd moved from the floor. He set them back down on the table. "If this idea of 'one above' and 'one below' gives you and Kai your greatest power on the equinox, assume the same for them."

I squeezed out the rag and draped it over the faucet. "Lovely."

Festos smacked the table, excitedly. "I think I can help with bringing the sunshine into your life," he said. "I'm just that good."

"Okay, oh modest one," I replied, giving him a playful shove as I returned to the table and sat down. "What's your plan?"

"Light boxes. Like, for depressed people."

I scrunched up my face in confusion. "Explain please."

Festos lit up. He found a pen on the table and began to sketch out a box with what I guessed were rays shooting from it. "People who suffer from Seasonal Affective Disorder use them. Basically, they sit in front of a box and expose themselves to specific wavelengths of light that mimic sunshine. You can use polychromatic polarized light, dichroic lamps, full-spectrum …"

After about ten minutes' worth of detailed explanation, Theo poked him. "Even I'm glazing over, babe."

Theo wrapped his hand around Fee's neck and leaned into him. "And I love when you get all techie."

"Spare me the foreplay," I muttered.

"At least mine talks to me," Festos shot back.

"Ouch."

He leaned over and kissed my cheek. "Anyhoo, I could build you a specially amped up wearable version capable of feeding you all the light you need."

"If it works," I pointed out.

He nodded. "Which is why we commence testing. Also, I may have something up my sleeve that I could quickly doctor."

"See?" Theo said brightly. "All is well in hand."

Theo's belief was so rock solid, it was hard to disagree. Also, I didn't want to. I wanted to face this with optimism and the conviction of my victory. I'd been off my game, but talking this through had helped.

As had the reaffirmation of everything we had going for us. In six more days, we were going to wrest power from Zeus and Hades and stop humans-as-expendables for good. Now, all I had to do was get Kai to talk to me and we'd be peachy.

I shot the boys a grin, as I scratched one arm through my sleeve. "Time to pick a fight with a god."

Four

To my surprise, Festos wasn't a fan of the idea. "Talking to Kai didn't work the last fifty times."

"This isn't talking. It's fighting. And I'll try harder." I started to rise from the table, but Festos pulled me back down in a iron grip.

"It's not about trying harder, honeybunch," he said, as I struggled to break free. "I'm worried about you. You're a mess." His hand snaked out and whipped up my sleeve.

Hot adrenaline flooded my system as Festos revealed my bare arm. I snatched it away, pulling the sleeve back down. "I'm fine."

But it was too late. Theo was staring at my arm in horror. "Soph?" he asked, quietly.

"It's nothing," I said. But I let him push my sleeves up again and examine my arms. Both of which were covered in an angry red rash, made horror show worse by the tons of scratch marks on top. I peered down at them. I'd avoided checking them out too closely up until now. I'd preferred the "deny and rub raw" approach. But even I had to admit they looked like I'd been through some kind of nuclear disaster. "It's a rash," I explained uselessly.

"I see that," Theo replied. "From what?"

Festos looked at him like he was nuts. "Really, Thesi? From this. All the stress she's been under." He shook his head. "If that's on your outside, I hate to think what your insides are like."

My insides were confused, angry, and seemed to have put spring on hold. But all I said was, "I could put some Calamine lotion on them."

Festos snorted. "Unless you're gonna brine your arms in a barrel of it for a few days, I'm doubting that's the fix. Why not take one night off? Get out and blow off steam. Actually enjoy yourself. You can talk to Kai tomorrow."

I raised an eyebrow. "At which point we'll have five days until I face Zeus and Hades. What if I have to sit outside Kai's door for two days until he opens up, huh? The clock is ticking here."

Festos cocked his head and looked at me. "What if I could guarantee that he'd speak to you? Tomorrow. Would you let me get you out of your head for one night?"

I stood up, more than ready to end this ridiculous conversation and get back to working on Kai. "How are you going to do that, Miracle Max?"

Festos and Theo did more of that wordless communication thing. It was highly annoying.

Festos looked at Theo. "It's her birthday," he said.

More meaningful glances with zero explanation.

I threw my hands up, turned, and walked toward to my room.

"Magoo," Theo called out after me before I'd gotten far.

I stopped and half-turned back. "What?"

"He's right. Celebrate your birthday tonight, like any other seventeen-year-old. It'll do more good than harm. Tomorrow we'll amp up with a vengeance. All of us. Including Kai."

I exhaled heavily. Then weighed the pros and cons. On one hand, I was very aware of how little time we had left. On the other, if Festos could guarantee that Kai would speak to me tomorrow, that would make the whole "putting the past behind us" process much much easier.

I scratched at my arms, then growled as I caught myself. Fee was right. I was a mess. Meditation hadn't worked. Focusing on what lay ahead hadn't either. And I *had* read about soldiers playing paintball to blow off steam, pump up adrenaline, let go of anger, and generally bond. Which would be perfect. "We could play paintball," I suggested.

"We could not," Festos replied, aghast. "Get ready to shake your booty, because we're dressing you up and taking you to the most exclusive club in the universe."

Nyx?" Theo groaned.

"Nyx," Festos confirmed, beaming at me. "It's going to blow your mind."

***

Two hours later I wanted to blow my brains out. Did that count?

You're going to be a laughingstock. That little pep talk

51

was the fifth one of its kind I'd heard in the past little while. Persephone's voice-in-my-head was on a roll, creatively magnifying all sorts of deep-seated insecurities. The fact that I'd already tried on every outfit I owned and failed to feel fabulous in any of them so did not help the situation.

Not to mention, Festos met each new ensemble with a variety of "ick" faces. He allowed me a dinner break without letting up on his constant chattering criticism of my utterly lacking fashion sense.

"Don't you have anything a little less … teen prom?" he asked, staring doubtfully at my latest pairing of a blue strappy number with a pouffy skirt. Over top of which, I'd added a red cardigan, since I was super self-conscious about my arms.

"My wardrobe is fine," I snapped. "I was a student. Not a club kid." I perked up as I heard Theo call out, "Incoming with Saul." Saul was his nickname for Hannah.

I grinned, pushed away from the table and skipped over to her. The two of us burst into gleeful shrieks while jumping up and down holding hands. Yup, totally channeling our inner eleven-year-olds here.

It had been almost a month since we'd seen each other. For the two of us, having grown up at boarding school together, that felt magnified by dog years. Students weren't allowed cell phones at Hope Park, and our Skype time had been limited. Seeing Hannah now? It was like having my other half back with me.

A piercing whistle cut through the noise of our reunion.

We glanced at Theo, whose arms were laden with dresses. "Where do you want these?"

Hannah and I exchanged a wordless look, in which we communicated an entire pros and cons discussion of leaving the clothes in the living room versus the bathroom versus the bedroom.

"Bedroom," we said in unison.

I felt somewhat smug that I had a silent psychic buddy, too.

Theo dutifully headed off with everything.

Hannah enveloped me in a giant hug. "Happy birthday, Kitten." Her eyebrows rose as her hand brushed my bicep. She gave it a squeeze. "And hello, Warrior Princess."

I flexed for her as we broke apart. "Me of all people, right?"

"We live in strange times," she said gravely.

"Yeah, yeah. Enough chit chat. More presents for pretty girls," I said.

She waved me off. "Later. Maybe."

I was *so* getting a present.

I held Hannah at arms' length to take her in. Being tall, blonde, and beautiful meant that she could wear a potato sack and be dressed to kill. Thing is, Hannah was a huge science geek who until recently, had preferred jeans and corny science pun T-shirts. Then she'd met and started dating Pierce, a.k.a Eros, the God of Love. Shockingly, she'd started dressing like a girl soon afterward. A very hot girl.

"You look even more disgustingly gorgeous than usual," I said.

"I know," she replied without an ounce of modesty. "Check out the attire." She ran a hand along her body. Her outfit consisted of a short, flowy, strapless babydoll dress with a sweetheart neckline, all in the palest gold. Her blonde hair was pulled back into a sleek ponytail and she wore the funky, hammered gold hoops I'd bought her for her sixteenth birthday.

I nodded. "Perfect 'get past the velvet rope and all you losers be damned' look."

Hannah exhaled hard. "Oh good. I was worried I was being too subtle."

I laughed and twirled my finger in the international sign for "turn around and let me check you out from the rear." She obliged. The back of her dress had a fat band across her shoulder blades, with a wide cut out section underneath. Strappy gold heels completed the hotness.

Festos gave her a wolf whistle. "I could turn straight for that."

Theo chuckled as he returned from my bedroom, his arms now empty. "You can't even draw straight."

Festos was right, though. Hannah looked amazing. But more than that, she glowed with happiness. She was a total goner in love with Pierce.

And I was really glad for her.

For the first hour she spent talking about him anyway. Then I wanted to shove my bestest friend out my bedroom window. Because, hello? She was dating the God of Love. Dude was the most romantic guy in the history of the universe. No date night of Playstation and a pizza. Nope, his latest escapade had involved taking her on a midnight picnic at some ancient ruins on a beach. Not what I wanted to hear right now.

Hannah zipped me into a little red number. "... Then," she continued, "I decided to come home for spring break this week since dad is tied up with a big case, which meant I'd have a ton of unsupervised time with Pierce." She half-sighed, half-giggled (who was this alien?) while I tried not to gag.

I nodded for her to continue as I made my way to my mirror.

"Guess what Pierce did on my first night home?"

I crossed my fingers and wished for *got violently ill with stomach cramps and couldn't see you for a while.* "I can't imagine," I murmured, pasting on a smile that I fully expected Hannah to expose as the fake it was.

She didn't even notice. She was too busy gushing. "He took me to Paraguay to meet these melanistic jaguars—"

"English, Pumpkin." I studied my reflection. The evil Persephone voice in my head laughed. I looked like a kid playing dress up in her slutty older sister's clothes.

Brilliant.

"Black panthers that he'd made fall in love. They let me pet their baby cub." Hannah's eyes gleamed fervently. Forget drugs, this girl's passion for dangerous wildlife was her addiction of choice. And Pierce had found the most impossibly perfect gift anyone could give her.

"Oh, he's good," I replied, fumbling for the zipper to better rip the depressing fashion abomination from my body.

She blinked at me. "Huh?" Her expression turned soft and gooey. "Ooh. Look at that."

I stepped out of the dress as I followed her gaze to where a little gray fluffball of a bird with a long tail sat outside on my window ledge.

"It's a Bushtit," Hannah said.

At her approach, the bird with the unfortunate name burst into song. Then its friend showed up and, I swear, they serenaded her. We were a millisecond away from a Disney moment with Hannarella trilling a tune with her woodland friends while I played Cruella De Vil in the corner, chain smoking and wearing coats made of puppies.

Freaking. Hell.

I strode to the window and banged on it. "Get lost."

The birds squawked angrily at me and flew off. "Thank God." I gave a sardonic laugh. "Which one of them, am I thanking exactly? Do I get to pick ..." I trailed off, spotting Hannah's "WTF is wrong with you?" look.

I shrugged and started to rifle through the rest of the dresses that she'd brought. I didn't realize I was scratching again until Hannah spoke.

"Why haven't you told me what's been going on with you?" She did not sound impressed.

I stilled, crumpling the dress in my hands. "Uh, you've been busy?"

She tugged the outfit away from me. "Seriously?"

That got my back up. "You have. Between your midterms, and Pierce, and me being here, we haven't had much of a chance to talk." Yes, there was a smidge of pity party in my tone of voice. It would have been nice if she'd found a moment or two in her perfect teen life to spare for me.

"I call BS. You're avoiding me so you don't have to fess up." She bestowed one of her patented gray-eyed glowers of death on me as she ticked off items on her fingers. "Headaches, horrible rash, throw in hair loss and your stress trifecta will be perfect."

"Sounds to me like your intel is already complete."

She wasn't letting up. "Assume I want to hear about it from the source. And apparently, I'm waaay behind on what's going on with Kai."

"Tonight's my happy night," I replied blandly. "Talk to me tomorrow." I picked up a copper colored dress and held it against me.

She cocked her head before giving it a definitive shake. "No. Washes you out. And if you won't talk about Kai then let's talk about how it's the middle of March but sure doesn't feel that way."

I scratched my right arm like mad as I reached for the bottle of Midol on my dresser. A dull throb had set up samba hour in my head. Damn childproof caps. I couldn't scratch and pop it at the same time. Frustrated, I snarled and tried to bite the thing off.

Hannah droned on. "… Weather patterns aren't right. It's too cold to plant anything, which is going to mean havoc for food supplies." She listed off several more global issues. My personal bad news report.

My palms tingled as my light vines tried to come out. *Some friend*, Persephone taunted.

With supreme will power, I dissipated my light and tightened my hold on the bottle of Midol, staring at the wall, until I was able to calm myself down and face her again. I cut her off. "Do you think I don't know all that, Pumpkin?" Finally, I got the cap off like a normal person, shook a couple pills directly into my mouth, and dry-swallowed them.

Hannah's face fell. "I'm scared for you," she whispered.

I set the bottle back down. I was going to lie but my eyes filled with tears, blowing a perfectly good strategy. "I'm scared for me too."

And that little admission broke me.

I'd tried so hard to keep a lid on my feelings. Keep everything going, and move forward with my eye on the prize. Ignore or deny whatever wasn't working, and focus on taking down Zeus and Hades. I checked the wards, and practiced the ritual. Not to mention all the physical training Theo had me doing, and the constant meditation to keep me all zen.

I'd been stressed, I'd been angry, and while I had to admit my iron will hadn't been all that strong given the rashes and headaches, I'd never felt the overwhelming panic that swamped me now. I started bawling. It was impressive. Giant snotty tears, body racking sobs, chest tightening anxiety, and through it all, Hannah hugged me tight, stroking my hair.

I cried out my fears that I would hurt Earth before I had a chance to save it, and that, when push came to shove, I didn't have the stuff of heroes. I cried out my heartbreak, finally admitting that my lifelong dream of having a mom who loved me and wanted me, was dead.

I wept for Kai and me, having gone so wrong when we

should have been so flush-with-new-love right. I mourned the fact that I'd somehow become that girl I'd always mocked; the girl that, six months ago, I would have smacked upside the head and told to get some pride and some backbone because she deserved better. I had settled because, in the face of everything else that had happened with my family, I was clinging to whatever love crumbs I could get.

And finally, I cried for my death. Which might sound weird, but was oddly freeing. Even if I went into this final battle with all the odds on my side, something could go wrong. Dying was a very real possibility. So I let myself feel that death. Grieve the end of my existence.

Once I'd done all that and still come out the other side, I felt better.

Plus, eventually, I ran out of salt water.

I snagged a tissue from my bedside table to blot my tears, then turned red, puffy eyes to Hannah. "Thanks."

She shrugged off my gratitude and gently brushed away a lock of hair that had plastered itself to my forehead. Then she reached for the gold beaded evening bag that she'd thrown on my bed. She rummaged around for a moment before pulling out a small box in purple wrap, and tied with a gold bow. "Happy birthday, Soph."

I unwrapped it, swiping at my still damp eyes with another tissue but eager to see the gift inside. Hannah and I had a tradition of giving each other cute jewelry for birthdays. "Whoa," I said, as I lifted the cover of the box.

Nestled inside, against the black velvet lining was a wide silver wrist cuff made up of interlacing vines and leaves. "It's gorgeous." I pulled it out, staring at it in wonder.

She took the bracelet from me and fitted it onto my right wrist. The weight felt comforting. "It's to remind you that you're the kick-ass Goddess of Spring. But mostly you're my best friend."

Girly hormone central. Apparently, I did have more tears left. And Hannah had to catch up.

Festos tromped in, pushing between us. "Ew! I am not having my arm candy looking like allergy sufferers. We have a birthday fête to attend." He pointed out the door. "Now get a hold of yourselves, go to the bathroom, and splash cold water on your faces. There is no crying in clubland."

At which point Hannah and I sandwich hugged him, getting tears all over Festos, too. "Aw, man." He complained, but his arms came around both of us, so we knew he didn't really mean it.

The night picked up from there. The flood I'd let loose made me feel loads better. My Midol kicked in, too, and we managed to find a long-sleeved dress that really made me look good. Finally, it was on to finishing touches. I leaned back against the bathroom counter, holding still as Theo put smoky eye makeup on me. "Do I want to know why you're so good at this?" I asked, as he expertly smudged the corners.

"Nope."

"Thesi used to wear eyeliner all the time," Festos said, watching the proceedings.

My mouth fell open and I jerked my head to Hannah,

totally incredulous. She stared back at me from her seat on the edge of the tub, her expression identical.

"You lie," Hannah accused Festos.

"Swear on the Styx," Festos replied, giving the sacred oath of the gods.

"And you kept this from us?" Hannah asked Theo.

"I wasn't going to wear eyeliner at Hope Park. Our school isn't that progressive. And thanks for moving your head," he groused. "Now I've got to do it over."

"But I could have been watching you wear it since we've been at Fee's," I protested as he clasped my chin in his hand to keep me still so he could fix his work.

"You get enough pervy thrills voyeuring when Festos and me kiss. I'm not encouraging any other kinks of yours."

Hannah cocked an eyebrow. "They been kissing much?"

Festos nodded enthusiastically before I could answer. "Tons."

Theo let go of my chin, stepped back, and looked at me for a moment. "We're good," he said and checked me over again. "Nyx good."

Fee squealed and turned me around to face the mirror. Staring back at me was a really hot stranger with whom I was quite willing to get more familiar. My eyes were huge and all mysterious. My royal blue dress was crazy scandalous. For me. The long sleeved top was loose and blousy, but it turned into an über-tight mini skirt at the hips. While the neckline in front was high, the back plunged down to my waist. There was no bra-wearing tonight.

Hannah had helped paint my nails and toes a matching blue, and I wore very low heeled silver sandals since I wanted to be able to dance. With all the running and weight training to amp my strength and stamina, my legs looked crazy sexy.

I wore my hair down, the loose curls tumbling to my shoulders in the best sultry bedhead imaginable. My only jewelry was Hannah's silver cuff over the top of my right sleeve. And of course my sapphire pendent, which I never took off. I had the pendent tucked under my dress. Shimmery lip gloss completed my va-va-voomness.

"I love it!" I clapped my hands in delight and beamed at my friends. "Seriously, you guys. Thank you so much. For everything. I really did need this. Need all of you."

They shrugged it off in varying degrees of modesty, except for Fee who announced, "D'uh. That's why I suggested it."

I flung my arm around his neck. "Okay hot bunch, let's dance, drink, and be merry for tomorrow—"

Theo cut me off with a shake of his head. "Don't even finish that bad paraphrase." He left the room.

We waited with Festos in the living room while Theo got dressed. Festos rocked a kind of retro 80s London vibe. He wore dark green slightly baggy pants that were a bit long through the crotch and rolled up at the ankle, revealing black wool socks and matte shoes. His shirt was the same green as his pants, topped with a short fitted charcoal jacket, and matching scarf.

He'd rolled the cuffs of both his shirt and jacket back in a jaunty "couldn't care less" kind of way and topped his blue hair with a fedora that matched the color and fabric of his jacket.

"Admire me all you like, kiddies," he encouraged from his sprawled out pose on the low red leather love seat.

We did, until we saw Festos bolt up, and turned to see what he was gawking at. My breath caught. "Hannah, I'm feeling wrong feelings."

"Indeed," she murmured.

Even the eye roll Theo shot us could not detract from the uncomfortable reality of how amazingly GQ incredible he looked.

He sported a black skinny suit thrown on over a black striped tone-on-tone T-shirt. He'd lost his glasses for the night and slicked down his usually dark spiky hair. Very *Mad Men*.

I'd seen Theo in suits before. Most recently at our school's Winter Formal. And he'd looked very handsome. But more "good boy for cleaning up so nicely and even buttoning up your collar." Nothing like this. Looking at Theo right now, so sleek and tailored, I realized this was the first time I'd seen him with some confident swagger.

I'd seen many sides of my friend; snarky, annoyed, loyal, and sadly—lately—far too serious. But Theo had never given off that vibe of supreme conviction that I was used to from other gods. An arrogant sense of self. Which made me wonder what he'd been like as Prometheus. And how much he'd tempered his personality to better fit in as a human. Being around Festos, maybe Theo was showing his true colors.

And those colors ran the full spectrum of man-candy edible.

I swallowed hard. Twice. And continued to stare dumbly at him.

"You never looked like this for us," Hannah sputtered.

By this point, Festos had limped over to Theo. He smoothed a lapel down and gazed at his boyfriend. "This one's all mine."

Hannah cocked her head toward the handsome couple. "Real hardship living with that," she said to me.

"I despair," Theo said as he grinned across the room at us. He took Festos' hand. Hannah and I took that cue to also link ourselves to Festos, and in the blink of an eye, we'd left Seattle behind as he transported us away.

Almost immediately, we found ourselves outside, under a starless night sky. Before us lay a black infinity pool full of flat rocks that pulsed with a gentle light. The rocks marked a path toward, well, even more darkness.

"You're sure this is the right place?" I asked.

"Oh, ye of little faith," Festos said. "Come."

Festos jumped from rock to rock across the pond with surprising agility, given his twisted foot and the fact that he'd left his cane at home.

The stones didn't sway at all but I was still glad I'd worn low heels as I made my way across. I yelped as I saw something slither in the water, rippling the still surface.

Theo glanced down. "A little something for unwanted guests."

Even though I was apparently worthy of attending Nyx, I reached the ground on the far side with a sigh of relief. Now that I was up close, I realized I'd been completely mistaken about the darkness ahead. There wasn't just night before me. More like an absence of everything, woven into a pulsating barrier.

"Yeah, so that's creepy." I craned my neck up, attempting—and failing—to see where the barrier ended. I looked down and scanned the section in front of me. There didn't seem to be a door or a gate. "How do we get in?"

I poked gingerly at the barrier, felt the energy pouring off whatever it was, and decided I really didn't want to be touching it after all. I tried to pull my hand away.

But I was stuck fast.

And that's when the barrier pulsated outwards and slithered over my arm.

Five

I shrieked, trying to tug myself free with all my might. Festos sighed and placed his palm against the barrier.

I shivered involuntarily but it didn't rip his hand off. Instead, threadlike strands of fiery purple and orange seemed to swim up from the depths of the barrier and wriggle their way toward Festos. The strands merged to form a glowing "N" under his palm.

I was able suddenly to pull my hand away.

Hannah gasped.

"Such theatrics," Theo said.

"I know," said Festos with a saucy grin, choosing *not* to interpret Theo's comment as a slight. Part of the wall slid noiselessly away to admit us, and just like that we were through.

The space beyond was filled with people. I stepped inside, bouncing on my toes in wonder.

"I get to say 'I told you so' now, right?" Festos sounded smug.

"I'll give you this one," I replied, half-turning, unsure

of where to ogle first. "Membership does indeed have its privileges."

I'd expected some kind of posh building. But no, we stood on the top level of a colosseum. Very much like the one found in Rome, including, I guessed, its size. The one obvious difference was that this space was set down into the earth, rather than sitting on top of it. So while I was on the fourth floor of the ringed arena, I was on ground level. I could see all the floors below me, sloping down and away, since the inner walls were only about waist high and topped with railings.

And this colosseum had a roof. The outside wall on the top tier curved up into a ceiling with a tiled pattern—thousands of white, dark purple, and lavender tiles, all seemingly lit from within. As I stared up, some tiles got brighter while others dimmed. I found myself getting lost in the trippiness of it all.

Theo waved a hand in front of my face. "Look at something else for a bit. You're swaying."

I *was* getting a little dazed so I turned my attention to the four levels. Through the archways ringing each tier, I saw that every level boasted a multitude of cozy seating areas in sleek, dark groupings. Balls of light—not flame, not torches, just golden balls of light—were mounted every few feet along the walls. They gave the impression of millions of candles, adding a much needed intimacy to the cavernous space. So did the oases of greenery centered around the flowing water features, that dotted each floor.

The electronica that played through invisible-yet-perfectly calibrated speakers grabbed me in my gut and in my hips, making me want to abandon myself to swaying sensuality. But the music took second place to the clientele. Gods, goddesses, demigods—this was the place for the Greek pantheon to see and be seen. Everyone looked young and beautiful in a way that mere airbrushed mortals could only fantasize about.

It wasn't all human forms either. I saw centaurs chatting up daemonae, and on the floor below, a siren held court amidst male and female admirers.

"Interspecies," said Hannah, her eyes gleaming, "very nice."

The waitresses were all nymphs with slender flowing bodies clad in seaweed, river pebbles, or leaves. Yet the flora these girls sported could have upstaged any Paris couture on the catwalk.

Silk dancers performed aerial ballets high above the dance floor. They spun and arced from billowing ribbons of silver and gold, like acrobats in Cirque du Soleil.

I squinted, my head tilted upward, trying to see what the silks were attached to. The answer, I saw was nothing. The silks were actually gossamer wings that sprouted from the dancers' backs.

"It's so beautiful," I sighed.

Hannah nudged me. "Check out the dance floor."

I leaned slightly over the railing and gazed toward the bottom level. The floor was packed with bodies jammed so tightly together that they appeared to be moving as one. Even from this top level, I could see the ecstatic expressions.

"They're all relatively human size," Hannah said.

"We're on Earth," Festos said, like it was the most obvious explanation in the world.

We were quiet for a little while. Lost in the music. Then, there was a voice beside me.

"My favorite patrons. Welcome."

My head swiveled around. All this gawking was quite the workout.

Beside me stood an androgynous figure that was definitely not human. It was slightly too tall, and its eyes gleamed yellow in its ebony skin. Its fitted black shirt and slacks did nothing to help me guess the gender. Neither did its close-cropped hair, dyed platinum blonde.

I felt both a centeredness and great power coming off it, so figured it was probably a god of some sort.

The being embraced both Theo and Festos warmly.

"Nyx!" Festos leaned in to kiss both cheeks.

This was Nyx? Goddess of Night and successful club owner?

Nyx read my face and gave me an amused smile. "Do not assume all goddesses come in the same flavor, little one." Her gaze swept slowly over me. "Hmm."

My eyes narrowed as I stared her down. Or rather up, since she towered over me. "Yes?" I said.

She cocked one perfect eyebrow. Perfectly. "A lot of chatter over you. I was not sure what to expect."

I shrugged. "Most don't."

"It appears much of the rumor is true."

"Probably, more is false."

Her smile grew genuine. "Enjoy yourself, Sophie. And welcome, finally, to Nyx."

With a sweeping bow, she left us.

I watched her go, puzzled. "Why finally?"

Festos made a face. "Persephone wouldn't be caught dead with this riff raff."

Her loss. Happily, I had better taste.

But no hearing, since with a delighted shriek, Hannah flung herself happily into her boyfriend's arms and shattered my eardrums. "Pierce!" she squealed.

I tried not to gape at his appearance like a slack-jawed yokel but I wasn't entirely successful.

Hannah turned to me with a raised eyebrow. "Something you want to say, Kitten?"

Yes. If I'd been capable of speech.

I was used to Pierce looking like he belonged in an Abercrombie catalogue what with his tousled sun-kissed hair, and amazing green eyes. But this was club porn. He wore slouchy jeans in the same pale gold as Hannah's dress. Giant gold wings extended from his back. Two bands of brown striped each one. And every feather was long and full. I tried very hard not to make inappropriate comparisons.

Festos shot me a smirk, so I knew that my smut-mind had company.

While the wings were definitely impressive, his chest was a masterpiece.

For starters, it was bare.

And ripped. Holy crap was he ripped. Compelled like a moth to a flame, I reached out a finger to touch his abs, but Hannah smacked my hand away before I could reach them. I shook it to take away the sting. "Possessive much?"

"Next time you lose the whole arm. And that's just because I love you."

"Yeah," Pierce said in the sexy British accent that moved his whole vibe into stratospherically hot territory. "You should see her around girls she doesn't like." He grinned, and I could see that it didn't bother him at all.

"It's time to dance," Festos announced.

Hannah waved him off. "You guys go." She stared dreamily at Pierce, her hand on his rock hard belly. "We're going to go sit and chat."

"Nice euphemism," I teased. I didn't begrudge her much because, well, most breathing females, and more than a few males, would want to euphemistically chat with Pierce too. All night if possible. But I couldn't help feeling a little hurt. It was my birthday. She didn't have to third-wheel dump me so blatantly.

"We'll catch up with you soon," she promised with a breezy wave.

Theo caught my hand before I scratched more than a couple of times "Come on, Magoo," he said. "Let's dance." He paused and then added, "I think I needed this too."

Theo had spent the past seventeen years watching and planning and keeping me safe. All without his god powers. He'd lived like a human boy, hidden from family and friends. I was glad he could finally have this night for himself. Sometimes, a bit of self-care can make as big a difference as all the tough preparation in the world.

I squeezed his hand.

In a birthday miracle, Theo pulled me into a huge hug and held me. Theo hated hugging. I mean *ha-ted*. Even

Festos could barely get more than a few seconds out of him. So this?

This was huge. This was Theo's "I love you."

My toes curled, I got a goofy grin on my face, and felt sunshiny joy pour through my body. Not all meltiness originates from swoony lover boys. Sometimes it comes from best friends. Because love is love and it is all great.

I pushed the moment by smooching Theo's cheek, at which point he shoved me away like I'd spilled hazardous waste on him. I winked at Festos, who watched the whole thing with evident amusement.

Then, with a "come on" wave, Festos led us through the club and down to the dance floor.

It was tropical jungle hot and steamy on that level. Also sardine packed. But entirely fabulous. The music and energy were contagious. Even snaking through the crowd, the three of us sambaed along.

I was so lost in my own little world—trying so hard to take in this fantastical place—that I collided with a hard body, and felt the slosh of a drink against my front. "Sorry," I said, looking up. I found myself staring at Anil Patel and did a double take. Anil was a classmate and former flirt buddy of mine. "I'm not sure which question to ask first." I said.

Anil gave me his familiar warm grin. "How about 'Hey human, how did meat like you get through the door?'"

I laughed. "Okay. Let's start with that." Last time I'd seen Anil, he hadn't known about the existence of gods and goddesses at all.

"I'm dating Cassie," he said, blushing.

"Really?" I tried to wrap my head around it. The popular star wrestler dating the kooky ginger misfit who also happened to be an Oracle. I failed. "That's uh—"

"Freaking weird. I know. It happened the night of the Winter Formal." His expression turned sheepish. "The night your mom dragged you out of school. Sorry about that, by the way."

"Not your fault." It wasn't. Anil had been unfairly screwed over that night, too. Underneath all his posturing, he was actually a nice guy. A friend. If he and Cassie had grown close, then I was glad that something good had come out of that mess. "Where is she?" I asked.

Holding two cocktail glasses, Anil gestured. A deep turquoise liquid pulsed and sputtered in one of the glasses, like angry waves in the ocean. I started as it crashed against the glass. The other drink looked like liquid sunset with streaky layers of red, pink, and gold that glowed magically. Anil caught me staring and brought me back to reality. "She's over here."

I looked around to tell Festos and Theo to go on without me, but they were already on the edge of the dance floor. So I headed over to Cassie and gave her a sneak attack hug.

She squealed when she saw me, her ginger curls bobbing over a cute green halter dress that made her eyes sparkle.

But that could have been her manic energy. "I can't believe you're here!" she said. "I didn't think I was ever going to see you again! What happened that night? I didn't want to ask Hannah in case you didn't want to talk about it. Are you doing okay about next week?" Her words were rushed and overly happy as if every statement deserved an exclamation mark.

"Are *you* okay, Cass?"

Anil gave me the tiniest shake of his head.

Cassie smiled brightly. "I'm fine! Ha! Ha! You know, getting closer to the equinox! Big day! Lots of prophecies!" Her smile wavered for a second before going extra mega-watt.

This was worrisome. Mostly for what it was doing to Cassie's mental well-being but also because new prophecies could mean new info I needed to have. "New prophecies?" I asked. "Like what?"

She waved me off. "Nothing really! Just the old favs!" She took the sunset glass from Anil and tossed it back in one gulp.

Anil leaned in to me. "She's upped her Ativan. Swears she's fine but I'm worried she's going to snap."

I braced my hand on his shoulder, spoke directly and quietly into his ear. "Anything happens to her, even if she only gets a tiny bit worse, promise me you'll take her to Hannah. Hannah can get her to me and Theo, and we can help." I hoped.

I'd always hated the fact that my goddess awakening had triggered Cassie's own prophetic abilities. I couldn't help worrying that I was still triggering stuff for her. That all my anger and unease were amping her up. And not in a good way.

I stepped back at Anil's nod, but stood gnawing on my lip.

Cassie noticed and placed her hand on my arm. "No worries, girlfriend! Tonight is about forgetting! Eat, drink, and be merry, right!" She beamed at me but I could feel the waves of anxiety coming off her.

"Right," I said. "You have fun tonight. Enjoy your guy. He's a good one."

Cassie blushed as Anil slipped his arm around her waist and pressed a kiss to her temple. I could see her relax. Maybe Anil was a talisman to keep her grounded. Man, I hoped so.

I smiled at them both and with a small wave, went to find the two boys who were keeping *me* sane. And alive.

I stood back from the dance floor for a minute, and took it all in. I saw Cassie bouncing to the beats, while Anil flailed like an enthusiastic puppy. Beyond them, deep in the crowd, I caught sight of Pierce's wings. He and Hannah had come down.

They moved beautifully. Big surprise. Even the stunning otherworldly beings around them noticed. But my friends didn't come off as snobby, or aloof. Hannah's arm was draped on Pierce's shoulder and he had one arm locked around her waist. They gazed into each other's eyes, huge smiles on their faces as the love flowed between them.

Everyone around them felt the effect, smiling and swaying toward them as if to bask in their glow. It was hard to begrudge that kind of love and happiness. And I really didn't. I guess I just wished there were two of Hannah so that Pierce and I could both have her attention.

I watched Festos and Theo, their hands on each others' hips, and grooving together. It meant they weren't moving around much, which probably worked for Festos since he didn't have his cane. Also, it allowed them maximum touching.

No downside.

Theo pressed his hand into the small of Festos' back, pulling him closer as he leaned in to say something. Fee's lips tugged up in a small grin. That's when Festos looked up and saw me at the edge of the floor. He crooked his finger, beckoning me to come dance with them.

So I did. I tried to dance beside them but, shockingly, it was Theo who would have none of it. He pulled me between them.

At first, I couldn't stop laughing. I was the center of this boy-sandwich, and Fee was acting exceptionally lewd. But soon the music swirling around us was too compelling to resist. We quit fooling around and lost ourselves in the sound.

The night progressed. We didn't leave the dance floor.

Friday night turned to the dark, first hours of Saturday morning.

Sweat poured between my cleavage. I'd lost my shoes hours ago, and the sprung floor was bouncy and warm under my feet. My mind was fabulously blank. I was alone in this moment, the music driving me forward through the night.

The beats got wilder, our dancing more abandoned. Festos' fingers threaded through mine, and our arms flew upward as we swayed together. Theo's arms snaked along my hips and held Fee's waist. My eyes were closed and my face turned to the lit tiles as I grooved between my friends, unsure of where I stopped and they began.

As much as it may have looked like the dirtiest of dancing, it wasn't sexual at all.

It was transformational. The ultimate sense of being free and alive and connected.

I was bliss.

The music changed, the melody shifting as our unseen DJ mixed "All You Need is Love" into the pounding rhythm.

My eyes shot open and I dropped my arms to my side. A prickling awareness came like an alarm over my skin.

Kai had arrived.

I pulled myself free of Theo's grasp, murmured, "Back in a sec," into Festos' ear and tried to make my way through the dancing throng to where I could feel him. I pushed deeper and deeper into the crowd, passing Hannah, who shot me a quizzical glance. "Want me to come?" she mouthed.

I shook my head and kept moving, barreling forward. As much as I wanted to see Kai, I didn't need visual confirmation to follow him. I could sense him.

I broke through the bodies and found myself all the way at the back edge of the floor. I scanned the area, trying to get a handle on where Kai was. I had to find him. It was no coincidence he'd shown up when that damn song had started to play. That song would always be tied to my visions, and so, to Kai. Or rather, the lack of Kai.

I couldn't see him, but I caught sight of a door and knew he'd gone that way. I hurried through it, finding myself in a stairwell. Taking the stairs two at a time, I jumped my way down one floor, the cement cool under my still-bare feet. I hit the next landing and burst through the door into a subterranean level.

The vibe was very different here. Instead of dancing throngs or, intimately chatting groups, I found myself in a long, wide corridor. The same balls of light were mounted on the wall, but less frequently.

Revelers streamed in and out of various rooms. I passed by a chillout room where a six-foot-tall musical fountain placed impossibly in a wild garden, pulsed to a mellow beat during a perpetual sunset. Club-goers lay around it on giant pillows strewn in lush grass, transfixed.

There was a dark room where goth patrons drank to the blast of industrial music at a bar built from scrap metal on a rooftop overlooking a post-apocalyptic megacity. And a room where masked dancers whirled like dervishes to the sound of drums in a moonlit courtyard. Molten streams of lava writhing around them.

One of the dancers held out a hand to me. I sensed keen eyes from behind her lavishly bejeweled mask. My heart kicked up into my throat. I desperately wanted to go in. But there was no time. With a regretful smile, I sped up, feeling the need to get to Kai. To see him. To talk to him.

I rose on my tiptoes, trying to find him above the crowd. Nothing. But I knew with absolute certainty that he was here.

The rooms blurred as I raced past them, until I stood before a closed door at the end of the hall.

Unfortunately, a beefy and rather hairy satyr barred my way. He was clad only in dark green genie pants embroidered with peacocks' tails splayed in full glory. "What's your hurry?" he asked in a rumbling voice, an amused glint in his eyes.

I forced myself to make eye contact, and not take a step back. "Just going in, thanks."

The satyr shook his head, laughing a laugh I felt deep in my bones. He wasn't being creepy. He just found me highly entertaining. The satyr gave me a gentle push back down the corridor. "The lava room is more your speed."

Never mind that I'd thought the same thing. "Presumptuous of you." I said, shaking him off and stepping forward. "Besides, my boyfriend's inside."

He sighed as if he thought going in was a foolish idea. "You're not going to find what you need."

I gave him a tight smile, really ready to be done with this and find Kai. "I need to talk to him." I pushed past and turned the knob. As I stepped inside the room, I heard him say, "You're wrong, baby. Love. That's all you need."

I whipped back around to ask him what he meant. Because hello, again with that song,

But he was gone.

With a sigh, I returned my attention to the room. The door clanged shut behind me as I realized there *was* no room. There was no club. There was no Kai.

I found myself in a rain slicked alley, late at night, still barefoot. I swung around and pounded on the door. "Hey! Let me back in!" I kicked for good measure, since I had no idea where I was and no desire to be out here alone.

I let out a *grrr* of frustration. My itchiness was back. Stomping along the ground, scratching, I searched for the nearest tree to get myself the hell out of here.

Lost in my thoughts, I almost jumped out of my skin when a car horn blasted at me. I leapt out of the way as a black limo careened to a stop and blocked my way. The back passenger door swung open. "Get in." I heard a familiar voice inside.

Damn.

Hermes had arrived and that could only mean trouble.

Six

I peered into the dimly lit interior of the limo, eyes narrowed. "Lovely to see you too, Jack, but I'm busy."

Media mogul Jack Wing, Hermes' public persona, regarded me with his shrewd dark eyes. "I don't like playing messenger tonight any better than you like having me, kid. Now get in already so I can get home to bed." He gave a sharp tug on a cuff of his perfectly tailored pinstripe suit, the image of wealth and power.

"What's the deal?"

"An official summons," he said steadily.

Great. "Tell Pops he can go screw himself. He gets his chance to kill me next week." I moved to slam the door, but Jack was surprisingly fast for a middle aged guy. Okay, middle aged *looking* guy. He caught the door and leaned out toward me, his gaze intense. "A meeting. Not an attempt. Safe passage guaranteed."

I raised my eyebrows. "I'm waiting."

Jack gave an exasperated huff. "I swear on the Styx."

I considered my options. Really, I didn't have any. If Zeus wanted to see me, he'd see me with or without my say in the matter. Besides, Kai was gone. And my birthday high was dead now. Might as well pick a fight with my father in time-honored teen tradition.

I scrambled into the limo and shut the door.

"Isn't the outfit a bit much?" Jack asked.

"It's my birthday. I was celebrating," I said flatly.

"Without shoes?"

I glanced down at my bare feet. "You try wearing heels."

Jack laughed.

"What does Pops want with me?"

He shrugged. "Not just your father. Hades too."

"Come on!" I glared at him.

He smiled. "Happy birthday."

I turned my head and stared out the tinted window. I could tell we were moving by the sights passing by, but I sure couldn't feel the road beneath us. This puppy was smooth. And the seats were plush. Might as well enjoy the ride.

We drove for several hours. The long ride must have been the gods' way of amping up my anxiety, by building my tension around the meet. We could have blinked directly to the location.

Eventually, we came to a small strip mall on the outskirts of some cookie-cutter suburb. It consisted of a discount shoe store, a dry cleaner, and Marina's Taverna, a Greek restaurant. The limo came to a stop in front of Marina's and the door on my side opened.

Jack saluted me. "Have fun, kid."

I got out of the limo. "Give my regards to Aphrodite." *The ditzy bat.*

Jack smiled, as if he knew what I was thinking. Then the door swung closed and the limo departed.

I really wished I was wearing shoes. If nothing else, I could grind a heel into my father's foot if he pissed me off. Well, there was no helping that now. I straightened my shoulders, held my head high, and strode inside.

I expected the worst Greek tackiness with plaster statues of gods, but the place was surprisingly tasteful. Airy with high ceilings. Rectangular blue panels were inset into white walls. The chairs were made of simple varnished wood, while white cloths covered each square table. A fully stocked bar, curved and gleaming took up one side of the interior, with the kitchen visible to the right.

The restaurant was empty except for a kind-looking woman in chef's whites who smiled at me as I entered. Marina, I presumed. "Come. This way," she said, with more than a hint of a Greek accent.

My heart stuttered. She sounded exactly like Demeter had when Jack had created an illusion of her to trick me. I'd been royally suckered and heartbroken. "Thank you," I said quietly, and followed her through the space.

She led me out the back doors onto a large patio, covered by a gazebo of white beams. Flowing white cloth had been woven to make the roof. The fabric also formed curtains, tied back to create half-walls.

A seating area with white leather sofas and tall cacti filled one corner. Large glass lanterns encircled the patio, fat pillar candles blazing brightly in each one. A tall patio heater kept the space toasty.

In the center of the patio, a dark wood table had been laid out, laden with yumtastic Greek tapas like pita wedges, pink creamy taramasalata, triangles of spanakopita, and a heart attack heaven of saganaki—fried cheese.

Zeus and Hades sat there munching in silence. Not even the tense "One wrong move and there's gonna be a hurting" silence you would have expected from two powerful foes who despised each other. Nah. More like "Eh, it's family and family is gonna push your buttons, but we're here now, so let's eat."

I took a moment to scope them out before I approached.

Most gods on Earth tended not to appear much taller than six feet. To blend in. But not these two. From the way they both dwarfed their chairs, I could tell they hit seven feet easy. Guess neither could stand to appear too human.

They looked ridiculous. Not just because of their height either. Hades had decided to wear pleated khakis, a plaid button-down shirt and a cardigan. Which sounded very golf dad but came off as bad-touch relative wrong when combined with his bloated alcoholic looks, and all around messed up energy. He wasn't giving off his usual charming, yet evil, vibes.

Pops, on the other hand, was his regular metrosexual self, all baby smooth skin and buffed mani. While I'd only seen him in linen suits and a fedora, his current outfit could have been taken off one of the club goers I'd just been with.

No girl should ever see her father in a suit that skinny,

shiny, or tight. Scouring that image from my memory banks might require therapy.

I slid into an empty chair between the two of them, glancing around to see if maybe Kai was here. "What's with the family reunion?" I asked. I could smell dad's citrus cologne, and knew better than to sniff for whatever brimstone Hades wore.

My father handed me a plate and motioned for me to load up. Ordinarily, I would have been happy to, but I was sulky that my dance-fueled peace had dissipated, and I didn't feel like breaking bread with two people who wanted me dead.

I set the plate down.

My father shot me a puzzled look. "Are you not feeling well? I know how much you like to eat."

Now I was definitely not eating. Which was a shame because I'd started to waver about the saganaki. "Such a charmer, Pops. Let's cut to the chase, shall we?"

"We thought we'd treat you to a last supper," Hades laughed. "Since you'll be dead soon."

I gave the smug bastard a tight smile. "So sure of that, are you?"

He nodded. "Yes. You've been outwitted and out-played."

Zeus threw him a sour look. "My progeny. Mine to tell. You got to tell yours."

Hades muttered something about big babies, but flinched when Zeus sat up sharply.

Zeus smirked then turned to me. "We've warded up your ward." He gave me an assessing glance. "Do you understand what that means?"

"Yeah," I ground out. It meant that Zeus and Hades had put a ward up around our ward, effectively blocking our access to Eleusis and the ritual location.

Zeus patted me on the head, like a particularly clever puppy.

I jerked my head away.

He smiled as Marina set a plate of steaming moussaka—a kind of Greek eggplant lasagna—in front of him and a lamb dish before Hades. Zeus' smile was for the food, not Marina. She was dismissed with a lazy wave and no thank you. I doubted my father tipped, so this night had to suck for her.

Hades picked up his lamb and tore into it. I turned away from that grossness and focused on my father's dainty bites. Which were equally disturbing. It was like there was no middle with these two. Everything in extremes.

"My brother and I have realized that fighting is beneath us. We are not the issue here." Zeus speared a tiny bit of ground beef and cream sauce, and popped it into his mouth.

I rolled my eyes.

"It's true," he insisted. "The issue is humanity failing to worship us as is our due."

Astounding. I ran my thumb around the rim of my water glass. "Maybe you're not relevant to humanity, you egotist."

Zeus shot me a pitying glance.

Right. How could *that* possibly be the case?

"Thus have we decided that on the equinox, at the moment of our greatest power, Hades and I will wipe out humanity and live in a pure world. A world of only gods."

"That's very Aryan of you," I snarled, trying to ignore the burning tingle along my arms. I'd learned not to show any weakness around these two. Not that they didn't generally ferret it out.

"We're housekeeping," Hades said through greasy lips. "Losing the clutter."

I smacked my hand against the table. "Are you hearing yourselves? You're going to wipe out mankind because they don't love you enough?"

"Worship, not love," Zeus corrected.

I shook my head. "I don't buy this for a second. The reason you've been fighting isn't because of people adoring you, it's because you both want to be top dog. How does this change anything?"

"With no Earth and no humans taking up valuable real estate in the Underworld," Hades said, pausing to slug back some wine, "we can unite our two realms. Gods and goddess can live freely and *we* will be rulers of the only two domains left."

I rose, fed up with the BS they were feeding me. "No. Here's what's really going to happen. You're going to kill all humans out of spite, and then fight it out until one of you is dead. And that second part, I highly support. But you are *not* harming any more humans on my watch. So thanks for the big reveal, but we're done."

I turned to leave but Zeus' hand snaked out and caught my arm. He yanked me back into my seat. "I wasn't finished speaking, child," he said in a mild voice that was totally at odds with his cold eyes.

I stayed put. And kept my mouth shut. This was not the moment to get snotty.

"The reason I shared this with you, is that you are still of my blood." Pops looked a little put out at having to admit that. "I have tried to guide you and teach you the error of your ways but—"

I straightened up, totally incredulous at that whopper. "By repeatedly trying to kill me?"

He shrugged. "Tough love. Much as Persephone went astray due to Kyrillos' influence—"

Hades growled at that.

"I hate to see my daughter die." Zeus leaned forward. "You can be part of this new world. If you stand down and don't perform the ritual."

"You and Kyrillos," Hades added. "He got the same offer."

Zeus' lips thinned but he didn't say anything.

Both gods turned their attention back to the food, giving me, I guess, time to think it over.

I tried to wrap my head around things. I could understand them deciding to kill humans, out of spite or lack of attention. That made sense. But I came up short at how they thought *I* could go along with this. I may have been a goddess, but I was also most definitely human. Sure, I had a vested interest in the well-being of my god friends, but in the division of these battle lines, I was Team Humanity all the way.

My head throbbed. Were they blithely assuming I'd say "Thanks ever so"? This was possibly the most insulting, condescending interaction I'd ever had with gods. And there had been many.

My arms now itched so madly that if I could have ripped the skin from my bones, I would have happily done that. Instead, I jammed my hands under my butt and shook my head. "Let's see," I said. "Uh, no way."

Hades snorted like he wasn't surprised, but Zeus actually seemed to be. "Perhaps you don't understand the choice I'm offering here. The correct decision brings you back into the safety and security of your family. The other ... does not."

That was actually kind of funny. "Secure? Like mob secure? One wrong move and I'm sleeping with the fishes?"

Zeus' brow creased in confusion. "Why would you sleep in water?"

Hades looked at his brother like he was a moron. "It's *The Godfather* ... Forget it. She obviously has a death wish."

"No. She doesn't." I said. I pushed away from the table and stood up, bracing my hands on the tabletop as I leaned toward them. "Since I very much want to live, how about this counter offer? Not only am I going to defeat you both, I'm now going to destroy you. I won't let your selfishness ..." I gripped the table, practically trembling in my rage, "your utter self-centeredness hurt humanity. No matter what it takes, I'll find a way past your ward, unite with Kai, and win."

I eyed a slender silver olive fork tossed in among the Kalamatas. I wanted to savage someone but its tines wouldn't inflict the messy, and therefore more painful, ongoing trauma I was after.

Zeus looked amused at my outburst. "You indolent whelp. Who do you think you are?"

I stood tall and steady. "I am the goddess of ushering in a spring in a world free from destruction of gods. A world that allows humans to bloom. But ultimately, Pops? I'm your daughter. And I am about to show you the true meaning of teenage rebellion."

I would have liked to leave on that high note, but Zeus had to have the last word.

My father toasted me mockingly with his glass. "Then eat, drink, and be merry for tomorrow you die."

"Next week," Hades interrupted.

Zeus glowered at him. "Yes, obviously, but I was using a metaphor."

"No," his brother replied. "You were paraphrasing. Badly."

That's when they lunged for each other, and I left.

Actually, I scurried out shaking with adrenaline, and then just shaking because the edges of my vision had begun to blur. I wanted to be away from the restaurant if I passed out.

What scared me the most was that, for all my talk of humanity, I'd never felt so inhuman as I had back there, so driven by a primal need to destroy blindly. I wanted to kill them and feel the weight of their deaths. Truthfully, I had no idea if they could be killed, but it didn't matter. All that mattered was how I had felt.

I stepped past a planter box, full of cacti. They burst into flame as I went by. Tears spilled down my cheeks. I was drowning in my anger, in my crazy emotions. The sense of not being able to reign myself in, get myself back under control, scared me. My heart sped up and I let out a small whimper, pressing my fists into my eyes.

Solid arms slid around my body.

"Shhh," Kai whispered into my ear. "You're safe." He turned me in his arms, holding me tight.

I buried my head against his chest, and let his steady warmth slowly counteract my insane emotions. I inhaled his spicy scent like a lifeline. Finally, I relaxed and came back to the parking lot, and the night, and him.

But I hadn't forgotten how things stood between us. Warily, I raised my head to look at him, unsure of how this surprise visit was going to play out.

He tilted my chin up to better study me. "Did they hurt you?"

I shook my head, not trusting myself to speak yet.

I felt his relieved sigh against my chest as I took the sight of him in.

Kai wore a fitted gray sweater that stretched tight across his chest. The denim of his jeans scratched against my bare legs. There was the faintest tinge of dark under his eyes, and his hair was mussed.

I wanted to smooth everything away and make him feel better, but I kept my hands to myself. Touching would not lead to talking. I waited.

Finally, he spoke the words I'd been hoping to hear. "We should talk."

We didn't have to have our loaded discussion in a strip mall parking lot. Kai took me back to his house. I'd been there before, but only outside, trying—and failing—to be let in. He hadn't had this place when he'd been with

Persephone. Even if I was imagining everything about her as an active presence in my brain, it was fun to think that my gloating was killing her right now.

I returned my attention to Kai's home. When I'd first discovered where he lived, I'd been surprised, expecting a flashy hi-rise in some major metropolis. "Why a tree-house?"

We stood on a deck that circled his round wooden pod, built high around the thick, mossy trunk of a massive cypress tree on the bayou. It was designed so that, from a distance, it would be indistinguishable from the rest of the tree. Not that there was anyone around to fool. The area was remote. Uninhabitable without god abilities to blink in and out.

Kai shrugged. "It fits me."

He spoke in such a low voice that I barely heard him. Morning had broken, and the sound of birdcalls was deafening. It wasn't peaceful exactly, but it was calming.

Except for the oppressive humidity. Despite the gray overcast sky, my dress felt clammy against my skin. I grasped my hair and twisted it out of the way, using it as a fan on the base of my neck. Talk about pointless. I felt like I was breathing soup.

To distract myself, I eyed the brackish water far below, and a tricky gator doing its best log impersonation amidst tufts of wild grass. In the blink of an eye, the gator lunged forward and snagged a fish. Pure savagery.

And yet, in its wild way, there was no doubt it was beautiful here. Dangerous, lethal even, but with a surprising fragility. A brilliant orange butterfly landed on the rail beside my hand. Hmmm. Maybe this place was perfect for Kai after all. So seemingly fierce, and yes, actually fierce, but still beautiful and vulnerable.

I watched the butterfly flutter a moment, and then fly past Kai's head, giving me a glimpse of the wistfulness on his face. He caught me looking and smoothed his expression into the poker face that drove me nuts.

Kai turned, opened the door, and stepped inside. Since he left the door open, I followed him.

His place was one big round room, with large, rectangular windows almost floor-to-ceiling all the way around. Underneath them were custom built cedar cabinets, which infused the whole place with a lovely sort of sauna smell.

The cypress' trunk came up through the center of the room, disappearing again out the top of the sharply pitched ceiling, which was inlayed with slender cedar planks.

To one side of the trunk, Kai had strung a huge hammock bed from an iron grid on the ceiling. The other half of the room was a lounge area, with comfortable seating grouped to take advantage of the view. There was only the most basic of kitchens beside it.

"No bathroom?" I asked as I glanced around.

Kai gave me the ghost of a smirk, making my insides clench in shivery delight. I knew he was remembering the last time we'd found ourselves in a high-end bathroom, and the flirtation that had ensued. He tilted his head. "Over there."

I looked past him to see a walkway connecting this pod to a much smaller one in a nearby tree. "Ah."

Awkward small talk out of the way, I sat down on one of the sofas, because no way was I going near the bed. Determined to keep this on a mature, adult level, I let him speak first. Also, he was the one with the explaining to do.

Kai took a seat on a chair beside me. He didn't speak for a moment, rubbing his thumb over his index finger. "I still love you," he said, finally.

"I know."

He nodded as if that was all he needed to say.

My eyes narrowed.

His brows raised.

I shot him a scathing look and drew my legs up to my chest. "You talked to Zeus and Hades? You know what they're going to do? What they *have* done with their ward?"

He nodded.

That was the sum total of his response. I snapped. "When we do this love ritual, is it going to work? Or is your Guinness World Record for pissed offness gonna sour the whole thing?"

Kai's face flashed annoyance. Maybe maximum snark wasn't the tone to lead with.

"I dunno," he shot back, equally sarcastic. "How far did Persephone's betrayal go? She must have known I'd come after her. So what was the plan? Kill me? Use one of Pierce's arrows to magic herself into being in love with me?"

I flinched at that last bit. At one time, I'd wanted to do the same thing. In my defense, I hadn't known Kai had loved me then, and it had been a major survival plan for keeping my heart in one still-beating piece.

Still, I didn't want to answer him either. I knew what she had felt. It wasn't pretty. "She loved you." I left it at that.

Problem was, Kai was no idiot. He laughed mirthlessly. "And she was going to kill me anyway," he said.

I flung up my hands in exasperation, and sat up, my feet slapping onto the floor. "What do you want me to say? Persephone was the universe's biggest bitch. And I've got Bethany—who tormented me for my entire life, tried to steal my boyfriend, stabbed me, and left me for dead—as a contender for second place. I'm sorry about what Persephone was planning, but I can't change it. So right now I'm telling you to put on your big boy pants because everything is falling apart and we can't let Zeus and Hades win."

Persephone and I had made entirely different choices. For better or for worse, I led with my heart. As opposed to letting my messed up goddess-essence-with-a-superiority-complex rule my life with knee jerk reactions. Could he say the same?

Kai didn't actually say anything for a bit. I hoped laying it on the line had gotten through to him, and was making him rethink his attitude. Then again, gods were notoriously stubborn. And touchy.

I decided to employ the "catch more flies with honey" approach, so I softened my tone and said, "For what it's worth, I doubt Persephone could have really done it in the end."

He shot me a sideways glance. "Could *you?*"

"Screw you, Kai." I pulled my pendent out from under my dress, bolted to my feet, and headed for the cypress' trunk. I could be back in Festos' apartment in a second.

Kai jumped up and grabbed my arm, knocking my pendent out of my fist. "Protest all you want, but you *are* her. And if she could do it, then the potential is in you."

I broke his grip. "You're as crazy as our fathers." I shoved at his chest. "Your kid self is in you, if you weren't hatched out of Hades' ass fully grown, or however you were spawned. So the potential for every stupid thing you've ever done is still in you, too. Does that mean you're going to go out and do endless stupid things? Because if you wanna start making lists, I'm betting I'm the one that needs to be worried here."

Silence. My chest heaved and Kai would have to be blind to miss my furious glare.

His nostrils flared. His jaw was so tight I worried he might shatter it. His eyes narrowed slightly and then he disappeared.

Days away from the love ritual we had to perform and this was the state of our relationship.

Humanity was screwed.

Seven

"Great," I said to the empty room. There was nothing to do except wait for him to come back because no way was I leaving without some kind of resolution.

I folded my hands in my lap and sat down on the sofa. My eyes snagged on Kai's bed.

I looked away.

Looked back.

It was a really big bed. Extremely comfy looking. I eyed it, gauging precisely how comfy. Thought about testing it out, since I was stuck here anyway.

I headed over to the kitchen first, grabbed a paper towel and doused it in hot water. I'd been barefoot all this time and my feet were filthy. I cleaned them off and threw the wad of paper in the trash.

Biting my lip, I snuck toward the bed. I paused a moment at its foot, then launched myself onto it, arms outstretched. Yowza, was it relaxing. Not too hot, not too cold. Not too hard, not too soft. It was baby bear's ultimate bed. I rolled over onto my back, enjoying the way I sank into it the perfect amount. It must have been one of those memory foam mattresses because it molded itself around me, swaying gently thanks to the massive hammock.

My, a girl could get used to this.

Shaking dangerous thoughts from my head, I sat up reluctantly and immediately felt a familiar weight knocking me back down against the mattress' fluffy perfection.

Kai lay over me, propped up on one elbow. "I love you." His voice was hard, his eyes burning with intensity. He pressed me into the bed.

I blinked. Stupidly. "I know."

"The ritual is going to work." I heard the absolute conviction in his voice and understood that his anger didn't overpower his love. That we were going to be fine.

Dumb boys and their inability to articulate actual emotions. As much as I would have liked to hear him say that, I could tell from the look on his face that those three words were as much as I was getting out of him. "Are you still mad?"

Kai hesitated. "Yes." He rolled onto his back.

I took it as my cue to leave.

His arms wrapped around me and nestled me into his side. "Stay." It wasn't a question. I would have bristled but he looped his finger into one of my ringlets and tugged gently. "Please."

It was *so* killing him to say that word. Which didn't endear him to me. But the accompanying tender look dissolved my brain into swoony mush.

Mostly mush. I still felt a core of deep resentment at how he'd treated me the last couple of months. How I'd allowed myself to be treated. It should have been the easiest thing in the world to open my mouth and tell him everything that had been wrong with his behavior. *Our* behavior.

I tried. I thought them silently. *If you'd been mad, you should have respected me enough to talk to me. Not just use me as a hook up. Not make me feel like crap.* I even progressed to mouthing the words. Until I finally got the courage to turn my head, look at Kai—and feel my resolve crumble. What if I broke what little connection we'd re-established? What gave me the right to be that selfish when, now more than ever, we needed to be in sync?

Persephone had been selfish and look where it had gotten her.

I was better than that. It could wait.

We lay there, not speaking, not even kissing. Just Kai playing with my hair and keeping me cuddled against him. Which was not great, but at least felt like we'd achieved a tentative level of all right. Maybe not the giddiness of the day we'd declared our love for each other, because there was still too much hurt on both our parts, but hopefully enough new closeness to get us through the battle with the rest of our lives to achieve Hannah-and-Pierce glowiness.

I lay my hand over his heart, feeling its steady beat, and the soft rise and fall of his chest.

"Happy belated birthday, Goddess." Kai kissed the top of my head and my chest tightened. He hadn't called me by my pet name since we'd learned of Persephone's betrayal. "I got you a present, you know."

I rolled over, hoping the delighted grin on my face would extend to real joy in my heart. "Really? Well, hand it over. Don't waste more time."

He laughed and the sound shot straight to my toes. God, had I missed knowing how much I amused him.

"I already did. I let Festos and Theo live even though I wanted to fling them off you while you were dancing."

"That's not a present, you caveman." I smacked him. "I knew you were at the club. Big coward, not facing me."

"I expected you to find me."

I gagged at the stupendous arrogance. That's what I got for dating a god. "I tried." There was a lot Kai didn't know. And I realized that I'd better catch him up.

To say that Kai was displeased—about my visions, me constantly hearing "All You Need Is Love", Festos coming with us to do a cleansing ritual while we held off all the minions in existence—would not accurately describe the glowery scowl of doom that seemed permanently etched on his face.

I decided not to mention my belief that I was no longer the Goddess of Spring and more the Goddess of Bah, Who Needs That Silly Season Anyhow?

We needed to get back to Festos' and speak with him and Theo. But I wasn't leaving without my present. I poked Kai. "If I am psychically intuiting my imminent death, then this would be a great time to give me my gift."

Kai looked at me with both fondness and frustration. I could live with that. He leaned over to reach under the bed. I enjoyed the view of his back muscles rippling in the process. When he rolled back up, he held a poorly gift-wrapped box out to me.

I took it and frowned. "It's wrapped in Kleenex."

He shrugged. "Wrapping is wrapping."

"And duct tape."

Another shrug. He really didn't get it.

But there was a present of some sort under there, so I ripped into it with nails, teeth, and a bit of viney light, eventually prying off the lid.

Inside was a bright red T-shirt with the word *Phospherocious* spelled out in glittery silver letters. I stared blankly at it.

"It's because all your power names suck," he explained.

I still didn't get it.

"You come up with the worst names for your light." Kai grinned, excitedly. "Then I thought, why not combine the word 'phosphorus' from the Ancient Greek for 'bearer of light' with 'ferocious', because when you wield your power you get all kick-ass. Which is hot. So you're phospherocious."

He sat back and waited expectantly for me to say something.

I stared at the shirt again. "You got me a T-shirt with a made up superpower name for my birthday?"

His grin faltered. "Was that wrong?"

"Are you kidding me?" I screeched. "Polar opposite of wrong!" I bounced up and down on the bed to appropriately display my enthusiasm for this most awesome of gifts.

Kai's eyes flared at the sight of all my soft jiggling bits.

I stopped and leaned forward. "Kai?"

His face broke into a wolfish grin. "Yes?"

I was suddenly very conscious of how short my dress was and how very close my boyfriend was. "Got a pair of sweats I can borrow?" His crestfallen face made me laugh. "I want to try on the T-shirt, but not over this dress."

Kai looked horrified. "I don't own sweats."

"Oh, whatever."

Kai grumbled, but he rooted around in one of his cupboards and pulled out a pair of jeans. I motioned for him to turn around.

He leaned back against his elbows with a look of unholy glee.

Not fazed in the least, I shimmied into the jeans while still wearing the dress. I had to roll them up and use the belt already conveniently threaded through the loops, but they stayed put.

I wasn't wearing a bra, though, and I wasn't giving Kai his own personal peep show right now. We had to get back to Fee's. Instead, I did the most awkward maneuver—pulling the T-shirt over my head to cover me, and then wiggling out of the dress before finally stuffing my arms into the shirtsleeves.

Kai gave a resigned sigh.

I looked down at it in sheer delight. It rocked. Even though the cotton was thick, it had that gone-through-a-billion-washings softness to it. And it fitted me to a T, pun intended. It also went very well with the cuff Hannah had given me. "I think the silver glitter brings out my eyes," I said, beaming down at myself.

I was so phospherocious, it was insane.

"I like you in my clothes," Kai said.

I grinned and launched myself at him. "I love you."

Kai yanked me close by my shirt front. "You and me? We're unstoppable."

And in that moment, I chose to believe that we were.

***

I tried valiantly to remember that feeling later in the evening, as Kai and I faced Festos and Theo. Their club gear was gone. They were back in their regular casual clothes, and looking grim.

Kai had brought me back a few hours earlier. We'd updated the guys, and waited anxiously while the two went to Eleusis to check out the new ward for themselves.

"There's no way to break it," Theo said.

"You're positive? You checked it from every angle?" Losing the war because we were essentially locked out of the ritual location? Lamest defeat ever, and not going to happen.

"Trust us." Festos sank onto the chair beside me. He moved more slowly and, I could tell, painfully, from his night of dancing without a cane. He used it now and it clattered to the floor as he lay his head down on the table. He had a smear of dirt on his cheek. "We examined it thoroughly."

I rubbed his back.

Festos sighed. "More to the right." He extended his left leg out, gingerly flexing his twisted foot.

Theo gave him a concerned look but kept quiet. They'd had the argument about Festos using his cane enough times. Theo straddled a chair. "Not being able to take the ward down is not the same as not getting through it. There could be … a back door."

"That's brilliant!" I shouted at the same time Kai said, "Absolutely not."

"Told you," Festos murmured to Theo.

Confused, I turned to Kai. Festos bumped his shoulder blade against my hand, so I continued the massage. "What's wrong?"

Kai waved at Theo. "Tell her."

Theo plucked his glasses off and polished them. "Zeus and Hades placed their ward pretty much butt up against ours. We can't get through theirs to get to ours. Therefore, we can't get to the ritual location."

"Okay." Still didn't get it.

Checking to make sure the lenses were clean, Theo put his glasses back on. "The wards surround an area that was once the Temple of Demeter—"

My hands froze, mid shoulder rub. "No way."

"Told you," Kai said to Theo.

Theo put on his let's-be-reasonable voice. "It's our only hope. Eleusis is like Demeter's ground zero. She still holds power over that place and if anyone can get us inside, it's her."

That may have been true, but it was irrelevant. "At what price?" I yelled. "Felicia already tried to kill me once!"

"Ow! Watch it." Festos shifted beneath my hands. My massaging had turned to painful excavation as I dug the heels of my palms into his back.

"She's not going to try and kill you," Theo said.

Kai made a sound halfway between disbelief and disgust.

Theo rounded on him. "Shut it. You've been useless and basically MIA the last couple months. You don't get a say now."

"I do when Sophie's safety is involved." Kai's voice had gone scary quiet.

Theo went for his chain.

I held up my hands, not wanting them to start brawling. Again. "Enough." I turned to Theo. "Why do you think she'd help us? The kindness of her heart?"

"Power."

"Hell, no!"

"You and Kai take out the big bads and let her rule like Persephone originally promised," Festos said. "There's no other way."

"There has to be." I jumped to my feet, my mind working furiously. There had to be some other god we could turn to. "What about Jack? Or Pierce?" Anyone but her.

For my entire life, my adoptive mother, Felicia, had made me feel unwanted. She had shipped me off to Hope Park when I was six and spent the next ten years with minimal interaction, and maximum exuding of disappointment, at my existence.

Then I'd learned I was Persephone. How amazing was that? And what was the one thing that even *I* knew about her? Her mother Demeter had loved her so much that she roamed the earth in grief when Hades ordered Persephone's abduction.

That's when I'd started to dream of the day that Demeter would come back and find me. I knew there had to be some reason she hadn't shown up. Knew that she would get to me as soon as she could, and shower me with love.

Two months ago, when I'd realized that Felicia actually was Demeter? That she'd tried to kill Persephone, lied to me, not cared at all about me, and put me at risk by pulling me from the one place where she knew I was safe? The one place where my friends actually loved me? And then for her grande finale, she'd gleefully dropped the bombshell that Kai and I had yet to recover from?

I was not inclined to crawl back to her and ask for help.

I scratched at my arms. "I swore I wouldn't. To her face."

"Really?" Theo asked. "This is going to come down to your pride?"

"This is going to come down to her having been a cow to me for my entire life. She doesn't get to win. Who knows what she'd do with that kind of power?"

"Probably not much," Festos said. "Demeter has always liked humans. She's not going to hurt them now."

How naive. "Yeah, she will. She said as much before. She'll do whatever is opposite to what I want."

At which point Kai and Festos jumped in, all three of us arguing.

Theo's fist slammed down on the table, shocking us all into silence. "I gave up my powers for you. My immortality for you." His voice was so cold I broke out in

106

goosebumps. He advanced on me steadily. Just as steadily as I retreated.

I was caught in the fury of his gaze. I'd never seen Theo like this and he was scaring me. Out of the corner of my eye, I saw Kai rise. Festos locked an iron grip on him, keeping him in place.

Theo's voice rose to a loud roar. "So maybe you could just *suck it up*?!"

I opened my mouth to fight back. But out of shock, or maybe an iota of wisdom, my brain took a moment to think.

This sucked. I hadn't asked to be saddled with this responsibility. To save anyone. But since it had happened, I'd stood up and shouted down anyone who doubted me. Every single time. Was I really going to retreat into whiney teendom now? Yeah, I wanted to pout and scream, but I felt the weight of Theo's words deep in my bones.

I would rather stick knives into my eyes than go back to Felicia, offer her everything she wanted, and face her smugness. Along with whatever other hurts she would force me to endure before oh so graciously accepting my offer. I felt sick at the thought.

I sank back down beside Kai. Theo was right. And I was so very very wrong. If I had to come back and curl into the fetal position for a few hours afterward, well, I'd survive. So all I said was, "Yes, Theo. I can. Let's go see Felicia."

Which was the correct answer given the situation, but did nada to ratchet down the tension in the room. I could tell that Theo was still pissed at me. And at Kai.

Who returned the sentiment in spades as he yanked his arm free of Festos' grip with a fierce glower at both of the guys.

Festos' fingers twitched. He obviously wanted to unleash his fire, as he pointedly stared Kai down.

A cold smile spread over Kai's face. His fingertips emitted a black glow. "Go for it," he said.

"Stop," I said, shoving at each of them in turn as I made my way to the kitchen. I wasn't mad at anyone, but I was feeling prickly. Ashamed and guilty where Theo was concerned, and still cautious with Kai. He had admitted that he was still mad, which made me nervous about doing the ritual. And, honestly? I was fed up with him being pissed. There was a small, hard festering ball of resentment in the middle of my chest.

I flung the fridge door open. "What's the best way to approach Felicia?" I grabbed a small hunk of white cheddar, ripped off the plastic wrap, and bit into it.

Festos limped over to me, his cane thumping with each step.

He shut the fridge door. "Honeybunch?"

"Yes, Fee?" I smiled at my friend as protein flooded my body and kept me from going postal.

Festos boffed me across the top of the head in a stinging smack. "You've never heard of a phone? Next time, don't disappear from your own birthday party leaving us searching the place like crazy people. We practically got our favored status revoked."

"Ow!" I rubbed my head.

Festos' eyes narrowed. "Pull a stunt like that again and you'll really understand the meaning of the word 'hurt'. Also, you'd better apologize to Hannah when you see her."

"Huh. She noticed I was gone?" My tone was indifferent but my heart was not. I focused my attention on Festos' cupboards, rummaging around until I found a box of crackers to pull out. When I faced Festos again, I held the box to my chest, as if holding it tight enough could keep my heart from splintering because I missed Hannah so much.

Festos' expression softened. "She's in love."

I simultaneously smiled, shrugged, and nodded. She was. That was good. What was I supposed to say?

Festos watched me for a moment, but he didn't push it. He limped over to Theo and placed his hand on his boyfriend's shoulder. "Can I keep Sophie tonight?" he asked. "I need to run some tests and figure out how to sustain her power. Can she go see Demeter tomorrow?"

Theo thought it over, then nodded his agreement. Guess I wasn't getting a say in this.

I was about to head into my bedroom and strip off my superpower T-shirt and Kai's jeans in exchange for something loose and stretchy, when Kai stopped me.

"Admit it," he said to Festos, gesturing at my T-shirt. "You covet. And hate the fact that I'm so cool and clever."

Festos gave a dismissive shrug, but he did glance longingly at the shirt.

Kai smirked and motioned for me to go. "That's all."

"I admitted nothing," Fee retorted.

"You want a made up superpower name?" Theo asked Festos.

"Have you not met him?" asked Kai.

I stuffed my hands in the pockets of Kai's jeans and looked between them. Kai was right. Of course Festos wanted a shirt like mine. But why would Kai, his kinda-enemy, know that?

"Go." Festos ordered me out, pointing toward my room.

I went. But it didn't stop my curiosity. I absolutely did not understand Kai and Fee.

***

"Ready," I said as I re-entered the living room, a few minutes later, in exercise clothes.

"Follow me," Festos said, standing by the door. He exited the apartment and I scrambled after him with Kai in my wake.

Festos took us down to the second floor. It was an open, unfinished space, like all the floors except the top one. In one corner, Festos had set up his work space, consisting of a large stainless steel table flanked by heavy, metal floor-to-ceiling cabinets.

A bank of large light therapy boxes dominated the middle of the room. They were stacked three high and fifteen wide, their white light angled slightly downward.

"Detonate," Festos instructed me.

I looked between him and Kai, anxious.

Kai smiled. "I'm harder to destroy than that."

"More's the pity," Festos said.

"Brace yourselves." I sent out a full body shockwave, feeling my usual utter exhaustion at the end. On the upside, a quick glance showed that I hadn't destroyed my friends, which boded well for the big day. Yay!

"Again," Festos said.

I shot out a puny vine of light that fluttered and disappeared.

Festos nodded and motioned for me to go stand in front of the wall of light boxes. After much trial and error, we discovered that I required ten minutes of light box rays to recharge enough for another full body shockwave.

This was great to know, but I had no clue how Festos would translate that knowledge and the light energy into something I could use. Kai and I would have every last minion attacking us from the second we showed up to perform the ritual, until Festos finished cleansing the location.

Not to mention, that they weren't going to stop trying to kill us and stand there respectfully while we chanted. We'd have to hold them off then as well.

We spent the rest of the day on the second floor. I fired my power any way I could while Festos paced around me making notes and taking measurements, talking under his breath.

Occasionally, Festos would wander over to his work area and pull something out. Sheets of sterling silver, buffers, soldering irons, jewelers' saws, wire, lighting tubes, everything ended up tossed on the table.

My eyes slid to Kai, sprawled against the wall the whole time. We may have made up, but neither of us was the type to just move on. There was still all this lingering baggage between us, and I wanted to speed up time to a point when all that festering emotion had finally worked its way through our systems.

Kai met every look with an encouraging smile. He also kept me fueled with food and water. On the surface we were great. In my gut, I still felt that we weren't.

I was acutely aware of the disconnect.

Eventually, I really had nothing left, light boxes be damned. Sweat matted my hair and my body felt rubbery with exhaustion.

Festos rubbed the back of his neck, his eyes blurry. "Scamper off. You're done for the day."

I shuffled over to his work table. "Can I stick around and see what you do?"

"No." As if that wasn't pointed enough, he gestured toward at the stairwell door with his cane.

"He's worried that if we see what he does, we'll realize any half wit could do it," Kai said, pushing to his feet.

"Or you," Festos shot back.

"Nah, I'm just charmingly decorative," Kai said, totally unfazed.

I was too tired for these two to get into it. Visions of pillows danced in my head. I tugged on Kai's hand and started walking. "Good night, Fee. And thank you."

"Yeah, yeah," he muttered, already lost perusing his supplies.

"I hate your friends," Kai said, as we headed back up the stairwell.

I patted his cheek. "I know, godling. But you'll make nice for my sake."

Kai hmmmd noncommittally.

I pulled open the stairwell door on the top floor and we stepped into the foyer outside the apartment.

"This is where I say good-night," Kai said.

I blinked. "Oh." I'd assumed he'd stay over. Just to sleep. My body ached to feel contact with him, to reaffirm our connection. We needed more bubbles of just the two of us—like we'd been back at his place. Time to breathe and be, without the world pushing in on us. But maybe he didn't feel the same way?

My brain went into furious over-analyze mode.

Kai smiled gently, as if he could tell what I was thinking. "You need your sleep if you're going to face Felicia. If I stay, that's not going to happen." His voice dropped to a low rumble there that did lovely shivery things to my insides.

"Ohhh," I said in an entirely different tone of voice. One with waaay more enthusiasm. I gave him my best wide-eyed adorable look. *Kiss the cute girl,* I thought.

Kai tugged me closer. "That's not gonna work on me," he mumbled against my mouth.

"What about this?" I kissed him for all I was worth.

Hah hah. Putty. In. My. Hands.

Kissing Kai had beat out eating as my favorite activity.

"Evil wench," he said several moments later, his eyes dark.

I smirked, feeling highly smug. This was teasing and flirty and positively normal.

"But one of us has to be noble enough to put what's best for the battle first," he said with a self-righteous expression and disappeared.

I laughed and reached for the door knob but before I could turn it, his arms grabbed me from behind and swung me around. Kai planted one last hotter-than-hell kiss on me that flared every single nerve ending I had to life, screaming "whee haw!" I actually staggered back when he released me.

Hot or feverish? Chemistry or overcompensation to try and pretend it's all okay between you? I refused to let my Persephone voice poison me with whispers.

"Sophie."

I snapped back to attention, and Kai who now took his turn looking smug. "Sweet dreams, Goddess." He disappeared again. This is what couples did. It was good. It was healthy.

So why where my hands trembling?

I entered the apartment and stopped, remembering that it was just Theo and me. "Hey."

"Hey," he said, his arms full of books. He began to stack them on a slender bookcase.

This sucked. I ran through a million things to say and discarded them all. "My behavior before was self-indulgent and childish. It won't happen again."

Theo shrugged and shelved another book. "It might. Felicia is a total bitch."

I barked out startled laughter. Theo turned my way with a small smile, which made everything okay. "Love you, Rockman."

He tilted his head toward my room. "Go to bed, Magoo."

So I did. I barely managed to change into my pjs and crawl into bed before a deep but content fatigue stole over me, and I fell into much-needed sleep.

Eight

"Up and at 'em, honeybunch," Festos said cheerily on Sunday morning, crawling onto my bed to seat himself against my headboard. I was so dopey with sleep that it took me a second to remember where I was.

He looked disgustingly chirpy, all clean shaven, dressed in a green sweater and one of his endless pairs of skinny jeans. No fedora today though.

"Ugh," I croaked, rubbing morning granola out of one eye. "What time is it?"

"Time to celebrate my sheer unmitigated genius." He jammed his hand into the pocket of his jeans and pulled out a silver ring, which he dropped into my palm.

I sat up, scootching against him. "Look at that." I held the ring up to inspect it. "Necklace, bracelet, ring. I've got a whole jewelry set."

The ring was really cool, with a wide, silver band. Attached to it was a flat silver plane, shaped like a shield, with a stylized sun engraved on it.

I slid the ring onto my middle finger and saw that the shield part went all the way up to my middle knuckle.

"Tres funky." I held it out to better admire it on my hand. "But how does said stylish accessory work?"

"Five minutes. Get dressed."

"Can I eat?" I asked as I scrambled out of bed.

"No." He left the room.

"I'm calling Amnesty International," I called after him.

I threw my fabutastic red superpower T-shirt back on. First, because I knew Felicia would haaaate it. But mostly because I could do with any extra confidence boost I could get before facing her. Truth be told, I was really nervous about seeing my mother again. I'd always known she didn't love me, but I had stupidly held out hope.

I didn't anymore.

That just made it worse.

I pulled Kai's jeans back on because, yeah, I liked wearing his clothes, and again, Felicia would despise our implied—*no, actual,* I corrected—closeness.

I made it to the living room in four minutes, partially to show off my punctual commitment to the cause, but mostly because I smelled bacon. The one reason I could never be a vegetarian.

Kai was already there, wearing jeans and a fitted red long-T. Tension simmered between him and Festos.

"We match," I grinned, indicating our outfits, hoping to change the vibe.

Kai smiled as he held up a take out coffee cup. "Espresso?" he asked, waggling it.

"Gawd, I love you."

"Doesn't take much," Theo said, entering the room, already dressed.

I shot back the espresso, my brain waking up as the hot caffeine hit. Heavenly.

Festos grabbed my hand. "Back to me and my brilliance ..." He led me toward the door.

I glanced over my shoulder at Kai.

"Don't worry, I'm coming," he said.

"No." I gestured vaguely with my free hand. "Bring bacon."

Theo snorted his laughter.

Kai shook his head and caught up with us in the foyer, handing me a couple strips of super crispy bacon. I bit into a salty, crumbly piece and my eyes rolled back into my head in delight.

Festos opened the door to the cold, concrete stairwell. Both he and Kai tried to take the lead, jostling each other for position. Fee whacked Kai across the back of the knees with his cane. In anyone else, he would have shattered something. All Kai did was shove Festos hard enough into the cement wall to crack it.

I pushed between them. "What is your problem?" I hissed. I understood why Theo hated Kai. Kai's kiss had messed up all of Theo's plans. Plus Theo knew how Kai had catted around after Persephone's supposed murder. But Festos and Kai seemed to have some kind of history that left massive chips on both their shoulders. Yet they bonded at the oddest moments.

"Well?" I demanded looking from one to the other.

Their expressions smoothed out and became totally unreadable. But they stopped behaving like bratty ten-year-olds, so I let it lie.

Festos only went as far as the third floor.

I shivered as we stopped in the middle of the large, unfinished, unheated space.

"Go for it," he said.

My moss green light flew from my body to fill the room with a bright flash, then immediately dissipated. Before I had a chance to experience my usual utter exhaustion at using that much power, the ring glowed and a warmth poured through me.

I felt fine.

"Again," Festos said.

I blasted another one. And another. I whirled on Festos excitedly. "Three! I did three in a row! That's never happened. This is a freaking incredible superhero ring! How did you do it?"

"I'm brilliant." He looked down his nose at me in mock haughty arrogance.

"Noted and agreed." I bounced on my toes, still feeling the warmth tingling through my body. "I feel like I could go on forever."

Festos shook his head. "More precisely, you could go on for another three minutes and thirty seconds. That's our maximum time for you two to hold off the Pyrosim and Photokia. For me to cleanse the location and let you perform the ritual before Miss Dramabomb runs dry and hotshot is left on his own."

"Worried I wouldn't save you?" Kai asked him.

"Well, you are fickle when it comes to your loyalty," Fee retorted.

I could practically feel the air heating up as the two of them inched closer to each other.

"Versus how you have no loyalty at all," Kai sneered.

Them seemed to be fighting words, because, with that, all hell broke loose. Festos didn't unleash his torrents of lava and fire. Kai didn't strike with his toxic, pointed black light.

I almost could have understood that.

This was a plain old brawl. Primal and visceral and way more "I want to kill you with my bare hands and enjoy it." The two of them lunged at each other and started pounding, landing brutal punches.

I ducked out of the way as Festos threw Kai about twenty feet, then barely scurried my butt to safety in a far corner as, with a roar, Kai raced back to deliver a roundhouse kick that should have shattered Fee's ribs.

"Stop it!" I screamed. And was completely ignored. I tried shooting my vines out to wrap around them, but they were moving too fast, a speeding blur. I wasn't quick enough to hold them.

Cement chips flew and concrete walls buckled.

It was terrifying. I'd shoved myself into a far corner, my back pressed as far as it could go against the wall, my arm shielding my eyes from flying debris. I hoped one of them wouldn't fire the other my way and end up decapitating me in the process.

Just when my fears turned to anger, when I was sure that they were going to collapse the building and kill us all, there was a piercing shriek from somewhere above us.

We all froze. Festos and Kai were red-faced with exertion, cut up, and bloody. There was going to be some pretty ugly bruising.

I glanced up at the ceiling. With a chill, I recognized the voice. "Hannah!" I gasped. I ran upstairs in record time, flung the apartment door open and skidded to a stop inside the threshold, with my chest heaving.

Hannah stood there in her pajamas, her hand covering her mouth, her expression horrified. Pierce was beside her in clothes that looked thrown on. The look of concern on his face chilled me to the bone.

I followed their gaze and couldn't believe what I saw. Cassie stood on the far side of the room, blood flowing from her eyes. She opened her mouth and, in a loud hollow voice, chanted, "Bring the fire, choke the spark, release the form."

Over and over again.

Theo ran in from the bathroom with washcloths to staunch her bleeding. Cassie didn't even blink as he touched her. Just continued her monotoned prophesying. "Bring the fire, choke the spark, release the form."

"Fix her!" Hannah demanded of me.

I was rooted to the spot, with no idea what to do.

Festos and Kai ran in behind me. Fee's eyes widened at the sight of Cassie's condition, but all he said was, "We need to sedate her." He headed for his First Aid kit in the kitchen, but Kai knew where he kept it. Kai shot past Fee, got it first, ripped it open, and rifled through it as he raced to Theo. Kai pulled out a small vial and held it up questioningly.

Festos nodded.

Kai tugged out the rubber stopper and waved it under Cassie's nose. She fell into Kai's arms in a heap, unconscious.

Silence.

No one moved. It was as if we were in a movie where the frame had been frozen. Then, with a lurch, everyone sprang back into action.

"Bedroom," Festos said tersely, already leading the way. Theo and Pierce went with him, Kai in the rear with Cassie still unconscious in his arms.

Which left Hannah and me.

"What happened?" I asked.

"She lost it," Hannah threw up her hands and started pacing. "Luckily she was on the phone with Anil. He freaked out and called me. Pierce and I went to collect her. She was babbling that sentence over and over again." Hannah shook her head at me, radiating disappointment and worry.

I felt bad enough without Hannah's supreme disapproval. That just made me testy. I jutted my chin out and met her eyes. "What's with the look?"

"You know she's tied to you. Maybe if you hadn't been holed up here, maybe if you'd been paying a bit more attention—"

My rash flared into life. I ignored it, gritting my teeth and curling my fingers into my palms.

"Yeah, sorry," I said, all nonchalant. "Paying attention would have cut in to my vacation time." I gave in then, my nails tearing at what felt like fire ants biting their way up my forearms. "Are you kidding me?" I shouted. "What do you think I've been doing all this time?"

Hannah gave an infuriating shrug. "I have no idea."

My heart thudded, achy. "Maybe that's because you're

so wrapped up in Pierce that you can't be bothered seeing what's going on in other people's lives."

Hannah looked wounded for the briefest of moments. Then she came out swinging. "You act like you have no power to make any choices, but that's *all* you have."

I stepped toward her, blazing. "One time when I've done that. Tell me one."

She came toward me, finger outstretched. "You let Felicia railroad you out of school."

"I *let* her?"

Hannah poked me in the chest hard, shoving me back a step. "Yes. You just conceded to whatever she wanted instead of stepping up for the sake of the bigger picture. Probably did it with Kai, too."

What does she know? For once, I was in agreement with my Persephone voice.

I knocked Hannah's finger away. "Big words coming from a girl who's biggest concern is who will adore her most today."

"You hypocrite," she screeched. "You're fine when it's all about you. But now that it's my turn? You can't stand not being in the spotlight. It's killing you to be happy for me, isn't it? Could you be any more selfish?"

Bethany stabbing me had hurt less.

I placed my hands on my hips and cocked an eyebrow. "What's really bothering you?" I sneered. "Can't stand the fact that for once you're not the most fabulous girl in the room? That I'm not in your shadow anymore? Your stupider, uglier sidekick?"

I could feel Persephone cheering me on, even as Hannah's face got stonier and stonier. These horrible things were spewing out of my mouth and I kind of didn't mean them but, yeah, I did.

Part of me was screaming at myself to shut up, but that part didn't seem to be in control anymore. My mouth just kept going. "Are you feeling your human limits now that you're hanging around higher beings? Word of advice? Stick to being the girlfriend. Don't even try to understand what it's like being us."

I felt a perverse satisfaction at her sharp intake of breath.

Then she laughed bitterly. "Don't kid yourself. You're not that complex. You never have been." And with that parting shot, she strode toward Festos' bedroom.

I wanted so desperately to call her back. To undo this mess. But when I opened my mouth, my throat wouldn't work. When I tried to follow her, I stayed rigid in place.

She doesn't understand. I pressed my fingers to my temples, not wanting to bond with Persephone right now, but still in agreement with her. *Show them what you're made of.* She was louder now, more insistent in my head.

"No."

"Sorry?"

I whirled around at the sound of Pierce's voice.

"Bit of a spat?" he asked, watching me carefully.

I closed my eyes briefly against the absurdity of that understatement. "Is Cassie okay?"

"No more bleeding. Still asleep. Figure she had to break, now she can mend." Pierce sat down on one of the sofas and tilted his head to indicate that I should sit down beside him. "She's your best mate."

Ah. Topic switch. "And your girlfriend, so let's guess whose side *you're* going to take."

"No sides. You haven't been a goddess for very long, so I'll give you some advice, yeah?" He regarded me for a long moment, his eyes more brilliantly green than usual. "Don't hold a grudge. Stick with love."

I crossed my arms. "What if I want to hold a grudge?"

He looked at me with pity and sadness. "Then you miss out. You end up hard."

I sighed and started worrying at the leather on the sofa. "She doesn't understand all the pressure I'm under, or how tough it is to deal with gods constantly undermining me. Never mind this basic struggle to survive. Why should I have to be the first one to apologize on top of all that?"

Pierce shrugged. "You shouldn't. But then it goes one of two ways. You end up as polite acquaintances who maybe spare a thought one day, wondering what ever happened to each other."

My chest tightened. That was a horrible thought. "And the other way?"

He waved a hand toward the bedroom, where everyone else was. "You find yourself knocking the stuffing out of each other because it's all been festering."

It took me a second to make the connection. I shot him a skeptical glance. "I don't know what the deal is between Kai and Festos, but they were never best friends."

Pierce gave me an enigmatic smile. "All I'm saying is that if you're going to be the savior of humanity, maybe you could start by saving a single friendship." He got up in one fluid movement and patted my head. "I'm going to collect Hannah and Cassie, and take them home. Think on it, yeah?"

I sat there for a few minutes after he exited, my head bowed and my elbows braced on my knees. I wanted to give Pierce time to leave with Hannah and Cassie because I couldn't face either one. I didn't have the guts to deal with my guilt and anxiety where Cassie was concerned. And I didn't have the heart to handle all the jagged, raw, tangled up emotions around Hannah. Maybe tomorrow. If she came to her senses, too.

As I headed toward Fee's bedroom, I wondered if Pierce was right. Had Kai and Festos been best friends at some point? Is that why they were so antagonistic now? Why Kai seemed to take a perverse delight in taunting Fee? I hesitated outside the bedroom door, then shook off my unease, and stepped inside.

Theo was perched on the large bed, one knee tucked under him, head bowed as if in defeat. Festos stood nearby, leaning heavily on his cane. In his other hand, he held the now-bloody washcloths, staring at them like he wasn't sure what to do next.

Kai held himself apart from the other two, resting against the top of the bamboo dresser and avoiding contact with the flat screen TV mounted on the wall behind him.

They all turned to face me at once, but no one spoke. The room felt loaded, though not because of the earlier tension. It was as if our encounter with Cassie had drained us profoundly, leaving behind a mix of sorrow and uncertainty and a kind of loss. My fight with Hannah coupled with the brawl between Kai and Festos, only worsened the vibe.

I latched on to the one tangible thing that we could possibly deconstruct without stepping into an emotional minefield. "Did anyone understand what Cassie was saying? About the flame and stuff?"

"'Bring the fire, choke the spark, release the form'. I have my guesses," Festos said, sliding Theo a sharp look.

Theo stood up abruptly, brushing off the front of his baggy pants. "It's about Zeus' and Hades' ward. How I'm going to take it down."

"Uh, no," said Festos. "We agreed I was going to cleanse the area. Which means I take the other ward down as well."

"You have your job, I have mine," Theo said.

I whipped around to face Festos. He looked like he might explode.

Shockingly, Kai pushed away from the dresser at this. With his right side held stiffly, he crossed to Fee in three steps. He waited until Festos met his eyes. "Prometheus started this. It's his to take down."

"His to be in danger. You would say that." Festos sounded, well, not angry exactly. More bitter.

I expected the fight to resume, but Kai let a fleeting moment of sadness pass across his face before his expression went scarily neutral. He gave a one shouldered shrug, almost indifferent.

What the hell was going on here? Kai never called Theo by his full name. Nor had he ever given a damn that Theo had been the one to save Persephone seventeen years ago and put all this into motion. Never mind whatever was brewing between Kai and Festos.

All of which I was about to say when Festos spat, "I'm leaving," and stomped out of the room.

Uselessly, I stretched out a hand to stop him. But he was gone.

Kai shifted his focus to me. "Ready to go see Felicia?" he asked.

"I'll get my shoes," Theo said, crossing into the hallway with only the barest of flinches as he heard the front door slam behind Festos.

"What was ..." I made a flapping motion, "that?"

Kai shook his head, his mouth tight. "Nothing you need to worry about." His expression softened. "Festos doesn't want to see Theo hurt."

I could certainly understand that. "If Theo has to do this, then we'll keep him safe."

Kai's response was a small smile. He took a few steps toward the door.

"Kai?"

He paused and half turned toward me.

"What happened to playing nice? Downstairs? With the fight."

This time I got a genuine smile. "See, now, I never agreed to that."

He went out, leaving me alone and still very confused and deeply concerned about what had just happened.

I could puzzle it out later. For now, I had to go face Felicia and hope she'd help us through the ward that

Zeus and Hades had put up, in exchange for handing Earth and its welfare over to her.

In other words, time for me to suck up to my pissed off mother and pray it didn't all go horribly wrong.

**

Theo, Kai, and I made a pretty impressive thwack as we rebounded off the glass and steel high-rise that was technically still my family home.

The fact that we were twenty-three stories up was not so great. Luckily, Theo had my hand, and I had Kai's, so he was able to blink us safely to the ground.

Snag the first.

My head started to throb. I went to the sidewalk and peered across the street, past the leafless branches on the row of trees ringing the park, and out to the frothy waters of English Bay, my favorite beach in the world. In summer, the water would be a brilliant blue, but today, in the gray weather, it was washed out and lifeless. The waves broke hesitantly on the rocky shore. Being here, seeing this usually filled me with such joy.

Now I was just cold. But that could have been the weather. I'd been expecting to end up inside Felicia's apartment and hadn't worn a jacket over my superhero T-shirt. I rubbed my arms to lose the goosebumps.

"You okay?" Kai's voice startled me out of my thoughts.

"I'll live."

He took my hand and threaded my fingers through his, giving it a reassuring squeeze. "If you want me to take her out, just tap your nose."

That got a smile from me. "Dispose of the body and everything?"

"Child's play."

"Appreciate it, but we'll hope it doesn't come to that." Because if it did, I was going to have the pleasure myself.

We walked back to Theo who waited by the glass front door. "Warded up. So no grand entrance. Got your keys?"

I dug into the pocket of Kai's jeans, pulled out my key and jangled it. I held the fob up to the security sensor and pressed the button, but the light stayed red. Which meant the door was still locked.

I tried again.

By the fourth time, I realized that the security system had been updated but my fob had not.

Kai nudged me out of the way. He held his index finger in front of the sensor and sent out a quick pulse of black light. The panel crackled and flashed, but nothing useful happened. Same with trying to blast the glass.

Since that was getting us nowhere, Kai tugged on my arm and I followed him.

"You have a plan?" Theo asked as we headed around the side of the building.

"One of us has to." Kai positioned himself at the edge of the driveway into the underground parking garage. "Look aimless."

Theo and I were more awkward than aimless.

Kai shook his head in despair. "You two are the worst layabout teens ever."

"Well there weren't a lot of 7-11s to loiter in front of at boarding school," I said.

Kai tilted his head at the sound of a car approaching. "New plan," he told Theo. "Play third wheel." Then, with his back to Theo, Kai kissed me.

Not that I was complaining but, "This is going to get us inside?"

He grinned as he heard Theo growl disgustedly and stomp toward the security gate. "Step one: Annoyed friend. Step two." He reached for me again.

"I still don't see how—" I mumbled against his lips.

"Would it kill you to play along?"

"Fine." I went up on tiptoe, grabbed his shirtfront, and fell into him.

Kai's arm came around me and he stumbled into the driveway, his kiss growing more intense.

A car horn blared. Kai startled away from me in a very un-Kai like motion. He ducked his head sheepishly and waved at the driver, as he tugged me out of the car's path. "Sorry, dude."

Huh? Computing ... computing ... Ah. Kai wanted us to get into the garage with the car.

The security gate across the driveway was rising. I stepped forward as if to duck under it. The driver glared at us. Kai gave another affable wave of apology and led me away down the street. "Keep moving," he said, as I tossed a confused look over my shoulder.

Once we heard the gate shut again, Kai stopped. He waited a moment then began walking back. "Step two," he continued, as I scrambled after him, "distract the driver so that the annoyed friend of step one fame—"

Theo's head popped out, as a door beside the security gate opened.

Kai nodded, "Is smart enough to slip inside while the driver isn't looking." Kai seemed pretty pleased with himself.

I grinned at him. "And all you needed was the cooperation of a willing and highly kissable female."

He scrunched up his face. "Really? Where?"

I elbowed him.

"Don't mind me," Theo said as we slipped past him into the underground parking lot. "I love being exposed to you two."

"You're just grumpy." I winced as I remembered that Festos had recently stormed off. "In general," I amended lamely. "Grumpy in general. Oh, look. Elevators!"

"Nice save," Kai murmured to me.

Theo jabbed at the button. "You think she'll be home?" he asked as we rode upward.

I checked my watch. "If she's in town, then yes. She's home. She likes to freshen up with a drink about now." If Felicia wasn't in, well, we'd be stopping by her place in Whistler next.

The elevator opened and we padded down the hall to apartment 2311.

Of all the emotions I figured I might feel at this moment, standing before my front door, absolutely zip was not something I'd considered. It was just a door. One that I was familiar with, but that was about it.

Funny. *That's* what made me feel sad.

Here we go, I thought, and slid my key into the lock.

Nine

I was shocked that my key still worked. I pushed the door open quietly and we stepped into the small marble foyer. I could hear voices and laughter coming from the living room at the far end of the apartment.

Theo raised his eyebrows at me and cocked his head toward the living room. I took a step forward, listening intently until I recognized the voices. "It's Felicia," I whispered, as we gathered in a tight huddle. "And her best friend, Kiki."

Theo suppressed a laugh. "You mean I finally get to put a face to the elusive Russian cougar I've heard so much about?"

"She's not that bad." I actually liked Kiki and her totally-inappropriate-for-kids jokes. Brash, overbearing, and loud she may have been, but she'd always been kind to me, cheering me up on more than one occasion after a fight with Felicia. My mother hadn't loved our bond but she hadn't bothered about it either.

"Does she usually stay long?" Kai asked.

Theo brightened. "She's a cougar. You could be prey."

Kai elbowed him.

I glared at both of them and motioned for them to follow me.

We crept down the hallway to the bright, all-white living room. "Lovely to see you as always, Felicia," I said as we stepped up to the threshold.

The shock on Felicia's face was priceless. As was her choking on her drink.

I took in my mother's appearance. She was as immaculately groomed as always in a rust-colored cashmere sweater and brown tailored trousers. Her honey hair fell to her shoulders in exact, blunt edges, probably fearful of being a fraction out of line.

"It would mean more, darling, if you didn't wear rags." Damn. She'd found her voice.

I turned my attention to Kiki, seated across from Felicia on the sofa. She dragged on her cigarette, one hand patting her pouffed up, red-hennaed hair. Her leopard print shirt, worn over a pair of black slacks, was unbuttoned to best show off her goods. She tucked her bare feet and red painted toes along her side.

Kiki exhaled. Her eyes narrowed as she took the three of us in, brazenly scoping out Theo and Kai. "You visit with such delicious friends, Sophinchka." Her voice was so gravely that I'd mistaken her for a guy more than once on the phone. But the sound of her familiar Russian accent was comforting.

Kai and Theo exchanged looks. Theo may have shuddered.

"Down, Kiki," I said. "Theo is gay and both are taken."

"I appreciate beauty." Said with the kind of leer that undermined any potential poetry in the statement. Kiki angled her cheek up and tapped her index finger against it. "Sugar me."

Obediently, I went over and kissed it.

Ignoring Felicia.

Who ignored me.

Kiki tugged me down beside her on the sofa. "What brings you home? Spring break already?"

Felicia shook her head in fond exasperation at her friend. I was very familiar with the gesture, since she'd directed it at me numerous times.

Except without the fond part.

Felicia swirled her drink. "You always encourage her. The only reason Sophie is here is because she wants something."

Yeah, but I wasn't about to go blurting out details in front of Kiki. "Could I speak to you privately?" I asked.

Kiki stubbed out her cigarette in a heavy crystal ashtray on top of the wide leather ottoman that served as a coffee table.

Kai and Theo flinched.

Kiki smiled at the boys. "Nichivo," she said in Russian. "No matter. You can speak freely."

I frowned, confused.

Kai edged toward me. "Sophie," he said in an oddly neutral voice, "A little warning that Kiki is Hekate would have been nice."

Ripping open a new pack of cigarettes, she paused to wink at me.

I open-mouth gaped at Kiki.

Hekate was the Goddess of Night, Magic, Witchcraft, the Moon, and—I racked my brain—Ghosts. Among other things. Hekate had also alerted Demeter when Kai took Persephone to the Underworld, and then been Persephone's companion. Talk about a long friendship.

"But you're Russian," I said, trying to process.

"Da. For now. I needed a new look, and, well, Moskva always provided such amusements." She slid a cigarette into her mouth with a practiced ease. "Light."

I picked up the lighter from beside the ashtray and flicked it. Something I'd done many times before. "Who do you like more?" I asked. "Me or Persephone?"

Kiki barked out a laugh. "You. Especially now that you have everyone's nuts in a twist." She glanced at Felicia, eyes glinting mischievously. "Present company included."

Felicia frowned.

I looked over at Kai and Theo, neither of whom looked happy at this turn of events. I couldn't understand the problem. Okay, there was yet another member of the Greek pantheon to deal with, but this one liked me. What was the big deal? "How'd you know?" I asked instead. They hadn't recognized her, so something else had given her away.

"The tattoo," Theo said in a flat voice. "When she stubbed out the cigarette." He mimed her sleeve riding up.

I glanced at Kiki's wrist. I'd seen that tattoo so many times that I'd forgotten it was there. The design featured a small circle inside a larger one. Between the two, there was a ring of three semi-circles, almost as if they were trying to keep the small and large circles apart. In the very center of the design, there was a stylized star. I touched the tattoo gently.

"You always did love tracing it," Kiki said.

I smiled, feeling a brief nostalgia for my younger self. "Hekate's wheel. Except I didn't know that then."

She exhaled again, turning her head so the smoke wouldn't catch me full-on in the face. "It's true. You do remember everything."

I nodded.

"Ochen horosho."

I was too distracted trying to figure out the dynamic between Theo, Kai, and Kiki to respond to her praise. Kiki patted my hand. "Don't worry. Kyrillos never liked me having the run of the Underworld."

"Or my father's ear," Kai said.

"I can't help my charms," she replied, with a sly smile.

Okay. That made sense for Kai. But Theo was scowling at Kiki with a hatred I'd never seen from him before. The only thing I could think of was …

"Holy crap," I gasped. Suddenly it all made sense. "You're the witch that took Theo's power."

Kiki tilted her head in agreement.

I grasped her hand, almost desperately. "Give it back. Please." The difference his power could make, to our battle and to the safety of my friend's future was enormous.

Kiki's look was almost sympathetic. "I can't, Sophinchka. That was the payment. The balance. I gave a human baby goddess power. I had to take a god's power and render him human."

"Titan, not god," said Theo.

"Regardless." Kiki took another drag. "I can't just give it back." She looked shrewdly toward Theo. "But I think you know that already, don't you Prometheus?"

Felicia had used our little catch-up chat to toss back her drink and get another one. She returned to her chair already making headway on the liquor. "Cut to the chase. What do you want?"

"We're here to make a deal," said Theo.

Felicia gave him a totally fake smile. "Delightful. I want to hear my darling daughter offer it."

Like mother, like daughter. I pasted on a beaming, fraudulent smile of my own. "I'd like nothing better." Our smiles were plenty broad but our gazes were combative.

"I grow old," Kiki said. "Speak already."

I kept eye contact with Felicia. "You wanted power?" I spread my hands wide. "It's yours. Original deal on the table. Kai and I take out Zeus and Hades, and let you rule." My throat caught as I choked that out, but choke it out I did.

From the way Felicia's eyes gleamed, she knew what it cost me to say it.

"Not quite," Kai piped up.

We all turned to him with varying degrees of surprise and—from me and Theo—a bit of suspicion.

"I want the Underworld." Kai's face twisted. "Hades is going down and I want him to know that I have everything he cared about. You can have Olympus and Earth. The Underworld is mine."

I exchanged an uneasy glance with Theo. This wasn't part of the plan. For a brief second, I worried that it would be a deal-breaker and that I'd come to Felicia for nothing.

But she lit up, thrilled. "Such bitterness. I can practically feel it eating away at you." She rested the rim of her glass against her bottom lip as she stared at Kai, thoughtfully. Then she set the glass down. "Don't worry, darling, it's an emotion I can appreciate. Agreed. The Underworld is yours. However, I'm simply burning with curiosity to know what's in this for you?" She swung her piercing gaze back to me.

I leaned forward. "Zeus and Hades warded up the ritual location in Eleusis. We need you to get us inside."

"Ah, my old stomping grounds." I swear to God, if she'd had a mustachio to twirl in evil glee at that moment, Felicia would have done it. "It seems that you need me far more than I need you."

Kiki tsked her, but a sharp look from Felicia kept her quiet.

I sat up straight. Beyond fed up. "Alright, Felicia. What's it going to take? You want me to beg? I'll beg. But despite how you feel about me, I know that you've always given a damn about the human race. So let's cut the BS and name your price, so we can stop this war on Earth and stop the human casualties."

Felicia crossed one leg over the other, as if we were enjoying a cozy chat. Her tone was anything but cozy. "Did you really think you could just waltz in here with old promises that you'd tossed away once before, and win me over so easily? Every action has a consequence. Something I've been rather lax in teaching you."

I ground my teeth so hard that I could hear the enamel destruction.

Felicia picked a piece of invisible lint off her sweater. "My price is this. When this is over, you never see Kyrillos again."

My breath hitched and, for a second, my heart stopped beating.

She smiled. "Yes. I think that will do nicely."

Never see Kai again? Intellectually, I knew I had to say yes. What was our love against the fate of the world?

But emotionally? My throat had closed up. A cold sweat beaded my brow and icy fingers of panic clawed at me. I couldn't say the words.

Kai had gone pale.

Kiki tsked again. "Demeter," she said, disapproving, "You of all people should not force this."

Something unspoken passed between them before Felicia relented. "Theo then."

My heart stuttered again. That was just as bad. Its furious pounding echoed in my ears.

"Done."

I swung to face Theo, who regarded me evenly. "This is bigger than us, Magoo."

"No!" I turned to Felicia, pleading. "Not Kai. Not my

friends. Anything else." Hot tears pooled in my eyes. "I'll be your slave. Whatever you want."

"You can't give me what I want," she said. Felicia turned to Theo. "You'll stay away from Sophie?"

"For the rest of my life," he mocked.

She grimaced, not finding him funny. "Excellent. We have a deal. Swear?"

Theo nodded. "I swear on the Styx that I'll stay away from her."

I was crying outright now, trying to make her take it back, arguing that I hadn't agreed to it. But neither she nor Theo paid me any attention.

Kiki ground out her cigarette and gave my arm a sympathetic pat. "It is done, Sophinchka." She rose from the sofa and crossed to the bank of floor-to-ceiling windows, gazing at some far point.

I buried my face in my hands. Tears coursed down my cheeks. I felt Kai sit beside me and take me in his arms. He stroked my hair. "It'll be okay."

But it was never going to be okay again.

"Soph," Theo said. I realized he had moved to sit beside me, too.

I raised wet eyes to his, wanting to ask him how he could have done this. Wanting to know if he could really just walk away from me? I saw that it was killing him, and he was doing it anyway.

Once I'd become a goddess, there had been a lot of points that I'd figured were tests. Big tests, small tests, it was the nature of the hero game. All of them were totally insignificant beside this one. With shockingly cold clarity, I knew that when Zeus had kidnapped me, when Demeter had almost ruined my relationship with Kai, even when I'd been bleeding out on the ground, I'd had one massively important thing that I didn't have now.

Hope.

I swallowed hard and wiped my eyes. Then I pulled Theo into the fiercest, tightest hug I'd even given him.

He didn't even resist. All he did was echo Kai. "It'll be okay."

"Can we talk details now?" At the sound of Felicia's voice, I released Theo from the hug, but kept his hand in mine.

I knew my father was a psychopath. And while I had lots of colorful names for Felicia, that wasn't one of them. Yes, Persephone had screwed her over and taken away her chance to rule Olympus, but still, watching her recline in her chair with an expression of mild boredom, waiting while my heart broke—I revised my opinion.

"Start talking." Kai had a take-no-prisoners tone. He slung an arm around me and hauled me against him, his body practically humming with tension, his eyes never wavering from her.

"Your little ritual ground borders my temple in Eleusis. Where are the boundaries of the ward you created? Is there overlap?"

"Yes," Theo replied. "On the southwest side."

"Good." Felicia nodded. "Beside the remains of the Lesser Propylaea," she said, using the Greek word for the monumental gateway, "there is a cave. Inside is an entrance to the Underworld. Or, conversely, an exit to Earth."

"You want us to go through Hades." Kai's disbelief was palpable.

"There is no other way for me to grant you inside access. Descend to the Underworld and make your way to the portal on that side."

"Hades will kill us," I piped up. My arms burned. I had to give up Theo and Felicia couldn't even find a non-lethal solution for us?

"Then you'll have to stay one step ahead. You've been quite successful thus far." The look she shot me was almost proud.

"I'll deal with my father," Kai said.

"Do you know where to find the portal on the Underworld side?" Theo asked Kai.

Kai thought about it a moment, then nodded. "Leave it to me."

"Then we time this as close to the equinox as possible." Theo stroked his chin. "We want to get through and take down Zeus' ward. Then we let Festos take down ours and cleanse the site in as little time as possible before you two say the ritual." He looked at Felicia.

"I'll open it early Thursday," she said. "It won't alert Hades or Zeus one way or the other. I will ensure that the way between the two realms is open, and that your passage through is safe. At which point you will be inside their ward and can proceed." She raised an eyebrow. "Are we done?"

"Swear on the Styx," I said, barely audible.

My body ached with the knowledge that my time with Theo was counting down, in a gut wrenching, marrow-of-my-bones kind of way. If I was going to have to endure this blinding heartache, and a future without my best friend, then I could bind Felicia to her word.

"I beg your pardon?" She sounded insulted.

"Swear. On. The. Styx."

"Such a petulant child," she protested.

"Swear, Demeter." I startled at Kiki's voice. Still standing by the windows, she had been so quiet that I'd forgotten she was still there.

Felicia looked like she couldn't wait to have this over with. "I swear on the Styx that it shall be as I decreed," she said, and tucked a strand of hair behind her ear. "Now you. I want you bound to give me power this time."

Whatever. Not like I had a choice. "Fine. I swear on—" A knifelike pain slashed across my left wrist. With a gasp I stared down, but it was unmarked.

"It's the oath," Theo explained. "The binding hurts. Just say it." He got up and rocked on his heels as if stretching out his back.

"I swear on the—" Pain flared across my right wrist.

"What'd I miss?" I knew that voice. Behind me.

Words failed me as my personal tormentor and classmate, Bethany Russo-Hill sauntered into Felicia's living room, in her usual ridiculously pricy yoga gear, all streaming dark red hair and deceptively innocent blue eyes. She gave Kai, Theo, and me a dismissive glance, and then plopped into a chair like she lived there. Which given Bethany's god groupie tendencies and Felicia's desire to inflict maximum emotional damage on me, may actually have been the case.

Felicia turned a doting smile on Bethany. "Sophie was just swearing to put me in power in Olympus and never see her little friend Theo again."

"Oh. Cool."

I waved my throbbing right hand between her and Felicia. "Are you kidding me?" I exploded.

Bethany rolled her eyes. "God, Demeter, you sure she's really yours? Such a drama queen."

Viney light shot out of my palms, snaked around Bethany, and began to squeeze.

"Sophie!" Kiki hurried over to me and smacked my arm. My light flew back into my palms.

Bethany rubbed her sides, giving that "poor wounded me" look that she'd pulled so many times before, back at Hope Park.

Take her out. Another moment of me and my Persephone voice in absolute agreement.

"I'm going to kill you," I said to Bethany.

She laughed. "Try it. I'm under D's protection."

I wanted to claw her eyes out. She was on such familiar terms with *my* mother that she'd given her a nickname. Whereas, I wasn't even invited to call her Demeter. I couldn't even look at Bethany because my hands literally shook with the desire to annihilate her. My Persephone voice screamed at me to do it.

My right wrist still burned. I hadn't finished the oath. My sight wavered. My body vibrated with rage.

"Calm down, Goddess."

I ignored Kai.

"Sophie, the rims of your eyes are turning black," he said, grasping my shoulders.

I shook him free. I didn't care.

"Finish the oath, daughter," Felicia said. "Then Bethany and I can chat."

There was a loud *crraaaack* from outside. Loud enough to be heard twenty-three floors up.

Everyone except me turned to the window. I kept my sights on Bethany and Felicia.

"Magoo," Theo said, his worry evident, "you just broke the branches on all the trees in a two block radius."

I barely registered him. My entire world had shrunk down to the two people before me. My body was rigid with the will power it took to use my words and not my fury. "The night of the Winter Formal you claimed to love me, Felicia. Was it all a lie?"

"No," she said slowly.

"Then how can you align yourself with someone who stabbed me? Murdering Persephone wasn't enough for you? You had to team up with likeminded others?"

Bethany chortled her amusement.

Later for you, I vowed.

Felicia uncrossed her legs and leaned back in the chair. "Well, darling, you do have that affect on people. Maybe you need to take a hard look at yourself and figure out why you prompt that reaction in so many. Now, the oath?"

I kept silent, my eyes hard and unwavering.

Felicia could tell I'd say nothing until she answered my question. "I wanted power, you refused to help me get it. Bethany is my Plan B. I help her achieve her goals—"

"Told you I'd be famous." Bethany didn't even bother to look over as she spoke. She was too busy braiding a thick strand of hair.

"And in return," Felicia continued, "with the world at Bethany's feet, she helps me rebuild the adoration I knew before."

"Your building your power," Theo cut in.

Felicia acknowledged him with a one-shouldered shrug. She picked up her glass.

"For what?" I demanded.

Felicia's grip on the booze tightened. "I answered your question. Now say the damn oath."

Ordinarily, the pain in my wrist might have been enough to make me say it. But I was so far into my own hurt and anger that I could absorb the fire I felt, and add it to my own hot indignation.

I could feel the pain sliding away. Out of my wrist, through my arm, and into my fiery core. My wrist stopped hurting. Flush with the triumph of that, I shook my head. "My end of the deal is off."

Everyone in the room looked horrified. "But you swore," Theo said. "You can't go back on that."

"Technically, I never finished."

"Yeah, but the spirit of the thing," he began.

"Can kiss my ass."

"Think this through, Goddess," Kai urged.

I funneled every ounce of rage and destruction into a megawatt smile, and turned it on Felicia. "I will die before I hand power over to you."

"That can and will be arranged," she said.

"Happy to take another shot at it," Bethany offered, starting a matching braid.

I ignored her and delivered the best part. "Here's the thing though, *mom*, you *did* swear. So I'll be taking that safe passage on the equinox."

Felicia was super ticked off now. She knew I had her. "Last chance, Sophie. Finish the oath or you'll be sorry."

The room was thick with tension.

"Bite me." My voice was steady, but inside I seethed.

"Then you leave me no choice." She looked at Kiki. "Make it hurt."

Ten

I didn't feel any pain but it did get exceedingly dark. Heavy, all-encompassing, like light was an alien concept here. Dark. Did Felicia make Kiki blind me? I tried to touch my face and realized I couldn't move. I lay on my back, my hands pinned to my sides and my legs clamped together.

I. Freaked.

Light blasted out of my eyes and palms in my panic, and I felt something fall away from me. But between the blinding flash of my powers, and the return to Situation Normal blackness, I couldn't actually see what it was.

Free from my bindings, I groped around until I found them. Cool, thin cloth had wrapped me like a mummy. Not strips of bandage though, one solid strip. That twigged something. I lay there, trying to grab hold of the elusive fact dancing just out of memory.

A shroud. That was it! But my satisfaction at remembering quickly turned to dread as the implications of that thought hit me. Shrouds were used for one thing. Burial.

My hand flew up and hit a heavy earth barrier above my head. I started to pant. Had Felicia buried me alive? Awkwardly, I contorted myself so I was on all fours, since there wasn't enough room to sit up straight. My legs got tangled in the flowing long dress that I now wore. Trust Felicia to ensure a wardrobe change.

Face tilted upward, I scrabbled furiously at the dirt, my blood icy with fear as I felt my oxygen draining away. My palms sweated, my breath managed to both hitch and hyperventilate. Loamy earth clogged my fingernails as I clawed at the earth to get out. But it was hopeless. I was trapped.

From my position on all fours, I collapsed face down, acking out the taste of soil. I inhaled a nose full of musty air, with an undertone of deep rot. That smell, more than anything, hammered home the finality of my predicament. This was it. Just like in my vision, buried alive. I felt hollow. The futility of it all, the stupidity and surreality of coming so close only to lose overwhelmed me in spikes of equal measures: fear and despair.

I lay there, a boneless heap, listening to my racing heart and every precious remaining breath. I thought about how I'd left things with Hannah. About how I'd been cheated out of what little time I'd have with Theo. And Kai …

Maybe it was better if I didn't think anymore.

I didn't want to lie there until I starved, or suffocated, or whatever. If I *was* buried alive, maybe there was a rock or something to knock myself unconscious with. In this situation, patience wouldn't be a virtue. Just scary.

My arms were bent up against my sides, my elbows hovering around my ears. I stretched out one arm, fully expecting to encounter more dirt. There was nothing but empty air. I stretched my arm out a little further, my fingertips exploring the absolute blackness. More air.

I pulled myself back up onto all fours and carefully examined my space. My back fit snug against the dirt ceiling. The sides were close in on me. I couldn't turn around to check behind me, because I was Alice-in-Wonderland huge here. I crawled forward then backward for a bit. Nothing stopped me. Not buried alive then. In a tunnel.

Just as I started to wonder where I was, and why I was there, I felt something skitter over my foot. Wonder later, get out now. I began my world record speed crawl to freedom.

"Kai? Theo?" Were they nearby? It was so dark, they could have been right in front of me and I'd never have known. But no one answered me. Which begged the question of where they were. Back at Felicia's?

It was crampy joint-stiffening work inching along like this. The tunnel was uncomfortably hot and stuffy. Every few minutes, I had to wipe the salty sweat from my eyes and stretch my neck as best I could, so as not to solidify into pretzel form. I felt like I'd been crawling for hours, the tunnel spiraling downward in long loops all the while. All this quality time alone in my head allowed me to progress through the five stages of dealing with my mother.

Stage one: Denial. The panic, the utter cluelessness about where I was—it couldn't be because Felicia had sent me tunneling to the Underworld, could it? Felicia had said we needed to cross through it to get to her exit. And a lot of the myths talked about how people descended to Hades. Was she really sending me there on my own?

That led to stage two: Disbelief. Seriously? Again? She'd screwed me over again? Showed not disinterest, but active desire to do harm. The more I thought about it, the more I felt certain that Hades was precisely where she was sending me. If the Underworld was like Manhattan, I was a single occupant driver in the Holland tunnel from Jersey.

Hopefully, there wouldn't be a toll booth. Because I'd paid enough.

Stage three: Rage. Lots of name calling. Lots of threats.

Finally, I swear it felt like I could have graduated and gone to college by this point, I saw a pinprick of light up ahead. I blinked to be sure that it wasn't some weird trick. Like my brain trying to fool me into seeing it. Wishful thinking made manifest.

But no. The light grew brighter and brighter until I could see a grate. And grateful I was as I made my way to it. Daylight filtered in from up ahead, which meant that I was reaching the end of this stupid non-scenic route.

I shoved my weight against the grate. Nada. It wouldn't budge. *Waa waa waa waaaa.*

Stage four: Laughter. Perhaps a tad unhinged. Because of course Felicia wasn't going to make any of it easy on me. Foolish girl for thinking otherwise.

The grate was made of crisscrossing metal bars, which were too narrow for me to get through, with the bars themselves unbreakable. And unshootable. My light did nothing except slip off of them.

I mentally shook myself and progressed into stage five: Determination. All right, I had to get through a grate. Could be worse.

The ground rumbled with low, deep menace.

And hello, worse.

Cerberus stepped in front of the grate, blocking out pretty much all the light. He reminded me of one of the Wild Things. Roaring his terrible roar and gnashing his terrible teeth.

"Nice boy," I said, soothingly.

Rumbling growls became ear-splitting barks. This was, however, a step up from the first time that I'd met Cerberus in my Sophie form. Back then he'd tried to snap me in two. I felt about as cuddly toward him.

I flapped one hand at him from the safety of my side of the barrier. "Quiet," I hissed.

He stepped closer to me and sniffed with two of his three heads. Then, amazingly, he shut up. He turned six black-as-pitch eyes on me and waited, heads bobbing expectantly.

Awwww. He was kind of cute in a stinky, knobby, death beast way.

I wasn't sure what he wanted. But I did know he was my best shot at help right now. Did I dare trust him to leave me intact? I had very limited options. I could either try and crawl my way back up and out of the Underworld with no guarantee that there *was* a way out on the other end or I could risk trying to get Cerberus' help and hope that he didn't tear me apart like a chew toy this time.

Desperate times. "Help me get out of here, dog." Seeing as he was a primal killer and not a reasonably intelligent orangutan, he sat there.

I stuck my fingers through the grate and waggled them at him, indicating he should come closer. I also called my light with a palmy glow, in case he turned on me.

His fur felt rough and matted as he nudged my hand. His muscles made lumpy ridges under his skin, which rippled as he opened one of his massive mouths and let out a stream of the foulest stench I'd ever smelled. Rotting eggs were minty mouthwash in comparison. It was like a thousand years of compressed decay.

I tried not to gag, failed, plugged my nose, and tugged him close until two of his snouts touched the grate. "Arrr. Arrr." I mimed biting the metal bars of the grate and tugging backward.

He got the picture pretty quickly, i.e. not at all. Ten minutes later, I was slumped in a dejected ball. "Come on, you dumb mutt."

More waiting on his part.

Okay, he was a dog. A scary one, but still. What did dogs respond to? I had no treats. Hand motions had done nothing. Maybe he just needed a simple command? I sat up and channelled every once of commanding that I could muster. "Cerberus, move grate."

The magic words. Go figure.

I hurried to cover my nose and mouth as his jaws opened again, which helped somewhat with the smell, but still made my eyes water. Cerberus bit down on the bars, and with an effortless flick of his heads, flung the grate out of the way.

I crawled into the Underworld and collapsed. The last time I'd been here, it had been night. I thought it would always be night, but now that I had my Persephone memories, I knew that Hades enjoyed sunlit days during which to strut his god's doucheyness, as much as he liked moonlit nights.

Worked for me, since the sunshine recharged my power. I looked up, a hand automatically shielding my eyes. Then I realized it wasn't that bright. Weird. Even though the sun was yellow and the sky was blue, there was no vibrancy or richness to them. More the faintest suggestion of color than the actual thing.

Color or not, this sun recharged me just fine. After a few minutes, I felt good to go. All I wanted was to find Kai and Theo—if they were here—locate the way to Demeter's temple, and get on with stopping Zeus and Hades.

But where might be the most likely place to find my boys? I looked to Cerberus who settled his heads on his paws, his eyes lowering sleepily. Nope. I wasn't finished with the mutt just yet. "Cerberus, play game."

He didn't exactly thump his tail in joy. Instead, he let two of his heads go to sleep.

I stood up and wiped some salty soil from my eyes. The dress, which had originally been a very nice shade of deep blue, was now streaked with muck. Well, Felicia shouldn't have stuck me in a dirt tunnel if she expected it to stay clean.

I approached Cerberus cautiously. I couldn't remember if I was supposed to make eye contact or not.

Hannah would have known.

No. Not going there.

With a beast this size, and this dangerous, it probably didn't matter. He wasn't worried about dominance. He *was* the top of the food chain.

I stopped in front of him, feeling his hot breath against my hand. Cerberus was massive but not quite as enormous as I remembered him. In *my* memory of fleeing Hades with my sapphire pendant, I must have built this puppy up to nightmare proportions.

I squatted down. "No rest for the wicked yet, buddy. I need you to find Kai. And Theo, but I'm betting you know Kai's scent better." I shoved at him. "Up and at 'em."

Cerberus dropped his middle head on the ground. His deep, ancient eyes looked back at me with a profound stare. It was a stare that said, "I have lived an eternal life and you are the biggest idiot I've seen."

"Seriously. Get up." I nestled against him, my nose wrinkled at his musky smell. I turned around with my back to his body, dug in my heels for leverage, and pushed. Complete with straining face and grunting.

That's when I heard Kai say, "There you are, kardia mou. I've been looking for you."

Kardia mou? "My heart" in Greek?

I looked up with a laugh, happy to hear Kai tease me with such sappy affection. But my laughter cut short at his perplexed expression. He hadn't been teasing—clearly Kai had no clue what I was doing, and he wasn't dressed like I'd last seen him. Now he wore a dark linen short-sleeved shirt over similarly colored linen pants. He was barefoot. And looking at me all kinds of weirdly.

I stepped away from the dog, stood up, and brushed myself off as best I could. "I know I look bad, but come on. That tunnel was a bitch."

He placed a finger over my lips. "Such language mars the perfect beauty of your mouth."

Was he kidding me? I eyed him, worried that maybe he'd suffered some kind of concussion on his way here. Maybe Felicia had done a number on all of us. "Enough, Kai."

Kyrillos. Persephone's voice rose up unbidden inside me. "Kyrillos," I found myself amending.

Kai gave me one of his cat-going-to-eat-the-canary-that-was-me grins. It put me at ease and had me on delicious, anticipating edge as he held out a hand. "I've blown off my father for the afternoon."

He took a step closer. "We can be alone, Persephone."

Persephone?!

Say what?! "Say what?"

Everything fell into place with a sickening lurch. Why Cerberus hadn't tried to kill me, why he didn't seem as large. Why Kai was acting off.

I glanced down at myself, praying this horrible impossibility was not, in fact possible. I saw that the ground was now much farther away than it should have been, and that the body I now rocked was definitely not mine.

Somehow, I had become Persephone.

I heard in her my head, full of spiteful glee. *I'm back.*

Oh. No.

Eleven

I bolted. As if I could somehow outrun this body I was stuck in. Molt it away with speed, leaving it in a dusty heap on the ground and my Sophie self all happy in the sunshine.

Yeah, right.

I ran through grasses in wide fields, their sharp tang tickling my nose. All the plant life had that dry, brittle, washed out look of a land that was in the throes of a long, deep drought. It was a million shades of wheat and gray, with no vibrant colors anywhere.

Eventually, I found myself on a dusty cobblestone road. I knew that it would lead me back to Hades' palace, where there were mirrors to confirm this change. But when I came to the shore of the crystal clear Akherousian lake, I realized that the water would work just as well.

One quick look into the lake was enough to leave me reeling.

It was true. Somehow, I was now Persephone.

Looking away quickly and looking back didn't change things. Neither did pinching myself, opening and closing my eyes, or wishing desperately. Since hers was the last face I wanted to be gazing on, I trudged off, continuing toward the palace and lost in my thoughts. All the while, I was trying to figure out why Felicia would want this?

"She said make it hurt." I froze at the sound of Kiki's voice.

She sat on a flat rock at the edge of an empty intersection, dressed in the same outfit she'd been in at Felicia's. Since I had Persephone's memories, I knew every inch of this place as if I'd explored it myself. Which I had, in a way. At any rate, I knew where we were.

Hekate's Crossroads.

Literally, it was an intersection with three roads branching off from it. The judged souls that Charon and his deadly ferry ride hadn't brought to their final destinations came here. If they'd lived normal lives, they shuffled off to the Fields of Asphodel. If they'd been evil, they went to Tartarus. Or over to the Elysian Fields if their good deeds had won them the afterlife jackpot. Hekate didn't need to be around to help them. The dead people would only be able to travel the appropriate path.

She patted the rock beside her. I'd always liked Kiki, but suddenly I was very wary of her. Because for the first time, I truly felt her power and knew what she was capable of.

She made a lit cigarette appear in her hands. "I'm not going to bite. Sit."

I sat. Since Kiki was still human-sized, and I was about thirteen feet tall, I dwarfed her. My bum felt massive on the rock. After an awkward moment of sliding around, trying to fit both butt cheeks comfortably, I gave up and stood. I gestured at my goddess body. "Why?"

Kiki squinted at me, almost like she was surprised I didn't know. "You did screw Demeter over."

I gaped at her, ready to argue.

She gave me the hand. "You did. She said the oath in good faith that you'd reciprocate. You didn't. Now you suffer the consequences. Balance out your choice."

I laced my fingers together, steepling them against my lips as I studied her. "The consequence that I'm Persephone now? How does that follow?"

Kiki was silent for a bit, smoking her cigarette.

I watched the red ashy tip grow larger, waiting for it to fall. But she tapped out the cigarette before it could. "Are you familiar with the phrase 'Those who cannot remember the past are condemned to repeat it?'" she asked.

"Yeah."

She slid off the rock. "Well, you're repeating it." Then she was walking away, her stride brisk. As if that was the end of the discussion.

Couldn't any of these Greeks bother explaining themselves in detail? I scrambled after her. "I remember everything about the past just fine. I have all of Persephone's memories."

"It's not about literally remembering, you foolish girl. It's about learning from past errors. Well, hello there."

A group of twenty-something man candy car crash victims dressed in soccer uniforms swaggered along en route to Asphodel. The lascivious leer Kiki gave them made her look like she was trawling for boy toys, not shepherding souls.

I waited impatiently.

Kiki gave them a come-hither stare with the full weight of her charm behind it and the one closest to her blushed from head to toe.

I wanted to pull her off the cobblestone road, away from temptation and distraction, and make her talk to me. Or even sling her over my shoulders and carry her away, since I could totally do that, but I was kind of afraid to touch her. She'd already turned me into Persephone. And that was with her liking me.

I sidled in close and spoke up, hoping she'd stop running her hand over the soccer player's bicep and answer me. "Learning what from my errors?"

Kiki trailed a fingertip down his arm and I tried not to shudder, since it was like watching my old aunt hit on a guy better suited to dating me. Finally, she smiled, pulled her hand away, and let them continue. "I have missed this place."

With a last tilt to appreciate the receding view, she returned her attention to me, jabbing a finger into my stomach to make her point. "You've got to reconcile with Persephone if you're going to fulfill that 'one above one below' prophecy. Keep going this way and things are going to end badly for you. And humanity. I didn't go to all the trouble of saving Persephone so that you could blow it." She punctuated that last bit with a few exceptionally hard jabs.

It was almost funny. Like a little terrier yipping its displeasure at a giant sheep dog. Which did not make me sound sexy in the least, but being this size took getting used to. You know, like being on top of a mountain. Or just being a mountain.

I bit down on my bottom lip, trying to make sense of this. Kiki had decided that me being Persephone fit Felicia's wish for me to suffer *and* helped me fulfill the prophecy. The first part made sense. Being stuck with Kai, with him thinking that I was his original love was so going to suck. I could even grudgingly acknowledge the sense in the second part.

I still grumbled. "It's all about Persephone. I should have known."

Kiki shook her head. "No. It's all about *you*. Persephone is part of your younger self. She's part of you, and you still share characteristics. But now you are you."

I let out a half-laugh. This was sounding eerily familiar to the words I'd flung at Kai.

"… Except you're way too hung up on the past. That's no way to have a future. And a heart full of hate can't love. You need love."

I narrowed my eyes at her. "Like The Beatles song?"

She blinked, then got the reference and smiled. "Yes. Exactly."

This was all too coincidental. The feeling of being buried alive in the tunnel. The song. "Did you plan all this? The visions? Has it been you the whole time?" I felt a little sick. My mind whirled with conspiracy theories as everything that had happened in the past few days started to look seriously shady.

To her credit, Kiki played confused very well. "You're affecting the present, Sophinchka. That's a danger to all around you. You will never be successful unless you work through it. This," she spread her hands wide, "is both you facing the consequence and me helping you learn from the past."

There wasn't time for this. The equinox was in four days. Which may seem like a lot of time but, trust me, when you're facing the battle of your life, it's not. The last thing I wanted was to deal with was some after-school special about "life lessons for a better you."

I put my hands on my hips, trying not let the fact that I *had* hips distract me. Persephone was a curvy girl. "The only help I want involves you showing me the exit to Felicia's temple so we can break the stupid ward. Can you do that?"

Kiki scowled at me. She gave great scowl. "This *is* the way out. The way to ensure your victory. But you need to prove that you deserve it. Sometime in the next few days, Demeter is going to murder you."

That stopped me cold. "We've gone back in time?"

"This is an enchantment," Kiki scoffed. "Everyone here is under my spell. To them, they're playing out these events for the first time. But the end can be just as deadly." She motioned for me to get off the path and onto the grass beside it as a busload of seniors went past. "Seventeen years ago, in the early hours of the equinox, I put Persephone's spirit into your body. At that moment, you and she were perfectly aligned. Now you're not."

"There's the understatement of the year." I focused on the procession before me. A widow on the prowl, hard scrambled grandma with a visor, lecherous old guy with an orange tan …

Kiki moved herself into my field of vision. "If you and she are not aligned once more by the equinox, you will fail. Save Persephone and the enchantment breaks. You're free to go through the portal and save the day. Don't save Persephone? You die here and no one knows Sophie Bloom ever existed."

That got my attention. "Not fair." My blood ran cold. "That's cruel."

"It's balance. You repeated the past when you betrayed Demeter by not keeping your word. Now Demeter has her chance to repeat the past and avenge that. It's up to you how it ends." She smiled and patted my cheek. "Have fun."

Kiki disappeared.

Fun? No. What I was going to do was get myself out of this stupid enchantment and back to reality. There were plenty of trees around to transport me. I felt under the dress for my pendent and, with its reassuring weight in my hand, headed straight for the nearest one.

Whacking my nose firmly against the rough bark as the pendant failed to do anything.

I cursed Kiki, rubbing my nose to take away the sting.

Evidently, short cuts were out. I was stuck here until the enchantment broke. Fine. I'd avoid going under the throne room to the gold room beneath it. Demeter couldn't murder me if I didn't show up.

And Persephone didn't suffer from heat rashes or migraines, which was going to make a pleasant change. I'd need my all my wits about me here.

First up then? Find Kai and Theo and make them remember *me*, Sophie. Because I now understood the way this would hurt. It wasn't being murdered again. It wasn't even being Persephone while around Kai.

It was that *I* wouldn't exist at all.

Which would seriously crimp my save humanity plans.

I touched the cuff that Hannah had given me which I still wore. As if to reassure myself of who I was and that there were people out there to whom I mattered. *Maybe.* Hannah had never fought with anyone like she had with me. Even if I wanted to apologize, which maybe I did and maybe I didn't, I wasn't sure she'd reciprocate. Maybe I no longer mattered to her.

Green light swam before my eyes. My palms got hot.

No! I shut my power down before I could blast one of my full body shockwaves. Which reminded me that I still wore the ring Festos had made me. Kiki had left it alone.

I unclasped my chain, slid the ring off of my finger, and threaded it on next to my pendant. I didn't trust my temper at the best of times these days, and especially not now. The last thing I wanted was to get mad and use up my recharge before the final showdown. I could only go for three minutes and thirty seconds and I wasn't about to waste any of it.

Now, where was the most likely place to find Kai and Theo? I glanced at Hades' palace in the distance. My stomach clenched with nerves. *Hades won't know it's me.* I recited that thought over and over as I made my way toward the palace. It helped keep the dread at bay. So did the realization that there was a definite plus to being stuck in enemy territory: I could ferret out any weakness that might help us during the battle. That cheered me up enormously.

But first, I needed transform myself into the most girly goddess imaginable. Become the pretty decoration that Hades expected, all the better to keep my secrets. Because if Hades realized who I really was before I could get Kai and Theo to remember, he'd kill me. And neither of them would know to stop him.

It was a bit of a trudge to get to the palace from the crossroads. The heat made me sticky, and by the time I reached Hades' home, I'd been wiping the sweat off my brow for ages. The sun may not have been bright, but it was still hot.

I stepped onto the large front lawn that preceded the palace gardens and looked up at the building. The dark green marbled stone had seemed forbidding the one time that I, Sophie, had seen it. But it had been night, and Theo and I had been breaking and entering.

Now, in the sunlight, the stone was warm and richly veined. It had depth and a kind of magnificence to it. Didn't mean I was planning to walk in the front door, though.

Thanks to Persephone's memories, I knew other ways in. I skirted around the stoney path that led to the gardens full of twisted silver trees and statues. I sidestepped the Pool of Lethe, and the ornately carved iron doors depicting the War of the Titans.

I ducked around to the side, giving the palace a wide berth until I found what I was looking for: a narrow path with a vine covered archway overhead. Provided Hades hadn't done a major reno, there would be hot springs where I could bathe.

I darted onto the walkway, feeling its wrongness. The filtered light should have had a green tinge, but it was flat. And not because of me. Which was interesting. So far, the only things I'd seen here with any richness to their color were the corrosive dark orange and red of the River Styx, and the green of the palace marble. It made me think that the Underworld was great with the evil color palette, but somewhat limited in the happier pigments.

I knew that Hades liked color. Kai had told me stories about how they would go to Earth to see all the colors it offered. But, for whatever reason, certain hues just didn't seem to stick here. Idly, I wondered if that was part of the reason Hades had fought so long for control of Earth.

Nah, that made him vaguely likable.

I fingered one of the smooth-edged leaves on the vines that wound up and around the walkway. But where the vines should have been twists of deep green, they were silver. Which was cool but, well, really wrong.

Grapes hung from the vines in fat bunches of the palest blush. Like someone had sucked the purple from them. What little color there was could only be seen at certain angles of sunlight.

Cautiously, I sniffed at them. I was starving and they smelled right. I snapped off a bunch and gingerly touched my tongue to one. No immediate convulsing from poison. I hesitated for a second, unsure whether eating anything would leave me stuck here, but I figured that if I was Persephone—for all intents and purposes—then that ship had already sailed. Greedily, I scarfed them down. Sweet, sun-warmed, and sticky, I filled up on their juicy yumminess.

Behind me, I heard a flat dispassionate voice. "You look awful." I practically choked on the grape I was eating. Seemed Persephone didn't like the owner of that voice any more than I did. And I wasn't even sure who it was yet.

I turned.

Oizys, Spirit of Misery, Woe, Distress, and Suffering, peered directly into my eyes. She took her image very seriously. Her jet black hair was pulled into a severe bun, with a short fringe across her forehead. Behind black, round glasses, heavy kohl ringed her green eyes, and her lips were a slash of deep purple against pale skin. She wore a black sweater, a black spandex mini skirt, and thick black tights with (shocker) black combat boots.

Okay, the boots were cool.

"Greetings, Goth Girl." I saluted her.

She blinked in confusion.

Yeah, I bet Persephone never spoke to her that way, but I figured that if I could keep everyone slightly off balance by being myself, it might work in my favor when it came to making it out of here in one piece. Hopefully, it would also twig Kai's memory of *my* existence. Besides, no way could I speak like Persephone and keep a straight face. Formal, flowery BS language.

I imagined her bristling at that. Well, truth was a bitch.

"Grape?" I held one out to Oizys.

She frowned. "They're not washed."

"Precious much?"

She nodded. "Yeah, you are."

Hang on. *Me?* It figured. Persephone probably wanted them peeled on a silver platter. Gag. I popped a last one in my mouth

"What's wrong with you?" Oizys touched a finger to some dirt on my dress and then touched her finger to her lip. "Why were you in the tunnel?"

My ewww, gross turned to huh, cool, when she figured that out. "None of your business," I said.

"Because you don't get dirty." She pushed her glasses up her nose in a gesture that was eerily reminiscent of Theo.

A pang of missing him so badly speared my heart when I remembered the horrible condition Felicia had imposed. I needed to find out if he was here. See him right now. "Yeah," I told Oizys, "well, I was cavorting with some deer and they led me astray." I brushed past her and continued on my way to the bathing pool.

"Using sarcasm to steer me away from what you're really up to."

She'd followed me and was still talking. Lovely.

"That makes you marginally more interesting," she said.

"I'm so thrilled you think so." I sped up, but she clomped alongside me no problem.

"Which leaves the question 'what, precisely, are you up to?'" Oizys' expression, like her tone, was bland. No. More like curiously detached. Like I was a science experiment. I swear, if she'd had a clipboard, she'd have been taking notes.

Hannah would like her.

I shoved that thought down, way far far away, and padlocked it tight. No thinking about people who may or may not remember their best friend with whom they had just had the worst fight of their lives.

Oizys kept pace.

I stopped, annoyed. "Back. Off."

An amused glint cracked the blank slate of her face. "And here all I thought you were good for was dancing among flowers and looking pretty."

Me too. "Me too." Involuntarily, I voiced Persephone's memory of that exact feeling. I frowned. I didn't want to feel for her. I closed my eyes briefly, trying for patience. "Just ... I need to go."

Oizys tilted her head and studied me for a long moment. "You'll keep your secrets longer if you play the part given you, Springtime."

With that, she spun on her heel and left me wondering if she could see through Kiki's enchantment. And what she would do about it if she could?

I killed that train of thought as I reached the end of the walkway, finding myself outside a long, low cedar hut. The air around it was warm and moist and full of that fabulous woodsy scent. I opened the door, glad that it was unlocked, and stepped into the vacant room.

My entire body sighed with relieved recognition. Smell was such a strong gateway to memory, and both were really powerful here. I was a tad worried that I might be assaulted with sexytime details but, thankfully, Persephone had only ever come here alone. It was been her place to unwind and relax.

And plot. And seethe.

Yes, well, I wasn't doing any of that. I slid the wooden latch on the door, locked it, and slipped the blue dress up and over my head, tossing it in a rumpled ball on the floor. The heat in the room gave my skin a rosy glow, and I could already feel sweat beading the back of my neck.

This was the first time I'd seen this body naked, so yeah, of course I totally gave in to curiosity and checked myself out.

Score one for Persephone. Light olive skin that was butter soft to the touch, even my elbows and the pads of my feet. Dangerous curves, C cup boobs, long legs ... Persephone's hair was longer than mine, falling down the middle of her back, but our hair color was the same.

I twisted around to examine my butt. From what I could tell, it was a perfect, perky globe.

So pretty much a twenty out of ten.

Body issues? I refused to be jealous of a dead chick.

Instead, I faced the pool. It was probably about fifteen feet in diameter with cedar planks around the edges and steam rising from the water. Baskets of towels and pale green soaps were placed around in easy reach.

I dipped a toe into the water. Yikes! Hot. I was in heaven. I loved hot baths. The hotter the better. We'd only had showers at Hope Park. Same at Fee's place.

Inch by deliciously painful inch, I slid in, gasping the entire time, until I was sitting with my head back, submerged up to my shoulders. I rested there, steam cleaning myself until I was lobster red and pruney. Then I soaped up, washing my body and my hair until I was squeaky clean and oozing lavender from every pore.

I pulled myself out of the pool, looked down at the less than clear water and waited for the neat trick I knew was coming. Sure enough the surface rippled, magically cleaning the pool of all dirt until the water was pristine for the next bather.

The Underworld did have some amenities I could get behind.

Toweling myself off, I picked up my dress. I didn't really want to put it on again but I had no other option. I was pleasantly surprised to find that the heat had done a steam clean number on it. I slipped it on and wrung out my hair as best I could. It settled down my back in glossy ringlets.

She even had good wet hair. Whatever.

I threw open the latch and headed out. I still wanted to find Theo, so when I heard male voices close by, I went to investigate.

Coming around the bathing hut, I saw a field in the distance with a soccer game in progress. There were a lot of spectators: dead humans, a variety of demigods and goddesses, and a few fantastical creatures varying from small and ugly to large and hideous.

Kai was there, shirt off, running toward center field with his arms spread out, like he was trying to get things moving.

My brain promptly started issuing stern instructions on keeping my dignity in the face of his male magnificence.

Don't stare.

No, not the head tilt!

Stop that! Straighten head. Close mouth. Act like the dig-nified goddess you are.

Now tear your eyes away.

Not down. Away.

Yeah, fine. It took me a minute to line up my intentions with my actions. But eventually, I was able to look at the rest of the field. I didn't recognize any of Kai's teammates but I did see Oizys playing on the other team. She was the reason for the hold up, juggling the ball on her knees and ankles in a very cool show. Her face was total concentration, until she suddenly grinned and snapped the ball to an approaching teammate.

My heart caught in my throat. It was Theo.

No, it was Prometheus.

Wow.

Twelve

Prometheus had the same height as many of the other gods, so about fifteen feet, with his familiar shock of spiky hair. His face was, well, it was like *my* Theo really was the teen version of this very hot male. His features were more ruggedly masculine.

And—my, my—Festos had been right. Prometheus wore eye-liner. No glasses, just these big, dark eyes ringed with black. Also, he had a six-pack so crazily well-defined that all I could think of, even in the presence of Kai, the love of my life, was that I wanted to drag him off and lick them.

Holy crap did I need to restore Theo's powers if it got him his proper body back. I'd be made a saint for that good deed alone.

"Staring at the wrong guy aren't you, Springtime?"

I didn't bother hiding my irritation as I turned to face Oizys. "Really got that ninja stealth walk going for you, huh?"

She looked amused, but there was an element of …

what? It was a gleam that I could only interpret as a challenge. Was she waiting to see how I would respond to her initial question?

I was going to protest. Say I'd been looking at Kai, only had eyes for him, but screw it. "It's enough to make me wish I'd been born male."

Oizys studied me for a long moment. She pushed her glasses up her nose and looked like she was about to speak, when—

"Yo! Zys! Scared you can't keep up with me?" Prometheus yelled out in a teasing voice.

"Any time, any place, Rock Boy," she called.

Rock Boy? Had Theo picked his last name partially in memory of Oizys? Had I been calling him something that was a constant reminder of the friend he'd been unable to see for all these years?

My entire reality was shifting. I had one foot on shaky ground and the other in quicksand. Any more upheaval and I'd be lost.

Prometheus made a taunting "bring it" gesture with his hands as he jogged backward. Then he smiled at her with this look of incredible love and affection. I waited for that smile to include me.

But it didn't. It transformed at the sight of me, to a polite nod, for a casual acquaintance.

My face fell. That nod was a blow to my soul. Four days from now, I was never going to see Theo again. The time we had left should have been about stockpiling as many memories as possible. Instead, it was about polite indifference.

I realized that Oizys was still watching me. Suspiciously now. She probably thought I was secretly in love with Prometheus. I took a shaky breath. "Better get back to your game." I turned toward Kai, gave a little wave to catch his attention, and kept my eyes on him until I sensed Oizys leave.

Kai looked concerned when he saw me. Probably wondering why I'd bolted off so suddenly before.

I nodded back at him, smiling to let him know I was fine.

He brightened and blew me a kiss.

I blew one back, but my heart wasn't in it. A best friend who didn't recognize me, and a boyfriend who treated me like I was breakable, rather than the flirty, funny, infuriating Kai who turned my crank.

It was a very long game.

I passed the time seated on the edge of the field, making appropriate cheering noises while my mind churned over ways to make Kai and Theo remember me. More than once, I caught my fingers viciously ripping grass stalks from the ground.

I sifted through Persephone's memories. But it wasn't as if I could sit here and recite every single thing she had ever known or experienced. And there was nothing useful in what I could remember right now.

I watched Kai and Prometheus tussle, both fighting for control of the ball. Kai managed to get it with a fake out, but Prometheus stayed hot on his heels as Kai wove deftly around players and launched the ball into the net.

Cheers and whoops abounded.

I figured Kai would turn to me after that, but he was gazing off to the far end of the field, his poker face on. I followed his line of sight and saw Hades watching with disdain. A couple of nymphs clung to him. He said something that made them titter with laughter before walking off.

Kai went completely still for a split second. Then, with an easy grin to a teammate, he jogged off.

I doubt anyone else noticed his flash of pain.

Hades was an asshat.

I ached for Kai. I wanted to call him over all sweaty, so that I could fling my arms around him and kiss him and take away his hurt with some snarky comment about his dad. Yeah, and bug him when he got all smug about his prowess. Except Persephone would never do that.

That just made me feel bad for her. As far as I could tell, she basically acted as precious as everyone expected her to. But given how she'd snapped in the end, that goddess was carrying around a lot of suppressed anger and resentment. She was the original Goddess of Spring with an edge.

A title I wasn't sure I wanted anymore.

The sound of a whistle brought my focus back to the game. Oizys had the ball, with Prometheus keeping close, trying to get her safely to the net. They worked seamlessly, passing back and forth at just the right moments, trash talking their opponents in tandem.

I was jealous. Bitterly, bitterly jealous. It burned in my chest and I had to swallow several times against the metallic taste of bile in my mouth. I wanted to run into the middle of the field and scream, "It's me!" I couldn't stomach watching them anymore.

The only bright spot was that the game ended shortly after. Pretty much everyone cleared out, until it was just me watching Kai and Prometheus play some one-on-one. More aggressive than friendly.

I drifted closer to them. My mind emptied of everything except the highly pleasing image of the two guys before me. Not that I'd ever admit this but, truthfully, I'd be hard pressed to say whether Kai or Prometheus was better looking.

A vague thought nudged its way into my brain. Some story about Prometheus and truth ...

Processing ... processing ...

I grinned in triumph it came to mind. Aletheia, the Spirit of Truth. Prometheus had crafted her out of clay and brought her to life. If he could go to her now, could she reveal the truth about *me*? It was worth a try.

I steeled myself to go speak to Prometheus, one friendly acquaintance to another. "Can we talk?" I asked him.

Kai snatched his shirt up off the ground and slung it around his neck. My mouth went dry,

"Can it wait?" Prometheus asked.

I tore my gaze from Kai. "No. Now."

Kai cupped my hip with his hand. "I'm going to get changed."

I didn't want him listening in on this. Plus his touch, with his shirt off like that, made me lose my train of thought. "Good idea," I said and waved him off.

He blinked dumbly at me for a second, then he left.

Prometheus laughed. "That was code for 'you were supposed to follow.'" He jogged off toward where his own shirt lay on the ground.

Whoops. I called toward Kai's retreating back in a lame fix. "My heart won't be complete until I'm with you." Oh. My. God. It was like I was possessed and this gibberish was just spewing out of me. But it was just my instinctive recall of how Persephone and Kyrillos had interacted.

Kai turned around, jogging backward. "I will burn until I see you again."

I gave him a weak smile and sashayed off, trying not to gag. What a difference seventeen years and a waaaay better girlfriend made.

I trotted after Prometheus. "Do you know who I am?"

"What?" He picked up his shirt and wriggled into it.

No wonder Festos kept trying to get that second date. I stared pointedly at the sky, and tried to stop objectifying my best friend.

"What's wrong, Persephone?"

Well, that answered that question. "I thought maybe you were mad at me or something. Since you were pretty cool when you saw me with Oizys."

He looked at me oddly but his eyes were kind. "Wouldn't do to have people suddenly thinking we're best friends or anything at this stage of the game."

"Course not." I guess I wasn't able to keep the hurt off my face. I knew that Persephone and Prometheus weren't friends like Theo and me. Sigh. With me stuck here, and in the face of that horrible deal Theo had struck with Felicia, yeah, I wanted more from Prometheus as compensation.

I wanted us.

"Not like you were supposed to sweep me up in your arms or anything," I teased, wishing exactly that. Even if only for one of his millisecond hugs.

"Definitely not part of our deal," he joked back.

Deal. Yeah. Right. That's all this was to him. A business arrangement.

Prometheus patted me on the arm. "Feeling nervous?"

I forced myself to stop moping about our lack of a friendship, and focus on getting the truth spirit here so Theo would remember me. "It's not that," I said. "I need you to help me put one more piece into place."

"Prometheus."

I shivered at that low voice. Hovering in mid-air beside us, was Thanatos.

Death.

Appearances were slightly deceiving. Thanatos looked like a winged baby. But no one would be cooing over him unless they were a serious psychopath. He was too pale, too self-composed, and he gave off the creepiest vibe of any being I'd ever encountered.

I took a step back.

Thanatos spared me the briefest of glances before he spoke to Prometheus again. "My Lord has a task for you."

"We—" I plucked up the courage to speak in Thanatos' presence.

"Are done," Prometheus finished in a hard voice, that would have anyone convinced of how little he wanted to be around me.

It's just an act.

He followed Thanatos away without a single look back.

I sighed.

The sky streaked with black as the sun set. I yawned and figured it was time to go find my room. I didn't relish the idea of making small talk with Hades, so crashing early seemed like a good plan. I didn't even have an appetite. Which proved more than anything what a number this day had done on me.

I entered the palace through a passage which, although on the opposite end from the iron front doors, still led into the massive throne room. The walls in here were hewn from the same large blocks of green marble as the outside. The last time I'd been here, the room had been empty. Now tons of godly beings roamed around chatting, seeing, and being seen.

How high school.

The room was unbearably stuffy and my nose wrinkled at the smell of so many bodies pressed into the space. Not sweat so much as competing perfumes and colognes. Very cloying.

I avoided everyone, weaving my way past the large throne, raised up from the jet-black obsidian floor on a base. The throne was obsidian too, cut from a single block and standing thirty feet tall.

Hades sat upon it, his attention on a selection of wines in crystal goblets that some monkey-like satyr held out on a silver tray.

Much to my relief, he didn't see me, and I managed to cross to the corridor beyond without any "Greetings and Salutations." Given some of the sneers directed my way, I wasn't Miss Popularity. Which suited me just fine.

I followed the wide, winding staircase in the hallway up to Persephone's room on the third floor. I breathed deep, enjoying the fresh air outside of the throne room. No over-sprayed bodies here, just a slight undercurrent of something woodsy, slightly spicy, and a tad sour.

Cypress. Any tree scent was reassuring to me. Especially these trees which grew so abundantly around Hope Park. They reminded me of home. Both happily and wistfully.

I stepped onto the third floor landing and glanced around. I was alone. I counted off three doors on the left, grasped the heavy brass latch on the fourth solid wooden door, and pushed.

It was exactly as I'd seen it in Persephone's memories. A rush of nostalgia overwhelmed me. This had been my room for years and years. And the memories weren't all bad. I squirmed, not wanting to go *there* right now.

The furnishings were simple. And colorful. The most color I'd seen in the Underworld. A moss green blanket—the exact shade of my light—covered a massive bed. Cranberry and deep blue throw pillows were piled high on top, and warmly lit by a bedside lamp. The walls were a creamy white, while the furniture was a rich cherry red. I sighed, the colors giving me nourishment and energy.

And the smell. As nice as the cypress wafting through the hallways was, this room smelled like spring. There was no other way to describe it. It was rich earth, fragile blooms, and sunshine. I wondered if that's how I smelled to other people. How Persephone smelled. If so, it was definitely my favorite thing about her.

Just as I was idly wondering how I could bottle that scent and bring it back home, Kai's arms came around me from behind and he nuzzled in the hollow on the left side of my neck. My happy spot. Okay, Persephone's happy spot too. Yet another reason to keep this all platonic. Something I had to repeat silently several times, as I wriggled with tingly sensations along every nerve ending.

Kai shuffled us into the room and kicked the door shut behind him.

Gulp.

He turned me to face him. "What's wrong, kardia mou?" he asked gently. "Worried about the plan?"

Enough with the "my heart" stuff. I kept waiting for him to crack up and not be able to say it with a straight face. But no. This was how these widdle sweetums talked to each other.

"All is well, matia mou." The endearment, literally "my eyes" or "light of my eyes", just tripped off my tongue. Because it was what Persephone had called Kyrillos.

Very different from the names I tended to fling his way.

Kai looked pleased to hear the pet name.

I, however, had an irrational urge to blast something.

Either he didn't notice or he simply attributed it to being nervous about the upcoming ritual. "I'll take care of everything. We'll be fine," he assured me in that sweet voice.

182

I'll be fine. Persephone's rage swelled up inside me.

Down, girl, I cautioned. There'd be no betrayals on my watch. But maybe there could be some closure for the past. I stepped away from Kai. "First, I'm not going to break. So you have to stop treating me like I will."

He tipped his head to one side and studied me. "Are you getting sulky again?" A slow grin spread over his face. "I can fix that."

Now I was annoyed on Persephone's behalf. Talk about small miracles. "Are you even listening to me?"

He nodded and made himself comfortable on my bed, lounging back, arms folded behind his head as if he hadn't a care in the world. "Always."

The hem of his shirt rose, exposing a tanned strip of perfectly sculpted abs.

I absolutely did not gape.

He motioned for me to sit beside him.

I opted to look off slightly to the left of his nose, ignoring his blatant invitation. I was thankful he was fully clothed. "Second," I said, "who said anything about you taking care of everything? We're in this together."

I had come close enough to the bed that Kai was able to hook a foot around my leg and yank me onto the mattress with him. Perfectly aligned with his body.

This was an extremely dangerous, super awesome place to be.

My brain went into high alert.

He chuckled, the sound vibrating against my skin. "Since when do you want to take care of anything?"

I stiffened and sat up. "You never give me the choice."

Kai propped himself up on one elbow. "You've never once indicated you wanted one. Even for the simplest decisions, you never offer up your own opinion." He sounded annoyed now. Much more what I was used to.

I would have refuted that, but I couldn't think of a single time when Persephone actually *had* offered an opinion. I deflated. "Forget it."

"Fine by me." And with that, he kissed me.

What a kiss.

What a perfectly disappointing kiss.

I thought he was toying with me at first. I mean, our lips pressed together, there were all the right motions, and it was fine.

But I'd never had fine with Kai.

I'd had "blow my mind". I'd had "melt my bones". I'd had "blackout ecstasy."

I'm sure the kiss looked very romantic from the outside but here in the middle of the action, it was all rather nondescript, kissing partner considered.

No wonder Persephone wanted to kill him. Except … there was nothing in any of her memories about this being a disappointment, or anything other than what she wanted. She hadn't had any complaints about their love life.

Where was the chemistry? The combustibility? Should I be glad it wasn't there? So confused.

There was a click as Kai turned off the lamp. The room was plunged into darkness, save for the silvery sliver of moonlight trickling in through the window.

My confusion grew. "It's bedtime," I said.

There was a rustle and what sounded like an item of clothing hitting the floor. "Exactly," he replied, as he took me in his arms. I pressed my hands to his chest realizing it was bare.

Kai tried to tug up my robe.

Holy! Crap! I grabbed it in a death grip.

"A little late to be playing hard to get, love," he said, amused.

"Very tired. Go back to your room now."

He laughed. "Are you taking over our bedroom?"

"Our?" They shared? Of course they did.

Another rustle and a heavier thump.

Nervously, I stretched out the tips of my fingers. And cringed as I felt more bare skin. The thump had been his pants.

Please be wearing underwear.

Tentative, I crept my fingers up his thigh—*how I loved his thighs.* I was relieved to hit boxer length fabric.

Unfortunately, Kai saw that as an invitation. "I need you."

Oh. *Ohhh.*

Yes, please!

Hell, no!

My brain intervened before my mouth could say something I'd regret. Although it had to put quite the smackdown on some serious cravings. It was a struggle, but in the end, my mind emerged victorious.

Kind of a hollow victory.

I bolted back to the edge of the bed. There was no way in Hades, Olympus, or any reality that my first time having sex—especially with Kai—was going to happen while I was in Persephone's body.

No getting intimate and interactive for us.

A very long silence ensued, during which I gnawed my bottom lip raw, and tried to figure out how to handle this without coming off as a tease or a prude. What was Persephone normal? "We should wait to have sex until after the ritual. So as not to dilute its power." There. I thought that was pretty good.

Kai sat up into a pool of moonlight. He raked his hands through his hair. "When we do the ritual, is it going to work? Or is whatever you're so mad about going to sour the whole thing?"

I flinched, hearing him parrot the words I'd said to him back at his house. I gave him a strained smile. "Don't be silly. Everything is fine."

"Uh-huh."

With a final assessing glance, he turned away and lay down.

I stayed on the edge of the bed, tense until, finally I heard Kai's even breathing and knew he was asleep. Careful not to wake him, I scooted closer and peered down.

Kai was tangled in the sheets, barely covered. In the moonlight, he resembled a fallen angel. He was ripped everywhere, from his long muscled thighs, up his abs and along the perfect V of his torso. Like a chiseled statue.

I braced myself against a sudden rush of giddy longing. My eyes roamed to his face. He must have shaved recently because his skin was free from stubble. His olive complexion so free of blemish that he could have made a mint as the poster boy for clear skin. His dark, thick lashes lay heavily on his cheek. He seemed so innocent.

So beautiful. I longed to touch him. But as me.

And since that was impossible, I curled into a ball on my side of the bed, leaving a good ten inches between us.

It might as well have been a mile.

Thirteen

I woke up Monday morning half sprawled on top of Kai and realized two things. One, he gave off heat like a furnace and two, he was pressing slow kisses into my shoulder.

"Morning." His voice was growly and scratchy.

I tucked my head against his bare torso, feeling the rise of his chest and the steady thump of his heart. Just like we'd been back at his house. Except that had been Sophie and Kai. This was Persephone and Kyrillos. Kind of.

I wanted the other way back.

I propped myself up on one elbow to look at him.

In response, Kai lowered his head, all the better to gain access to my neck, His dark hair was totally mussed up.

"Kai—," I caught myself. "Kyrillos, look at me."

He rolled me onto my back and looked into my eyes. "I see you just fine, kardia mou."

You're not seeing me at all. But I wasn't sure if that

thought came because he didn't see Sophie, or because he didn't see Persephone.

He leaned in slowly. I knew he wanted to kiss me, and that he was checking to see if Persephone was still upset. Which was sweet. I guess.

I needed to know if the tone of our previous kiss had been a weird one-off, so I allowed this one. My eyes fell closed and Kai moved in.

His kissing has gotten better in the past seventeen years. Or is it just that he had the right person to kiss? Well, he did have a lot of practice after she died. And, ew! How much did he practice? Because he went from little league to the World Series. But yay for me, Sophie, being on the right end of it!

It's not good when you can hold entire conversations with yourself in the face of your boyfriend's kisses. And that's all we were doing. Kissing.

Kai and I would have been tearing at each other's clothes by now. And we hadn't even had sex. These two had. There was just none of the madness between *them* that there was between us. Maybe that was a good thing? Maybe that's how normal couples did things? Were we just so zero-to-a-billion about everything that all my perceptions were skewed?

Kai paused to smile down at me, just as the sunlight surrounded him, his hair perfectly tousled. I slid my eyes sideways, noticing our just-so rumpled sheets, the way a strand of my hair fell across his arm.

It was a freaking movie moment. That's what their entire relationship was like for me. Cinema pretty. Not real world messy.

I wanted the messy back. So I bucked to push him off me and sat up. I had to find Prometheus and see about getting that truth spirit to pay a visit. "Busy day," I said. I'm not stupid. I could tell Kai was getting suspicious of me holding him at bay, so I pressed a soft kiss to his lips. "The equinox is in three days. I'm just edgy."

He seemed to accept that. Or at least not press the subject.

I threw him a bright smile. "Hungry?"

He swung his legs off the bed, got up, and threw on jeans and a worn green T-shirt. It molded to him, but left many good things to the imagination. "I'll get you your coffee," he said.

Before I could add, "Great, that'll hold me until I get some real food," a spurt of rage flooded my system. A memory hit me.

Kyrillos entered the room, a large mug in his hands. Sleepily, I propped myself up against the headboard, hoping against hope that today would be different.

I fisted the edge of my blankets, but kept a smile on my face.

He reached me and held out the mug. And just like every morning, I felt disappointment unfurl deep within me. Coffee again. Not hot chocolate.

I accepted the cup, the bitter aroma making my stomach turn.

I hated coffee. But he delivered it to me every day with a smile.

He was no better than the others. Only wanting whatever image of me suited him best. Not really seeing at all.

Persephone's simmering anger rose in me, a snarl twisting my lips. It grew, dancing inside me until my back arched and the emotion of the memory thrust me back into my vision. My body tensed as I saw that this time, there was a twist.

Sophie stood across the garden, immobile on the rock. The lava bubbled and flowed freely around her. But where I was, all was light and fire, falling away to nothing.

I burned, stretching out my awareness to fuel the flames and the lava and the destruction. I would die but everything would go down with me.

"Persephone?"

I don't know how long Kai had been calling me before I came to, but as his face came into focus, I saw him flinch.

Persephone's memory, her deep seated resentment for Kai had snapped me into a version of the vision that was truly terrifying. My brain couldn't process the lingering after-emotions of it. Never mind being here, in front of the person who fueled that fury.

I needed Kai gone. To think through what it meant. To be able to shake this off without his very presence leaving me at the mercy of *her* feelings.

I forced myself to relax the granite glower carved into my face. Uncurled the talons that my fingers had become. I blinked up at Kai with a pleasant smile and hoped he wouldn't see how fast I was breathing.

I caught sight of the steaming mug that Kai was still holding and felt a irrational surge of hope—maybe it was hot chocolate. I hated feeling like I was losing myself to

Persephone, as evidenced by my hesitation before reaching for the coffee I loved so much.

"Here." As he prompted me to take the cup, there was a flash in his eyes for the briefest of seconds. A glint.

I stared but his now-affable expression didn't change. And that's when I realized he knew. The bastard knew Persephone hated coffee, and he gave it to her every day anyway.

Why?

I took the cup from him with a pleasant smile. *Just like I always did.*

His expression hardened. He threw me a rakish grin and bent briefly to kiss my brow. "Come to me soon," he said. And then he left.

The sheets fell away as I awkwardly struggled up, with the cup cradled close. For the moment, the astoundingly passive-aggressive dynamic between these two took a back seat to whatever had just happened with the vision.

I'd *been* the freaking pomegranate tree, for crying out loud. And it hadn't felt like dying. Well, yeah, it had, but it wasn't a gentle go-out-with-a-whimper ending. I'd been fueling the destruction.

Was this my confirmation that I ended the world? Was I the instrument of destruction? And if so, in the end, was it me or Persephone who would ultimately be in charge? Was the vision hard proof that the past repeated itself? That this enchantment didn't end, and Sophie Bloom ultimately failed to exist?

Was I going to lose all awareness, leaving Persephone and her destructive impulses to take over? Would the volatile combination of Persephone, Zeus, and Hades end humanity?

I took a sip of the coffee, my head spinning. Persephone may have hated coffee, but funnily enough, it was exactly the way I liked it. It was drip, not espresso, which would have been better, but it had the right amount of milk and sugar. Maybe Kai did recognize me on some unconscious level?

Don't get stupidly hopeful.

I closed my eyes, savoring the taste, turning my anxiety about the the vision into a chance to sift through memories and understand why Persephone had never spoken up about the coffee. It was obviously part of something much bigger.

Demeter and Zeus had fueled Persephone's sense of very conditional love. Instilling her desire to please, to be told what a delight she was. There was my answer. As was remembering her anxiety to always live up to that label. In my experience, most gods didn't follow the "nothing you can do will ever make me love you less" school of parenting. All of this had brought her into a passive-aggressive standoff with Kai, where she couldn't speak up and he wouldn't ask.

Just because I always give in doesn't mean I always want to. Her long-ago thought echoed up to me now. I remembered Persephone in a way I hadn't before. And all it seemed to do was accentuate the differences between us.

I would have spoken up had it been me. *Yeah, like you did about your situation with Kai these past few months.*

That was different. At least I'd tried. *Not very hard.*

I put a smackdown on the negativity. I was different and this proved it. Persephone and I were never going to be aligned. Couldn't even understand how the other moved through the world. Hekate's decree to get in sync with my goddess self seemed impossible.

I set the cup down on the bedside table, the coffee off-putting. This morning's events were just more extremely pressing reasons to find Prometheus and get Aletheia here. I swung my legs onto the ground and stood.

Then I went to her closet, doubtful about finding something to wear that wasn't totally unacceptable. Surprisingly, the selection wasn't horrible. Just predictable.

Flip ... long flowy gown ... Flip ... long flowy gown ... Flip ... somewhat shorter flowy gown ...

I scrambled into the most bearable choice: a light blue dress that was—wait for it—flowy, hitting about mid-thigh. I paired it with black, flat sandals, and headed out.

My priorities: find Prometheus, get Aletheia to reveal Kiki's enchantment, take Theo and Kai to the exit, and make sure it was in exitable condition, in order to stop Hades and Zeus.

See where things stand with Hannah. Say good-bye to Theo.

One thing at a time.

I pulled my hand away from my cuff, not wanting the reminder of Hannah. I forced myself to stick to "find Prometheus" before I curled into a ball of dejection.

I marched down the stairs, hoping I'd find Prometheus in the breakfast room. I had no idea which bedroom belonged to him. But I had memories of seeing him at breakfast, so that's where I started. Also, it was no hardship to follow the smell of bacon.

I swept into the bright room and skidded to a stop at the sight of Hades hunched over a plate of food at a massive wooden table. He was dressed much like Kai had been yesterday, in dark linen pants and button up shirt. The effect was nowhere near as fabulous, but he did have a compelling charm of his own.

The way Hades' eyes burned into me, I was positive he'd realized I was actually Sophie.

"Yes?" His voice gave away nothing.

He was still waiting for an answer so I said the first thing that came into my head. "I'm hungry." My stomach rumbled and I blushed beet red.

To my shock, Hades actually laughed. "Even the Goddess of Spring suffers the same base needs as the rest of us." He flung an arm out toward the full buffet, where silver chafing dishes promised breakfasty delights.

I sighed happily. "Bacon."

Hades raised an eyebrow. "Are you actually going to eat swine?"

I should have declined. I had no memory of Persephone eating anything other than the lightest of meals. Like fruit.

Screw that. "Nope. I'm going to feast on it."

He dug into his own breakfast. "Help yourself."

I intended to. I picked up a plate and began the joyous journey to discover what lay under each silver lid. Oh bliss! Oh taste bud heaven. Not only did I find bacon, but also eggs and light-as-air waffles. Sausages and tiny pan fried potatoes tossed with salt and oregano. I piled my plate high.

"You can get seconds," Hades said in disbelief as I set everything down precariously on the table, willing my leaning Tower of Breakfast not to fall.

"I could. But that would be greedy."

He laughed again. I did too. We blinked at each other in surprise.

Seriously. This was uncharted territory for me, Persephone, and Hades. We hastily returned to our breakfasts.

For a while, there was no sound other than eating. "Where're all your suck ups?"

Hades eyes blazed from under his heavy eyebrows. "They leave me alone until I've had my coffee. Or get thrown in Tartarus."

I stiffened. *Touchy.*

"I'm kidding." He shook his head. "No one ever gets when I'm kidding."

He looks lonely.

No, see, I didn't want to think that about him. Didn't want to feel bad for him. *He wants humanity dead. Wants Earth destroyed.*

I chewed on a sausage almost viciously, trying to hang on to my hatred. I thought about how he treated Kai. That helped. "Your son would get your humor. If you ever bothered with him."

Hades scowled and slammed a fist down on the table, sending a crack out along the foot-thick wood like a ripple in a pond.

I clamped my knees together so they couldn't shake.

"Don't ever talk to me about my son. You've made him soft. Whipped him around your little finger. After all I've done ..."

Now I was indignant. "Ignored him? Insulted him? Emotionally abused him?"

Hades tilted his chin up, the gesture haughty and proud. "I made sure he survived."

Understanding took my breath away. In his own twisted way, Hades *loved* his son. He really thought he was being a good father. Just like Zeus had thought that sending minions to kill me if I didn't fall in line counted as tough love.

No wonder Kai didn't break the passive-aggressive stalemate with Persephone. Because as much as Persephone had been raised to never disappoint, Kai had been raised to be tough. To show he was strong. To play a different predetermined role. They were locked into a dynamic they wouldn't, couldn't, break. To break it was to speak up, and make themselves vulnerable.

And vulnerable was unacceptable. Instead, they both pretended everything was fine.

I bowed my head, busying myself with pushing food around my plate and studying Hades through lowered lashes, while my thoughts spilled over each other. Did Hades act that way toward Kai because taunts and mockery were the only connection he knew how to make? And if I took that thought further, did this entire war between Hades and Zeus boil down to the fact that fighting each other was the only way they could stay connected?

If that were true, messed up as it was, it was still sad. Man, I didn't want to feel compassion for the old goat. "Don't you want more for Kyrillos than just survival?"

Hades sneered at me. "Awww, does he need a hug?"

And back to thinking you're an ass. "You don't need to be such a jerk." I took a grim satisfaction at his startled expression. I'd talked back to the Lord of the Underworld.

Hades pushed to his feet and gave me a low, mocking bow. "I will throw a party celebrating the greatness that is my son. How about that?" I tried not to be too subtle in conveying my thoughts on his doucheyness.

But Hades wasn't paying me any attention. He zoned out for a moment, and then pronounced, "I *will* throw a party. A masquerade ball starting at midnight before the equinox." His gaze turned distant and soft. "He used to like parties."

I choked on a bite of food at seeing this side of him. Which swung his attention back to me.

Hades' eyes gleamed and he smiled slowly. "Such an art to picking the right mask, don't you think? The wrong one can reveal so much more than it conceals." He swept from the room, bellowing for some creature or another to start the planning.

Games and roles and masks and agendas. Give me high school backstabbing any day.

On the upside, my belly was full and I'd survived my first encounter with Hades. Maybe my luck would hold in finding Prometheus. My chair scraped over the flagstones as I stood.

Crossing to the door, I heard a chirping. I looked around, expecting some trapped little bird but there was nothing. I took a couple more steps. The noise got louder. More insistent.

Another look around. This time I found the source. A gray gecko with brown spots and brilliant green eyes clung to the wall, close to the ground. I bent down to peer at him. "Hey, little guy." I would have dismissed him as a cute wildlife encounter when I realized what his presence meant.

Demeter was here.

The gecko was her messenger. I knew it. I remembered it. These creatures were considered sacred to her. And whenever she'd wanted to meet Persephone in the Underworld, she'd used one of them to arrange a meeting.

I narrowed my eyes. "Mother dearest wants to see me, does she?" My palms started to sweat and I tugged at the neckline of my dress. I swear it had shrunk and was the reason I suddenly couldn't breathe.

My first time seeing Demeter while she was still the loving mother of legend? How nerve wracking was that? What if I ended up blubbering the whole time? Or punching her? Either was possible.

And since refusing the summons was not an option, I was about to find out which it would be.

Fourteen

One of the many fun facts now at my disposal with the return of Persephone's memories was that while in the Underworld, she and Demeter had always met in Tartarus. Not exactly the field trip I wanted to take.

Ever.

I stifled a half-panicked breath. *Calm* ...

I had to meet with Demeter. This was my chance to make sure she didn't end up wanting to murder Persephone. Therefore, I would be the absolute delight that she expected. "Lead on," I told the gecko.

He crawled out of the room, and I obediently followed.

The gecko hugged the low edge of the wall, leading me through the palace via its twisty back hallways. He had an unerring sense of timing, turning into corridors just as voices faded off ahead of us and feet padded away.

He moved fast for a little guy too, never stopping to see if I was keeping up. Which I was, but barely. When we stepped outside, I was only dimly aware of the heat beating down on my head, and the ticklish twitching in my nose from the acrid tang of the dry grass.

Between the nerves and the total focus on not losing my tiny guide, I didn't realize we'd reached Tartarus until the overpowering smell of sulphur had me gagging. I flung an arm up to cover my nose and mouth, but the scent was insidious. It snaked its putrid way inside me.

My lizard leader came to a stop. Before us was a bronze fence that stretched up and away as far as the eye could see.

I glanced down at the gecko. "Couldn't you bring her out here?"

He waggled his head at me.

Uncertain, I placed one hand against the fence's ridged surface, and practically buckled as the cries of the damned knocked the breath from me.

Tearing my hand off that gate was like trying to detach myself from the strongest magnet ever. Every molecule of me felt stuck, plastered to it in despair for all eternity. It magnified every self-criticism, every negative thought and fear into infinity.

Instrument of our destruction. Instrument of our destruction.

The mocking laughter from my vision filled my ears.

I slid down the fence, the skin on my legs pricking sharply as I hit a tangle of thorns. The pricking crept down my ankle, getting more frequent. Dully, I glanced down to find the gecko nipping at me.

I could almost hear him chittering at me to get up.

It was crazy hard but I managed to stagger to my feet.

The gecko kept up his chatter, nipping at me every few feet to make sure I didn't stop.

My limbs felt heavy, my gait sluggish. I was doing a pretty excellent zombie shuffle.

The gecko prodded me along for a bit, finally stopping at a gap in the fence. No, a small door that stood ajar. He ran through it.

I don't know how Persephone had managed to keep coming here, because I couldn't make myself take that first step into Tartarus. I had to take my hands, wrap them around my leg, lift it up, and set my foot down a step ahead. Over and over again. I stared at the ground, my willpower taxed to its limit.

The heavy clunk of the door shutting behind me let me know I'd made it through.

Unwillingly, resentfully, apprehensively, I looked around. Everything was black. From the mud on the ground, to the air itself.

Black roses with deadly thorns grew in wild tangles—the only foliage I could see. They looked like the drawing Jennifer had made for my tattoo. Guess I knew what I'd been channeling when I'd asked for them. Fleetingly, I wondered if I'd ever go back and get artwork that really suited me.

I forced myself to move deeper into Tartarus.

The air was ripe with sulphur, but I was getting used to the stink of rotten eggs now. Somewhat. I still sucked my nostrils together as best I could, as I made my way forward trailing the gecko.

Worse than the blackness, or the stench, or the despair I felt, was the identically frozen expression of utter hopelessness on every person I passed. Eyes wide and lost, they moaned and keened from the depths of their souls.

I sped up. There was no consolation to offer them and I was scared that if I stopped moving, their cries would suck the life from me. Also, the thought of them touching me was plain creepy.

At least I had no time to be nervous about seeing Demeter again. It was all I could do to keep my mind blank as I wound my way through this land of wretchedness and despondency.

Until I was enveloped in my mother's arms.

She smelled sweet. Almost fruity. It cut through the Tartarus stench like a balm to my heart. That was the first thing I noticed. The second was that she was shorter than me.

Until now, my parents—especially my god ones—had been larger than life. Figuratively and literally in the case of Zeus. I'd never imagined that Demeter would be smaller than me. Not by much, but it gave her a fragility I hadn't expected.

Her hug, however, was firm and loving and pure mom. It was the hug I'd been waiting for all of my life, and the hug I would have loved to savor. But I felt Persephone gnawing at my skin like a darkness. The tiny hairs on my arms—*her arms?*—bristled in seething resentment at Demeter's touch. I had to suppress the overwhelming urge to rip myself free of her embrace.

I understood mommy issues. I had my own. In spades. And with the same mother. But despite everything I had experienced at Felicia's hands, I still wanted to feel Demeter's love.

If only for a second.

Even if it was borrowed. Even if it was just magic. Or fake, or whatever. Because I'd never had it and, with every fibre of my being, I wanted to savor that amazing feeling that I'd missed out on for so long.

I took it all in. How, when she hugged me, she slung her left arm over my right shoulder and her right arm under my left armpit, to kind of cocoon me in a sling of affection. How her cheek felt slightly flushed as she pressed it to mine. How, before she released me, she gave me a final tight squeeze.

I stockpiled it all in *my* memory. And I hated Felicia even more for having deprived me of it.

Jack had gotten every little detail right when he'd created a fake Demeter to trick me. Her dark hair, the crow's lines around her eyes, the slight lilt of her Greek accent as she spoke my name and brushed a strand of hair from my face. I memorized her appearance.

"Has he contacted you?"

Demeter shook her head impatiently at my look of confusion. "Your father, Persephone. Has he bothered with you at all lately?"

"No. Of course not. But mama—" Instinctively, I had reverted to Persephone's name for her.

Demeter cut me off before I could steer the conversation around to the equinox and what was or was not going to happen. "Selfish, arrogant man."

"I prefer psychopathic narcissist," I muttered, but she was on a roll.

Demeter gripped my hands, her eyes glittering. "Four

days, kopella mou. We will have everything we want and he will have nothing."

There was the familiar rush of rage. "Everything *you* want."

"What we both want." Demeter's voice was firm.

Anxiety warred with anger. *I cannot disappoint her. Thus will I play the perfect daughter until it is time for her to learn.*

I closed my eyes to center myself. I was at the mercy of Persephone's emotions. I had to get on top of this. Murder just wasn't gonna happen a second time.

My very existence was at stake.

Think, Sophie ... I frowned. I willed my breath to stay steady, my power to remain contained as I sifted through Persephone's memories for something that could help. I only half-listened as Demeter spoke again. But when she said, "Tell me where you and Kyrillos plan to recite the ritual," I came to full attention.

"The less people know, the better," I hedged.

Demeter gave a familiar grumble and smoothed her hair. A gesture I'd seen from Felicia many times.

My heart twisted.

"Now is not the time to be coy," she said. "I want to be there. To make sure your father understands how his promises and lies have brought about his defeat."

I was lost. There was nothing in Persephone's memories about Zeus having promised anything.

Demeter's lips were tight. "He wants it all. He will have nothing. No one. You think she will want him when he is no longer ruler? He will see how I was the only one who truly loved him, but it will be too late."

The bitterness in her voice stunned me. That's what this was all about? The fact that Zeus wouldn't leave Hera for Demeter? The fury of a woman scorned?

She had been betrayed in love and now she expected me to do the same thing to Kai? This had to stop. "Mama," I beseeched her, "let it go. He's not worth it." But even as I said it, I knew she wouldn't listen. It had always been about him. Even my abduction—*Persephone's abduction*—was about making him notice her. It was the only reason she cared so much.

I was losing it. I felt like Persephone was blindly taking over. Not a voice I had made manifest, but a personality alive and well and righteously pissed off. She dwarfed me with her fury, and I no longer knew where she began and I ended.

Rage and hopelessness and destruction. She was me and I was her and Tartarus worked its oily evils upon us both.

"He is everything." Demeter's words, combined with the cold look she gave me, allowed *me*, Sophie to regain the upper hand. "I won't betray Kyrillos," I said. The words were thick in my mouth. Almost impossible to speak. Persephone didn't want me to say them and Demeter didn't want to hear them. "There has to be another way." One where we all got out of this without any collateral damage. I twisted my fingers, welcoming the tight pain.

"You will do as you promised."

My ears rang with Persephone's howling, her grief and pain swallowing me completely. "You're drowning in hate." I wasn't sure if I was speaking to Persephone or Demeter.

Demeter flicked me a contemptuous glance. "Don't be ridiculous. I love him. But he doesn't know how to love. Which is why you and I will defeat him. Then we will have each other." She bestowed a smile on me that promised sunshine and happily-ever-after as a loving family.

It was all a lie.

Because most of these gods didn't understand love. For them, it was all selfish passion. Not the glorious connection that humans immortalized in books and songs and movies. That was about giving yourself freely and willingly.

I *wanted* that scary free fall where your heart is in someone else's hands and theirs in yours. Instead of making you weak, it was the most precious, most secure place to be.

Most gods couldn't see that. For them, love was only allowed from a position of power. And any hurt would be paid back tenfold with ultimate destruction. They had it so wrong.

But I had no clue what to do, other than what Persephone had always done. I put a smile on my face and said, "I want you to be happy." At least Demeter would think I was still in line with her plans.

Demeter's expression softened as she took my words for agreement. "My girl." She pressed a hand to my cheek. "Go back now. Before you are missed."

"But—"

Demeter kissed my forehead. "It will all work out fine."

I hesitated but, at her small nod, gave a final hug and headed back toward the door out of Tartarus. I couldn't ignore the feeling in my gut. It wasn't going to be fine at all.

On the bright side, every step away from the despondency of Tartarus made me feel lighter, until I was practically skipping my way along the cobblestones back to the palace. Granted, it may have been kind of a manic lightness. After my encounters with Demeter and Hades, I was a mess.

I laughed, partially in amusement at how wrung out I felt, and partially in relief at being far away from that place.

"I like to hear you laugh."

I spun around to find Kai sitting on a low branch of a tree. His grin was so full of tenderness that my insides began a happy patter. Until I remembered that those feelings were for *her*. That sobered me up. I straightened and adopted my best pleasant tone.

Yeah, okay, no. I didn't do any of that.

Seriously. I was a sad sad case. I stared at him, drinking him in. Not that I needed to since every detail was burned into my brain. From his eyes, to his voice, to the tiny scar on his hand.

My ribcage tightened. My breathing constricted. This was killing me. I needed Kai to know me. Maybe, if things were all honeymoon happy between us in the real world, I could have sucked this up, and we could laugh about it later. But back *there*, we were still working through the very betrayal that I was desperately trying to avoid *here*. Everything was still so fragile between us.

I dropped my head. My energy zapped.

Kai dropped to the ground, moving so silently that I didn't even realize he'd come to stand next to me until I felt his hand splay across my belly. I leaned into his warmth. Into his strength.

He tilted my head up with his finger. "I prepared a picnic for us."

The sun slanted down on his dark locks, making a halo around his head. His magnificence in this moment temporarily soothed even Persephone's clawing animosity.

Yeah, she loved him too.

I reached out for him, not knowing if I was driving this train, or if she was.

Kai beamed at me like I'd just handed him Christmas. "Beautiful love." He took my hand. "Let me adore you."

It was tender and romantic and made me feel like I'd been doused in cold water.

Because Kai, *my* Kai, would never in a million years say that to me. Not without both of us laughing. It wasn't us.

I didn't want it to be us.

I wanted that arrogant sly boy who could match wits and mouthiness with me. Who seemed perpetually amused and annoyed by me, and couldn't stay away. I put my hand on his chest, emboldened by the wariness in his eyes. Yeah, Persephone wasn't a "make the first move" kind of girl.

I clutched Kai's shirt, the soft fabric spilling through my fingers. I knew this was madness. But some deeper, essential part of me needed to be recognized. I hoped that maybe I could spark a connection that would make him see who he was really with.

Me.

I didn't want to be *her* anymore. I leaned forward and gently bit his lip.

His body jerked and his breath hitched.

I pulled back slightly, my body vibrating as he jerked me back against him.

Remember me! I held his gaze and pushed the thought with all my might. I swallowed, my pulse kicking up as I saw that wild darkness in his eyes. Then I kissed him as hard as I could, willing him to know me in every touch.

Kai devoured me. There was no other word for it. It was like the dam between us had broken. His arm tightened around me, holding me in place against the length of his body, while he kissed me over and over again.

This may have been a new dynamic for them, but gawd was it awesome for me. I was in sensory overload heaven: the fullness of his lips, the possessiveness of his hands, and his unique scent that was my own personal aphrodisiac.

I shifted closer to him, whimpering when he broke contact. Heart racing, breath heaving, I looked at him and saw my questioning mirrored in his eyes.

But not the good questions like, "Do I get more of that?" and "How soon?"

Kai stared at me like he couldn't figure me out.

Of course he couldn't. Because I was acting like myself and he had no idea I, Sophie, existed. I closed my eyes, blinking back a furious wetness. Then I shoved at his chest hard and brushed past him.

"You're leaving?" He sounded incredulous.

I nodded, hurrying off because I didn't trust myself to speak. Besides, what was I going to say? "Every time I kiss you and you don't remember that I'm actually a seventeen-year-old human who happened to get your dead girlfriend's essence stuffed inside her, a part of me wants to die?"

Yeah, right.

"Goddess—" he began, sounding exceedingly annoyed.

I whirled, scowling. "Do NOT call me that." That was Kai's name for *me*. I could take all the Greek endearments he wanted to throw at Persephone, but no way did I want to hear him call her "Goddess." I couldn't handle it.

I broke into a run.

Kai didn't follow.

I hadn't really expected him to.

I ran out of steam back by the shores of the Akherousian lake. I strode into the water, not even bothering to kick off my sandals or hitch up my dress. I glared at the reflection of Persephone's perfect face.

I smacked at the water, and watched her ripple. "Damn it! I am Sophie Bloom." *Smack!* "I am Sophie Bloom." *Smack!*

I think the technical term for my watery assault was

hysteria. Every time I looked down and saw her face staring back at me, I felt disconnected. My skin prickled with the fear of not belonging in my own body.

Every time I shouted my name, I felt more and more depersonalized in the face of the unyielding reality of her, well, face. My emotional turmoil reached a fever pitch and I was utterly unmoored.

My peripheral vision faded and I was thrust back into my vision.

The rock on which I stood rose up, molding around my legs to entomb me. With growing horror, I watched it become a box to encase my entire body.

The pomegranate tree had burned to an ashy skeleton that threatened to crumble into nothingness.

John Lennon sang louder and more insistently but he was wrong. This wasn't love. This was getting buried alive.

There was a grinding noise and I watched wild-eyed as a heavy stone lid swung shut over me. I pushed against it with all my strength, but my arms bowed uselessly against it.

The world went black.

Fifteen

I came to on the grass. Prometheus sat beside me, watching me warily. "Want to talk about it?"

I shook my head, my limbs shaky. Revisiting my entombment was the last thing I wanted to do. I curled into myself instead, trickles of anxious sweat beading down my spine. "Why are you doing this?" I blurted.

"Why are you?"

Because Persephone is crazy with rage and wants to take everyone down didn't seem like an appropriate response.

Whatever Prometheus thought he saw in my expression made him chuckle. "I know you hate Zeus and Hades." He shrugged. "Fine by me since it suits my purposes."

He'd nailed my feelings for those two, and I was happy to let him think that was what had set off my hysteria. "I know your agenda," I said. "You want to save humanity. But why?" Here was Prometheus, willing to talk to me in a way that Theo wouldn't. Or maybe he just found it too hard after everything he'd been through.

Prometheus' dark eyes were wistful. "Wouldn't any parent do whatever they had to do to keep their kids safe? I was there for the birth of mankind. I nurtured them with the gift of fire and watched them achieve beautiful impossible things." He wrapped his finger around a dandelion stem. "Terrible things, too. But so many of those, as misguided and immoral as they were, came from a place of hope. Of believing in a better tomorrow and fighting to the death to achieve it."

"You don't want the gods messing with that," I said.

His expression hardened. "I don't want gods killing humans in the name of bloated egos and power plays because they fail to see their worth. I want humanity left alone to succeed or fail on its own. That is their right." He yanked the weed from the ground and flung it aside.

"But," I fumbled for a way to say this delicately, "you already paid a price. Being chained to the rock just for giving them fire. Imagine the consequences if we fail this time."

His smile dazzled me. "Which is why you won't."

There it was. The pure faith that connected this Titan and my human friend. "How can you be so sure?"

"Because you are prophesied."

Huh? I was confused. In this enchantment, Cassie hadn't dropped her "one above one below" prediction yet. I plucked a wet strand of grass from my leg, searching for a way to have Prometheus clarify without giving away knowledge I shouldn't even have.

"Why do you think Zeus let you stay here?" Prometheus waved a dismissive hand. "If he'd wanted you out, he would have marshaled all of Olympus to bring you back. He knew it was foretold that one of his children would overthrow him. It was a closely guarded secret."

My mouth was dry. I couldn't believe that Theo had never mentioned this. I mean, sure, it made sense, explained why he'd been willing to lose his powers over me. But still. You'd think it might have come up in conversation. "*You* found out about it."

Prometheus nodded. "And more. Zeus was never entirely sure which of his children it was going to be. When I learned that you had a way of stopping him and Hades?" His smile turned ruthless. "Let's just say I called in some favors to verify it was you."

Still … "Prophesied doesn't mean guaranteed." Zeus himself had said as much.

He stretched out his legs. "I know you're nervous, Persephone. You're hesitant to let me in on the exact nature of what will take them down."

It wasn't nerves. It was secrets. Persephone didn't want him to know about Kai's involvement in all this. Or her imminent betrayal of Kai and Demeter.

"But you've trusted me with your safety," Prometheus continued. "My one job is to get you out of here tomorrow night. I've secured us passage. Once we're out and you accept that you're safe in my hands, you can fill me in on the next stage."

I thought all this through. If Persephone had needed Prometheus to get her out of the Underworld, then she'd known that her pendent wouldn't work. She'd might also have known that even Kai wouldn't be able to help with that.

Theo had said he'd been supposed to meet Demeter on the night Persephone had been killed. I was willing to bet she was the secure passage. Which meant he'd struck the deal to exit to her temple grounds before.

Except, back then, Kai would've had to go with Persephone. She'd still needed him to do the love ritual. So she couldn't have harmed him until afterward. But once she'd killed Kai, there would have been a witness. The very being who had spirited them out.

Prometheus.

I dropped my head. Felt ill. Persephone had been planning to betray Prometheus, too. My resolve hardened. That hadn't happened, and it sure as hell wouldn't happen this time as long as I stayed in control. More reason to have Prometheus get that truth spirit here and break this enchantment. I spoke up. "Prometheus—"

"That's right," he said. "You had something you wanted me to do."

I did, but first I wanted him to know exactly where he stood with me. I took his hand. "I trust you," I said insistently. "More than anyone."

He didn't break contact. Instead, he squeezed my hand tighter. "I will see you through this, keep you safe no matter what." His eyes were solemn as they stared into mine. "I swear."

It was a super intense and highly charged moment.

Which was pretty much the worst possible way that Kai could have found us. "What have we here?" His voice was a smooth purr. It caressed my skin like silk, then slid under it like ice.

I'd never heard this voice before. It terrified me. Because after that horrible night two months ago, I knew how mad Kai could get.

This sounded worse. Felt worse.

Prometheus let go of me and pushed to his feet.

Leaving me scrambling, brushing the dead grass from my dress. "Nothing," I said.

"What are you up to, kardia mou?" Kai's breath was warm against my ear as he twined around me in a tight circle, like a cat.

I shivered.

His hand caressed my hip for a fleeting second.

I shrugged, bored, and played the same "dislike" card that Prometheus had pulled out when Thanatos had interrupted us on the soccer field. "Nothing. He's a jerk."

Kai paused and placed his index finger against his lips. "Hmmmm. Thing is," he gave me a sweet smile. "I don't believe you."

Yeah. I wouldn't have either. This was bad. Dread to the tips of my toes, bad. I folded my fingers over my sweaty palms and opened my mouth to speak but something cut me off.

Out of the corner of my eye, I saw Prometheus give an exasperated shake of his head and turn to leave, but Kai shot a blast of black light and totally eviscerated the ground beneath Prometheus' feet. He stumbled, barely staying upright.

"Another inch and it's your legs," Kai said, not taking his eyes off me. He flicked a hand. "Imprison him." His tone of voice didn't change. But his eyes flashed with the same fathomless black that I'd seen in the barrier around Nyx.

A dozen Pyrosim showed up to form a fiery guard around Prometheus. They arranged themselves in a tight flaming square, completely blocking him in.

"I'll take you down with me," Prometheus swore as he got to his feet. The minions were pressed too close for him to do anything other than stand, if he wanted to remain untoasted. His skin flushed red from the heat. And maybe his anger.

Kai laughed. "Try it. I dare you. I'll bury you so deep that you'll be forgotten." There was absolute promise and sneering certainty in his voice.

It made Kai sound more like his father than I'd ever heard him. *That* was terrifying.

I whipped my eyes away from Kai, so he couldn't see my panic.

Prometheus walked backward, facing me through the flames of his prison as the Pyrosim marched him off. "Believe," he mouthed.

I grabbed Kai's arm, more than ready to beg. "Don't take him. Please. It's not what you think. There's nothing going on between him and me. I'm not even his type." I didn't want to accidentally out Prometheus if Kai didn't know.

"You think I'm worried about that?" he scoffed. "But there *is* something going on with you. You've been different lately." He bit down on the edge of his bottom lip, lost in thought. "I figured I was imagining things, but the way you acted yesterday and today? Holding me at arms' length?"

Annoyance flared hot and hard inside me. "Is this because I wouldn't sleep with you? Why would I want to with all your passive-aggressive games?"

Kai went poker-faced. "At least I wasn't manipulating you."

"Please. That's your middle name." I remembered a fraction of a second too late that Kyrillos had never manipulated Persephone. Kai had messed with Sophie. And right now, Sophie failed to exist.

He inclined his head. "If that's how you feel, then perhaps this is our cue to end all our partnerships."

I grabbed his wrist. "No. What? This is our chance. We have to help humanity."

Kai's face broke into a very cold smile. Almost snakelike. I'd sprung his trap. "That confirms you're working secretly with Prometheus." He brushed my hand off, his knuckles grazing my skin. "Because we both know you don't give a damn about humanity."

"That's not true!"

"I wonder," he murmured.

My eyes closed against this onslaught of emotion—the feel of his lips humming against my skin; the seductiveness of his misguided words. I was losing myself. My brain couldn't process everything that Persephone and I felt toward Kai. Anger, attraction, revenge, desire.

My eye twitched. If only I could smack myself upside the head and reboot. Or end this enchantment, get out of here, and start dealing with the regular teen variety of angst and hormone fueled attraction.

219

"Were we really going to rule together? Or did you have a very different agenda?" Kai asked. He lifted his face to bore into me with his eyes.

Harder to say whose jaw was tighter at this point. His, given the way it looked, or mine, given the way it felt.

He cocked his head to the side. "Why did you get my father to throw a party? A *masked* ball. Why would you want to avoid being seen as we head into the equinox?"

I pushed against his arms, sending him back a couple of steps. "Are you kidding me? I was defending *you*, idiot. Trying to get your horrible father to treat you properly. Which, of course, he twisted into this stupid idea of a—"

"Stop lying to me."

I jumped at the fury in his voice, shrinking back at the flat blackness in his eyes. I kept a careful watch on him as I spoke. "I'm not lying!"

"I want the truth. You owe me that much."

"Truth: I love you. I didn't mean to upset you."

He searched my face carefully. "Who are you?"

That was the jackpot question, wasn't it?

My mind boggled. I realized we were having the same conversation we'd had after Kai's kiss released my Persephone self last Halloween.

Ironic.

And unfortunate that he couldn't do the same thing for my Sophie self here and now.

I brushed my palm across his cheek. "You know who I am. Better than anyone."

He leaned into my touch. We stayed like that, connected, skin to skin, for only a moment. I let my hand drop as I felt him pull away. "Are you going to imprison me, too?" I dreaded his answer.

Kai bowed his head. "I can't hurt you." He raised his eyes to look at me and I saw that truth reflected in them. And the pain of it. "But I want you gone. After we do the ritual, take down Zeus and Hades," he waved a hand between us, "this ends."

Good luck with that. "Like you could stay away from me."

His eyes narrowed. "I don't trust you anymore, Persephone. If I didn't know how badly you wanted to knock Zeus down, you'd be in cuffs until I could drag you to the ritual site."

"Which you'd need me to lead you to. Seeing as you don't know it."

Kai bristled. "Add that to everything else you're not sharing these days."

I was going to shoot my mouth off again, but I remembered that it didn't matter. This was an enchantment. Kai and I could return to our regularly scheduled issues once this was over. I raised my hands, as if in surrender. "Fine. We play nice 'til the equinox, then go our separate ways."

"I expect you to keep up appearances until then."

"And if I don't?"

"We find out how much you'd miss Prometheus."

"Right," I scoffed. "You can't kill a Titan without anyone noticing. Or consequences."

Can't I? Kai's look dared me.

I crossed my arms, and held his stare.

Kai smiled, thinly.

What was it with everyone trying to separate Theo and me? I glared at Kai but he simply stared back, totally unflappable. "Fine. You do your part, I'll do mine. We done?" I may have sounded flippant at the supposed end of my big love affair, but it wasn't real, so whatever.

He gave me a final "who are you and what have you done with my girlfriend?" look, and shrugged. "We're done." He may have seemed indifferent, but his voice was cold. As was his last look at me as he walked away.

Idiot.

I slowly paced along the shore of the lake, not really seeing anything. It was all so muddled. I wanted out of this rabbit hole where I felt sorry for Hades. Where I'd found out that all Demeter had was her woman-scorned bit. Where Kai wasn't my Kai, and Prometheus didn't really know me, and I'd lost them both.

I wasn't upset. Not even angry. More incredulous that I'd managed to screw things up so badly. I had a billion more mistakes to undo before I could get the truth of this matter out in the open.

The clock was ticking.

I rubbed my hands roughly over my face and straightened up. *Get yourself together.* There was only one thing I could do now.

And it had nothing to do with Oizys tackling me and punching me with a hard right to the gut.

Sixteen

"What have you done?" Oizys demanded, her fists up and ready.

One hand clutching my side, I elbowed her off of me.

She rolled herself to her feet, and I scrambled to mine. I wasn't about to let her tower over me. "You want to get mad?" I swept my arm out. "Get in line. But if you want to do something useful, then help me break Prometheus out."

Oizys stilled, taking me in slowly.

I shook my head and started walking. I'd had enough.

"There's something off about you, Springtime," she said.

I almost laughed. How right she was. On so many levels.

Oizys caught up to me, puzzled at my amusement. "You don't have your usual energy."

"My happy goddess delight?"

She shook her head. "The darkness that is usually deep within you."

That was disturbing. I stepped back. "You don't know what you're talking about."

Oizys watched me intently. "It's tempered by a fire now," she said.

The vision ...

My body went cold. I clasped my trembling hands behind my back and kept moving.

Oizys saw my shock and nodded. "Misery and pain. I see this in you. Or I did. Something fundamental has changed."

She could try and puzzle it out all she wanted. No way would this denizen of Hades guess who I really was. Kiki's enchantment was good for that much.

"Are you going to help me break him out or not?" I needed Aletheia to come reveal the truth, and it would make life a lot easier if Oizys played on my team.

She gave a sharp nod. "Only because I want to crack your secrets."

Fine by me.

My stomach rumbled. I realized I hadn't eaten since morning, and judging by the fading light, it was heading into evening. I was starved. "Let's eat, and then we can go back to my ..." I was going to say "room" but no way was I going back there. I shared with Kai. My brain tripped over *that* thought, and I trailed off. "We'll eat," I said, finally.

We continued back to the palace in the deepening gloom. I was happy to feel the last rays of warmth on my face, even as a chill nipped at my ankles. The air was rich with the scent of dry grass and scorched earth.

There was a rustle of wind. Enough to bring the faintest echo from Tartarus. I shivered and stepped up the pace, marveling at the silver trees around the deep, black, silent Pool of Lethe. We crossed the garden to enter the palace through the front, and I let one finger trail over the cool relief of the ornately carved iron front doors depicting scenes of gods in battle.

Once again, the throne room was packed. Oizys and I raised a lot of eyebrows and heard a lot of whispers at the sight of us together. "We shouldn't be seen together," I said. I didn't want anyone getting suspicious about a newfound alliance between us.

"Works for me." She veered sharply out of the room, headed for the large alcove adjoining it. Inside, there was a heaping buffet of dinner choices.

Atkins dieters would be in roasted protein ecstasy. I went to the opposite end of the buffet, filling my plate with the most recognizable foods. I pretended to focus on my dinner, eating at my own empty table. I kept one eye on Oizys at all times.

She kept to herself a lot. That surprised me. If she was going to win Miss Congeniality anywhere, I would've thought it would be here in the Underworld. But she avoided the other deities, and they her.

I felt a pang of sympathy. Being a misfit here had to suck.

I let Oizys leave first, then snuck out after her. All right. I wasn't all that secretive because the only ones who seemed to care where I was going were a couple of intimidating looking Infernorators who puffed up their flames at me.

Two Pyrosim were child's play for me. And I knew that beyond making Persephone's life miserable by forcing her to stay in the Underworld, Hades didn't allow any actual harm to come to her here—because Kyrillos had insisted on that. Of course, if anyone could end up breaking that rule, it would be me. Since I wasn't about to test my luck, I ignored the minions completely.

A few minutes later, I spied Oizys in an empty corridor. She sped up at the sound of my approach.

I sped up, too, until I had come flush alongside her. I slung my arm around her shoulder.

She didn't go into full rigor-mortis-stiffening at my touch, but it was close. "How do you feel about a roommate, Goth Girl?" No way was I going back to that stupid shared bedroom. I hoped Kai would freeze, all alone under the covers.

Oizys shrugged my arm off, shot me a disdainful look, and picked up her pace. "What happened to not being seen together?"

"Nothing. But we're alone now." I waggled my eyebrows at her for good measure.

She stared at me, like she couldn't figure me out but would love to try. Preferably using pointy instruments that would cut my head open. "No. No roommates."

I let her think that she'd had the final word. Didn't argue at all when she made her way toward her room. I let myself zone out to the sounds of far off voices and the random hum of activity in the palace. And I followed her.

Oizys put up with me dogging her heels until we

reached her bedroom door, in a wing far from my own, though it looked much the same.

She hovered on the threshold. "Much as I wish otherwise, we can't do that thing ..." She gave me a pointed stare. "... tonight. It's too dangerous to go traipsing around now. We'll reconvene in the morning."

I nodded. "Sure."

As she turned, I hip checked her, and she stumbled into her room. Quickly, I stepped in and shut the door. All sound from outside the room was cut off. The room itself smelled surprisingly floral. Girly.

I surveyed her digs. "Love your use of monochrome." Everything was the same dense shade of black. I ran a finger along one wall. "Although I hear accent colors do wonders. Consider a little blood red, or rat's eye pink. Classic choices in the goth palette."

Oizys folded her arms. "Get out."

"Nope. If you and I are going to plot, I'm betting this is the safest place to do it. You're a natural born citizen of the Underworld. I'm just a landed immigrant with dodgy papers. Probably a lot more breathing room on your side of the palace."

Oizys sank onto her bed and tugged off a combat boot. "Points for stringing together a logical argument. But no. I don't room with anyone. Especially not goddesses of spring."

"It's not a communicable disease. Trust me. You're not going to get suddenly flowery and smiley." I sure hadn't and I *was* the Goddess of Spring. I leaned back against her door, my palms pressed to the wood. "I'll be honest."

She paused, boot in hand, and looked up at me, visibly pained. "Must you?"

"I can't go back to the room that I share with Kyrillos. Which means I'll have to wander the halls, stealing naps where I can, and being entirely inefficient in springing Prometheus."

Oizys pulled off her other boot and waggled her toes as if delighting in the cool air. "Good. Then you won't get in my way. You've done enough damage."

"Oh no," I scowled. "*You're* the sidekick on this little mission."

"I don't think so." She fixed me with her best Spirit of Misery and Woe glower, and rose to her full height. It was an impressively quelling look, but once a girl had death squads trying to whack her ass on a regular basis, evil stares failed to pack a punch.

"Partners then." I settled myself onto a daybed in one corner. Instead of the usual wrought-iron rosettes, curlicues, and colored glass that often made up the sides and back of these things, this one looked like a massive iron spiderweb. Complete with evil metal spider awaiting its prey.

I bounced up and down on the mattress to get a rise out of Oizys. "It's a little macabre but it'll do in a pinch."

Her lips flattened so thin, they were practically nonexistent.

"Look," I said, relenting, "it's only for tonight. Tomorrow, we'll find Prometheus and break him out." This was a total lie. Until that truth spirit showed up to break this farce of an enchantment and let us out of here, I was bunking with Oizys.

Not that I'd tell her that.

Oizys pulled on the cuffs of her sweater so that they slid over her hands, covering them. "It'll cost you," she said.

I rolled my eyes. Of course it would. There couldn't be the simplest transactions with these Greeks without payment due. "What?"

"Tell me why Prometheus matters so much to you."

I leaned back against the daybed's scratchy sheets— black of course, like the rest of her bedding—and considered how best to answer that.

I felt the mattress creak as she sat down beside me. Felt her expectant stare.

I couldn't tell her the truth. First off, she'd never believe me. Second, no matter how much she cared about Prometheus, I wasn't about to risk the well-being of humanity by telling her anything that could be used against us on the equinox. Or get me imprisoned now.

So not the plan.

Which only left one explanation. "In another time, another place, he was my best friend. And whatever we are now, I'll always love him." Even if we never saw each other again, Theo would always be my best friend. I would always love him, and I refused to give him up without a fight. There had to be some kind of wily loophole in the Theo agreement. Like telephones. Technically, I wouldn't be seeing him, right? I couldn't give him up. He was a part of me.

I let myself get lost in mushy memories for a bit.

"He never mentioned you." Oizys said.

229

I blinked a couple times to clear my pictures of the past, then met her eyes, the fingers of my left hand crossed behind my back. "Because he loves sharing so much, does he?" It was a long shot, but given how close-mouthed Theo was, I was willing to bet that the same was true for Prometheus. Which meant he probably didn't go around talking about his life in Olympus.

She bought it. I could tell by the way that her jaw relaxed. "Fine. You can stay. But annoy me and I'll throw you into the Styx, and happily watch you dissolve."

On that cheery note, it was bedtime.

On Tuesday morning, I woke up the polar opposite of refreshed. Part of it may have been the fact that I was wearing yesterday's clothes, since I dreaded going back to my bedroom and running into Kai. Part of it may have been my nightmares, where the world burned and I was forced to watch, held in place by one enormous spider leg.

Mostly though, it was the equinox was in two days and I had a massive amount of stuff to accomplish: free Prometheus, break the enchantment, get through the portal safely, take down the wards, do the ritual, save the world, and not die anywhere in the process. I was somewhat daunted.

I couldn't let myself dwell on that, because, well, thinking led to getting overwhelmed, which led to angry feelings and the possibility of uncontrollable destruction.

Back there in reality, I'd managed to throw Planet Earth into a seasonal limbo. I'd made plants burst into flame, and broke branches off trees from twenty-three stories up. Not to mention dealing with an internal rage that was ripping me to shreds. Literally, given the way I'd attacked my arms.

Here, I was so busy trying to keep Persephone's emotions at bay that mine hadn't had a chance to suffocate me. And I planned on keeping it that way. If *my* off-kilteredness somehow managed to leach through and combine with all of Persephone's issues? That sounded like a recipe for disaster. The makings of a Sophie/Persephone megabomb.

Which was why, as much as I could, I focused all my thoughts on what I could do, what I *had* to do, not what I was feeling. And my immediate problem was freeing Prometheus. "We need to know what obstacles we face in the great prison break," I told Oizys. Also, how would I buy him time to get the Spirit of Truth here without Kai mounting a manhunt—or rather, a Titan-hunt?

"Where are the dungeons?" I asked. We'd returned to Oizys' room after breakfast for maximum plotting privacy. She'd needed to eat as badly as I had.

She sat at in front of her mirror, re-applying eyeliner in heavy black lines.

I was on the floor, my back against the daybed, chin resting on my hands. I was hopeful. Neither Kai, nor Hades had crossed our paths. Yet. Out of sight, out of mind seemed like my best policy where those two were concerned. While I understood that Kai—and Kyrillos—didn't want me hurt, who knew what consequences our newly strained relationship might have.

My breakfast suddenly felt heavy in my stomach. I shifted, uncomfortable.

"There are no dungeons," Oizys said.

Her voice startled me out of my thoughts. "Where do they imprison people then?"

She tossed a flat stare over her shoulder. "They don't."

Queasiness morphed to all out panic. I bolted upright. "They killed him?!"

Watching her reflection, I saw Oizys roll her eyes. "Don't be stupid. If Hades or Kyrillos were going to pull a power play like that, everyone would know." She examined herself a final time before turning on her padded stool to face me. "We just have to figure out where they would put him."

"Tartarus," I said, and shivered automatically. I did not want to go back there. Plus, the place was huge. "Let's rule everywhere else out first."

Oizys raised an eyebrow. "Scared, Springtime?"

I snagged a pillow from the daybed and wriggled it under my butt. "Uh, yeah. And don't even try to convince me that you enjoy hanging out there. Because there's gloom and doom, and then there's just plain stupid."

"Nobody enjoys hanging out there," she said, sounding more than a little convinced of my stupidity.

"Dead people and Olympians don't," I said. "Your kind might think it's a happy fun park."

I got an annoyed sigh, but no actual response. I crossed my legs and thought it over. "He wouldn't be in the palace. That's too obvious. The first place I'd search."

"Somewhere that would cause Prometheus maximum pain," said Oizys, rising to root through the jumble of stuff on her dresser.

"His rock." We said it in unison. And then, just as quickly, we both shook our heads. "No. Kai would want to keep Prometheus in the Underworld."

We stared at each other, both somewhat startled. "Great minds think alike," I murmured.

"Then I don't know how you reached that conclusion."

I waved my hands around, faking scared. "Ooh. Insults."

A corner of her mouth lifted ever-so-slightly into a grin. I had to look really hard, but it was there.

When she spoke, though, her voice was as matter-as-fact as ever. "Even if Kyrillos didn't actually bind him to the rock again, he could recreate the psychological trauma of it. Briareos, Kottos and Gyes, the Hekatonkheires who helped subdue him initially, live—"

"In Tartarus," I finished, glumly. "It fits. Kyrillos turned Prometheus over to the giants' keeping. We have to get him out of their hundred-handed clutches."

"Three hundred-handed clutches," Oizys corrected, snagging a tube of lipstick. "A hundred hands each. Along with their combined hundred and fifty heads."

"Thank you so much for clarifying that," I snapped. "Because we wouldn't want any hope going into this."

She uncapped the tube to paint her lips purple. "Best to know what we're up against."

I sighed. "You're right. I don't suppose there's a handy map of Tartarus anywhere?"

Oizys pointed to herself. "Spirit of Misery and Woe, here. If those giants are doing their jobs properly, Prometheus' pain will call me to him like a beacon." She sounded pretty miserable about that.

I didn't blame her. "Okay, so what do you need to—"

"Shut up for five minutes." She tossed the lipstick back onto the dresser and moved over to her bed.

I shut up.

Oizys hung backward off the bed, her hair sweeping the floor. Her eyes were closed but it didn't look comfortable.

For a few minutes there was no sound except our breathing. I looked around the room, trying to spot the source of the lovely floral aroma. Given the clutter strewn over the bed, the daybed, the dresser, and another low table, it could have been anywhere.

Oizys raised her head, her eyes bleak. "Found him."

My heart sank. "And he's in ..."

She rolled herself into a sitting position. "Yeah."

"Then it's field trip time. We'll need ear plugs. And possibly gas masks." Because I doubted I could withstand long-term exposure to either the sounds or the smells of the damned.

Oizys pointed at my ugly dress. "First, you need some proper clothes." She strode to her closet and flung the door open. Inside was a whole lot more black. She flipped through her stuff, pulling out a black T-shirt and black cargo pants. "Change."

It wasn't a suggestion.

But since it was a damn sight better than what I was wearing, not about to get an argument from me. I stood up, took the clothes, and headed into the bathroom, sponging away any stinkyness as best I could, and using my finger as a toothbrush. With the help of her bathroom mirror, I smoothed the more obvious snarls out of my hair, grimaced at my reflection, and decided this was as good as it was going to get.

Truthfully, it was pretty good. My Sophie self would have looked like something the cat dragged in, but Persephone looked like a slightly tired supermodel.

I stuck my tongue out at her face, and headed back into the bedroom. "Ready."

Oizys smirked. "So you didn't burst into flame wearing black, huh?"

"Sorry to disappoint. Do I get boots?"

She snatched up her glasses from her dresser and put them on. "I don't share footwear."

I didn't have any memory of Persephone owning anything other than sandals. Great.

I looked around. "Thoughts on the ear plugs and gas masks?"

"Yeah. Suck it up and suck it up, princess."

"Bite me."

"Ohhhh," Oizys pursed her lips. "Springtime shows her thorns."

I felt a momentary pang. This was just an enchantment, and when things returned to normal, we'd probably be mortal enemies. Too bad. I liked this chick. I allowed myself a small smile at how easily Oizys could take Bethany down a notch or two. Then I crossed to the door and opened it. With a flourishing arm sweep, I motioned for Oizys to lead the way.

We kept to the back stairways and corridors as much as possible. Seeing the two of us together, especially when I was dressed like Oizys' Mini Me, would raise too many questions. Luckily, it was fairly simple to get out undetected. The souls we passed on our way to Tartarus didn't know us. And frankly, they were more concerned with being dead than finding out what we were up to. All of which allowed us to get within nose-hair-blistering distance of Tartarus relatively easily.

We stopped in front of the bronze fence. This was nowhere near where I'd gone through to meet Demeter. The section was totally smooth, with no door in sight. I debated whether or not to mention that I knew a way in, but figured it would lead to questions I wasn't about to answer. So I kept quiet and let Oizys take the lead.

She placed her hands on the fence. A violent shudder ran through her.

I moved to push her back, remembering how the cries of the damned had chilled me to the core. But she kicked out at my leg.

"Ow!" I rubbed my calf. "Fine. Touch it, you psycho."

Oizys looked at me. Her eyes glowed red.

I took several steps back and brought out my green light.

She just laughed. "Like you could take me." In a feat of insane strength, even for a supernatural being, she dug her fingertips into the bronze, and shredded it like paper.

My eyes bugged as Oizys tore a jagged opening.

"Go."

I hesitated, taking in her ragged breathing. The red in her eyes had dimmed somewhat. "Touching the fence powered you up, didn't it? You got strength from their pain."

Her fingers tightened on the rough segment of fence. "It's fading fast," she said. "If you don't want me to kick your ass so I can amp up again, I suggest you move it before I lose my grip."

I hopped through the hole, staggering back as a wave of sheer despair overwhelmed me. This was way worse than wherever I'd met with Demeter.

I gritted my teeth. "Lovely."

Oizys ducked through the opening and let go of the fence. It snapped itself back into place with no sign that it had ever been disturbed.

"Impressive."

She gave me one of her flat stares and wiped her brow with her arm. Then she tromped past me toward a large boulder.

Awesome traveling companion. I gagged on a particularly vicious waft of sulphur, and an image of a burning pomegranate tree slammed up inside my head.

No way! I knew scent was a trigger but this was a terrible time to get hit. I hustled my butt to catch up with Oizys, keeping my mind on our task and trying to forget the putrid smell.

Oizys strode around the boulder. Without pausing or checking to see if I was still with her, she veered sharply left and entered a low cave.

I scowled at the blackness in front of me, just as the beam of a high-powered flashlight popped on inside.

"Figured you'd be afraid of the dark, Springtime."

I headed into the cave, making sure my voice was pure sweetness. "What dark? I was going to wrap you in my light vines and use you as a lantern. But a flashlight works too."

That shut her up.

I peered around as best I could. It didn't seem too bad. We were in a narrow tunnel made of craggy, black stone. A bit musty, and reeking of old rotten eggs, but at least it was dry.

Famous last words.

My next step went down. I stumbled, just managing to stop myself from falling into a puddle of warm, murky liquid. "Do I want to know?"

"The rivers converge to trickle through here."

"And you let me go in sandals? What if my feet melt?"

I could practically hear her indifferent shrug. "Next time, buy proper footwear."

"You're a real joy." I shuffled along behind her for a bit, trying not to think about what might live in the water to feast on my toes. I kept moving. There wasn't much more than a slight prickly heat. I didn't feel corrosive acid eating the flesh off of my bones. "Can you tell if … well, if they're hurting him?"

"Yes."

"*And?*"

"They're leaving him alone. For the time being. But that means that my sense of him is fading. So pick up the pace."

That was the best I could hope for. A jog was more than a fair price to pay.

We continued in silence for a while. I tried not to think about how fast I'd be smushed if all this rock came crashing down on me. Or what was waiting at the other end of the cave. Mindless chatter seemed like the best plan. "Are you going to Hades' masquerade ball?" I asked.

"Like I have a choice." Oizys sounded totally disgusted.

Best not to mention I'd inadvertently given him the idea. I picked my way gingerly along. The water had risen to just above ankle height, and there was a eye-watering stink of dead fish. "You got a costume yet?"

"I'm not wearing one."

"Way to take all the fun out of it."

Oizys stopped abruptly. I stumbled into her and whacked my head on her chin when she turned to face me. We both swore.

"There is nothing fun about one of Hades' parties," she said, shoving me back a step. "It's all backstabbing and plotting and secret agendas."

I rubbed my chin. "Which is different from any other day around here, how?"

"I keep to myself," she hissed, and she went on walking.

True. I'd noticed that. "Your anti-social tendencies trump your evil ones." I trailed my right hand against the stone wall to keep my bearings, since Oizys held the flashlight in a low beam that only helped her.

"I'm. Not. Evil."

She actually sounded hurt. "Sorry."

"Do you think Kyrillos is evil? Your boyfriend is heir

to this kingdom, but I don't see that stopping you from jumping into bed with him."

I wasn't jumping into bed with anyone. But I got her point. And she was right. "I think many varied things about that boy," I muttered. "None of which have to do with his birthright."

"Then don't paint me with that brush." She whipped around, momentarily blinding me with the flashlight. "You Olympians. You're all so judgmental. So self-righteous."

"Like Underworlders aren't? You thought all I was good for was dancing among flowers."

"Poor baby," she mocked, adjusting the light so I could see the sneer on her face. "Someone thinks you're pretty and useless. Cry me a river. You don't have everyone automatically assuming you're evil."

With that, she stormed deeper into the tunnel.

I stood there, the fetid water swirling around my feet. Maybe, sometimes, I could be judgmental. Even if I was, weren't we all? Did that make it all right? If anyone had asked me, I would have said that Hades' gang was evil and Zeus', what? Good? Less evil? Opposite, somehow.

I took a few faltering steps forward. Oizys had sounded hurt. Like this actually mattered.

I guess it wasn't that black and white.

I sloshed along until I'd caught up with her again. "Is that why you like Prometheus? Because he doesn't judge you?"

"Isn't it why you like him, too?"

I didn't know about Prometheus, but Theo hadn't.

Did we spare the people we loved? No, because I certainly laid a whopper of a judgement on Hannah. I squirmed, self-loathing and guilt rearing their ugly twin heads in a bitter knot in my stomach. I didn't want to have this conversation anymore. I sped up. "You need a costume for the ball."

"Maybe I'll borrow your clothes and go as you."

I snorted out my laughter. That was unexpected.

Oizys turned, balancing the light so she could see my expression. "You don't care?"

I put a hand on her shoulder, trying not to double over laughing. "Care? I think it's brilliant. Can I do your make up?"

Oizys stared at me like I was insane, but I distinctly heard an amused, "Maybe" before she disappeared around a corner and made what sounded like a smothered yelp.

My adrenaline spiked and I stupidly ran after her. I flew into the next section of tunnel, made it about three feet in, and dropped like a dead weight into nothingness.

Seventeen

At first I screamed. And then a howling drowned out the sounds and storm winds battered me against the cave walls like a bouncy ball.

It. Hurt.

Also, I was wet, and trying very hard not to think about all the grossness in the water that drenched me. I was tumbling down a hole, alongside the river, where it turned into a waterfall.

I called up my vines and fired one toward the walls. Luckily, the light held against the wet stone, and I could control my descent to Oizys. I fired another vine down into the gloom and prayed for a hit.

"Ouch!"

"I got you." Carefully, I lowered myself down with one hand and reeled her toward me with the other.

She was flailing on her end of the line, the vibrations making it that much harder to keep my descent steady in the gale force wind that whipped up the tunnel. My knee banged a sharp outcropping of rock. "Stop struggling," I yelled. "You're causing tension."

"It's the wind. I'm getting seasick," she said, when I managed to pull even with her.

A gust swung us right under the waterfall. I swung us out again as fast as I could, but not before we were both sputtering noxious water. "Try not to get this stuff in your mouth," I said.

"No kidding." She looked a little queasy so I picked up the pace.

The beam of the flashlight pointed down, so I could see we were maybe fifty feet from the ground. Bright flashes of lightning lit the way as I lowered us to the exit below. Talking was impossible. The winds were so strong and so loud that it was all I could do to keep us moving.

I focused on descending inch by painful inch, as the wind smacked us against the wet walls, and blew our faces into crazy funhouse mirror distortions. What should have taken seconds, took about ten minutes. Oizys lost her grip on the flashlight, and it hit the ground, going out. Not that it mattered, since we still had the lightening.

I glanced down to check our progress and realized that what I had mistaken for the bottom of the tunnel was just a ledge of rock with an exit to the outside. The tunnel continued downward to the left of the ledge, the water roaring down the canyon alongside. I had to land us on terra firma or risk continuing on to who-knew-where, along with the nasty river water.

We hit the ground in a bumpy heap.

I had never loved dirt so much.

We were bruised, wet, filthy, and judging by the scene

outside the cave entrance, about to find ourselves in the midst of a violent storm.

I tested my limbs. Nothing seemed to be broken but everything hurt.

Oizys and I exchanged glances. Then she tipped her head toward to the entrance and raised her eyebrows, in question.

I nodded. *Here goes nothing.*

We got to our feet. Bracing our shoulders against the wind, we pushed our way out of the cave.

It would have been beautiful if it wasn't so terrifying. Above me, streak of purple and black smashed against each other, while lightning snaked in jerky tendrils. I could only stare at it through slitted eyes. There was too much dirt flying around.

I tugged the collar of my shirt over my nose and mouth, against the twin scents of sulphur and electrical dust. I held it in place with my right hand, and hurried to take in our surroundings.

We stood at the edge of a vast pitted crater. All around us, the sides curved toward the sky. We were like ants against this vast backdrop of destruction.

And anguish. Did I mention the anguish?

The wind literally wailed. The air felt charged with an electric despair, so entrenched, so heavy, that every step was like trudging through a misery swamp. The wind would have severely tested the foundation of even the strongest building. But there was nothing to knock down. Only Oizys and me, as we struggled from boulder to boulder, bent double, looking for Prometheus.

The ground rumbled beneath us.

We grabbed on to each other for support, riding the quake out like a wave. Once it had subsided, we edged closer to the center of the crater, one eye out for the hundred-handed giants.

The next blast of lightning lit a rock formation. Prometheus' chain bound him to the middle stone. But this time, the chain seemed to be made of fire, which was a new trick, and had to majorly suck for him.

Oizys and I broke cover and dashed for the rocks.

Prometheus' stone was a wide, fat slab, like a sacrificial table that had been tilted upward at about a forty-five degree angle. His clothes hung off him in tatters, his flesh raw and blistered from the flaming restraints. Luckily, he was unconscious.

I wanted to throw up.

I tried using my power to free him from the chain, but neither Oizys nor I could do anything to break it. We couldn't even put out the flames, burning hot and fierce against his skin.

Suddenly, Oizys grabbed my shoulder and yanked me down behind the stone table. She pointed to the left. The giants Briareos, Kottos, and Gyes lumbered down one side of the crater with ground-quaking steps.

I craned my neck up to see the tops of these enormous creatures. Simply put, they were massive. Like a condo developer would have killed to build on their heads, just for the view. And I do mean heads.

Fifty of them.

Each.

Not to mention their hundred hands each. I lost count at forty-three on the first one.

I had to yell directly into Oizys' ear to be heard over the noise of the storm. "Now what? We can't free Prometheus. There's no way we can get him back up that tunnel, especially unconscious, and no way grabby and his brothers won't see us if we move."

The monstrosities neared, the expressions on their faces ranging from hideous leers to sneering smirks. My God, they were ugly. How fortunate that they were so large that I could see every single boil, snotty nose, and grimy finger in lifelike clarity.

I must have raised myself up a little too high over the back edge of the slab—all the better to gape at the uglies— because Oizys pulled me back down, glowering.

"Get caught and I leave you for their dinner." She sighed. "I didn't expect the chain to be like that. We can't take Prometheus until we find a way to unbind him without hurting him."

Or killing him. That's what she really meant. I didn't want to leave Prometheus. But she was right. His best hope was for us to get out of here and find something that could unbind him. Not just break the chain but do it without letting the fire consume him.

I also didn't want to stay here because every passing second was a head trip for my psychological well-being. I could feel Persephone's gnawing anger bristling the hairs on my skin. "Much as this place sucks," I said, "short of getting ourselves back up that tunnel, how do you propose we get out of here?"

Oizys pointed up, toward the top of the crater where the giants had entered.

It made sense that they had their own way in and out of Tartarus. But I couldn't see how we could sneak up there, past all those watching heads. I leaned in to voice this concern, and my head snapped back as Oizys' fist connected with my jaw. I hurtled through the air, hit my head on a rock and everything went black.

I came to in her room, feeling like, well, I'd been bashed in the head with a rock.

Oizys perched on the metal side rail of the daybed, peering down at me. "It was the only way."

I tried to struggle into sitting position, but the room swung with a vengeance so I gave up and stayed flat on my back. "Was that an apology? For punching me? For splitting my skull open? Because I could help you rephrase it so it sounds somewhat more ... what's the word? Apologetic." I glowered at her, then decided that made me queasy, and closed my eyes.

"Sorry," she said.

"It would be more convincing if you actually sounded like you meant it."

"It really was the only way out." I felt a coolness against my temple as she pressed an ice-pack to my head. "I had to convince them that you were trying to free Prometheus and that I had been sent to detain you."

I opened my eyes and took over holding the ice pack. "You could have filled me in. I could have pretended to be unconscious."

She gave a one-shouldered shrug. "Wasn't sure you were that good an actress."

She had no idea. I repositioned the ice pack. "You're lucky I don't have a concussion."

She stood over me, hands on her hips. "And you're lucky I found a more convenient way back to Prometheus. Which I would not have needed to do had you not gotten him captured in the first place."

"Mee mee mee mee mee mee mee."

"Really?"

"Screw you. My head hurts." I rolled over onto my side, icepack firmly in place, and willed the constant pounding to go away. Also, the room could stop moving any time it liked. "Even if you did find a way out—and yeah yeah, yay you—how are we going to get Prometheus out without being seen? They have, like, three hundred eyes."

Oizys smiled faintly. "Simple. If their drunken singing was any indication, Hekatonkheires are huge lushes. We can use that. Kyrillos won't let them leave for the ball, so I can take them some goodwill nectar, specially doctored up."

I thought it over. "The ball *would* make great cover. Kai will be keeping an eye on me so the more people and activity to distract him while we slip out, the better." It would mean cutting things close: freeing Prometheus, having him come back with Aletheia, getting to the exit, and passing through the wards to Demeter's temple. Not to mention making sure Festos was there to cleanse the site. All between the ball starting at midnight on Thursday and the equinox at roughly 7PM.

I'd had worse deadlines.

I looked up at Oizys. "Which just leaves the problem of how to unbind the chain."

"Yeah, well, if you can stand up, we may have a solution to that too."

"Bah." I let the icepack slide onto the daybed and held out an arm for support.

She took it and helped me to my feet.

I braced my hand on the bed for a second, but my nausea was at deal-able levels. I leaned on Oizys, my head throbbing like crazy. I would have much preferred to be horizontal. Did they have Advil in this place?

"Speak," I said.

Oizys shot me a smug look. "Who better to know how to break the chain safely than the one who forged it?"

I did a double take. "You mean—"

She nodded. "Hephaestus is here."

Fee! I stifled my squeal of delight and scrunched up my face. "He doesn't like me much." I'd faced Festos' bitch factor before, but given how he felt about Persephone, I suspected I was about to experience an entirely new level of condescension.

Oizys didn't seem perturbed. If anything, she smiled. "Then I'd refrain from mentioning that you got the love of his life tied up while you weasel out a way to break the chain."

"Why can't you do it?"

"Olympian," she replied.

"So's Prometheus."

"He's different. Speaking to Olympians is ... frowned upon."

I shook my head. Bad idea. My stomach lurched. "I'm an Olympian and we're having all kinds of chats."

"Not willingly. Besides, we don't want anyone questioning why we suddenly seem so friendly."

"'Friendly' meaning 'in the same ten foot radius' as opposed to actually being friends."

"Exactly." She tossed me a wadded up floral dress. "Change first. Appearances are everything around here."

No kidding.

I hadn't seen this ugfest in Persephone's closet last time, but I had no doubt it was hers. Not only was it dotted with tiny sprigs of pink and blue flowers, it was mid-thigh baggy. Persephone was lucky. She was so beautiful that no one noticed her sucky fashion sense.

When I was ready, Oizys looked me over with a critical eye, then strode to the door and opened it for me. Like she couldn't wait for me to leave.

"I will be coming back, you know," I said.

To her credit, she didn't argue the point. Merely shoved me out the door.

I headed downstairs to the throne room. It was slow going because I still felt wonky from my encounter with the rock. I kept stopping to rest my face against the cool wall. Although the feeling wasn't as bad as being hit by lightning.

The fact that this was a step up—just a rock to the head—was a sad comment on my life.

When I finally reached the throne room, I paused at the threshold and gaped. Then I laughed. Which did nothing for my head. And Prometheus was still in terrible, agonizing danger, so I felt a little guilty at finding humor. But Hades had transformed the space into a white and gold parody of Zeus' statue room in Olympus. It was funny.

Statues of my father, in varying sizes and poses, were everywhere. On each one, different features had been exaggerated into grotesque caricature. I sent up a small prayer of thanks that there were no naked ones. That might have sent me over the edge.

Two daemonae, gray, lanky, and wrinkled, brushed by me. "... He's encouraged all his guests to dress as Olympians," one said and threw me a barely concealed sneer. "But he's open to creative interpretation." They were both baiting me now, waiting for me to crumble in humiliation.

I shrugged.

They snorted, gray gusts bursting from their leathery nostrils as they walked away.

I skittered backward, not wanting any of that stank up my own nose. Seemed like Oizys could go as me after all. No idea who I was going to dress as, though. Something that wouldn't call attention to me, so that I could easily slip out to get Prometheus when the time was right.

I stepped further into the room and looked around, trying to spot Festos. I found him about halfway across the floor, directing some malevolent creature who stood on a ladder to measure the ceiling.

I approached cautiously, using the ridiculous statues as cover, because I wanted a chance to take Festos in before he saw me and wrecked our reunion with insults.

He looked good in god form. Although not all that different from usual, because Fee in any form was so arrogantly confident that his inherent sense of superiority never actually left him. Mostly, he was just taller. Requiring a longer cane. Even his clothing style was close to how he dressed these days. Maybe a shade more Rat Pack than hipster, but still with his fedora at a jaunty angle. Although his hair was actually a normal dark brown.

As I got closer, I realized that Festos was under constant guard. Several Pyrosim floated nearby, their attention laser-focused on his every move.

I slid behind a statue of my father reclining on a bed. He looked seriously constipated. I imagined Hades giggling as he ordered that one. But it hid me well.

Festos stood about five feet away from the front corner of the statue. He seemed more annoyed than afraid of his flaming guards, but I could tell from way he eyed them that he wasn't entirely comfortable being here. Hades must have really wanted whatever contraption Fee was getting ready to install. Hephaestus was so clearly in Zeus' employ that his entrance into the Underworld wouldn't have been granted otherwise.

Fee gave a final command to his helper, who lumbered away. The Pyrosim remained as Festos regarded the ceiling a moment longer. "If Hades thinks I'm reporting back to Zeus on this little farce, he's extremely mistaken."

I startled at Festos' sneering sentiment. For a second I thought he'd seen me. For another second I thought he *knew* me.

But neither was the case.

Festos spoke to Kai, who had come to stand beside him, casually surveying the buzz of activity in the room.

"Hades thinks you're a lot of things, Fee," Kai replied. "A rat is not one of them."

Fee?! My mouth fell open. That was *my* name for Festos. Wasn't it? Had I heard Kai use it back when I was Persephone and that's why I did, too?

"Said as if you have a differing opinion, Koko." Festos offered Kai a tight smile.

I shoved my fist in my mouth to cover my laughter. Koko? I was *so* calling Kai that sometime. Sooner than later.

Kai stiffened at the nickname, and I could see that he hated it. I could also see from Fee's angelic smile that he was well aware. Kai didn't comment though. All he said was, "I don't think you're a snitch."

Festos leaned onto his cane. "But dirty vermin?"

Kai shrugged. "That's something else entirely."

I was dying to know what exactly the deal was between them. Because they were sniping like a pair of exes and I knew Kai didn't swing that way. Nor would he ever be Fee's type.

I strained against the edge of the statue, hoping neither would see me so I could continue to blatantly eavesdrop.

"Well, we're even now, honeybunch, aren't we?"

Kai fixed Fee with an infuriating superior-yet-innocent look that even I wanted to smack off him. "About what?" he asked.

"Drop the act." I could practically hear Festos' teeth grinding in anger. "Was getting back at me your prime motive for imprisoning Prometheus, or just a happy benefit?"

Whoa. Word traveled fast. Although Fee had always had up-to-the-moment intel where Theo was concerned, so I guess I shouldn't have been surprised.

Kai's hands fisted at his sides and he took a step back. "You want to keep destroying yourself over that asshole? Go nuts. Not my problem."

"Nope. You made sure of that." Festos' fingertips shot red sparks.

My breath caught. I looked around, but no one else seemed to be paying them any attention.

Kai poked Festos in the chest hard enough to send him staggering back a few feet. "Contrary to your delusional belief-system, my entire reason for being is not to screw you over."

Festos gave a bitter laugh. "No, it's to make a fool of yourself with that waste of a goddess."

Hey. No one got to call Persephone a waste but me. However, as this was neither the time nor the place, I smothered my indignation before it could get me caught.

Kai shrugged. "Persephone and I are done."

So much for keeping up appearances.

"While I'm thrilled you finally dumped the dead weight, it changes nothing." Festos sounded venomous.

My palms got sweaty. I was suddenly very concerned about how much of his animosity toward Persephone may have been silently festering around me, Sophie?

These Greeks played long, deep end-games. Was I totally wrong about our big platonic love?

"... Because you're a stubborn ass."

Damn, I'd missed the first part of whatever Kai had fired back at Fee.

Festos scowled. "Better an ass than a bad friend. O, judgmental one."

Kai snarled. "Screw you, Fee. You want him? Go get him. But whine to someone else when he fails to give a damn about you. Again."

With that, Kai spun and stormed out, fury pouring off him in waves.

I exhaled, pressing my back against the cool statue, and processing everything I'd just heard.

Pierce was right. Kai and Fee had been friends. And it seemed like differences in opinion over Prometheus and Persephone had torn that apart. Thing was, once we got back to normal, Fee and Kai would be with Theo and Sophie. And while Kai didn't like Theo for lots of reasons, the big historical one—how he'd treated Festos—was gone. In Sophie-time, Fee and Theo were great together. So maybe there was hope for these two former besties yet, if they could get over their stupid pride.

Pierce's words floated back to me. *All I'm saying is that if you're going to be the savior of humanity, maybe you could start by saving a single friendship.*

He was right. I did have to save a single friendship. Well, a couple of them actually. Because, while I was going to do everything I could to mend the friendship between Kai and Festos, I needed to listen to myself and make up with Hannah, too.

I stepped out from behind the statue, one hand resting against it. I scowled. Damnit! It was so much easier giving advice than taking it.

"What's your problem?"

It took me a second to realize that Festos was talking to me.

"You." I shoved at him. "Waste of a goddess?"

He blinked, startled, then glowered at me. "A rude waste of a goddess, eavesdropper."

"Fine. Since I'm rude I can tell you straight up you're being an idiot. You and Kyrillos. If you let a friendship die because of your significant others." I raked gaze over Festos, watching his shock. "Or continuing *non*-others. Unless you get your act in gear."

His nostrils flared. Good. I'd gotten him riled up.

He shoved me out of the way and strode toward the Pyrosim, his cane thumping against the ground with each step. "The chandelier I brought," he snapped at them. "Time to install it."

Guess he thought our chat was over.

Guess again.

I grabbed his sleeve.

He shook me off.

I grabbed him again and tugged him around to face me. I brought up my light vine with my free hand. Just enough so he could see the glow. "Take one more step and I'll gift wrap your ass."

His fingertips sparked red and he smiled mercilessly. "Try it."

I tsked him. "Temper, Fee."

256

He bristled. "Don't. Ever. Call. Me. That."

"You'd be amazed at what I call you. And you love it."

Festos blinked, obviously confused.

I rolled my eyes. "Not like that, idiot." I leaned in and lowered my voice. "I'm breaking Prometheus out tomorrow night. During the ball. And I need your help."

He pried my hand off of his arm. "On so many levels, why? Should I believe you? Should I trust you? Should I help you? Should I care?"

"Because you love him."

Now Festos looked outright shocked. He turned to the Pyrosim and snapped, "Go find someone to bring in the chandelier or I'll personally hand Hades the fire extinguisher to put you out."

The minions floated off.

Festos grabbed my arm and dragged me off to stand beside a twenty-foot-tall statue of my father prissily soaking his feet. Complete with giant, bunions sculpted in loving detail.

Gross. I averted my eyes.

Festos' gaze drifted over the route Kai had taken out of the room, as if he expected to see him standing there, and feeding me info.

"Kai didn't say a word."

"*Kai?!*"

"Kyrillos. I said Kyrillos."

Festos stared at me, obviously suspicious, and leaning heavily on his cane. "Who are you? You're not Persephone, so don't even bother pushing that lie." He ran the tip of the cane in a sweeping motion up my body. "You got the outside right. But the rest? Way off base."

I thrilled at the fact that he'd had realized even that much, except it made me wonder whether his hatred for Persephone was so strong that he noted any little deviation in her personality. Which made me wonder about him and me, which led me to shutting down that train of thought. "Yeah," I said, "I'm vastly improved. Which is why in reality you and I are friends, I'm not stuck in this stupid body, and you're dating Prometheus."

"Doubtful," he muttered.

"You are so friends with me."

He planted his hands on his hips. "How do you know that's what I was referring to?"

I just stared at him.

"Whatever. Besides, there is no reality in which I'm dating Prometheus."

"Okay, that's true."

He looked crestfallen.

I relented, resting my arm along the statue's knee. "His name is Theo. He's lost his Titan self. He loves you. This?" I waved a hand around the room, "Is all just an enchantment. Long story."

"Summarize." His tone brooked no argument.

I summarized.

He opened his mouth, then shut it again. Then spoke. "I have no idea what part of that I believe the least."

I tapped a finger against the statue, impatiently. I needed Fee on the same page here. "Just believe that I love that stupid Titan, too. I have a way to break him out but for this enchantment to end, everyone needs to see the truth of the situation. Which is where you come in.

Have you been invited to the ball?"

His lips thinned. "As help in case my party favor malfunctions. As if it would."

"Boo hoo. Get over it. Can the help bring a helper? Like Aletheia, the Spirit of Truth?"

"Truth is not really welcome in the Underworld."

"But you could smuggle her in?" I smiled sweetly at him. "I know how clever you are."

He smiled back with twice the sugar factor. "Yes, I am." Then he dropped it. "So stuff the kiss up."

I made a "get on with it" gesture with one hand. "And?"

"Theoretically. Yes. I could smuggle her in. If so inclined. Which I am not yet."

"Please." I brought my hands together in time honored begging formation. "The fate of humanity depends on Aletheia revealing the enchantment."

"Eh." He shrugged, indifferent.

"The fate of you ever getting to have hot kisses with the guy you love does, too."

His eyes narrowed. "While that second part is all fine and good, *you* got Prometheus thrown into Tartarus."

My face fell.

He smirked. "Yeah. Didn't realize I knew that part, did you? Tell me why would I take any of what you're saying on faith alone?"

My shoulders slumped. I didn't have proof. That was the problem. I rubbed nervously at my neck, and my fingers felt the cool silver of my chain. *The ring!*

I pulled it out from under my shirt and showed it to him. "You made me this."

Festos peered at it, then held out his hand. I hesitated, reluctant to part with it. "Hurry up," Festos hissed, at the sound of stomping on the far side of the room.

I yanked the chain over my head. Placed it and the ring in his open palm. Then I turned to check out the commotion.

Some other smaller giant—not one of the three busy guarding Prometheus, but a thirty footer nonetheless—clomped slowly across the room, holding a massive wrought-iron chandelier. The thing must have weighed a ton, with its dozens of metal scrolls, hundreds of candle cups, and thousands of glittering crystal teardrops.

But that wasn't what was slowing him down. The chandelier blocked his view and he was trying not to squash the now-scattering creatures in the hall. Each painful step was a teetering accomplishment.

Four minions floated behind him, with another flying by his head. Presumably to guide the giant to where the chandelier belonged.

I turned back to Festos who was busy examining the ring.

He tested its weight. He held it up close to his eye. He licked it. Then, he returned it to me. "It's my work. But I don't understand how."

"Doesn't matter. Just do me the one favor. No, two."

"Don't push it."

"Get Aletheia here in time for the ball. If I'm wrong, well, you can do your worst."

He thought it over for a moment, keeping one eye on the quickly approaching work force. Luckily, the throne room was as big as a football field, so even the giant took a bit of time crossing it. "I'll do my best. What's the second thing?"

"How do I break Prometheus out of the chain you made, and is it supposed to be on fire?"

"Fire?" he screeched.

"Shh!" I glanced nervously around. The giant was making so much noise with the chandelier that no one paid Festos any attention.

"Kyrillos is dead," he muttered.

"He did that?" Kai and I would be having words when this was over.

"It's overkill," Festos snarled. "The chain is strong, and painful enough without adding fire. That was just to hurt Prometheus." Fee's eyes glazed red.

"Forget Kyrillos," I said hurriedly, not wanting Festos to erupt. "Focus on Prometheus. What do I do?"

"Nothing." I started to protest but Festos shook his head at me. "*I* do it." His expression softened, and he stared into the distance. "I can whip up what I need, but barely on this timeline, and not until I finish up with *that*." He threw an annoyed look toward the chandelier before returning his attention to me. "Meet me under the throne room at 2AM Thursday morning."

"Thank you," I sighed. I turned to leave, but froze as he gripped my arm, his fingers digging into my skin.

"But if you're wrong and you've made me hope for the impossible?" He leaned close to my ear. "Not even the gods will be able to help you."

I shivered at the malice in his voice.

Then, he released me and strode off toward the giant, hollering directions.

I rubbed my stinging arm, and took a deep breath. Then let it out hard as I realized what I'd agreed to. Meeting Festos under the throne room in the early hours before the equinox. Site and rough time frame of Persephone's murder.

Way to go, clever girl.

Eighteen

Five minutes later I was still kind of paralyzed, with worry. I tried to get Festos' attention, but he blatantly ignored me. He was testing jets of fire and lava from each individual candle cup on the chandelier. That was one way to light up a room.

I'm sure the result would be spectacular, but I'd leave my close up *oohing* and *ahhing* for the night of the ball. Besides, the one time I did manage to make eye contact with him, Festos tossed me a look that promised burns from the dancing plumes of flame if I came any closer.

Since I had zero desire to take him up on that experience, I kept my distance. Besides, there was no need to panic, right? I mean, Demeter and I had left on perfectly good terms. She'd kissed me.

Hmmm. Mafioso kissed people before killing them, too, didn't they? My pulse spiked. I brightened a little when I figured that, even if she did come to whack me she might have second thoughts doing it in front of a room full of witnesses. At the very least, I'd be with Festos, Prometheus, Aletheia, and possibly Oizys. Although it wasn't like Demeter had to worry about getting arrested so what did witnesses matter?

Jaw set, I scanned the room, looking at all the faces. Fact was, I didn't have a single friend here. I watched Festos as, with a flick of his hand, he made the chandelier come alive with fire. Then, he pointedly turned his back on me. Again.

I saw Kyrillos, surrounded by fawning suck ups, while minions hovered protectively nearby. He spared me one hard look before charming his posse with a grin.

Not even my friends were my friends here.

The whole situation felt so unreal.

Dazedly, I wandered farther into the room. I felt one second out of synch with everyone else. The chatter around me sounded like a buzz, coming through a long tunnel. Colors seemed teeth-jarringly bright. Even walking felt too languid. Like I was streaming through a river of molasses.

I couldn't breathe. I pressed a hand to my side, taking in gulping breaths of air, desperate to get my lungs to expand.

"Did you get his help?" Oizys asked. Suddenly in my way.

My chest loosened at the sight of her, and I took a much needed breath. "Yes. And you don't need to sound so doubtful."

She shrugged. "You dance in flowers. That doesn't scream 'competent'."

"Give me a freaking break. I'm Goddess of Spring. I celebrate occasionally in a meadow. It's not like I prance around with floral arrangements. Nor do I just get bored with people and forget about them. Guy in chains suffering? Who's that?" I held myself stiffly, chin up, and added, "For your information, Hephaestus is coming to free Prometheus personally."

She pursed her lips, displeased.

"Now what?"

"Prometheus isn't going to be happy."

Maybe for five minutes. Until Aletheia revealed the truth. At which point Theo would probably even hug me for bringing Fee to him, given how they'd left things.

My last hug?

Oizys took a step back, eyes huge.

Which made no sense until I realized that, in thinking about Theo and what lay ahead for us, I'd worn a dark enough look to bother her.

I smiled, thinly. Good.

Hurt flashed across her face.

And my stomach sank. I balled my fists. I was not going to apologize. She got to be as crabby as she wanted to me.

Guilt.

She didn't even like me.

More guilt.

I sighed. "I have a lot on my mind. Look, there's still stuff we need to take care of before the ball. Like the nectar, and getting us both a costume."

"I want a floral arrangement." Her voice was even. "For the costume."

"You're going to milk this, aren't you?" I was resigned. But not really annoyed.

"Yes." She headed off in typical stomping stride.

"Okay then. Just checking." I trotted after her.

Oizys led me me through winding hallways that got narrower and narrower, until the two of us stood squeezed together like sardines in a stone can in front of a simple wooden door.

"Use your light to open it," she said. "We need to get into Hades' cellar and liberate some nectar. The good stuff."

She probably didn't mean for me to blast the thing off its hinges, but I was not in a subtle frame of mind. The door blew back into the room, arcing through the air to take out an entire rack of glass jugs before it smacked against the back wall hard enough to make my teeth rattle.

We stood there staring at the carnage of broken glass and pale peachy liquid streaming onto the floor. Slowly and deliberately, Oizys looked from the mess, to me, to the mess.

"Whoops." I stepped inside, and carefully picked my way to an intact rack. I scanned the jugs of nectar. Each one contained several of gallons of booze, sealed with a metal cap. A date, probably of bottling, was written across each jug on a neatly scripted label. "Moonshine of the gods," I said.

Over my shoulder, Oizys squatted on her heels, examining some labels on the bottom row. She planted her feet firmly on the ground, grabbed a jug and slid it off the rack. "This ought to do the trick." She stood up.

"A fine vintage is it?" I asked.

"Fine is a relative term." Carefully, she uncapped it for me to take a whiff.

I leaned in, sniffed, and recoiled, wiping my eyes. "What is that? 400 proof?"

"At least. Drink any of this blend and you'll go blind. But the Hekatonkheires love the stuff." Oizys cradled the brew in her arms and led me out.

My sandals left sticky footprints as we walked away. "Where to now?" I asked.

"We need to put this away for safekeeping. Rule number one in the Underworld? Never keep incriminating evidence in your room." Her hands full with the jug, Oizys elbowed me away from a corridor full of voices.

We waited, tense, as they came closer. Thanatos, the creepy death baby, was directing one of the Infernorators.

Oizys held herself stiffly. She glanced back, searching for a hiding place but it was all wide stone corridor, devoid of any convenient doors.

I held my breath, sliding behind Oizys as if she could shield me from discovery. But at the last second, the voices faded off again.

We waited a moment longer, totally still. Then I peeked around the corner. Thanatos and the minion must have gone into the hallway that branched off the one we needed.

We scurried around the corner, and stopped at a thick stone door with a brass handle. I pushed down on the latch, shouldered the door open, and stepped into the last rays of evening sun. It was still weird to see sunsets that pretty much consisted of black streaking the sky in bigger and bigger swatches until all the daytime color was gone. But I had to say, they kind of grew on me.

The air held the last vestiges of heat, with just a slight nip. Hopefully, we wouldn't be out here too long, because the flimsy dress I wore did nothing for warmth.

Oizys led us into an overgrown garden. It was mostly thorny vines and weeds, all tangled together, with a narrow path in the middle. She crept to the far end, at which point she stepped off the path and through a gap in a scruffy hedge.

I followed, and found myself in a tiny clearing.

She set the jug down and arched her back, stretching. "Now we doctor it, so the giants have a nice long nap."

I looked around. "You going to use some plant to make a sleeping potion?"

"Yes. The bulb of the poppy, plucked by moonlight as its petals close. Ground by the stone of the dragon and set into the waters of the Styx." She unscrewed the cap.

"Really?"

"No." She pulled a small bottle of of white powder from the pocket of her pants. "Sleeping pills. Precrushed." She uncapped the bottle, and dumped the powder into the nectar.

I watched it dissolve. "You just carry that around, do you?"

She smiled, enigmatic. "I carry all kinds of interesting things around. Hope that you never find out what."

This chick was worse than Hannah. That was worrisome.

At the thought of Hannah, my shoulders sagged. There was nothing more I wanted in that moment than to fling myself down on my bestie's bed and talk about the inanities of our day. Make our stupid jokes and bitch about homework and be living the most staggeringly normal Sophie existence imaginable.

I ached with missing her. But I couldn't deny that I was still upset. What was so massively infuriating was that, as long as I was stuck here, there was no way we could even try and resolve our issues.

More than ready to be done with this stupid enchantment now. I blew a lock of hair out of my face. Reliving the past was pointless, especially when there was so much on the line in my future. Trouble was, before I could solve any of those problems, I had to extricate myself from this one.

Oizys capped the nectar and brushed her hands on her pants. "We're done. This is safe here until the ball." She pushed past me. "I need to eat."

Since the throne room was being decorated for the ball, dinner was waiting in the breakfast room. I was expecting Greek, Greek, and a side of Greek on the menu. Or some more vaguely identifiable roasted meats. But I guess Hades liked to mix things up, because it turned out that Tuesdays meant Chinese food.

Spicy green beans, chicken with cashews, ginger beef, green onion pancakes, chow mein—I'm not ashamed to say that I loaded up two plates. Feeding a body this size required serious amounts of food. And everyone was already judging me anyway.

Balancing one plate in each hand, I looked around for somewhere to sit. Oizys had gotten her food and was busy ignoring me. Even if there had been space beside her, I wouldn't have taken it. Sadly, there were no empty tables either. This was a billion times worse than any high school cafeteria nightmare. Sitting next to the wrong being didn't mean plain old verbal humiliation. They weren't just going to glare at me, or suddenly spread way out to make sure I couldn't slide in next to them.

These beings could kill me without taking their eyes from their plates. My only comfort was that, as far as I knew, Kai's edict was still in place. No harm could come to Persephone.

Suddenly, keeping up appearances seemed a very good idea.

I scanned the room for my darling boyfriend, ignoring the pain in my wrists from holding the plates. Maybe two trips would have made more sense.

Bingo. Kai was sitting with Hades in a semi-private alcove. Hades wore a red satin bathrobe, straight out of the Hugh Hefner collection. That made sense given the nymphs he surrounded himself with.

Thinking of Hades that way, was kind of amusing. But what wasn't as funny was how chatty Kai seemed to be with his father. They sat close together in a plush, burgundy, velvet banquette, talking insistently.

Time to find out what that was all about.

I made my way over to them and dumped my plates on the table. Hades barely spared me a glance. "When you decide to eat, you just go for it, don't you?"

Kai most definitely looked at me. Especially after I slid my arm around his waist and slipped in close to press a kiss to the corner of his mouth.

"Appearances," I whispered, seeing the curiosity on his face.

He scanned the room. "Taking your chance with the devil you know?"

I fluttered my lashes. "Something like that." Then, I raised my voice so Hades could hear me. "Don't let me interrupt your conversation."

They both looked at me suspiciously.

I focused on my food. "Mmm. Peking duck," I said, biting into a mini pancake filled with crispy skin and a liberal dose of Hoisin and green onion. Yum yum. *See the goddess eat and not care at all about what conspiracies you're hatching.*

They resumed their little chat. It wasn't what I expected. The two of them were gossiping like old Italian widows, watching the village go by and giving their unique judgy comments on everyone who passed.

It was harsh. Funny, but whoa. Who would have guessed that the one thing the two of them had in common was utter derision toward pretty much everyone in the Underworld?

The more I listened, the more I realized this wasn't just good old rumor-mongering. In systematically discussing (dissing?) each denizen of the Underworld, Kia and Hades were actually deciding who needed closer watch, or could be useful for something. I frowned.

"What's wrong?"

I shifted in my seat to better face Kai. "I didn't know you were so caught up in the daily dealings here."

Both he and Hades looked at me like I was simple. "He's heir to this realm," Hades said. "Of course he takes an interest in things."

Persephone must never have paid much attention to what exactly Kai did in the Underworld. And I'd assumed that he didn't do anything, since Hades always held his ascension to power out of reach.

Their relationship was a lot more complicated than I'd imagined. Because, if what I was hearing was any indication, Kai was totally up-to-date on Underworld business. Or at least had been, before Persephone's murder seventeen years ago. But more than just having current intel, Kai actively discussed people and events. And on some level, Hades listened.

Hades may have intended to keep Kyrillos dangling for eons. But before Persephone died, there was still some sort of relationship between them. In my current reality, where Kai had stolen Theo's chain and personally gone after Hades seeking revenge, it was pretty clear there was nothing.

All because of Persephone?

Which left me especially astonished. She hadn't troubled herself to learn what exactly her big love did in the Underworld. She'd existed in this narcissistic bubble. Which was fairly typical of all gods, but still. Given how long they'd been together, you'd have thought she'd take an interest. If only, because it was important to Kyrillos.

But she hadn't. I don't think she once asked him if

he enjoyed the politics of it. What he saw for the Underworld and his role in shaping that future.

I set down my fork. I hadn't asked either. I could blame that on the fact that we'd only been in a relationship, such as it was, for a couple of months. And that, during that time, there hadn't been a lot of in-depth sharing going on. But, honestly, I wasn't sure it would ever have occurred to me to ask Kai about ruling. Or what kind of ruler he'd be. Or, well, any of it.

Maybe that's why I'd been so surprised when he told Felicia he still wanted the Underworld. I'd never bothered to find out one way or the other. I shifted uncomfortably, faced with the very real awareness that I was possibly as narcissistic and self-absorbed as all the rest of the gods.

"Don't worry your pretty head." Hades lifted his goblet and gulped back some wine.

Now what? "Excuse me?"

"About Kyrillos' involvement. He still has plenty of time for you. Focus on what you do best. Being decorative."

That wasn't even thinly veiled insulting. The insult was right there. My face flushed. I wanted to snap at him. To tell him that Persephone wasn't actually stupid. Just frustratingly pigeonholed. But that would have been way out of character—and I couldn't afford to get him suspicious.

Kai gave me an odd look—like he was still trying to figure me out.

Since there was no way he would come to the correct conclusion—that this was all a giant, magic muck up—and since anything else would fuel his suspicions, I smoothed out my expression, killed all further personal insights, and went back to the last bites of food on my plates.

"Enjoying dinner?"

I gave Hades a vapid smile. "Your chef is a keeper."

"He should be. He cooked for Emperor Wu himself." Hades shrugged. "Before he tried to poison him. He's a deft hand with poison." He looked pointedly at me.

I choked on my duck. Coughed.

Kai pounded my back. My eyes teared up. "Water," I croaked.

Kai pushed a goblet toward me.

I grabbed it and slugged down half the contents. "Nectar," I sputtered.

"Yeah." His play at innocence didn't fool me for a second.

Nice try. He wasn't going to get me liquored up and spilling secrets. Like Persephone's upcoming betrayal. If I thought he'd believe me about Hekate and the spell, I would have shared that way earlier and saved myself a lot of trouble.

I dabbed my eyes with my napkin. "Great. Thanks." I took a moment to compose myself. During which I tuned out my dining company entirely. I could feel the nectar flowing through my body, warming my blood. I was a bit light-headed but that was probably because Kai had casually draped his hand on the back of my neck and begun to knead. His fingertips made teasing circles against my skin.

Maybe the conversation wasn't scintillating, but it was all good. My limbs were tingly and I felt warm and full and happy. And … tipsy, I realized.

"More nectar?" Kai asked, nudging the booze toward me.

Yeah, right. I'd drag you up the stairs and then roll over for you like a cat in heat.

Kai choked on his laughter.

I'd said that out loud. My face flamed. Time to die.

At least Hades hadn't heard.

"So, you did inherit my charm?" he said to Kai, nodding approvingly.

Spoke too soon. *Now* I could die. I glared down at the ground, willing it to open up and swallow me any old time.

"She can't resist me," Kai answered.

I glowered at him and saw that he was amused. Tipsy was headed downhill toward grumpy. The meal had been swell, but the company gave me indigestion.

I tried to get up, but Kai's grip kept me pinned. "Appearances," he murmured.

I gave up. And gave it ten minutes, max, before Hades blew their chumminess with an insult.

Try ten seconds. Hades stood. In a loud, bored voice, he said, "Cigar." Immediately, Hypnos—otherwise known as Sleep and twin to Thanatos—strode over, brandishing one. As a bearded naked guy, it was hard to see Hypnos' resemblance to Death, but they did both have wings. Even if Hypnos' sprouted from his head. One of the Pyrosim floated behind him, I guess it was his job to light the cigar.

"Outside." Hades didn't bother with good-bye. He turned his back on us and walked away.

Kai's hand tensed on my neck for a second. Other than that, he didn't show any reaction to Hades' sudden loss of interest. "Speaking of appearances, my love," he said, his voice wrapping around and through me.

I shivered in delight.

"You didn't sleep in our room last night. Has Prometheus lost his worth already?"

I balked at Kai's sheer unmitigated gall. He still thought I was going to bunk with him? Maybe I was supposed to play *really* nice and win Prometheus' freedom that way? What kind of giant skank did he take me for?

I hit him with my brightest smile, dripping scorn. "It seems to me, *my love*, that you broke that deal when you outed our status to Hephaestus."

Ha. That got him.

"You eavesdropped?" He went into thundercloud mode.

I stroked a hand over his chest and purred, "Every last word, Koko."

I thought he'd freak. Instead, he leaned back the banquette in a lazy slouch and regarded me through slitted lids.

I was not fooled. This was not a happy, relaxed Kai. Just him getting the lay of the land before he struck.

Like a snake.

But damn, if he didn't look pretty doing it. And by pretty I mean hot, tense, and smolderingly male. As a look, it worked.

"You're enjoying this." He sounded puzzled.

"Parts of it." I batted my eyelashes. "Immensely." The rest of it sucked, which was why it was time to lose Kai and find Oizys.

He stroked my back. "Forget Hephaestus. He isn't going to talk. So our deal about appearances still stands. Tonight you're back where you belong, roomie." That last word slid against my skin like a touch.

I didn't let him see how he affected me, meeting his eyes with bland indifference. "Think you need to look up the definition of that word," I said. I'd had a roomie for most of my life. And Hannah and I were definitely not up to the antics that the gleam in his eyes promised.

My brain chanted *lalalalalala* trying to ignore the feel of his fingers brushing over me. The fabric barrier did nada to prevent his touch from searing my skin. I willed my heart rate to stay slow and steady. "I don't sleep with business partners."

His hand skimmed up my side. "Technically, we aren't broken up until after the equinox."

I clasped a hand over his, stopping him cold. "You've got to be kidding me."

Kai dipped his head, peering at me through those damn thick lashes. "You're ... different." He lingered on my lips. "Compelling."

My heart sped up again. Not because I found it particularly romantic or anything. His heat didn't promise hearts-and-flowers romance. But my heart didn't speed up out of lust either. Fact was, the "difference" that intrigued Kai was me. Sophie. Even if he didn't know it.

Me. Not Persephone. I wanted to groove a happy dance. But I was still annoyed with his presumptions around our sleeping arrangements. And everything that went along with them. "Sadly," I said, "I don't return the sentiment."

His grin kicked up.

So did the flush on my skin. Except I'd been down this road with him before. Affection and animosity. Much as I wanted Kai to recognize me, no way was I getting into this destructive pattern again.

Kai didn't notice my distress. He was too busy being infuriatingly smug. "You lie," he said. And kissed me.

I blasted him with my light.

I'm not sure who was more shocked: him, me, or the dozens of heads that swung our way when my power lit up the room. It had been a totally subconscious move. "Oops." I scrambled away, out of the banquette and felt my Persephoneness hum in delight. *This is not a bonding moment*, I thought at her.

The minions flew at me, fiery tentacle arms outstretched and ready to destroy on Kai's command.

He stopped them with a raised hand, and stood up. "I'm just that good," he said, pure cockiness. He chucked me under the chin with one finger.

The room broke out into laughter, and I blushed as if on cue. I shot daggers with my eyes.

And the minions stood down.

I took advantage of Kai's gloating distractedness to bolt, but I didn't even make it one whole step.

Kai hauled me up against his body.

Use him. Use them all.

Down, psycho goddess. Was it asking too much to only have one voice in my head right now? Mine? Or to at least have the other one be friendly? "Let go," I said. "I have to find a costume for the ball." I looked across the room to the table where Oizys had been sitting. But she wasn't there. I'd have to track her down.

"I want you where I can see you. Make sure you don't cause any trouble." Kai laced his fingers through mine and started to tow me off.

I tried to dig in and stop him but I ended up sliding along the floor in his wake. "Don't force this."

"Or what?"

"You'll find out just how painful my light can be."

He gave me a crooked smile. "My kick-ass light-bringer," he murmured. "All phospherocious."

I froze. "What did you say?"

Kai shook his head slowly, almost as if he were dazed. "I don't know." He looked uncomfortable, speeding up as we hit the hallway. Compensating.

Was he remembering? "Think," I insisted, grabbing his arm.

He broke free and scowled. "It was nothing."

I sagged. He wasn't going to remember anything else. And trying only made him cranky. Damn, my eyes were getting hot and wet. I stomped up the stairs to our room, blinking furiously. Why couldn't he see how much being close to him-yet so far away-was killing me? Why couldn't he see me?

Kai stopped on the second floor landing. He brushed the pad of his index finger under my eye. "You're driving me crazy." He spoke so softly, I thought I'd imagined it. He kept going then, his grip on my hand as firm as ever. Which left me speaking to his back as we walked.

"I don't mean to," I said. I wanted us to have five minutes in a world where we were ourselves, no one wanted to kill us, and humanity wasn't on the line. "I want us to be like we're supposed to."

"I don't know what that is anymore," he said.

I could have happily throttled Hekate for forcing me to go through this.

Forcing *us*.

Although I felt somewhat less bad for Kai, when he pushed me through our bedroom door.

Alone. And warded in.

Nineteen

I flew to the door but it was locked tight. "Let me out of here." I pounded on it. Shot at it. Nothing. I laid my fingertips against it in defeat. I swear I could feel Kai on the other side. Feel his fingers pressed to mine. "Please."

The silence was long enough that I supposed it was just wishful thinking. Then he spoke. "See you in the morning, kardia mou."

"Argh!" I kicked at the door. But he didn't open it.

I spun and focused on the window, but he'd planned ahead. When I touched it, a sharp electric shock ripped through me. My power did nothing, and the lamp I threw bounced harmlessly off the glass, before hitting the floor and shattering.

Great.

I sank onto the bed, my hands on my knees. Sometime before the equinox, in less than forty-eight hours, my mother was going to try and murder me.

Again.

Even if she didn't succeed, my big prize was to stop Zeus and Hades and save humanity. And how did I get to psych myself up for all that? Watch my relationship fall apart, save one best friend from further torture, and wonder if the other remembered that I existed.

I buried my head in my hands. Helplessness and hopelessness choked me. I wished I could stuff those feelings in my emotional lockbox, and deal with them after the battle. When I had the luxury of collapsing in a massive heap of PTSD.

But the box was so stuffed with other emotional crap that, when I visualized adding one more thing, it exploded all over my imagination in millions of messy fragments.

Even my denial/coping mechanisms had been pushed too far.

I lay on the bed, knees to chest, arms wrapped tight around myself. A puddle of misery and doom.

Which turned out to be the best course of action. Because in the next instant, Oizys tore a hole in my door and popped her head inside. "Quit wallowing," she said. Her eyes were bright red and she was breathing faster.

Okay, maybe this wasn't spending time with my friends and loved ones in the face of impending death, but I felt a rush of fondness at seeing her, right then.

She shimmied through the hole in the door, and seamlessly repaired the wood. Happily, her magic had screwed with Kai's ward.

I swung the door open and closed a few times, pleased at my new freedom. But I'd have to make sure to leave the bedroom before Kai came back to check on me. With a final look around to make sure no one had seen anything, I closed the door behind Oizys and waited for her to settle herself.

It took her a moment to lose the demon eye and calm down.

Mostly calm. She got miffed when I suggested that we raid Persephone's closet for a costume. It was the best and most obvious choice, and she knew it. Although, I may have prolonged the selection process because it was so damn entertaining to see how uncomfortable she was in the parade of flowery gowns.

"They all suck."

I pursed my lips in a "huh" kind of way. She was right.

Knock. Knock.

I hesitated before grasping the knob. It wasn't Kai. He wouldn't knock and I couldn't imagine Persephone having friendly visitors here. I gestured for Oizys to hide behind the door. I cracked it open a smidge, one hand braced on the jamb with my light at the ready. "Yes?"

Hypnos stood there in all his naked glory, a box tied with a jaunty red bow tucked under one arm.

More disturbing than glorious. I forced myself to keep my eyes on the wings sprouting from his head.

He offered me the box. "My Lord requests you wear this at the masquerade ball." Hypnos' voice had the same smoker gravellyness as Kiki's. Maybe they smoked the same brand. *Hellfires*, I thought, amused. I could just imagine the tagline. *I'd sell my soul for a Hellfire.*

Hypnos stood there waiting for me to take the gift.

Oh, brother. I leaned my shoulder against the door-frame. "And if I refuse?"

He arched an eyebrow at me. Amazing how one little eyebrow can promise so much pain.

I took the box, trying not to think of it making contact with his bare armpit. "Understood," I said and firmly shut the door.

Oizys leaned in close as I put the box on my bed and opened it.

It was a dress. And oh, what a dress it was. Oizys' blanching look of pure revulsion was almost enough to put a little happiness in my heart.

The floor-length gown was woven from flowers. Fresh flowers somehow perfectly alive and full of blossoming joy. There were yellow and orange daffodils, deep purple Hyacinths, and red tulips. Pink anemones formed a sweetheart neckline and, although it was neatly folded, I caught a glimpse of white crocuses along the hem. It was surprisingly gorgeous.

I frowned down at it. "It's too pretty. You think it's poisoned?"

Oizys brightened. Like that somehow made the dress more attractive.

If that was the case ... I looked between her and the dress. Considering.

Her eyes narrowed. "You could kill me, peel my clothes from my cold dead body, leave me naked in middle of the throne room, and I'd still fight you if you tried to put that monstrosity on me."

I gave a tight smile. "Tell me what you really think." I lifted the dress, intending to to hold it up against her for size. But the second I picked it up, all the flowers started to die.

Oizys smirked. "That's more like Hades."

I grimaced. "Of course it is. Dying springtime." The petals felt dry and brittle. Their edges curled in on themselves, brown, droopy and wrinkled. I waited to see if they would start falling off, but despite looking like they were on their last gasp of life, they held on, not going anywhere.

I brightened. "On the upside, it's just your style now. Life-sucking. It would fit you perfectly. And look. There's a matching mask."

There was, but I don't think she was convinced. Oizys crossed her arms and gave me that flat stare that I was kind of getting fond of. "Why should I wear it? What will you be doing?"

I gave her a sweet smile. "Freeing Prometheus."

Red tinged her eyes.

"It's our best hope," I said, soothingly, and took a few steps back just in case, the dress held out like a shield. I had no desire to be ripped apart as easily as she scrapped wooden doors and bronze fences. "With you wearing this, I'll appear to be at the ball all night. The perfect plan." I put the offensive dress down on the bed.

Oizys looked like she couldn't believe what I was saying. "Hades wants you to wear it."

"He won't know the difference."

"He's not an idiot," she fired back. "We look nothing alike."

"Really?" I waved a hand between us. "You're just as curvy as I am. We're basically the same height. We'll dye your hair and arrange it so that it looks like some updo that I'd have. You even have green eyes."

"That are blind without my glasses," she protested.

"Don't move around much."

"That's your solution? One conversation and he'll know it's not you."

"Listen and nod. He likes that better anyhow." I lay the dress down again.

Oizys shook her head, making for the door. "No."

I pounced before she got to the knob. "Stop being so stubborn and think about it. The only one who actually has to go rescue Prometheus is Hephaestus. He's the one who knows how to unbind him."

Oizys twisted free. "Not true. I'm the one who knows how to get in and out. I'm the one that the Hekatonkheires will recognize and accept the nectar from."

"So I'll dress as you. Festos won't go with just you, Underworlder. He won't and you know it, so don't even bother to argue. And if Hades wants me at the ball, then our only option is for you to impersonate me and tell me the way back to Prometheus."

She pushed her glasses up her nose and glared. "You want me to let you go with Festos and drug the giants, while I play dumb at the ball?"

"Play goddess," I corrected.

"Same thing."

I motioned at her with a very specific finger, taking petty pleasure in her surprise.

Honestly? I didn't think she was actually going to agree. I mean, it was kind of a harebrained, Olsen-Twins-movie-of-the-week idea. Except for the part where we weren't twins. But it was really our best hope at this point.

A crafty look stole over her face. Like she'd found my deal breaker. "What about Kyrillos?"

Yeah. That was the one potential disaster. Not enough to scrap the plan though. I wagged a finger at her. "Avoid him. At all costs." He'd know in a second. "He wouldn't out you to Hades, but he would try and find me. Stop me from getting to Prometheus."

"I'm not kissing him."

I eyeballed her. "Good. 'Cause you do and you lose your lips."

She shrugged. "Long as we're on the same page. You really think this will work?"

I nodded. "Yeah. Crazy as it is, I think it will. People see what they want to. Anyone looking at you in that dress will see a humiliated goddess. And anyone who sees me, will be looking at the scowling goth princess they know and tolerate." I held out a hand. "Deal?"

She ignored my hand. "Deal. But when it goes horribly wrong, I'm so killing you."

I busied myself with the dress, oddly hurt at her dismissal of me. "Yeah, yeah."

That's how we spent the next twenty-four hours. Prepping for the equinox masquerade ball, and hiding in Oizys' room to avoid Kai. First, we had to dye our hair. That was the easy part. Oizys had a hard time moving around without her glasses. It wasn't pretty. She kind of held her hands out and shuffled forward.

"We're going to have to tell everyone you're drunk," I said, watching doubtfully.

"That's not a bad idea."

At least the preparations kept me from dwelling on all the insanity that was going to rain down on my head soon enough. I was grateful for every minute of Wednesday. Aware of each precious second that counted down to midnight, and the ball, and the start of all the madness, because these hours were the last normal ones I'd have until I defeated Hades and Zeus.

And even *when* that happened, the giant blank slate of my future was almost scarier. Since last Halloween, I'd been dealing with one crazy adventure after another. Planning and training, and then throwing all the plans out the window and starting again. Many many times.

But at least I'd been goal-oriented.

What was I going to wake up to on Friday morning? With no school, no home, no family, and a question mark where my future was concerned. What exactly did a girl do for an encore after saving the world?

Those thoughts made up most of my Wednesday afternoon. Honestly, they weren't any less terrifying than thinking about freeing Prometheus, breaking the enchantment, and fighting the battle itself.

Just different.

Late afternoon. I stared out Oizys' window, drumming my fingers in a slow rhythm that worked as a kind of white noise to keep me calm.

Eventually, the sky turned to full black and night fell.

"It's time."

I startled out of my reverie at Oizys' words and pressed my hands to my heart with a delighted gasp.

"Don't. Say. A. Word."

"You're so pretty," I cooed. "The dead flowers really bring out your eyes. And now we get to do each other's make-up."

"This is the worst day of my life."

Lucky her. I wished I could say the same.

***

"Shut up and stop blinking. I can't do your eye shadow properly." I had paired the dress with the girliest makeover imaginable, painting Oizys' face in hues of pink ranging from Bubblegum (lipstick) to Princess Poo (blush). I'd mentally dubbed the pale pink glitter on her lids as "Fairy Spew."

Her hair was now dark brown and curled into frothy ringlets. I topped it with a giant tiara. I'd pinned her bangs off her face so that no one could tell she had them at all.

"It itches," Oizys groused.

I slapped her hand away from her hip. "Stop plucking."

Finally, she grabbed my wrist to keep me from applying one more shiny coat to her lips. "Enough." Her eyes glinted. "It's your turn now."

She dolled me up in her clothes, cut my hair to give me bangs and then pulled the rest of my new black mass back into the same tight bun she wore. I wouldn't be able to wear her glasses, but we figured that copious amounts of eye-liner and purple lipstick would sell the effect.

As Oizys applied my make-up, she detailed my route in and out of Tartarus. She made me retrace the path, and repeat what I would say when I met the giants over and over, until I had it down pat.

Once I was fully made up, she cocked her head and looked at me critically. "A pale imitation, Springtime."

"Right back at you." I studied us both in her mirror. Unless we were standing side by side—under scrutiny, we looked pretty convincing. Normally, I would have found my resemblance to an Underworlder disconcerting. But if I could handle looking like Persephone, all else failed to rate. "It's going to work. Except ..." I glanced down at my bare feet. "Pony up the boots."

"No," she whined.

I gave her my sternest look. "Oizys, Spirit of Misery and Woe, I demand that you suck up your foot issues and hand me a pair of your stupid boots."

She muttered something mean and flung a pair my way. "I hope they pinch your toes."

I grinned and, shockingly, she grinned back. I felt a deep pang of regret. Maybe Oizys and Persephone had come to some kind of weird truce, but I knew that wouldn't hold when she found out who I was.

The Persephone in this enchantment hadn't betrayed anyone yet. Hades had no idea that she and Kai were planning anything for the equinox. The Underworld didn't hate her. Maybe they did on principal, but not with any specific vendetta. Once the enchantment was broken, this Persephone wouldn't exist anymore. Which would just leave me, Sophie Bloom, mortal enemy numero uno.

Regardless of how Oizys felt about her fellow Underworlders, she wouldn't stay loyal to me just because we'd had a magically induced moment or two. I'd rather not see the look on her face when she decided to get in on the "kill Sophie" action, too.

"For a daemon who feeds off other people's misery, you're not so bad," I told her.

"Yeah, well, for a goddess who cavorts in meadows," she shook her head. "Nah, you still suck."

Damn Hekate. And damn this enchantment. I wished I'd never met Oizys. She was going to be one more loss in my life.

By 11:30PM, we were as perfect as we were going to get. I tied the accompanying mask around the back of Oizys' head. It was a simple black thing, but dotted with pink sparkly crystals. While the mask itself obscured much of her face, enough of her pretty pretty makeover was visible that the overall effect sold her as me.

"I think it's perfect," I said, forcing her to do one last pirouette. "In that make-a-total-mockery-of-Persephone way that Hades intended."

Oizys gave me a weird look. "Talking about yourself in the third person now?"

Whoops. Luckily, I had just the thing to distract her. "Hang on. There's one last piece." I scrambled under her daybed and pulled out a pair of sparkly gold heels that I'd snagged from Persephone's closet.

Oizys stared at them in abject horror.

"You didn't seriously think you were going to wear any shoes *you* owned, did you?"

Poor Spirit of Misery and Woe. She looked like she wanted to die as she shoved her feet into the shoes.

Correction. She looked like she wanted to kill me. Either way. It would add to her aura of deep humiliation. Which would, in turn, delight one and all.

I wanted lots of attention on her. I wanted Hades entertained by her embarrassment. The more he was distracted, the better the chance I had of sneaking out with Fee to free Prometheus.

I put my hand on her shoulder. "Good luck."

"Bring him back safely or die." Oizys flung my hand off of her. "And don't get caught."

With that, she stomped out.

"Less lead foot, more goddess floating," I called after her.

She tossed back a rude name and headed out of sight.

I gave her ten minutes before I went downstairs myself.

I was lost in the throng of guests long before I got to the throne room. Costume-wise, all of the Olympians were represented, most of them in multiple versions. Except for Zeus. One guess who had decreed that costume for himself.

The outfits were lavish. Sumptuous. Also twisted, lewd, grotesquely exaggerated, and highly, highly offensive. Everyone's body language reflected their contempt. Looking around, you'd think all the beings in Olympus were limping, flailing hunchbacks.

The few people that bothered to look my way only rolled their eyes like the lack of a costume and the killing of buzz was exactly what they expected from Oizys. Her reputation served me well.

It was easy enough to keep to the fringes unobserved, yet totally observing everything. While the throne room may have mimicked Zeus' statue gallery, Hades had opted to drape the rest of the main floor in bordello chic. Not a decor I'd seen during my stay in Olympus. This meant red velvet brocade wallpaper, divans, plants, knick-knacks, and lots of gold gilt and zebra print furniture. Taaaacky. My head throbbed looking at it all. It didn't help that Zeus' own clean citrusy cologne was gusting into the room in hissing puffs.

I did my best to breathe through my mouth.

Finally, I managed to skirt my way into the throne room. After all that red velvet, the white and gold that Hades had used to transform it into Zeus' statue room was blinding. I blinked a few times to adjust my eyes.

When I could see again, I slinked to the far corner and hid behind a massive statue of my father plucking a fig from a tree, while a bird in the branches pooed on his head. The tree had been sculpted in such amazing detail that I was actually able to climb it and hide myself among its marble leaves. This was the perfect vantage point. I had a clear view of the entire room over everyone's heads.

Some of the guests had obviously gotten a jump start on their drunken festivities. Their costumes were already slightly askew. Masks were already tilted, eyes were too glittering, voices too loud, and too slurred. The buzz of conversation was loud, but from where I sat, just tolerable.

Hades held center court, dressed, just as I'd suspected, as Zeus, in a cream linen suit and matching fedora, that strained against his bloated frame. At first I wasn't sure how this made a mockery of his brother, until I realized that the suit wasn't some costume Hades had made for the occasion. It was Zeus' actual suit and fedora. His favorite outfit. Hades had stolen it somehow, and was wearing it with great pride and swagger. He just had to touch his brother's things, didn't he?

He plucked a goblet of wine from a passing minion's tray and slugged some back. Wine sloshed onto his lapel. I could just imagine his glee when he returned it dirty, ripped, and stained—to my anal retentive, metrosexual father.

An Infernorator glided over to Hades, Oizys in his wake. The minion presented her to his master and floated away.

I watched, curious, as Hades leaned in close to speak to her.

She stiffened, but Hades didn't notice, or didn't care. With a pat to her shoulder, he turned from her to get more wine.

I couldn't imagine what was going on, but whatever he'd said kept her close at his side.

And glowering. Her eyes sliced through the room. She looked ready to kill.

Maybe I was projecting that part, since her mask covered much of her face. But I didn't think so. I had a sinking feeling that her death rays were intended for me. I'd gotten her into whatever Hades was up to.

Well, I couldn't worry about it now. Everything, for better or worse, was in motion.

I watched them for a few more minutes, but nothing changed.

Nor did Kai appear.

Which begged the question of where he was.

I didn't see Festos either. I hoped he was off convincing Aletheia to show up. Gotta hand it to him, his chandelier was one of the most spectacular things I'd ever seen. The light hung high overhead, its candle holders and metal twists spanning a good ten feet.

It reminded me of dancing fountains, like they have in Vegas. Or rather, hundreds of tiny dancing fountains, all held in their own individual candle cups. They were made of lava and fire, and they syncopated in a gorgeous ballet of reds, oranges, and blues. Hundreds of teardrop crystals reflected all the color and heat into endless prisms of light.

It was mesmerizing.

I couldn't believe that nobody found it as entrancing as I did, but everyone else seemed too engrossed in being as loud and obnoxious in their Olympian impressions as possible.

Except for Oizys. Even from half a football field away, I could see how still she was. Looking for me. For a second, I thought she'd found me. Her gaze seemed to hold on my area of the room.

I pressed myself farther behind the marble leaves and into the shadowy corner. I held my breath. I don't know what would have happened if she'd had even one more second to glower my way, but a sudden blare of trumpets made everyone turn toward Hades.

"Friends and honored guests," Hades boomed out, his voice reaching even this far corner, "Welcome to my ball." His words were drowned in a cacophony of cat-calls, whistles, and stomping feet.

He held up a hand for silence. "On this eve of the spring equinox, we celebrate the union of light and dark. And what better way to start the evening's entertainment than a first dance between the Prince of the Underworld and a Princess of Olympus?" He shot Oizys a sly look, as if the dance was just the first of many "entertainments" he had planned for Persephone tonight.

Oh, crap! My stomach lurched.

A darkly sensual waltz played. The crowd parted and there was Kai. He stepped into the circle, clad in all-black, save for a glittering red mask. So much for avoiding him at all costs

Oizys stood there, chin jutted out, tense.

It was like a car crash that only she and I knew was happening. Our entire charade was about to be blown.

I had to get out of here before Kai could find me. I dropped out of the tree. The sound of the crowd "ooo-hing" with delight at the obvious tension between "Persephone" and Kai, worked in my favor. Everyone was focused on them.

I skittered around the edge of the room until I was in line with the throne itself, sparing a glance for the dancing couple. One look at their body language—Oizys unnaturally rigid, and Kai holding her in an iron grip and wearing that stupid poker face of his—and I knew the jig was up.

I shoved my way through the throng, and over to the base of the throne. It wasn't 2AM yet, but I figured the best place for me to hide was in the room underneath it where I was to meet Fee. Of course, this meant hanging about in the place where Persephone had been murdered seventeen years ago. And now that I had all her memories in glorious living color, it was going to be quite the trip down memory lane.

I put my hand to a specific stone near the back of the base and pushed. The heavy obsidian swung open and I slipped through. It whispered shut behind me.

The room was as impressive as ever. As black as the outside of the base had been, the inside of the room radiated a warm gold. Because it *was* gold.

Other than the door I'd used to get in, and a hallway that sloped under the room, there were no other entrances or exits. There was, however, a giant pile of cushions to lounge on. Or hide under. I flopped down onto them, ready to scurry underneath at a second's notice.

So. Here I am again.

I tried to keep my mind blank but it was hard. My eyes kept dragging up to the black iron chandelier that hung on the ceiling. It wasn't remarkable in any way. Not fancy or dancing with lava jets. Just a plain lighting fixture. It was only noteworthy because it was the last thing Persephone had seen as her life drained away.

The night Demeter had come after Persephone, the throne room outside had been deserted. Even though I knew that it overflowed with partygoers tonight, I still felt very alone here. And very vulnerable.

I burrowed deeper under the pillows. My eyes scanned left and right, all my senses on high alert for any approaching visitors. My entire body was tense. My heart pounded so hard and fast that I felt like it was going to burst free of my rib cage like in the movie *Alien*. I stayed that way for what seemed like eons.

"She wouldn't come."

I screamed. So much for hyper-vigilant. Festos had appeared and startled the hell out of me. He was dressed in gray slacks and a slightly lighter gray sweater. It was perfectly nice but not at all what he normally wore. "Servants' garb," he muttered at my stare.

I had barely recovered from the shock of his appearance when I realized what he had said. I jumped to my feet, scattering cushions. "No! She has to come!" I jabbed my finger at him. "Go back and convince her."

Festos frowned. "You're obviously distressed, which is the only reason why I'm not going to hurt you for touching me."

I rubbed my hand over my face. If Aletheia didn't show up, then my only choice to break this enchantment was waiting for Demeter to show up and try to kill me. What if she didn't show? Or if she did, but it didn't give us enough time to put everything in place for the ritual?

"I need to break this enchantment." I was utterly frantic. "Fine, let's free Prometheus and then he can try to get Aletheia here. He created her. Maybe she has to listen to his commands."

"If she listens half as well as you do, you're in for quite the wait." That was Kai.

Great. Before I could bolt, he'd grabbed Festos and I by one arm each.

"Hands off the goods," Festos hissed; sounding fed up, he tried to transport out.

Except Kai was still holding on to us.

The air rippled, a wave of pain sliced through my temples, and none of us went anywhere.

"Now what have you done?" Festos glowered at Kai. Then caught sight of me and looked suddenly confused.

Kai's grip had slackened, so I stepped back warily.

He'd gone pale with shock.

I glanced around the room trying to figure out the problem. When I turned back to Kai, I found him totally focused on me.

And angrier than I'd ever seen him. With everything that had happened, that was a pretty impressive and worrisome feat.

Now what?

Twenty

"Walking. Suicide. Mission." Kai sounded caught between relief and fury. "I swear I'm locking you up so you can't get yourself into more trouble. You've outdone yourself on this one, Goddess."

Goddess? Did he mean ...? I snuck a look a Festos, who stared at me so hard he seemed to be trying to see through me.

My heart raced. In hope, not fear, which was a pleasant change. I glanced down at myself. I was still Persephone and Kai was still not my Kai so I wanted—no needed—to be sure I understood him correctly. Understood that exasperated tone of voice correctly. "You know it's me? *Me*, me?"

Kai pressed his forehead to mine and put his arm around me. "Yeah. I know."

I wanted to weep. My entire body sagged. If Kai hadn't been holding me, I would have collapsed. Knowing that Kai and Festos were now firmly back on Team Sophie? Well, it made this entire situation so much more bearable. An incredible tension left my body. My shoulders felt like they dropped a good couple inches down from my ears, finally relaxing.

My mind whirred. The enchantment hadn't actually broken. The fact that I was still in Persephone form, and that all of Hades was not on my tail, was proof. But it had been pierced, which was good enough for now. I stepped away from my boyfriend and started down the corridor that led away from the throne room. We could talk en route to Prometheus.

"Spill," Festos said, keeping pace alongside of me, his cane thumping off of the green stone with every step.

"Wait. Where are you going?" Kai took hold of my hand and tried to pull me to a stop but I tugged him along, determined to keep moving.

"We need to go get some nectar."

"What for?" Kai asked. He refused to let go of my hand, and the look on his face made me think he might never, which filled me with a happy glowiness.

I explained the plan and he laughed. "Soph, I'm Prince of Hades. I think I can get them to let Prometheus out."

I mewled and he looked at me, concerned. "What? What's wrong?"

"Nothing," I sighed happily, pushing open a door that led us out into the night. "You called me Sophie."

"Which I know you are." Festos rubbed his temples, "Visual aid to the contrary. Explain already."

I poked Kai. "You going to save some time and transport us into Tartarus?"

Kai shook his head. "Can't. In and out of the Underworld? If you have that privilege? Sure. But not within Hades. It's forbidden. Big painful consequences." He smiled dryly. "Paranoia. My father doesn't like people sneaking up on him."

Now wasn't the time to get alert Hades and set him on our heels. Not yet. Not until I knew the enchantment was definitely broken and I could leave the Underworld. Guess we were walking. Briskly, because I didn't want Prometheus there a second longer.

Compared to all the noise of the party, the grounds were still and quiet. The air felt cool and refreshing after the stifling heat inside. The night was overcast, but there was enough light to pick out our route to Tartarus.

"Do you both remember everything that's happened down here?" I asked.

The guys nodded.

"Fee, what happened between you leaving your place, and getting sucked in to all this?" Theo, Kai, and I had been together when Kiki threw down the magic. But Festos hadn't been there.

He scratched his head, looking thoughtful. "I was pretty mad when I left. I just wanted to get out. Walk around. That's what I did." He laughed a little. "I was commiserating with the Fremont Troll."

Kai looked confused. "Seattle has trolls? Trolls exist?"

I smiled. "It's a massive statue under a bridge. There's a roll holding an actual VW bug in his hand."

"Ah."

Festos went on. "Eventually I ran out of steam. When you guys didn't come home that night, I figured you'd just decided to exclude me from the action." Fee's expression turned sheepish. "I was still mad. I didn't start to worry until the next day. Monday. I was about to go find Pierce and see if he could help me track you all down, when I was suddenly in a workshop space here. Working on the chandelier because Hades had me on deadline."

"You didn't wonder about that?" I asked.

Festos' forehead creased. "It didn't even occur to me to question it. It was just where I was and what I had to do." He frowned. "And it seems that Hekate must have spanned the enchantment between here and Olympus because when I went back to speak to Aletheia, she was caught up in it, too. Or I somehow carried it with me when I went to her."

Kiki's powers were impressive. All the more reason to believe that my only way out of this mess was to face Demeter. "Here's what you missed," I said, and filled them in on everything that had happened, starting with me in the tunnel. Talking kept me from thinking, which mostly kept the knot of dread in my stomach from getting too big.

Kai and Festos both thought my sleeping-arrangement anxieties were hilarious. Although I smugly noted their grins dropped when I reminded them of their little spat.

I shoved at Kai. "Fee was your name for him. And you never told me."

"Yeah, Koko," Festos said with a glint. "How remiss."

"Shut up," Kai said.

"You two need to resolve your issues," I ordered.

Their expressions grew stony.

"I mean it. I love you both, but this fight is stupid."

"Can we not talk about this while you still look like her?" asked Festos. "I do love you, honeybunch, but the optics are clouding it a bit."

I rolled my eyes. "Fine. I'll finish the story." I felt the ground go boggy under my feet and scooted back on to terra firma. I wasn't about to short cut us through the Stygian Marsh, even though the detour added a bit more time to our journey.

"You know, seeing me seeming to work with Kyrillos is just going to confirm every bad thing Prometheus ever thought about me." Now that he knew the entire story, Festos looked glum.

"It won't be for long," I assured him.

"Only until Demeter shows up to try and kill you again." Kai was not impressed.

I patted his arm. "I'm not thrilled about relieving that moment myself, but I'll have you two. You won't let anything happen to me."

Kai frowned. "Yeah, well maybe you should have thought about that sooner and tried telling me what was going on."

Great, now he sounded hurt. "Like you would have believed me? Hello? Enchantment."

"You told Fee." In Kai's agitation, he didn't even realize he'd reverted to his nickname for Festos. "But you couldn't tell me?"

"To be fair," Festos piped up, "I didn't exactly believe her."

"Irrelevant." Kai's voice was clipped. "She didn't even try."

304

Anger burned my cheeks. He did not get to be mad. *I'd* been the invisible girl. *I'd* been the one who had been stuck here in the body of his previous girlfriend. And it had killed me in a soul-destroying way every single time he'd failed to see me.

So yeah, I hadn't tried to tell him because hearing his dismissive laugh, or seeing that "get real" look when, of course, he didn't believe me?

It would have finished me.

But I wouldn't and couldn't voice all this. Instead, I shoved past him, and stomped ahead on my own, all the way to Tartarus.

Oizys had drilled me well on how to get there, so I didn't have to concentrate too much on directions. Which was good because I was so mad, so fully consumed with righteous indignation, that I barely had the energy to focus on anything else. My palms burned. My skin glowed with my green light.

To make matters worse, I felt Persephone's dark desires working on me again, straining to unleash. I was so set on limiting my actions to walking and fuming, that I didn't even realize we had arrived until the bronze fence loomed up before us. But the cries of the damned didn't work their usual soul-deflating mojo on me right now.

Seething worked like a protective shield. Good to know.

I motioned toward the door in the fence. "Who wants to blast it open?"

Kai muttered something, veered left, and started walking.

"Where are you going?" I demanded, scrambling after him.

"The son of Hades does not break into Tartarus through a back way."

He had a point but he didn't have to sound so imperious about it.

The ground here was rocky and the moonlight dim, so I worked on not breaking an ankle.

About ten minutes later, we arrived at two enormous gates. The official way in. There were no guards, just a lot more bronze and despondency.

The land around the gates was desolate. Windswept and barren. The ground sloped steeply down toward the River Styx, foaming and sizzling with corrosive orangey black water. I recognized a dock battened to the shore. I'd passed it on Charon's raft when I'd snuck in with Theo to retrieve my pendent.

Kai placed a hand on the left gate. All the bronze seemed to leech into his palm, as if his skin were a sponge. It left the fence oddly colorless. I don't know if it was verifying his identity, but the bronze suddenly flowed back into the gate and it swung open.

A number of dead people rushed us, misery spewing from their mouths in howls. They stopped, frozen in their tracks as Kai strode toward them. With a single imperious look from him, they bowed low, scampering backward, eyes on the ground.

Kai didn't even check to see if Festos and I followed. He pushed forward, the gate closing behind him as he moved deeper into Tartarus.

"He's in fine form," Festos said, as we jogged after him.

If I hadn't been so worked up, I might found it mildly entertaining to sweep along in the Princeling' royal wake.

No one dared approach him. Or us by association. Even the inhabitants seemed to mute their cries of despair in deference to his majesty.

Kai stopped beside a smaller yet still fine-means-of-containing-people gate. Without speaking a word, he pushed that one open as well.

We stepped through and I found myself back on the bottom of the crater, under the violent sky. It was crazy because there had been no sense of the storm outside the gate. But in here, it was absolute and everywhere.

Prometheus was still bound to the rock, still unconscious, the chain still flaming.

Festos ran for him, brutally shoving Kai out of the way. We followed close behind.

Prometheus looked worse than the last time I'd seen him. His clothes were little more than ragged threads, exposing the burns on his skin as the flames danced across his torso. He was pale and waxy.

Constant contact with the elements hadn't helped matters either. The air swirled against *my* skin so hard, I felt like I sandblasted by dirt and tiny rocks and chaos. How much worse must it have been for him?

I held my whipping hair out of my face, eyes slitted against the debris.

Kai didn't say anything, a muscle in his jaw twitching at the sight of Prometheus.

"Yeah, you should feel bad," I said, yelling over the winds. That earned me a hard look.

As Festos went to work on freeing his real-world boyfriend, the ground beneath our feet shook. The three Hekatonkeires were lumbering toward us.

Lightning arced across the sky. As long as it wasn't trying to hit me, I didn't care. Besides, between the winds knocking me sideways and quaking at my feet, I was too busy trying to stay upright.

The Hekatonkheires reached us and the ground went still. All of their shaggy, bristly, hideous heads snapped to attention when they saw Kai. "My Prince." The closest one saluted him in a voice so loud, it made the wind sound like a lullaby. To be clear, the head farthest from us, on the closest giant, saluted him.

I didn't pay too much attention to the other one-hundred forty-nine heads, because they were too wide a swath of ugly. The head that spoke, despite a festering boil on the side of his lip, was the heartthrob of the group.

Speaker Head looked at Festos, then back to Kai, waiting for clarification.

Kai looked to the sky. The giant flicked a hand at it and the storm stopped. It would have been impressive, but the stillness in its wake made me feel like we were in limbo. The sky froze in a savage swirl. The silence was so absolute that it was kind of freaky.

I didn't trust it. This sudden stoppage so we could have a little chat. My eyes darted left and right, waiting for the destruction to return.

"I am moving the prisoner, Gyes." Kai sounded indifferent.

"But my Prince, we have prepared—"

"Enough." Kai's voice was cold and commanding.

It shut up the giant.

Thing is, now I was curious. "Prepared what, matia mou?" I asked in my sweetest voice.

Kai turned to me, matching my syrupy ugh. "Nothing you need trouble your pretty head with, kardia mou."

"Bite me," I said through a smile, in a voice low enough that only he could hear. "What did you have planned for Prometheus?"

"It doesn't matter now. I'm not doing it."

"Tell me," I insisted. I wanted to know how far Kyrillos would have taken his imprisonment.

"Don't push me, Goddess," Kai warned. "I'm not feeling very charitable right now."

"Back at you, sweetheart."

Kai's eyes glittered angrily.

See now, there was the dynamic I knew and, well ... knew.

Gyes lumbered off to his fellow giants for a little confab. One of them shook himself, much like a dog, flinging off water, and making all his very many bits jiggle.

Their spines must be made from titanium to support all those parts. I waited, one eye monitoring Fee's progress, the other on the giants.

The three of them returned, presenting a many headed, many handed, united front. "We will not allow the Olympian to take the prisoner," Gyes' speaker head informed us.

We swung to face to Festos, who had just freed Prometheus and scooped him up in his arms. He was still unconscious, head splayed back, arms and legs spilling limply. It couldn't have been easy for Fee, holding this enormous dead weight. Especially since in order to hang on to Prometheus, he couldn't use his cane. It was tucked under one arm. But Festos stood tall, firing an imperious look of his own. "You will do as your Prince commands you."

Never thought I'd hear him defer to Kai like that.

A look passed between them.

It spoke of past secrets and mayhem, and made me uneasy.

Kai looked uncertain.

Festos looked insistent.

I probably looked confused.

The giants stopped looking, broke formation, and came roaring after us. The storm resumed its crashing above our heads. Winds howled around us, churning up a dust thick enough to choke me.

I sent out a full-body shockwave of light.

It did nothing. To the storm. To the giants' approach. Nada. Just temporarily lit up the sky so I could see where I was about to die. I swallowed, my throat dry and sticky with terror. I edged backward, clutching Kai's arm.

Sky and earth clashed. I was losing all sense of what was up and what was down, and it didn't matter because every direction promised death. I crept farther behind Kai. I hate to admit it, but I probably would have thrown him under the proverbial bus at that moment, if it had meant keeping me safe from those monstrosities.

You face enormous walls of teeth and grabby hands, and then give me crap for poor behavior.

It may have felt like hours but it was seconds between the storm's reappearance and the first enormous hand grabbing at my head. I shrieked and flung my arms around Kai, holding on for dear life.

I felt him sigh. And in the blink of an eye, with me still clinging to him like a baby koala, he slashed through all three Hekatonkheires with his deadly black light. Toxic ash fell on the field.

I gasped.

"Are you insane?" sputtered Fee, sidling up alongside us with Prometheus. "I didn't mean kill them. Great. Hades is so going to be on your fat ass, and my pretty one, now."

Kai's cheeks flushed with anger. "What exactly do you think the alternative was?" He took a step toward Festos. "Bitch at me for chaining Prometheus up, or bitch at me for helping to free him. Make up your damn mind!"

Insert squabbling here.

I tuned them out, still kind of shocked that Kai had just destroyed those giants in order to help Theo. Because that's really what it was about. I slid out from behind Kai to peer at the ash before swiveling to look at my boyfriend.

"What?" he demanded.

"Boys who slay monsters for their friends are dreamy." Shoot. Had I said that out loud?

Kai gave a cocky grin. "That's more like it."

Festos grunted, shifting Prometheus' weight. "His breathing is erratic." Fee's voice was barely controlled panic. He gave Kai a pleading glance.

Kai nodded. "We'll have to risk it." He grabbed all of us, transporting us away from the crater and back to the palace.

We landed in our bedroom.

The ball was still going strong. Thumping music vibrated through the stone walls and shook my floor. None of us had been missed.

"You blinked us here. What are the consequences?" I asked.

"Expect a visit as soon as Hades can be roused from the party." Kai's mouth twisted in a wry grin. "We may have a bit of time." He motioned toward Prometheus, and Fee laid him gently down on the bed. "We need to get him some help."

"No kidding." I jumped as a new voice spoke. At first I thought it was Hades. Or Demeter. But as she walked farther into the room, I was relieved to see that is was Oizys, framed in the early rays of dawn.

The gown of flowers was gone, replaced by her usual black sweater, fitted skirt, and combat boots. She scathed at me. "Took you long enough," she said, and shouldered past me to stand beside Prometheus.

"Um, hello?" Festos sounded totally unimpressed as she elbowed him out of the way. "You would be whom, exactly?"

Oizys took Prometheus' hand in hers. "His best friend. Which is a lot more than I can say about you."

Oooh, girlfriend had attitude.

"Best friend?" Festos shot me an incredulous glance. "Are you hearing this?"

I gave him my best "shut up" look, since Oizys had no clue as to the real situation. Also, I didn't really want to debate when my time with Theo was seriously running out.

Riiiip. Oizys tore open the tattered remains of Prometheus' shirt. The raw, chafing wounds did nothing to detract from his magnificent six-pack. Although this was not the time to drool. "What are you doing?"

She pulled out a small jar and uncapped it. "I brought a salve with both medicinal and magical properties for when you returned. This should get him back to normal in no time."

Smart thinking.

Oizys scooped out some of the amber cream and began to smooth it over his body in firm circles.

Fee made a strangled noise.

I moved over to our dresser and fished out some of Kai's clothes for Prometheus to change into once he recovered.

It took a while for Oizys to cover him with the salve, but it healed his skin instantly.

With a quiet moan, Prometheus finally began to stir. His color, his breathing, the lack of burns, it was all good. He looked around the room, confused, then sat up groggily, holding his side. "What ...?" He saw Kai and lunged.

Instinctively, Festos grabbed him.

Prometheus stiffened like he'd been jolted with a thousand volts and shoved Festos off him.

"That's it," Fee declared. "We're going. Now."

"Good riddance," Oizys said, as she helped Prometheus into the clothes. The salve had obviously helped a lot but he still winced.

"Yeah," Fee retorted. "To you." He jerked a thumb toward Prometheus. "He's mine."

"In no universe whatsoever," Prometheus growled, as he stood up fully dressed.

"You'd be amazed."

The situation was turning ugly. "A little help," I said to Kai.

"Oizys, return to your room. Prometheus, you're coming with us," he ordered.

"No," they both said at once.

"For Olympus' sake," Festos muttered and grabbed Prometheus' arm.

Prometheus retaliated with a fist to Fee's jaw. The *craaccck* was deafening, knocking Festos back several feet.

Fee rubbed at the red spot. "You get one. And only because you're currently clueless. Now we're leaving." He stepped toward Prometheus. And then Oizys jumped on Fee's back.

I let my vines loose and wrapped them around her, yanking her off of him. She struggled like a fish in a net.

"Enough!" Kai thundered. "Goddess, release her."

Reluctantly, I did.

"Return to your room," he told Oizys.

She didn't move a muscle.

"Now."

Yikes. That was every ounce the Prince of Hades and more. I'd never heard Kai sound so commanding.

Guess Oizys hadn't either because her eyes widened. And with a last a petulant glower, she stomped out of the room.

"Sorry," I mumbled.

She ignored me.

Kai turned to Prometheus. "If you're well enough to hit him, you're well enough to move."

Prometheus stuck his chin out, his expression hard. "Or what? You'll chain me up again?"

Festos tossed him back his chain.

"No." Kai's eyes narrowed. "I'll leave you with Hephaestus."

Prometheus' defiance turned to distaste. "I'll move."

"Thanks so much, Koko," Festos muttered. "I wouldn't have given him back the chain."

"He agreed, didn't he? Let's bail."

"It won't work," I said glumly. "I can't leave the Underworld until Demeter shows up. As per Hekate's decree, I can't go anywhere until she makes her appearance. Which means no ritual."

"What decree?" Prometheus looked at us, expecting to be filled in.

Kai ignored him to speak to me. "Then we go find her. The more people providing distraction when this all goes down, the better." He looked at me like he wanted to say something, or shake me, then his shoulders sagged and he flung open the door, waiting for us to step into the hallway.

"What's his problem?" Prometheus asked quietly, hesitating to get too close to Kai.

"He's worried that he's going to see his girlfriend murdered," Festos answered.

So was I. But not the girlfriend they thought. I hadn't shared the fact that if Demeter managed to take Persephone down again ...

It was bye-bye Sophie.

Thus did it suck when I took the lead, strode from the room, and walked directly into the point of Demeter's poisoned blade.

Twenty-one

I froze. Demeter had managed to grab me and spin me around, the knife pressed against my neck.

She edged me out into the corridor.

Kai's fingers twitched.

"Try it." Sounding amused, Demeter pushed the tip of the blade into me just hard enough to break skin. "One of you could probably take me out. But you risk the knife slipping that half-millimeter. To the coated poison part."

I felt a dot of blood bead on my skin and remembered the sensation of that poison killing me the first time. I tensed. Didn't want a recap, thanks.

"All you have to do is swear on the Styx to give me what I want and no harm will come to you," Demeter soothed.

"You think there is any chance of that happening?" When I spoke those words, something inside me broke. I'd been fighting Persephone's fury for so long, but now it rose to claim me. It settled on my skin like a shield and I spat her hatred at Demeter. "You were supposed to put me first. Me. Your child. But you abandoned me here because it suited your purposes."

My voice boiled with bitterness. The more I spoke, the more I knew that it wasn't just Persephone talking to Demeter. It was me pouring out my hurt to Felicia as well. For a lifetime of being abandoned, and neglected, and kept in the dark about who I really was. And who she was to me.

"For what?" I continued with a sneer. "A man who doesn't even care that you exist? *I* cared. But all you did was use me. And you think I'd return that favor by handing you your heart's desire? I'll die before I see you rule Olympus."

Demeter tensed against me at these words.

Prometheus gasped. Fee sighed.

But Kai? His eyes burned with sympathy for me.

I looked away. I wanted my anger right now. Needed it. And that look threatened to undo me.

I always came second. But no more.

In that moment, I realized that Persephone and I had something fundamental in common. Persephone never truly believed in her mother's love. Not the all-encompassing love she'd wanted. The love we'd both wanted. And needed. And that every kid had a right to.

My entire understanding of Persephone's life rearranged itself with a sickening lurch. Persephone hadn't been prized. Demeter had judged her value based on how close she kept the two of them—Demeter and Zeus. At least that's how Persephone saw things.

And me? Well, Felicia seemed to think that I had no value at all. I'm not sure which was worse. But one thing was clear. As Demeter or Felicia, this woman had done a number on us both.

Meantime, behind me, Demeter had gone still. Too still.

I knew that in the next second, she'd strike.

Kai's fingertips sparked black.

I gave him a tiny shake of my head. This problem was mine to solve. One way or another.

I knew what Persephone wanted. My green glowing palms were evidence of that. But I couldn't kill Demeter. I covered the hand holding the knife with my own. "My father is a jerk who will never love you properly." Using all my strength, I pulled the knife slightly away from my neck. "I'm sorry about that. But asking me to betray Kyrillos is not the way."

I couldn't wriggle free of her. But she hadn't killed me yet, so at least she was hesitating. I'd gotten through to her on some level. "Please." I squirmed, turning around just enough to meet her eyes. "I love you so much."

I did love her. Even now.

Persephone did too. That's why she was so mad. That's why all these gods were willing to do whatever it took to come out on top. Not because they didn't care, but because they cared too much.

They just didn't understand the right way to show it.

The knife clattered to the ground and Demeter disappeared.

I shuddered violently. Shock probably. But before we had a chance to process what had just happened, footsteps thundered toward us.

I took a sharp breath. Hypnos, Thanatos, a bunch of minions, and Hades himself were all approaching at once. "Kill them," Hades said. He gave Kai a dismissive glance. "All of them."

We ran for our lives. It was too risky to try and transport out while we were under attack. We had to get somewhere quieter for at least a couple of seconds. Because if one of us was hit, that could keep all of us from going anywhere. Make us sitting ducks for a deadly instant.

The violent shudder I'd felt when Demeter disappeared must have been me returning to my real form. Sort of annoying since Festos and Kai retained their godness, while Theo and I reverted to human state and fell quickly behind.

Fee and Kai doubled back for us, firing lava and black light down the hall, and buying Theo and I time to get away. We were wearing the clothing we'd been in back at Felicia's place. For Theo, the typical baggy black skater clothes. But I'd gone back to rocking my *Phospherocious* T-shirt and Kai's jeans.

Theo and I had to race full out to keep up with Festos and Kai in their god forms, but there was no way either of us would let ourselves by picked up like babies. That also meant I had no breath left to talk to Theo. I kept looking over at him, until I finally felt a squeeze on the hand he was holding. It would have to be enough for now.

I pressed a hand to the stitch in my side as we skidded around a corner, milliseconds ahead of everyone else.

It was enough. Kai grabbed us and we blinked out.

Our next steps put us outside a cave entrance. Kai and Festos had returned to human height. They still wore the same clothes but they'd shrunk to appropriate size.

Oizys awaited us, blocking our path, and with every inch of her thirteen feet, denizen of the Underworld that she was.

I tensed. Was this where she raised the alarm? Killed me herself and brought me back to Hades back like a prized trophy?

She hesitated for a fraction of a second as she saw me in Sophie form. "Told you I'd figure out your secrets, Springtime."

I edged closer to my friends. "Question is what are you going to do with them?"

She looked at me for a long moment, her eyes unreadable, before turning to Theo without answering me. The two of them were frozen, staring at each other, like they'd just lost their best friends. Which they were about to do. Again.

"Was it worth it?" she asked.

One side of his mouth quirked up. "Guess we'll find out."

"I could order you to move," Kai said.

I glanced over at him. He watched her carefully but didn't look particularly alarmed at her presence.

"You could," she said.

"But you won't," Theo added. He stepped forward, closer to Oizys. "I didn't get to say good-bye last time."

"I hate you."

He nodded. "I know."

Her face twisted with an instant of hurt, then she crushed Theo to her, bending down to hug him. It was a fierce hug. And Theo returned it.

I didn't begrudge them. Nor did I think about whatever good-bye he and I would be saying later today.

It was all very sweet until Kai reminded us. "They'll be here any second," he said, and I knew we had to move.

I grabbed Theo's hand and tugged him away. "Oizys ..." There was so much I wanted to say to her, but she cut me off with a sharp shake of her head.

"Get out of here," Kai instructed her. "Don't let them see you."

Oizys looked surprised at this, but she nodded. Then she turned to Festos. "Take care of him."

Festos snatched up Theo's hand. "Always."

I waved. "See you soon, Goth Girl." It came out more wistfully than I'd intended.

She left me the ghost of a smile. "Not if I see you first, Springtime." With a final nod to me, she blended back into the shadows around the cave. And just in time. It seemed like half of the Underworld was stampeding toward us.

We raced into the cave. "Demeter kept her word," Kai said, pointing to a glowing light in the next chamber. "The entrance to her temple is open."

She had to, I thought with grim satisfaction. *She was bound by the oath.* I wondered how Demeter felt about almost killing me all over again. Did it matter to her at all? Was she glad I lived? Or sorry she'd failed a second time?

My chest felt tight. Sorrow spread through me like a virus. Settling into my bones. Add it to my nervous breakdown list for later. I wasn't being flip. I just didn't have the luxury of grief right now. Because if I started, where would it stop? With Demeter? Zeus? Theo? Hannah? The cyclone that was Kai and me?

And what would be left of me in its wake?

So no. No grief. Anger-fueled determination. That was good. I could work with that.

Still, I felt a brief pang as I wondered if the time I'd spent with Demeter in the Underworld would have any effect on the next time I saw Felicia. Right now, I had to get to the battle site. Which meant going through the exit into the Temple of Demeter in Eleusis.

My stomach turned as I stepped into the next chamber in the cave and stared at the light. Of course, it wasn't some nice portal to just jump through. Nope, we'd have to dive into a pool of water so deep and dark that light only highlighted the shadows, and potential shadowy monsters, beneath the surface. I jerked away from the pool.

"Nothing to be afraid of." Kai pointed to a lip of rock overhanging the water. "All you have to do is swim under that ledge, and through a short tunnel. When you surface, you'll be inside the Temple of Demeter."

"I'm not afraid. Just understandably cautious."

"Thesi first," Festos said, kicking off his shoes. "Safe and sound. Go." He'd obviously had enough of Theo being in danger in the Underworld.

"Festos," Theo began. He sighed and rubbed his hands roughly over his face.

Poor Theo. He'd had no time to process. No time to deal with seeing Oizys again, or transition from a world in which he hated Festos to a world in which he loved him. Not to mention the torture.

Again.

"Sorry." I knew how hard it was for Kai to say that one word to Theo. But it was clear that he meant it.

Theo acknowledged the apology with a slight nod, but kept his distance from Kai.

Festos wrapped his arms around Theo, and leaned in. "Please." It was more a breath than a word.

Theo touched Fee's cheek. "We'll go together."

"Or you could let me take you home. Right now." Festos gave Theo his most encouraging smile, but Theo shook his head.

"I can't."

I murmured to Kai. "Fee is still really worried about Theo undoing the ward that Zeus and Hades put up." It worried me too. I knew it would be dangerous. Everything about this situation was dangerous.

But Festos' expression was full of resigned heartbreak. It scared me.

Kai kissed the top of my head. "Theo will be fine. Come on, I'll swim with you."

That was probably as good as things were going to get. I kicked off my shoes, really glad that my math skills were not up to calculating how much water per square inch of denim my jeans would soak up once we were in the water.

Fee went first. Since there was no gradual beach entry,

he flung himself in. Then resurfaced, his cane thrashing the water as he howled "Cooooold!"

Theo, of course, stepped into the water with a minimal splash, swam toward Fee in a perfect front stroke, and wrapped his arm around him. "Stop wasting energy."

Festos rolled his eyes, but stopped his melodramatic splashing. "Count of three. One, two, three."

They ducked under the water and swam for the ledge. I watched until they were out of sight.

"Our turn!" I ended with a yelp as Kai swung me up in his arms. "Don't. You. Dare," I said.

He grinned and tossed me in the water.

I came up sputtering. My hair plastered to my face in long strands. As I swiped it out of my eyes, I felt Kai's arms around my waist.

He pressed his face into the back of my shoulder and held me, both of us slowly treading water.

A minion rushed into the cave, all fire and fury.

"Hang on," Kai said. He swung our bodies around so that I had no choice but to fling my arms around his neck.

A fireball sizzled past our heads.

I barely had time to take a deep breath as Kai dove under the water, taking me with him.

It was very dark. That didn't matter so much since I decided that squeezing my eyes shut was a good idea. But I hadn't taken a big enough breath. Actually, I don't know if that would have been possible without transplanting a bigger set of lungs. As Kai dragged me through the frigid water, concern that the minions had found us, turned to concern that I might not have enough air.

Which turned to absolute certainty.

And progressed to burning panic as my lungs tried to explode. Or implode. Maybe both.

Until finally—on the verge of my "this is it, here I go, drowning now" moment—we broke the surface on the other side. I took an enormous gulp of air. Never had I been so thankful for the gift of oxygen.

Festos and Theo were already out of the water.

The portal light began to blink.

"Hurry," Theo urged. "It's closing."

I let go of Kai so he could get out, but before I could go anywhere, fire shot up my ankle.

It appeared Pyrosim could not only swim, they could keep flaming in water, too. And grab on to people's legs. It pulled me down.

The portal light blinked faster and faster.

I looked up toward the surface and tried to shake the minion free. Its other tentacle snaked around my waist. My T-shirt had floated up so his fire was in direct contact with my skin. My body jerked in pain. If I screamed, I would drown.

Enough of this.

I had no problem unleashing some fury on this minion right here, right now. I fired my light vines and spun the little bugger into oblivion.

Highly satisfying.

More minions poured through the tunnel. The closest Pyrosim stretched out its tentacles to grab my other leg.

There was a blinding flash. And not from me. Which meant the portal was closing.

I stretched my arm up and fired a vine, hauling myself out of the water and out of minion range. Just in time. I swung over the now-dark pool, breathing heavily. The portal had closed. With the minions trapped on the other side.

"The Temple of Demeter," Theo said. "We're safe."

I lowered myself to the ground, avoiding the water. Not like I hadn't brought enough of it with me in my clothes. I lifted the hem of my shirt to better see the tentacle damage. A lovely burn mark wrapped half-way around my waist. I touched it gingerly and hissed. It would heal but it still hurt.

"We match." Theo sounded grimly amused.

I sent him a faint smile. "I beg to differ, Rockman. You got the magic salve. There's no more marks on that pretty skin of yours."

I wrung out my shirt. We were all sopping wet. I only spared one covert glance for Kai, to check and see if his already body-hugging outfit had gotten more defined.

It had.

Yum.

Nice as that image was, I was happy to see that Fee had a blazing fire going to dry us all out. Having the God of Fire and Volcanos around was pretty handy. I squelched my way over and sat down, enjoying the feel of the heat on my face. Now that I was momentarily safe, I relaxed enough to take in my surroundings.

We were in a cave. Empty of everything except a dirty floor. "How unspectacular," I said.

"Well" Theo said wryly, "we're essentially in an ancient doorway, so I'm not sure what you expected."

"It doesn't get much better," Festos said. "We're present-day again. The glory of this temple is long gone. All you'll see are ruins."

I looked toward the cave entrance to confirm his words. All I saw was Kai, framed in the frail pink light of sunrise, and staring outside.

"We're not going anywhere yet." Theo glanced at his watch. "It's only 9AM."

I stretched my hands toward the flame. "Are we safe here?"

He nodded, sitting down cross-legged beside me. "Yeah. We're inside our ward, too. Not just theirs. Now we wait. We don't want to appear too early and give them time to see us. Mess with our heads."

I rested my head on Theo's shoulder.

He relaxed against me.

Gawd, I loved him so much. How was I supposed to let him go? "I don't think I can do it." I didn't mean facing Zeus and Hades, and Theo knew it.

"You have to, Magoo."

My lip trembled and I bit down on it to keep from bursting into tears. Making Theo feel bad about our impending good-bye wouldn't help him take down the ward. This was bigger than us.

Theo must have understood how much keeping silent was costing me, because he pulled me in and held me tight.

I sat there, enjoying our closeness.

No, memorizing it. Memorizing every last detail about him. How he smelled. How the knuckles of his right hand were weirdly more knobby than his left. How, without his glasses, I could see how deep and shining his eyes were.

But mostly, I just committed the feel of him to memory. So that on those days when his absence hit me like a physical ache, I could pull this time up and lose myself in it.

The fire hissed cheerfully. There was none of that woodsy smell I liked, since Fee had simply sprung it to life, but it sure was beautiful to watch.

We waited. The time would have been almost peaceful, except for Fee's incessant pacing.

"Babe," Theo said. "Sit down already."

"I can't. I'll go mad sitting here for what, another nine hours?"

"Seven hours, thirty two minutes," Kai said, barely turning his head. He seemed welded to the entrance.

Festos made another strangled sound.

"Okay, that's it." Theo gently disengaged himself from me and pushed to his feet. "Let's go."

Festos looked startled. "Where?"

"For a walk. We have some things to work out." Theo turned to me. "You two stay here. Even though our ward is strong, I don't want you out in the open until it's time. I'll take down their ward a few minutes before the equinox. You know where the ritual happens, right?"

Kai finally moved from his position at the mouth of the cave and nodded. His eyes locked on to mine. "Yeah.

The pomegranate tree west of here."

My mouth fell open. The pomegranate tree in my vision was real, and about to become center stage for the showdown?

Screw. Me.

Twenty-two

"We're performing the ritual under the freaking pomegranate tree?" I was incredulous.

Kai grimaced. "You didn't know."

"You think?" I brought my knees into my chest and then beat my head against them. "There's a garden, isn't there?"

"Not so much anymore." Kai stuck his arm between my head and my knees. "Quit it. I don't need you getting concussed."

Instead of using them to beat myself senseless, I rested my head on my knees, this time pressing my cheek against my damp jeans to look at Kai more closely. "How did I not know this? I was the one who knew where the ritual was supposed to happen."

"When did you start having the visions? How soon after you remembered?"

I'd been out of it for a while, healing from Bethany's stab wounds. But the visions had started pretty much once I was back on my feet. "When Theo started getting the ritual details from me," I said.

Kai nodded. "He never pressed you for more specific info on the location though, did he?"

"No. Why not?"

"Because back when you told us that we had to perform the ritual in Eleusis? We all knew exactly where. It was the only place near the Temple of Demeter that made sense. You did know," he added gently. "Even if you didn't, or couldn't consciously remember it."

I scratched at my jaw. "But you thought I actually knew and just wasn't talking about it."

Kai sat with his knees also to his chest, mirroring me. He propped a fist on top and rested his chin on his hands, staring into the flames. "Yeah. I mean, you were so freaked out by your visions. I thought that was part of the reason why."

"No. They were disturbing enough on their own."

He touched my arm, his face turned to mine. "It's just a place. It doesn't mean anything."

"It means something." I wrapped my arms tightly around my legs. "You weren't in the vision. If things ended well and we did what we needed to, why weren't you there? Why did I feel like I was dead? Or everyone was? Or both?" I gave a ragged laugh. "Ohmigod."

Helplessness flashed across Kai's face before he shrugged. "I don't know." He gripped my hands. "But I swear to you, Sophie, I won't leave you."

He had though. He'd left me back when we fought Delphyne, and he'd stolen Theo's chain to go after Hades. He'd left me when Felicia told him about Persephone's betrayal. Yeah, he'd come back but, not emotionally. Not completely.

I wondered if he held that crucial final piece of his heart back from me even now.

Sadness washed over me. My palms prickled. Not with rage, but nervous fear. Was Kai capable of loving me in the way I wanted? In the way I deserved? In the way I loved him? How much difference did me being human make to our fundamental understanding of how this relationship should go.

"What you thinking, Goddess?"

I tugged my hands from his. "You called me that, you know."

He squinted at me. "What?"

"In Hades. You called me, Goddess. Well," I laughed, kind of. "You called Persephone that. Seeing as you didn't remember I existed."

"Because of an enchantment," he said, watching me carefully.

"Yeah, yeah. But see, I thought that was your name for *me*." I was appalled to realize how much this mattered to me. My eyes misted up. "Not a left-over." I waved at some smoke coming off of the fire, using it as an excuse to wipe my eyes.

"You have her memories." Kai sounded exasperated. "Did I ever once call her that?"

I thought about it. "Not that I recall now, but—"

"Do you remember what I said that day when I first told you that I loved you?"

Every single word. "Maybe? What in particular?"

Kai's amusement said he knew I was full of it. "That goddesses are easy. They're vain and temperamental, but that I know how to handle them. When the truth was …" his voice twisted, "Seventeen years ago, Persephone was going to betray me. Kill me, for all I know, and I had no clue. No suspicion at all. I was totally played."

"What's your point?"

"I also told you that *you* were this mouthy human that I couldn't figure out, and couldn't make fall in line."

I was starting to cramp in this position so I sat up, shaking out my shoulders. "Don't forget how I kept getting under your skin," I said.

"Trust me, I couldn't forget that." He straightened, and raked his hand through his hair. "These past few days? Five minutes with you and I knew something was wrong. You made me so angry and nothing about you was easy. It drove me crazy. I knew it wasn't her. I called Persephone 'Goddess' for the first time ever because on some level, I recognized *you*."

I wanted to believe him. He sounded sincere enough. Plus, he was giving me that look like I was chocolate and he just had to indulge his very serious sweet tooth.

Perhaps I could give him the benefit of the doubt.

I shifted so that I was facing him straight on and leaned in. I curled my fingers into his shirt and tugged him closer. "Kissing me is also so much better."

He blushed.

It was simultaneously the sweetest and hottest thing I'd ever seen. My heart melted.

I kissed him.

Fireworks, earthquakes, fairy dust, it was all that and a heap of jaw-dropping magnificence.

"I love you," I said against his lips.

He pushed me softly to the ground. His eyes heating up as he leaned over me. "So much and more. My phospherocious girl." His voice was so tender.

Neither of us moved. Something profound had just shifted between us. The air itself felt weighted. Charged. Not with chemistry, but with something more real and scary and wonderful.

The heat was intense. And not from Festos' fire.

This was the moment we should have had after Kai had first said he loved me. But maybe we had needed the misery of the past couple months to get here. Without the pain, we couldn't have had the joy.

As I stared into Kai's eyes, I was lost. My heart raced. Whatever this was, it was so precious. And I was suddenly so afraid. What if I'd finally gotten what I wanted only to have it snatched from me? What if the vision was right and soon I'd be dead, or alone or ... "Kai—"

Kai shook his head. Almost violently. "Don't talk." He pressed into me for a kiss that was deeper and slower than any we'd ever had.

I was floating. Only the soft, gentle pressure of his fingers splayed against my stomach kept me from rising up and away. The kiss was sweet and heavy and longing. I trembled, twining my fingers into his hair to bring him closer. Make our two halves whole.

My skin flushed. My body tingled under the onslaught of this electrifying, spine-tingling, butterfly-inducing amazingness. Under this kiss of pure love.

Kai pulled away. "Try to sleep. We're going to need

all our energy." He curved his body around mine, his hand resting across my waist.

I relaxed into him. I needed this. The rest, the closeness.

Us.

I woke up warm and sleepy, laying on my other side, still snuggled into Kai. We were face to face now. Our noses almost touching. He still had one arm flung over me and our legs were tangled up.

"Sleep well?" His voice sounded scratchy as his eyes crinkled in a smile.

I smiled back, too drowsy to speak.

He brushed the tip of his nose against mine. "You're adorable when you sleep."

I scrunched up my face and ducked my head, embarrassed.

Kai tipped my chin up with his finger. "You're blushing." He traced the curve of my jaw and along my throat.

I squirmed. "Well, you're pretty cute when you sleep too."

Kai propped himself up on his elbow. "You watched me?"

I mirrored his gesture. "Yeah. Back in Hades. You were beautiful, sleeping in the moonlight." I looked at him, my heart in my eyes.

Kai ducked in for a kiss. A lovely wake up kiss.

"Ahem." Festos cleared his throat.

I blushed for entirely other reasons and tried to twist out from under Kai.

He didn't budge. "Go away."

"Trust me, I'd love nothing more. But we have a problem."

With a sigh, Kai rolled off of me. He got to his feet, held out a hand, and pull me up.

Festos strode over to me. He gave my shirt a sharp tug to straighten it and ran a hand over my hair, smoothing it down. "Just ratcheting down your wantonness," he declared cheerfully.

I removed a twig from his hair. "Aren't you in a good mood."

He blushed.

Adorable.

"Follow the leader. I'm leader." Festos pivoted and left the cave.

The air was cool and gray. What a surprise. Although, maybe, the sun really would come out tomorrow. Clear away our sorrows and all that jazz.

"What's up?" I asked. I was glad I'd banked all that fireside time. Instead of feeling all goosebumpy, I was pleasantly cool. I stretched out my arms, feeling a tightness in my shoulders. "What time is it?"

"About 4:30," Festos said. "We all crashed pretty hard."

Theo stood in the distance on a slight rise, waiting patiently for us to arrive.

"I thought he didn't want us out in the open."

"Yes, well. Best laid plans blah blah blah." We continued in silence until we had reached Theo.

I gasped. From this angle I could see that we stood inside an area ringed with flames. "What happened?"

"Hmm?" Theo peered at the fire. "Oh. No. That's just their ward."

"It hasn't caused mass panic among the townspeople? That this ancient site is on fire?"

"They can't see it," Kai explained. "It's magic. It doesn't hurt them."

Which would explain why the sky wasn't filled with smoke. Why I couldn't smell fire, just see it. "Then what's the problem?"

Theo pointed over to his left. "Do you see a pomegranate tree?"

I shook my head. "No."

"Exactly." He looked at Kai. "The ritual had a precise location. Care to guess where it was?"

Aw, jeez.

"How could our place marker disappear inside our own ward?" It didn't make any sense to me. Yes, Zeus and Hades had set up a ward of their own but it ran outside of ours. "The entire point of our ward was to stop them destroying the location. So how did someone manage to do exactly that?"

"It's not destroyed, exactly," said Festos. "Just a wee bit harder to locate. The garden is still there." He scrunched up his face in confusion and looked to Theo. "I could have sworn we saw the tree when we originally set up our wards."

"Yeah. We did."

"Felicia," I groaned. "It's her temple. She's the only other person who could have gotten to the tree. She probably wrenched it out of the ground with her bare hands."

"And ruin my manicure? Please." We all jumped at the sound of her voice. She looked as perfectly groomed as ever. Her meticulously coiffed hair brushed the shoulders of her short, cognac-colored jacket with fur trim. It was odd seeing that color on her clothing instead of in her glass.

Felicia stretched out a hand to peer at her nails, as if to assure herself no harm had come to them. "Bethany and an ax worked just as well." She smiled at me with glittering malice. "You know how effective mere mortals can be. Especially that one."

I am the bigger person. I am the bigger person.

I shot my vines out.

Felicia laughed and sidestepped them easily. "Not very effective when I see it coming a mile away. Don't telegraph so much, darling."

"But I don't." Kai gave her his snake smile. "And I haven't shown my displeasure at Sophie's personal time with your knife."

Felicia went pale.

Damn, that was satisfying.

"Blame it on Kiki," she said, recovering quickly with a flippant wave. "It was her ridiculous enchantment."

"Other than gloating, did you want something?" Theo asked. He stood in his usual slouchy stance, hands jammed in his pockets. But I was not fooled. His chain could be in his hand and doing serious damage in a second, if he thought the situation called for it.

Felicia smiled faintly. "Many things, dear boy. Right now I'm just curious to see how this all plays out."

I wrapped my arms around my chest. Mostly so I wouldn't blast her again. "If I lose, mother dearest, I'll probably be dead. And while I'm certain you'll enjoy celebrating my end, just remember that Zeus will be celebrating, too. With his beloved Hera at his side." Apparently, despite my love for her, I still had more than my ongoing share of petty desire to hurt my mother.

I'll give her credit. She didn't even flinch at that barb.

It was a good speech. Too bad I'd trembled slightly as my tangle of emotions—around her, around us—got the better of me. I dug my nails into my sides and let the sting keep me steady. I had to ask. "Why would you destroy the tree and actively help him win?"

"It was a fit of pique." Her eyes flicked down to my fingers, curved painfully into my skin, and back up to my face. "Things could have been different," she said.

"Why weren't they?" That came out a bit harsher than I'd intended.

My mother considered me for a long moment. Then she shrugged. "Despite your childish refusal to give me what you promised, I haven't totally knocked you out of the game. Just made it more difficult. The tree may not exist, but the location most certainly does." She glanced at her watch. "You have more than three hours to figure it out. Oh, and to say good-bye to Theo." She patted my cheek and disappeared.

"Come on," Kai said. "Let's see if Bethany left any trace of the tree."

We tromped down to the garden.

The sky grew dark. I looked up, knowing I wasn't going to find storm clouds. Sure, it might look that way to humans, but I could clearly see the thousands of Pyrosim and Photokia hovering outside the second ward. More arrived every second. Well, we'd known they'd all be showing up. Dwelling on it wasn't going to change anything.

I turned to face to the garden. I think I would have preferred to stare at the minions. That dead garden, wild and choked with weeds, was downright forbidding. Icy tendrils snaked through my blood. Every step closer left me with the irrational fear that, at any second, the ground beneath me would cave into a field of lava. My friends—and even the minions—would all disappear and I'd be left here. Alone.

The lack of a pomegranate tree didn't relieve me at all. It just made me more anxious. As if I'd already lost. The sight of the flames burning from Pops' ward made me feel worse. They came extremely close to the garden. With the pomegranate tree gone, I couldn't help thinking that if anything was going to be consumed by flame, it would be me.

The terror grew like a weight until I stumbled under it.

Theo grabbed my elbow. "Steady, Magoo."

I clutched his hand, my eyes focused on the garden. I could only manage shallow breaths. No matter how hard I tried to suck in oxygen, I felt like I'd never get enough air again.

Kai stepped into the garden first. He paced slowly through it, meticulously searching for any trace of the tree.

"It was along one of the edges of the garden," I said. And so was I. I'd go in if I had to, but not a second before. It hadn't occurred to me that I'd have to psych myself up to perform the ritual. I'd always just assumed I'd be so eager to defeat Pops and Hades that I'd be raring to go.

It's just a place. I tried to hold on to that thought. It couldn't hurt me. A lot of things in and around it most definitely could, but the garden itself couldn't. Not unless I gave it the power to.

"Tree cutting and yoga, who knew Bethany was so multi-talented," Theo said.

Festos limped into the center of the garden. "Demeter helped her with some kind of magic tool. Trust me. There's no way that child could have obliterated every trace of the tree otherwise."

Kai looked over at me. "Soph? Anything you remember that could help here?"

I forced myself to step into the garden. Nothing happened. I wasn't consumed by lava. No stone grew from the ground to twist up my body and seal me into a sarcophagus.

Hang on. The stone that I'd stood on in my vision. "Look for a low flat rock. One wide enough to stand on comfortably. "

We all took a corner of the garden and started searching. My patch contained a lot of weeds, that yielded no stones underneath. There were a couple of boulders, but they weren't the right size.

"Honeybunch?"

I looked at Festos. He held a tangle of vines aside with his cane, peering down. I hurried over to him. He'd exposed the edge of a stone that could be the one we wanted.

"Can you knock some more of the vines out of the way?" I asked. I bent down and scrabbled in the dirt to pull out some of the plants myself, while Fee hacked at the others.

In a few minutes, the rock was exposed. I squinted down at it. "I think that's it. The one in my vision."

Wimpily, no matter how much I assured myself that it was just a rock and not a tomb, I couldn't step onto it. I stood in front of it instead. "Since I was facing into the garden when I saw the tree ..." I spread my arms out in front of me. "Follow my arms. It was somewhere between them on the other side."

Theo and Kai started walking. I held my breath until Theo looked up with a grin. "They were good. But not perfect. Come see."

Festos and I hurried over.

Theo stopped us. "Look. There. Don't disturb the ground. That's the X-marks-the-spot placeholder."

It took me a minute to see it. The rest of the dirt was untouched save for pockmarks of scrub, but there was a small circle, maybe three inches in diameter, edged out of the brush. It was too perfect to be random.

Kai squatted down for a better look. "Must have been where Bethany took out the root." He scooped up a few small stones and made a little pile. "There." Then he stood up and brushed his hands off on his pants. "Solved.

So, what should we do for the next two and half hours?" And then he gave me a look that made it abundantly clear what he *thought* the two of us should do.

I shivered. Sadly, it wouldn't be good to get that distracted. Also, I wanted to stay with Theo. "We stick together," I said.

We went back to the cave. None of us wanted to hang around and watch the minions gather.

It would have been nice if, during our last few hours, Theo and I had gone for lunch in Paris. Or swimming by moonlight on a tropical beach. Rode roller coasters and laughed hysterically. Even binged on too much cookie dough and watched dumb movies. Made one incredible memory that could sustain me after I said good-bye to Theo.

It wasn't just that I'd never get to see him again. This deal with Felicia was going to change everything. I wouldn't be able to see Festos if Theo was there. Hang out with Hannah if he was around at all.

Hell, even Kai could go hang out with him if he wanted. Not that he would now. But if he ever made up with Festos, then it could happen. I'd be cut off from it all, though. And yeah, Theo would too. In reverse. It would change the dynamic for all of us.

So no, hanging out in a cave wasn't amazing in your typical memory-making way. It wasn't what I wanted. But at least it was Theo and me. Stripped down to our essence.

When Kai said, "It's time." I wanted to refuse. Beg for five more minutes.

I was strong enough to take on any god that came my way. But I couldn't let Theo go.

Tears ran down my face. I didn't care. I couldn't stop them if I tried.

Theo pulled me to my feet. "Love you, Magoo."

"Love you," I said in a broken whisper.

He pressed his lips to my forehead.

Festos turned away, wiping his eyes.

Theo stepped away from me. I felt colder already.

He looked at each of us in turn. "The second I take down their ward, the second I'm out of here, Festos will take down our ward and start the cleansing ritual. Soon as that happens, you become vulnerable. The minions will attack."

I nodded and slipped my chain off of my neck. Fee's re-charger ring was still threaded on it, next to the pendant. I took the ring off, slid it onto my finger, and put my sapphire back on.

"We good?" Theo asked.

Festos opened his mouth and then closed it again. "No."

Theo took his hand.

I took Kai's.

And for better or for worse, the four of us walked outside to begin the battle.

Sunset had hit. This didn't mean the fight would happen against a backdrop of splendid oranges and pinks which might somehow have fueled our hope and courage. Nope, it just meant that the sky turned a darker gray.

Light leeched away with every second. Which sucked. Who wanted to fight in the dark? I'd gotten used to the lack of sunshine lately, but, psychologically, I found it way easier to do this with at least a little light on my skin. Night time was when the monsters came out. Literally and metaphorically.

I pressed closer to my friends.

Theo explained that it didn't really matter where he took down their ward. But it made sense to do it where the two wards came closest to our ritual location.

We needed to be pretty much in place. Especially since, once the wards came down, we only had three minutes and thirty seconds for both the cleansing and the ritual. That was the maximum recharge on the ring. All the time I had to fire my full body shockwaves and hold the minions at bay.

Fifteen feet from where the pomegranate tree used to be, we stopped. The ward fire blazed. I couldn't understand how humans couldn't see or feel it, when I had to throw up a hand against the heat.

Fire is a slippery thing with many faces.

The fire that Festos had brought to life back in the cave, while no less magic'd than this one, had been cheerful. Comforting.

These flames promised power. And annihilation.

"Bring the fire, choke the spark, release the form." I repeated Cassie's words. Had it only been a few days ago? It felt like a lifetime. I looked from the flames to Theo. "So? How does this work?"

Theo gave me a tired smile. "Simple."

See, I didn't understand. Anything.

Not why Kai bowed his head as if he couldn't bear to look.

Not why Festos moaned as if in great pain.

Not why Theo stepped into the flames.

No.

He held up a hand to us. Like a good-bye.

But ... *no*. I started to hyperventilate. To shake my head harder and harder, as if one good snap of my neck could knock the image of the flames swallowing my best friend from my brain. Wake me from this grisly nightmare.

Theo was consumed.

The flames blared hot and bright and fierce and then winked out.

The fire was gone.

Theo was gone.

And all I was left with, in the gloomy night air, was the radiance of his memory.

Twenty-three

A sound tore from my throat. Not a scream. Something darker. Inhuman-cry. I lunged toward the spot where Theo had just stood, my arms reaching out.

Festos grabbed me. I registered it dimly, and only because I felt his cane bang against my shin.

The world around me began to pound under the assault of endless minions.

Bring the fire ... Prometheus had brought fire to mankind. *Choke the spark* ... Theo had done that, dousing the flames with his own life essence.

Release the form ...

I twisted away from Fee and screamed, "How can you stand there?"

Why wasn't he raging too? The love of his life had just died. But it wasn't like it didn't matter to Festos. The pain on his face was raw and real, and agonizing to watch.

Then I saw the flash of guilt. "You knew," I said and kicked away from him, wild-eyed. That's why Festos had been so upset, so furious, after Cassie had made her pronouncement.

"Sophie," he said quietly.

I threw my arm across my stomach, as if I could stop the pain knifing through me. "You. Knew."

"Leave him alone." Kai pushed between me and Festos. His voice was harsh. "You think this was easy on him? You think Fee wanted to know that he was going to watch Theo die?"

Ohmigod. I stuttered out a sob. "You knew too." When Kai had left me, back in Delphyne's cave, I thought I'd understood the pain of betrayal. But now? They had both known what Cassie's words meant and not told me. No wonder Theo had made the deal with Felicia. It hadn't mattered. He wasn't going to be around anyway.

I stood there. Unable to move. Unable to breathe. Unable to do anything except feel the torment pounding inside me in time with the onslaught from above.

"Don't let Theo's death be for nothing," Kai snapped. "Honor him. Honor your friend who is standing here dying." He motioned to Festos, who looked shell-shocked, "And fight."

I stared dumbly at the spot where Theo had been and a memory overtook me.

"That new kid?" Bethany threw her thick braid over her knit dress. She snickered at Veronica who was, as usual, stuck to her side. "Weirdo." They walked past us, on the school's back field.

I hoped she wasn't going to bug us. There wasn't much

349

time left in long recess and I just wanted to play with Hannah.

Yay. The girls ignored us and headed over to the rest of their dumb friends, like Anil and Jackson. So annoying.

I stuck my tongue out at Bethany's back.

Hannah looked up from trying to coax an earthworm back into the glass jar filled with grass that she'd made as its home, and grinned. "At least she's in Miss Cohn's grade two class. Not ours."

My stomach growled even though we'd just had lunch. I flopped down and prodded the worm.

"He looks lost."

"Huh?" I scrunched up my face, not sure who Hannah was talking about.

She stared off across the field. "That boy. Maybe we should say hi."

I looked over at where she was staring. The new kid. Bethany was kind of right. He was sort of weird looking. His dark hair stuck up like he'd shoved his finger in a socket. He wore a T-shirt with a robot picture on it. And the black glasses on his face kept sliding down his nose.

It didn't seem to bother him, because he just kept pushing them up to look around.

"Come on." Hannah bounced to her feet and headed toward him, expecting me to follow.

I rolled onto my back. Didn't want to move. I wanted to lie in the sun. And not talk to strangers. I had Hannah. I didn't need another friend.

I waited for her to come back so we could keep playing. But she brought him with her.

"This is Theo. He's going to be our friend."

We'd see about that. Groaning and moaning, I pulled myself up and looked at him.

He tilted his head, kind of studying me.

I didn't like that. So I gave him my best prickly look. Imagining I was a porcupine with my quills standing up.

"Yeah. You're okay." He grinned and folded himself down beside me.

Hey, wasn't I the one who should decide if he got to stay? He was the new kid.

But then he peered at the home we'd made for the worm and said, "You need to make a better hole in the lid. Get some rocks and leaves and stuff." It just felt right for him to be here then. With us.

With me.

I relaxed and listened to him talk about the worm.

Bethany skipped past and rolled her eyes. "Figures."

"Shut up, Bethany," I warned. "Theo's our friend."

Yeah. We had our group now.

Bam!

The air vibrated hard enough to jostle me sideways, knocking me back into the battle. I wanted to stay in that happy past, not this horrorshow present.

I swiped at my eyes. Kai was right. Here. Now. I would fight. And later, I would fight with Kai about what he'd kept from me. But at this moment, I had a job to do. No way was Theo's ... *absence* going to be for nothing.

Absence. I didn't even want to think the other word. It made my insides twist as if Demeter was killing me a billion times over. I swear I felt bits of my heart breaking off and hitting the ground. I could hear the hollow thunks.

"Sophie!" Kai yelled. He stood, tense, in position next to Festos.

I blew a kiss toward the last place I'd seen Theo alive. And vowed that everyone who had brought this about would pay. Then I looked at Festos and nodded. "Do it."

Festos spoke the words and brought our ward down.

I raised my face to the sky, feeling the wind on my cheeks as the minions swarmed to the attack. The war had begun.

Now. Persephone's voice swirled in my head. This time, I let her have her way. I mentally removed every block, every civilized impulse I had, and unleashed my full furious power.

Kai and I fell into a pattern. I blasted shockwave after shockwave, clearing the sky momentarily with each discharge. But in seconds more came back. That's what happens with an endless supply of minions.

My ears rang with each explosion, until I felt like I existed inside of an endlessly ringing bell.

Kai handled the minions that got too close to Festos. He was Fee's personal bodyguard, keeping him safe while he chanted the cleansing ritual.

I could see Fee's body trembling with grief, but he kept going. And if he could, then I could too. His determination in the face of such insane loss, recharged me just as much as the magic ring on my finger.

I fired again and again, staying rooted to the spot, and forcing extra power from deep within the earth. I wiggled my bare feet into the dirt, digging my toes in deeper.

At least it didn't stay dark. Between fireballs, lightning strikes, my shockwaves and Kai's black light, it was quite the dazzling illumination.

My eyes closed. I didn't need to see the Photokia and Pyrosim to know where they were. I could sense them, millions and millions, swarming me. More than I could count. More than I could process.

It was a plague of minions. The world was so thick with them that I was amazed there was still room for air. Their fireballs burned my skin and sparked my hair. Their lightning arced through my body.

The air was heat and smoke and burning destruction. Every particle glided over my skin in electric vibrations that shocked the tiny hairs on my arms. Black ash rained down, covering me in a blanket of soot. I took it all in and used it. Turned it around and sent it back with every shockwave I fired.

I felt untouchable. Even with all the hits I was taking, my healing abilities kept up pretty well. I had never been more a goddess, more every-inch powerful, than in this moment. I felt Persephone settle into my skin, connect to me in a way that had never happened before. For this moment, at least, we were in perfect synch. We were the vanquishers and our enemies would go down tasting our wrath.

Until I heard the laughter. The mocking from my vision. It rolled through me with such contempt that I could taste it. My eyes shot open and flicked to Kai. I wanted to know if he heard it, too. But there was no way to ask over the roar of noise. Over the ringing in my ears.

He understood though. He nodded and tilted his head up.

Zeus and Hades had arrived. They landed on the ground with perfect grace, about twenty feet away. I'd seen them both in their towering god forms, but this was different. For all the times when I'd confronted them and mouthed off to them and mocked them? There was nothing vaguely amusing about either of them now.

I shivered. A splinter of doubt wedged its way into my heart. I may have been a goddess, but they were truly the lords of all gods.

They weren't even angry. It was as if we were as much beneath their notice as ants. Suddenly I knew where the laughter—in my vision and in real life—had come from. We amused them. Kai and I. Their silly children throwing a temper tantrum. Zeus and Hades looked at us with exasperation and resignation. Like our fun was over now. It was time for the grown-ups to dole out the punishment.

I wondered how I had ever been deluded enough to think myself equal to them.

Except ...

Since our punishment was death—ours and all humans—so that the gods could freely roam, I wasn't going to roll over and accept whatever they intended to dish out. I sidled over to Kai and Festos, still blasting away at the minions. The magic ring may have been recharging me but using so much power made me feel wonky. Light-headed.

My human form strained to contain my power. My limbs trembled. My skin felt tight, stretched to its limit and ready to tear. My light wanted to break free, unhindered by my puny mortal body.

I was burning up. Sweat streamed down the back of my neck and under the elastic of my bra. My hair was plastered in limp, damp strands. Moss green spots danced in front of my eyes. More and more with every shockwave I fired.

I stumbled, anxious that my power would kill me before the gods did. We'd been so happy that Festos had found a way to recharge me, that we hadn't stopped to consider whether or not I could handle a continuous re-up. Whether perhaps the reason I had to rest between blasts was because my body couldn't take it.

If this were a video game, my life bar would have been blinking red. And I'd be ignoring it. Voluntarily shortening my life span to keep firing at the minions. Keep trying to save the world.

I burrowed my feet deeper into the earth and looked over at the guys. Festos had finished the cleansing, which meant that Kai and I were good to go. *Seconds, Soph. Hang on a few more.*

My head cleared enough to hear Kai yelling at Fee to leave. Festos shook his head and Kai grabbed him by the shoulders. "Go!"

Fee took in the situation. He knew that it was down to Kai and me. And despite all his power, his presence was now a distraction we couldn't afford. He looked at me with dull eyes and I forced myself to nod. As much as I wanted him here, not to fight but to comfort, I couldn't lose him, too. One more reason to wrap this up as fast as possible. Fee and I were going to need each other tonight.

He understood. Blowing me a sad kiss, he disappeared.

Kai took my hand. Resolve flowed through me. Let Hades and Zeus do their worst. Kai and I had love on our side and we would win. We'd make the minions ours, turn them on our fathers, seize their power, and save humanity from destruction.

It would all be over.

Kai threw up a shield of black light as we stepped onto the ritual location. I stayed on alert, ready to keep blasting even as I spoke. Between us, we'd deal with whatever they threw our way.

It was a good thought. In theory. Thing was, they didn't throw anything at us. Instead, Zeus and Hades began to chant. The wind picked up and the air grew cold. But beyond that, not much happened.

A wide smile broke across Kai's face. "They're trying to start the apocalypse. One above and one below. But it's not working."

I felt hope blossom within me. Zeus and Hades chanted more insistently, their faces clouded, turning splotchy with anger. I could have danced. The big top gods were achieving squat. Kai and I were going to win. I knew it. I felt it.

I squeezed Kai's hand, turned to face him, and spoke the first line of our ritual. "*Katabaino.*"

"*Anabaino,*" he replied.

Zeus roared and fired a thunderbolt that burst Kai's shield into thousands of fragments of toxic light. It knocked us to the ground, our momentum rolling us away from my father's next killing blow.

A staff appeared in Hades' hand. He struck the ground twice. Jagged cracks opened up in the earth, sucking everything into their depths.

We got to our feet, hands still clasped, and ran. Forget staying in place to do the ritual. Our lives depended on outdistancing the earth that came toward us like a wave. I prayed that saying the words in the general vicinity would be enough.

"*Di'erota, sthenos gignetai,*" we chanted.

The ground disappeared from beneath Kai's feet. He stumbled and went down.

Ironically, it was only the shockwave coming off Pops' next lightning strike that kept me from falling into the hole as well. It hit and hurled me sideways. The mocking laughter started again.

Kai. I had to get to Kai. The total and absolute terror of him not by my side, of losing him while my vision unfolded before me, gave me the jolt of adrenaline I needed to keep moving.

Dazed and bleeding, I crawled to the lip of the hole on my belly. Nothing else mattered in that moment. Nothing but Kai. Without him, there could be no victory. I didn't care that the minions continued to swarm me with their deadly assault. I fired another shockwave. almost carelessly, clearing the skies for another moment. But I wasn't re-charged with the same level of light.

Festos' magic ring was running out of power.

A shadow fell over me. Zeus raised his thunderbolt ...

... and missed as Kai shot out of the hole to physically tackle my father out of the way.

It bought us precious seconds. Our eyes locked and in perfect unison we chanted the last line of the ritual. "*Di'erota, menos gignetai.*"

The world went still. The minions hadn't returned. I think that Zeus and Hades were too shocked that we'd completed the ritual to do anything. We all stood frozen, waiting to see what would happen.

The ground beneath me bucked with a force no Richter scale could measure. Kai and I couldn't get to our feet. The world shuddered so violently that we were flung around like rag dolls.

I couldn't understand what had happened. We'd done it. We'd said the ritual. We'd stopped Hades and Zeus.

Hadn't we?

A roar split my eardrums. It wasn't just loud. It was all-consuming. The noise slithered into me and punched me from the inside.

My eyes bulged at a tsunami of water rushing toward us. So much that I wondered how there could be any left in the ocean. It was one atrocity too many. My mind snapped and I stared, hypnotized.

Stumbling to his feet, Kai scooped me up and jumped a hundred feet out of the torrent's wake. Another jump. More distance.

With each leap, my bones jarred and my teeth rattled. But it snapped me back to attention. I gaped as Kai kept us heartbeats ahead of the deadly wave. A final jump. He landed us on a cliff overlooking the temple grounds. We were safe from the water.

But when I finally let out a relieved breath, the sky burst into flame.

It creeped me right out of my skin. My nails dug into my palm and I scrambled backward through the black ash covering the ground. Tiny puffs of it burst up with each step, settling back down to coat my feet in fine black powder. The world smelled like electrical smoke and burnt dust.

I heard Hades laughing hysterically. Like he'd just heard the best joke in the world.

Water, fire, earth. air. Every single element heralded death.

I stared in confusion. In horror. Desperate to make sense of the senselessness.

Zeus closed the distance between us in a single stride. The destruction didn't affect him one bit. He squatted down to speak to me, eyes glittering with amusement. "One above. One below. Alive. Awake. A key. It is no more. It is no more."

"What have you done?" I screamed, hanging on to Kai for balance as the earth continued to break around me. I swung my head to look at him and shivered. I'd never seen this expression on Kai's face.

Dread didn't cover what I felt seeing my all-powerful boyfriend stare at the sky in perfect horror.

"We've brought the apocalypse." Kai turned stricken eyes to mine. "You and I."

That was impossible. *I* was the *savior* of humanity.

Cassie's words about me being the instrument of destruction echoed back to me.

Zeus chuckled and patted my head. "You've done such a good job. Earth will be free of humans in no time. Maybe I'll let you live after all, daughter."

I didn't get a chance to respond because, at that moment, the very fabric of the air around us shredded. I flew into my father's leg with a hard jolt, bouncing off of his shin to land on my butt in the dirt. Blood streamed from my ears. I put a hand on my stomach, certain that the violent rift in our atmosphere had torn my organs from my body.

Standing, moving, doing anything beyond gaping up at the swirling, churning, burning depths above, was impossible. I saw the end of everything.

Man, was I pissed.

I clawed at my arms. Everything we'd gone through? *Theo*?! For what? The end of the world? The end of humanity? I refused to accept it. There was no way we'd been so wrong.

I peered through the smoke toward Demeter's temple far below. There was nothing left. Just a raging torrent of water.

Winds buffeted us. Fire writhed all around me, mocking with its flickering dance. *Instrument of our destruction.*

I looked into the depths of the rift. How could we be responsible? In the face of all the hate that had surrounded us, Kai and I represented love. Didn't we?

Persephone's voice raged in my head. *They must not win.* My arms burned and my head felt ready to explode.

The rift grew larger and larger. It was angry.

So was I.

I faced my last seconds of existence and thought about everything I'd experienced since I'd become a goddess. How my fury had grown with each new challenge. Had it really been any different than the rage that the gods had felt?

Look at how much raw anger Kai had held on to. For his father. For Persephone.

For me.

Despite all our protestations, were we any different from the rest of them? What if Kai and I had performed the ritual from a place not of love, but of hate? What if we'd taken the right actions—a love ritual to stop Zeus and Hades—but with wrong, angry intentions? What if the means hadn't justified the end, and in wanting to prove those gods wrong, we'd given them exactly what they wanted? A world free from humans. A gods-only existence?

In which case ... what?

Fight harder. Persephone shouted from inside me.

I pushed her voice aside. Tried to focus. *One above. One below. Alive. Awake. A key. It is no more. It is no more.* How did I stop this? What did the prophecy mean?

Persephone stole my breath with her rage. It speared through me, my own anger calling up in response to hers.

The rift swirled faster. Like it was reacting to my churning emotions. This was a billion times worse than me sending spring into limbo. With that thought, I understood what had to be done.

Kai and I were not the prophecy. Or rather, we were. But the destructive one.

The version that could *save* the world? It applied to me. And Persephone. She was above. I was below. My realization was the key. The key to stopping this apocalypse and all godly destruction. Making sure it was no more.

I finally understood what Hekate had meant by Persephone and me being in synch. What my visions meant by insisting that all I needed was love.

Humans knew that love got you everywhere.

Love gets you nowhere. That was Persephone's—no, *our* secret fears. And it had gotten us nowhere.

Overhead, the rift expanded in an ugly crackle, consuming entire heavens. It had gotten us worse than nowhere. I flinched.

I was the synthesis of god and human. And it was *my* rage, *my* fire, *my* hate that had to be extinguished right now. My path was clear. I knew what had to be done. Fighting our fathers? Taking control of the minions? It was just more destruction and powerplay. How could I have believed that my outcome would have been anything other than this? No. Destruction was for Hades and Zeus.

I had to relinquish the role of warrior. My path was creation.

I'd said as much to Zeus and Hades before. I was the goddess of ushering in a spring free from the destruction of the gods. A world that allowed humans to bloom. I'd just been trying to do it with a blowtorch instead of a green thumb. It was time for me to remember who I was and what I truly stood for. Human and goddess selves alike.

It was time to forgive. Time to love.

I looked at Kai. Maybe a minute had elapsed since he'd realized what we'd done. He was rooted to the spot, watching the end, his expression shattered.

I touched his arm.

Kai stared at me, glassy-eyed. "How could we have done this?"

"It's okay. I know what it needs." I smiled at the questions in his eyes. "Love, baby."

Then I threw myself into the rift.

Twenty-four

I'd like to think that Kai was back there screaming a clichéd slow motion "Noooooo!" Maybe even combined with a run toward me, his arms outstretched, the pain at my sacrifice etched across his face. But the truth was, I jumped, got my teeth rattled as the rift knocked me around, and then I found myself back in the garden.

And oh baby, was it glorious. Gloriously terrifying. My vision had come true with a vengeance.

A carpet of lava bubbled over the ground, consuming everything except the rock on which I stood. The air hung so heavy with smoke and ash that the sky looked night-dark. But the lava burned so brightly, that I threw a hand up to shield my eyes.

Fat orange bubbles popped, turned black, hardened, and were swept away. Geysers of molten lava jetted, reminding me of Fee's chandelier. This was no less beautiful, but the jets spewed upward to heights of thirty or forty feet, infinity times more deadly. Fragments of molten lava flew through the air.

In the middle of it all, the lava swirled around the furiously blazing pomegranate tree. The fruit, the leaves, everything was gone save for the most barren skeletal outline visible in the flames.

I shook in the face of this devastation. It's amazing I didn't wet myself. Major life-realization-heroic-moments are all well and good, but my heart hammered and my brain screamed, "Are you freaking insane?!! You just threw yourself into the heart of darkness, idiot!!! And look where you ended up!!"

All of that combined in a hell of an endorphin rush that left my limbs rubbery. I'd been so certain that jumping into the rift was the way to stop the apocalypse. But this? I didn't understand this.

Lava splashed my skin, blistering it. I protected my face as best I could, but I had to get out of here, or risk death. I tried to step forward, not even sure where I could go, since the lava fountain danced all around me. But that was irrelevant. My foot was stuck fast.

Panic clawed at my throat. The stone twined itself around my feet, as if it was fluid. I knew how this ended. With me in a sarcophagus.

I fought back. Blasted the stone. Again and again.

I had a visitor. Kiki stood beside me on the rock. She didn't look particularly goddessy with her low cut zebra print top tucked into fitted jeans, and stilettos on her feet. Her red hair was as pouffed up as ever. But I didn't doubt her power for a second. "Stop fighting it. You had the right impulse. Don't ruin it all now." A lit cigarette appeared in her hand. She inhaled with an oddly delicate flick of her wrist.

"Go ahead," I said. "Enjoy your smoke. Don't worry about me being entombed or anything." I flung myself violently from side to side, hoping to break free.

The stone rose up to my knees.

"Sophinchka." Her voice was stern.

I stopped struggling long enough to stare at her. "What? You have something to say to me, Kiki? Some great wisdom to impart? The vision is real. Happy now?"

She blew a smoke ring to the side of my face. "This ... manifestation. It did not come from me. You saw the consequences of your actions. You didn't heed the warnings. Now you live them."

I slammed my hands down on the stone, now at hip level. As if I could physically hold it back. My body was a block of icy terror. Which was ironic since the air around me was so hot, that it had to be amping my core temperature.

The tree wasn't doing much better. I watched branches disintegrate and fall away into nothingness.

I glared at Kiki. "I needed love. I gave in to love. To compassion. I understood the gods. Realized I had to take another path. What more is there?"

She looked at me, puzzled. As if she couldn't understand how I could fail to understand. "You are missing the most important piece."

"What?!" I felt the stone cement my belly button.

"All *you* ever needed was love."

I screamed in frustration. That was no help. I knew that already.

The stone slithered up to my chest. Lava splashed

against it, hardening into chips. Great. I could be a freaking art piece in Zeus' statue room when this was over.

Kiki stood there, watching like she'd handed me the key to this whole puzzle and was waiting for me to unlock it.

I forced myself to take a breath, which wasn't easy, since the rock was crushing my ribcage. All right. I needed love. No, wait. She'd emphasized "you." I needed people to love me? Well, I had some. Maybe not all the ones I wanted, but good ones nonetheless.

The stone rose to my armpits. The tree had lost all its branches now. Only its spindly trunk remained. Poor tree. Poor Persephone. I felt for her. "She never felt loved enough. Never loved herself enough."

I hadn't either.

"Talk to me," Kiki said.

"Where to start?"

"Where it began."

I tried in vain to break free of my prison. "There wasn't much to it. To me. Sophie Bloom, the girl who flew under the radar. Hoping to feel worthy one day. With my mom. Then with Kai."

The words tumbled out. The stone slithered over my shoulders. I wouldn't be able to talk soon. "History repeating indeed. Persephone and I were exactly the same. When nothing worked to make us feel better, we raged and fought and ignored and yearned and hurt."

But what about filling that need with love for ourselves? Had anyone ever asked me that, I'd have scoffed at them. Of course I loved myself, blah blah blah. But I hadn't.

Not really. Even once I'd been restored to my goddess status, I'd spent so much time trying to find external validation.

My chest grew hot and tight. Persephone and I? We were worthy and worth love. Anyone who thought otherwise or tried to make us feel that it was conditional? That was their problem. Not ours. "We never believed how powerful we were. Not like superpowered. Amazing. Alive. We couldn't because we never loved ourselves."

A knot deep in my chest, deep in my heart, loosened, and I cried. For lost years. For broken hearts. For never feeling good enough, when that had never ever been the case. Ugly soul wrenching tears poured from me.

My compassion for Persephone felt absolute. Utter alignment and understanding. Her and I were one and the same.

The stone stopped moving at the base of my throat. The pomegranate tree had burned down to a twisted stump. But there was still life in it. Seeing that, my crying changed. It was no longer about grief. It became about hope.

Kiki sensed the change. "Say it."

I could barely get the words out. To me, always so flip, it was terrifying to say something this real. Part of me was still scared that if I voiced the words, the mocking laughter would return. I believed what I was about to say, but it was still so fragile. Its roots in me were still so shallow that this new Sophie ecosystem could be destroyed in a breath.

The rock rose to press against my jaw. It was now or never.

"It's not about being the best Sophie *and* Persephone, or even the best Sophie *or* Persephone. Just the best person. And for the first time in my life, I love that person. All of her." I could barely speak. The stone choked me, distorting my words.

But no one laughed. I was going to be all right.

Better than all right.

I raised my chin up and met Kiki's eyes. "I am divine." On every level.

Kiki beamed at me. "That's all you ever needed to understand." She pressed a kiss to my forehead. "Now end this."

In the next breath I found myself back on Earth.

On fire.

But I was free of the rock.

It was hard to tell if the apocalypse was still in full swing, or who was fighting who, because the flames consumed me. Happily, they were of some magical variety that didn't hurt, but I could still only see orange and blue dancing before my eyes. Only hear a crackling roar.

This was it. The final piece. The way to defeat Zeus and Hades. And why I was on fire. I had to become the ward of love that would keep Earth safe. So many times I'd pulled fury and fire and lightning into myself and projected it back to the world. Now, I simply loved.

For the first time in my life, I truly understood peace.

I felt flames shoot from my body to the heavens and beyond. Felt them burrow deep into the ground as I created a ward to not only keep Earth safe from the gods' destruction, but also to heal all the damage they'd taken in the name of their war.

"All You Need is Love" played over and over in my head. The happiest of soundtracks.

I lost all sense of time as I surrendered. To the flames, and to love. I closed my eyes. My heart felt calm and full.

Creating the ward felt like having a blood transfusion. My ordinary plasma was replaced with some new elixir that pounded warmth and strength and hope and fabulous life through my veins. The stronger the ward grew, the stronger the earth grew, the stronger and better I felt.

It was a rush. One I hated to leave. But I couldn't stand there impersonating a bonfire forever. I had a life to live. And what a magnificent life it was going to be.

As the orchestral sounds of The Beatles' song ebbed away, I knew it was time to bond the ward into place. The flames flared bright and hot, and then winked out.

I opened my eyes and smiled. I was in back in the garden of my reality. But it was no longer overgrown and forlorn under a gray sky. Spring had come. Full-on "sunshine warming my skin, birds chirping, flowers in flourish, trees budding, all-over-gorgeousity" spring.

The pomegranate tree stood tall once more. The sight of its budding, red, star-shaped-blossoming self made me smile. There was no trace of the waters, or the fire, or the rift. The sky was blue and the only things it in were fluffy, lazily drifting clouds. Earth had survived a cold, hard night of destruction and on this colossally fabulous morning of Friday, March 21, all was right with it.

I checked over my body. Not a scratch. Even the scar I'd gotten from Bethany's knife had disappeared. I was as shiny and whole as the world around me.

I was very pleased that my *Phospherocious* T-shirt had come out with only minimal soot smudges. I ran my fingers over the letters as I bounced on my toes, euphoric.

There was no sign of the minions. No sign of Zeus or Hades. I had done it. There would be no more godly battles on earth. No more innocent human casualties. Invisible though it was, I felt my love blaze in a protective ring around the planet. No gods intending harm would ever be able to get through.

I'll admit it. I burst into a happy dance.

Very clever, daughter. I jumped at the sound of Pops' voice in my head, mid butt-shake.

I straightened up. "Told you, I'd win." There was more than a trace of cockiness in my voice.

Hmm. This won't be our last encounter. I'll be keeping an eye on you.

As will I. Great. Hades had joined the telepathic hot line. He sounded a lot more grumpy than my father. Which didn't mean Pops was any less mad.

I felt their disapproval burning into my brain.

Oh well. "Sorry to break up the party," I said, "but the rates on these long distance conference calls are a bitch. So bye-"

Toxic black light struck the earth beside me, knocking me off my feet.

Kai stood before me, his eyes two burning black coals.

I stood and readied my light. "Are you evil twin Kai now?" What had happened to him while I'd been off with Kiki?

"Do you even think before hurling yourself at death?"

Another blast of light flew from his fingertips, exploding scarily close. If Kai wanted me dead, I'd be dead. He was missing on purpose.

"Is this because I jumped into the rift?"

He growled, his entire body vibrating with anger. Light exploded from his hands.

I jumped out of the way. "Yeah. But see? I'm fine." I stepped toward him, one hand held out as if to soothe him.

He fired another blast near me.

"Love's not supposed to hurt, Kai. Use your words, matia mou." I batted my lashes at him. I thought he'd laugh.

Wrong. My words infuriated him even more. His face was like thunder. I felt bad for the guy but nothing could shake my bliss vibe.

I grinned and flung my arms out. "Gimme some sugar. I just saved the world." Exhilaration flowed through me, making me giddy. I wanted to celebrate.

From the tension in Kai's body, I could tell he was keeping himself from killing me only by extreme force of will. His fingertips flickered, an occasionally deadly spark flying free. His chest rose and fell with ragged breaths. "I watched you burn."

I dropped my grin and took another step toward him. "I'm sorry. But I had to. And for those few minutes, it didn't hurt." My body went soggy with ecstasy as I remembered the feeling.

"Twelve hours."

My eyebrows shot into my hairline. "What?"

"I watched you burn for twelve hours." He shook with the effort of restraint.

Yikes. My mouth fell open but no words came out. Really, what could I say to that? I reached for him.

Kai took a step back and disappeared.

I bowed my head and sighed. Better Kai take a time out than smite me because he was pissed. Not that I blamed him. It couldn't have been easy thinking he was watching me die.

I'd only watched Theo for a moment, and ...

Theo. All the fabulous rush left me.

"Honeybunch?" Festos spoke in a tentative voice.

Oh, Fee. He'd had to deal with Theo's loss all by himself. Guilt and sorrow rushed in to swamp me as I realized that, in my high, I'd forgotten about Theo. I felt like the worst friend around.

"You forgot about me in your world-saving gloat, didn't you?"

I went rigid at the sound of the voice behind me. "Theo? Are you a ghost? Because I'll kill you if you've come back to dispense some kind of magical wisdom in phantom form. Seriously, I'll kick your spectral ass."

I couldn't handle a civilized chat with my floaty friend. It would send me on a one-way ride to nutsville. Although, I wondered if visiting with dead Theo breached the terms of the deal with Felicia.

He chuckled. "Not a ghost."

Slowly, I turned to face him. "Not Theo either."

Prometheus was back.

Twenty-five

Prometheus stood in front of a wild spray of spring-blooming poppies, their delicate centers ringed with pearly white. Festos hovered nearby. Despite the beauty of the garden, he only had eyes for his boyfriend.

Even though Prometheus was Theo-height, back at about six feet, this was most definitely his god self. He oozed that same supreme confidence, rocked those same gorgeously eye-linered eyes. Although I missed the glasses. His dark hair still looked like he'd been shocked into tiny spikes, and while he still wore all black, his clothing rode his hard planes like a second skin.

"Prometheus," I began.

"I'll always be Theo for you." His eyes met mine.

That did it. I crossed the distance between us in three steps and hugged him as tight as I could.

"Let go." He squirmed but I held fast.

"No. You didn't tell me what Cassie's prophecy really meant. You made me watch you die. This is your punishment, you rat bastard." I buried my face in his chest and squeezed harder.

"You got me tortured," he said wryly. "I think that makes us even."

I didn't care if Felicia was going to show up with some horrible punishment for breaking the deal. It was worth it, seeing Theo alive and well and fidgeting in my arms.

"I couldn't tell you." He broke free. "You needed your head in the game. Knowing wouldn't have helped anything."

"How are you even here? There was nothing left of you when the fire went out. Not that I'm complaining."

He motioned for us to sit down on a small wrought iron bench. Theo took the middle with Fee and I pressing close on both sides. Massive invasion of his personal space, but I doubt either of us cared. I needed to feel the solid warmth of him beside me to convince me that this was real, and not some dream.

I think Theo knew that because he let us crowd him. "You heard Cassie. 'Free the form.' It didn't mean my death. Exactly. Although I did die. Well, my human self did." He fell silent.

I gave his leg a sympathetic squeeze. Just the thought of Persephone's death upset me, and the only time I'd ever been in her body was during Kiki's enchantment. Theo had lived and breathed his mortal form for seventeen years. It didn't matter that he was now restored to his true self. Not grieving his own death would mean he was insanely psychopathic.

Festos beamed. "But like a phoenix, my Thesi rose from his ashes better than ever."

"Too far," Theo and I told Festos together. But Theo clasped Fee's hand in his and didn't let go.

There were no words to describe my joy. My blood felt like it was made up of billions of bubbles, a fizzy warmth that promised to let me walk on air. But I'd be lying if I didn't admit to a bit of old resentment. "So when you made the deal with Felicia?" I twisted away from him, unable to make eye contact. "No big deal to agree, right? Since you were going to die."

Theo leaned into my line of sight. He waited for me to acknowledge him. "Regardless of ... my death, no, it wasn't easy to agree." He winced sheepishly. "It hurt me as much as it did you. I knew Felicia would demand a price. You know your mother. Better me than Kai." He held up a hand to stop my next question. "I needed you to believe it. If you didn't buy it, she wouldn't have either."

I pouted. "You make it very hard to hate you."

He smiled. "I told you. I believe in you, Magoo. And I was right to."

I basked in his approval, squirming happily in my seat. "I did good, didn't I?"

"She's going to be insufferable now," Festos groused, slipping an arm around Theo. "Good thing we don't have to put up with her anymore."

"Wh-what?" I stuttered. Were they kicking me out?

Festos pursed his lips in mock sympathy. "She's got that kicked puppy look."

"Felicia and I had a little chat," Theo explained. He leaned back against Fee. "She reinstated you at Hope Park. If you want to go."

I literally sagged backward at the news. I could go home? Because more than anywhere else, that's what

Hope Park was. At least for now. I sighed in relief. But the warmth blossoming in my chest was tempered by the butterflies in my stomach at the thought of seeing Hannah.

"We still have visitation rights on holidays," Festos said cheerfully. But his eyes were sharp, watching me.

Ah. That meant that Felicia didn't want to see me.

I understood my mother in a new way now. I'd seen her pain and vulnerabilities. And I forgave her. For all her actions toward me, over our thousands of years as mother and daughter. Complicated didn't cover half of our relationship. Maybe one day we'd get to a place where we could finally put the past behind us and build something new. But if that day wasn't today, I was okay with that. Hannah, Fee, Theo, Kai—they were my family.

I may not have known what I was going to do with the rest of my life, but I knew it involved loving the ones most precious to me, and never taking them for granted—as much as I would never take myself for granted either.

Having Fee's place as my second home was fine by me. Hang on. That meant— "I get to see you?" I squealed. "Both of you? Felicia killed the deal?"

Theo shook his head and my happy bubble burst. He laughed at my obvious dismay. "No, Magoo. It was fulfilled. Think back. I said the deal was for the rest of my life. She thought I was being snarky." He grinned. "I wasn't."

My eyes lit up with respect. "You wonderful diabolical boy."

"Titan," he corrected. He shifted in his seat and his shirt rose up slightly. He tugged it down again, but not before my gaze dipped briefly down to those work of art abs.

"You are such a sad perv," he said.

"And you're a dummy who could have done more to mold your puny human form into this." I smacked his arm. "I could have been looking at that six-pack all these years."

Festos shot me a smug grin. "Why do you think I hung in there all this time? Despite his very bad attitude?

"I'll have you know I am more than my six-pack." Theo didn't sound particularly upset, though.

Fee and I exchanged dubious looks.

Theo elbowed his boyfriend. Then kissed him hard.

Fee looked a little woozy upon release. "Yeah, there's that going for you too."

My heart practically burst with joy at the thought that I was going to get to be around this for the rest of my life.

Theo stood up and held out a hand. "Come on, let's get you back to our place. You can't go back to school until morning anyway."

Fee wrinkled his nose. "Change, shower, generally don't reinforce that whole drug addled, runaway look you had going for you."

I swatted him. "Your concern is touching." Though he had a point. The last time my classmates had seen me, Felicia had been dragging me out of the Winter Formal under the pretense that I was high, and that the school had failed to take care of me. Ha, freaking ha.

Festos let Theo blink us back. It was pretty cute seeing how happy Theo looked being able to do it.

It was nice to be back at Fee's. Moonlight streamed through the far windows since it was about 1AM there, with the time difference in Athens. The place was still kind of a disaster. All our battle-prep stuff was strewn everywhere.

Festos walked the length of the apartment, slowly taking in the state of the place. I nudged Theo. "I give him three hours before he's hipstered it back up again."

Theo's mouth twitched. "You're being generous."

"I heard that," Festos said, already taking down the first whiteboard. "Less insult, more action, Titan." He clapped his hands together. "Old dusty books. Begone them now."

I scurried out of the room to shower before he could press me into service with Theo.

"Princess," Fee said.

"Goddess," I called back.

Back in my bedroom, I stripped off my clothes and headed for the shower. Never had hot water felt so good, or so deserved. I stood there, a ball of lathery joy, until I felt the water cool. Reluctantly, I rinsed off.

I padded back into my bedroom, giant towels wrapping me in mighty sexy fashion around my head and body. I had the best of intentions. Do laundry. Start packing a few things to bring back until Fee could move the rest of my stuff.

I threw on my pjs, proceeding to half-heartedly putter around the room and toss items I'd bring back to Hope

Park on my bed. But I couldn't focus. I felt restless. Incomplete. Which I could have attributed to a massive adrenaline crash after my most excellent humanity protection victory. But that wasn't it.

I sat down on my bed and glanced at my right wrist. At the cuff from Hannah. I stretched out my left one, turning my palm up to examine the bare skin. It looked so naked. *I* want a tattoo. I bit down on my lip, considering. A sense of urgency, of rightness streamed through me. Without a second thought, or a word to Theo and Festos, I slipped my shoes on and crept out of the apartment. Minutes later, I was standing in front of Jennifer's cabin.

Even though it was the middle of the night, the forest didn't seem creepy. Just peaceful and calming and gorgeous now that spring had come. Leaves were in evidence on all kinds of trees. Buds and delicately blooming flowers were curled tight in the moonlight.

It was perfect. I even enjoyed the brisk air on my skin, although I wished I'd thought to grab a jacket before I'd bolted over here. But my excitement made the shivers worth it. I approached the cabin, taking the stairs at a skip, and knocked on the front door.

Jennifer opened it. She didn't look surprised. Or sleepy. Or anything other than gorgeous and perfectly put together. Maybe she simply existed in a constant state of wonderful.

"You're back." She stepped away from the door to let me in.

"I came to finish what I started."

She blinked at me. "The roses? Yeah, all right. I kept the design."

I shook my head. "No. I had something else in mind."

Up in her studio, she frowned at my idea.

I faltered, losing a bit of the confidence to go through with it. "You think it sucks," I said.

She picked up a piece of carbon paper. "Surprised is all."

There was no painful fire arcing across my body this time. Just the normal sting of a needle permanently etching ink onto delicate skin. Trust me, that was enough.

Less than an hour later, the tattoo was done and I was back in my bed. My accelerated healing abilities meant that I'd skipped the scabby stage. The tattoo was pristine. I lay propped against my pillow and admired the design. Written in purple script around my left wrist were the words, "All you need is love." I sighed, utterly content. Seeing those words, the permanence of them, gave me comfort I was really truly going to be fine, for the rest of my life.

Whatever happened.

With a smile on my lips, I closed my eyes. I came to many hours later, with Fee lounging in my doorway. "Morning, sunshine. You snore."

"Do not."

He grinned. "I figured you'd want to get back to the other one in your misfit trio." He pointed at a large roller-board suitcase. "So I packed up a few things for you."

I yawned and stretched, feeling a delightful pull all through my body. The thought of seeing Hannah made me want to both sing and hide. "You're sweet."

Fee sat down on the edge of my bed. "You need to go see him today."

I pushed my hair out of my face. "I thought I'd give him time."

"No. Koko doesn't do well with time. He just shuts down even more."

"It's back to Koko now, is it?"

Fee ducked his head, sheepish. "The whole Hades experience. Both of us watching loved ones burn. It bonds a guy."

"You've missed him, haven't you?"

"He was my Hannah. Of course I did."

I gnawed on the inside of my cheek. "Was it really Theo and I that caused your friendship to fall apart?"

He patted my head. "Naw. Might have cemented it. He was from the wrong side of the tracks. Or maybe I was. Whatever. It was took its toll as we got older."

"And now?" I tilted my head, hoping to hear that things were fine between them. I loved them both so much. They needed each other.

Festos shrugged. "One day at a time, honeybunch. I'll go see him later. But you need to talk to him first." He wagged a finger at me, dad-style. "Now get dressed. You have school."

It felt heavenly to put on a totally me outfit: leggings, a short skirt, and a cute red sweater. I wore my red flat boots, accessorized with Hannah's cuff and Fee's ring. My sapphire pendant lay snug and warm against my skin, hidden against my skin. And my tattoo, my love of all that mattered, would be right there with me forever.

I looked out my window. It was a beautiful day. I had a feeling there were going to be a lot of those for a while. Scanning the bedroom that had been my refuge, I knew I'd always have it to come back to. But I was ready to go home.

I entered the living room and found Theo typing rapidly on his cell. "Hey, downward facing phone," I said. "I'm ready."

"It's not just a pose. It's a lifestyle," Festos joked.

Theo looked at me and slid the phone into his pocket. "Just emailing Hannah to let her know you're coming."

My stomach sank. "Thanks," I said, full of fake cheer. I'd been hoping to spring my return on her. You know, to avoid her requesting a room change or something before I got back.

"You saved the world. You're scared of facing your best friend?"

"D'uh." I grabbed my suitcase and rolled it to them.

Theo clapped me on the shoulder. "Don't stress, grasshopper. You'll be fine."

They insisted on accompanying me back to Hope Park, depositing me where the road to school met the road to town. I shivered, wrapping my arms around myself. The day was warm enough that I didn't need to wear a jacket, so I couldn't even blame my chills on the weather.

"Go see her," Theo said. "Festos will bring the rest of your stuff over later." He cast a final look at Hope Park. "The old broad looks pretty good," he said wistfully.

Theo wouldn't be able to go back to Hope Park. There would be too many questions. He was still recognizable, yet definitely not his old self. While I'd miss him being with me at school, that didn't matter. We'd have the rest of the world to hang out in together.

"Group hug," I said and flung my arms around them. We stayed like that for a while, locked in our embrace. Happiness pumped through me. I hoped I'd never come down from this high.

Festos planted a loud kiss on my head and broke the hug. "You good?"

I grinned. "I'm great. I'm the chick who saved the world."

"Definitely insufferable," he said, and took Theo's hand.

Theo gave me one last squeeze. "Later, Magoo."

"You know it, Rockman. Oh, and Theo?"

He raised an eyebrow.

"Go see Oizys." I grinned. "And tell her I'll be harassing her soon."

Theo laughed and gave me a small salute. "Will do."

They disappeared and I began the walk up to the front doors of Hope Park.

Seeing my school standing there so solidly reassuring in the sunlight, I should have felt excitement. Instead, my heart hammered. My palms sweated. I couldn't believe how nervous I was. It was ridiculous.

I marched up the stairs, hands in a death grip on my suitcase to keep from shaking. I flung open the front door and strode into the warm, familiar foyer with its red and white checkerboard tile. The school's essential smell of lemon polish and bleach soothed me to the depths of my soul. My hands relaxed.

A moment later, Principal Doucette emerged from the front office. "Welcome back, Sophie," he said with a warm smile. I teared up at the sight of him. His dreads hadn't gotten any grayer in my absence, which made me pretty certain I'd been the cause of it in the first place.

He chuckled. "It's not that bad to be back is it?"

"No. Not at all." I took a deep breath, drinking everything in.

Doucette's expression turned serious as he studied me. I tried not to squirm under his scrutiny.

Part of me wondered exactly what he saw? Could he sense, on some level, who I was? What I was? What I was capable of?

He put a hand on my shoulder. "Whatever you experienced these past few months? It's made you stronger. You're going to be just fine, Ms. Bloom." His eyes crinkled with amusement. "Mr. Patel, Ms. Jones. I'm certain there's a class you are both supposed to be in."

I spun to find Anil and Cassie, waiting for me to notice them.

Cassie bounced with happiness, all her floaty clothing swirling around her. Beside Cassie, Anil wore his sweats. He probably had wrestling practice at lunch. They were such an oddball couple, but the sight of them made my heart swell.

I was so glad to see this welcoming party.

"I trust that you'll escort Sophie back to her room. Directly back."

"You bet," Anil assured him.

Doucette nodded. "Then we'll talk later. For now, go

put your suitcase upstairs. Get yourself moved in today."
He patted me on the shoulder and headed into his office.

The second he left, Cassie and her mop of ginger curls rushed me with a crushing hug. "You did it."

"Cass, she may be a goddess, but she still bruises." Anil tugged her away gently.

I tossed him a grateful look. "Good to see you, Patel."

"Back at you, Bloom." He took the suitcase from my hand to carry it upstairs.

I smiled my thanks.

Cassie pulled me toward the stairs up to the girls' dorm, peppering me with questions about what had happened. Anil kept us company, not talking, just looking entertained as Cassie did enough babbling for both of them.

"How bad did it get here?" Hope Park didn't look damaged but I hadn't walked the grounds. Yet.

"The skies opened up," Cassie said.

"More like ripped open," said Anil.

We turned the corner, continuing up toward the second floor.

Cassie shook her head, remembering. "It poured. Like, this is rain city anyway. But I'd never seen anything like it. I thought we were going to have to start collecting two of every animal. And the wind." She shivered.

My gut churned. "How long did it go on?" How much had been destroyed? How many lives had been lost?

Anil paused when we hit the third floor landing. "That was the weird part. The bad stuff? It didn't last long at all. Then everything just kind of went away."

"Which made everyone freak out worse," Cassie said.

Anil nodded. "Some of us were watching online. Social media was going nuts." He grinned. "You should have heard some of the conspiracy theories. Probably still going on. They're calling it the March Miracle."

I snorted. "It was a lot of work and pain for a miracle, let me tell you."

Cassie put her hand on my arm. "But you're okay?"

"I'm fine. How are you?" I peered at her, worried. "Last time I saw you. Yikes."

She laughed. "That was a low point. It's all good." She took Anil's free hand. "I had a lot of TLC to get me through."

He went beet red.

They were awesome.

"Pretty brave of you to come back." Bethany awaited me. Goody. As beautiful and haughty as ever, she leaned against her doorframe. Well, it wasn't a welcome home party unless the evil neighbor showed up.

Cassie and Anil tensed but I shook my head and stepped forward. This was my situation to handle.

I looked at Bethany. Really looked at her, this girl who'd bullied me, tried to steal my boyfriend, stabbed me, and then attempted to take my place in my mother's life. Bethany, who had been the source of so much pain.

And I felt nothing. No rage. No thirst for revenge.

This girl before me? She was going to waste her life on anger and a burning desire for things that were never going to fulfill her. Never going to make her happy.

I pitied her.

Bethany may have sensed that because she took a step back, looking confused.

I didn't need to have a showdown with Bethany. It wasn't worth it. She wasn't worth it. "It's over, Bethany."

Her expression hardened and she opened her mouth. To threaten me, or to threaten to kill me—I had no idea. It didn't matter. She couldn't touch me. "It's really over."

It was her turn to study me. "You're more powerful. What did they give you?" I don't think she meant to, but she sounded hopeful. Like, if I'd been given something, maybe she could get something, too. She could have what I had.

It was doubly sad because Bethany was the one who always spouted all the New Ageisms about inner peace. If she could only believe her own message, maybe she'd be okay.

I smiled, totally serene and moved on. I could tell that my utter failure to engage—my total dismissal of her existence burned her.

It. Felt. Fabulous.

Petty? Oh, well.

I heard Cassie exhale as we continued down the hall. "Tense," she muttered.

"Cool," added Anil.

I slowed as I reached Hannah's room. Our room. Hopefully she'd still think that. If she was even inside. "She's probably in class. I mean, it's class time. I'll just put my suitcase in. Or not. I could wait until I come back with everything else and—

My palms were clammy with sweat. My throat was dry and I couldn't remember how to swallow, which was interesting considering I couldn't stop babbling.

Cassie nodded encouragingly. "You'll be fine."

I took a deep breath. I'd faced Zeus and Hades. I'd saved humanity from destruction. I could do this.

I wiped my hands on my skirt. "See you, later?"

"Not if we see you first."

Anil handed me my suitcase.

I took a deep breath and flung my shoulders back. Then I reached out, twisted the doorknob, and stepped into my room.

Twenty-six

M&Ms pelted me painfully. I jumped around, trying to dodge them, and flailing my arms to knock them
away. I didn't see Hannah because I was too busy pro-
tecting my face from candy coated missiles.

"You. Are. A. Giant. Bag." Apparently, she had not
yet reached warm fuzzy reconciliation mode.

"Ow! I'm sorry. Quit it."

There was a momentary lapse in abuse. I thought she'd
accepted my apology but I heard a crinkle, and candy
once more flew. "Did you stock up just to attack me?!"
I grabbed the corner of her comforter, held it up like
a shield, and stretched out one hand, letting my palm
glow. "I can hurt you."

"Rule number one." A pillow whacked against my
head. "No hurting humans!"

Tentatively I lowered the blanket, wincing as she
smacked me full in the face. "Is this because of the apocalypse?"

Hannah lowered the pillow. She glowered at me.

I held very still. In case she was going to pounce and tear my throat out.

She breathed heavily. But she looked as fabulously Hannah as ever. I noted that, while her jeans were a cuter cut that she used to wear pre-Pierce, she had on one of her punny science T-shirts, instead of the stylish tops she'd started to wear. This one read "Zoologists do it with animal instinct."

I tamped down a hopeful smile. I wanted to believe that she'd put the shirt on for me. A nod to our pre-boyfriend, pre-goddess days. "I didn't mean for anyone to get hurt," I said. "I'm sorry."

Hannah scowled deeper. "I know that. Do you think I'm stupid? Because I'm not a high and mighty goddess?"

Right. Not mad about the apocalypse. "You're worth a billion of any god."

Her glare softened a bit, but her fingers tightened on the pillow.

I put every ounce of sincerity I had into my face. "Everything I said to you. It was horrible. I'm so so sorry. I'll do anything to make it up to you."

She gnawed on the corner of her top lip. At least she was thinking it over. Then she smacked me again. "You cut me out of your life. I was stuck here not knowing if my best friend was alive or dead."

"You remembered me?"

She froze, the pillow held in mid air. "What? Of course I remembered you, idiot. We had a fight. I wasn't lobotomized."

I sank onto her bed, relieved beyond anything. "You don't understand."

I heard her clothes rustle as she sat back, waiting. "Then explain it to me."

So I did. For the first time, I told her everything that had happened since the night Bethany stabbed me. Everything I had felt. All the way through my time in Hades. Into the rift and the burning garden.

I must have talked for hours. By the time I finished, we had moved to the cafeteria. Had eaten lunch and seen the room empty out. French fry remnants sat on the plates between us. I'd been fortified with caffeine and sugar.

Occasionally, a teacher wandered through. But they left Hannah and me alone. I guess she had some kind of free pass from classes today, since I was back.

It made me appreciate how supportive this school really was. *I'm really home.*

I looked at Hannah. I'm not sure what I was expecting from her. Sympathy or horror or forgiveness. Whatever it was, I certainly didn't think she'd be staring at me like I was stupidest person ever. "Nice look."

"That's how I look at morons," she said. "And you're the poster child."

I kicked at her leg. "For what?"

She kicked me back. "Not believing in yourself. Not loving yourself. Gawd, Sophie, it took you almost getting killed to realize that?" She tossed her hair out of her face. "Pathetic." But she said it with love.

A laugh bubbled out of me. Surprised. "Ingrate."

"Annoying." She tossed a fry at me. "And I get the last word because you were really really mean to me."

I could live with that.

"Are you gonna move your stuff back in or what?" Hannah was back to glowering.

"Yeah. Give me five seconds. Jeez."

Hannah pushed her chair back. "I want to hit biology class. But you're here now, right? For good?"

"Yeah."

She stood.

I did too. Then the two of us rushed each other in a mutual crushing hug. When she spoke, there was a waver in her voice. "Don't ever do that again. Any of it."

"Promise."

I practically skipped up the stairs to our bedroom. I was giddy at the thought of unpacking. I flung open my door and skidded to a stop at the sight of Kai sitting on my mattress.

Man, he was in über poker-face mode. "I've been thinking about you and I," he said.

"Okay." Thinking about us was good.

"And how the two of us caused the apocalypse."

My heart sank. That wasn't the kind of thinking I wanted him to do. That was the kind of thinking that led to talks ending in, "I think we should just be friends." Suddenly my skin felt like it was the wrong size.

I sat down across from him on Hannah's bed, matching him perfectly in give-away-nothing blank expression, and waited.

He fidgeted, almost as if he were nervous.

That was sweet, but no way was he going to cute his way out of this. *He'd* come to *me*. And if he didn't have anything genuine to say, then maybe there really was nothing left for us to say at all.

Under the sleeve of my sweater, I stroked a finger over my tattoo. My reminder that I'd be okay eventually, no matter what went down in the next few minutes. But also my hope for our love and happily-ever-after.

Kai watched me, but couldn't see the tattoo. After a long, massively awkward silence, he spoke. "On a scale of one to ten, one being, 'of course I could never hurt you, my beloved', and ten being my imminent phospherocious destruction, where, exactly, do I stand?"

"Thirty seven."

He nodded. "That's pretty good. I thought you'd be angrier at me."

I waited for something more. This time, I wasn't giving him an inch.

Kai braced his hands on his lap. "Watching you, engulfed in the flames like that? It wasn't just your death I saw. It was the death of this twisted thing that I'd been holding on to for so long."

Whoa. I'd wanted genuine and this was as real as it had ever gotten with him. I kept still for fear of jolting him back into his usual mode of suck-ass communication and general disappearance.

He kept going. "I've spent so much of my life defining myself against my father that watching you, understanding what you were doing ..." He looked directly into my eyes. "Yes, Sophie, I did understand the significance. I was furious. At you. I felt like you had wrested control away from me and were resolving the situation without any discussion about my place in it all."

I twisted my hands together. "I kinda was. But I didn't have a choice."

"Let me finish," he chided. "Overriding my anger, was fear. I was terrified you weren't going to survive. Because it didn't look like Theo had. Terrified that, even if you did, what would my purpose be then? How was I supposed to go take the Underworld from my father after that?"

"But you don't have—"

He slid over beside me and clapped a hand over my mouth. "Like, five minutes without butting in?"

I nodded that I would be good.

He took his hand away. "When I saw you emerge from that fire unharmed and lit up with such joy when I felt so," he growled in frustration, then sighed. "It was too much."

I didn't know how to interpret this. "But you came to find me here," I said.

He straightened his shoulders. He was steadying himself. "Yeah. Because I realized that the main thing I felt was relief that you were alive. I want to be here. With you."

Cautious delight. "You're sure?"

He nodded. "Positive." Kai kissed the tip of my nose. "Your turn. What happened after you jumped?"

I filled him in on my conversation with Kiki and all that had transpired in the garden. "You know, Persephone had been trying so hard to live up to a certain image of herself that it snapped her. But I was just as bad. I thought I'd been living my life, kinda giving Felicia the finger, but I hadn't. Once all these other gods came into my life, my desire to be seen a certain way, to get validation in a certain way ... It just got worse."

I pursed my lips, thinking it over. "Ultimately, my big 'whoa' moment was realizing that everything I'd gone through just made me the best person I could be. I became whole. If that makes sense."

"It does." Kai pulled me onto his lap.

I leaned back into his strength, and his warmth, then twisted to face him. "Everything that was happening with Persephone? That was happening with me and sending spring into limbo ..." I laughed at the look on his face. "Yeah, forgot to mention that. It was because we forced ourselves to fit all these ideas everyone had about us. In the end, though, it warped us. In Persephone's case, to a point when she was willing to take everyone down because there was nothing left but her rage."

I stroked Kai's arm. "I hate that you got caught in that fallout."

His eyes sparked. "I lived. Maybe it helped me figure stuff out in the end."

"Hmm. Thing is, I'm probably going to spend the rest of my life figuring myself out, but it's for me to figure out. Just me. I'm okay with that. I started out feeling like a nobody and ended up feeling like a—"

"Goddess?"

I shook my head. "No. Better."

He nuzzled against my cheek. "I love you."

"So much."

He exhaled hard and grinned. "Good. Because who else would I match with?"

I scrunched up my nose. "Huh?"

Kai tugged up my sleeve, then his own. He brought our wrists together. Mine was palm down, his palm up. That made it easier to read: "All you need," across mine, and "is love" across his.

Incredulous, I stared at our identical tattoos. Like down-to-the-ink-color identical. "When? How?" I turned his wrist over to examine the full inscription. No wonder Jennifer had been surprised when I'd asked for those words. She'd already tattooed them on Kai.

Kai linked our hands together. "A while after I left you in the garden. After all we did, good and bad, I finally accepted that I didn't have to prove anything to my father anymore." He smiled at me with the full wattage of his love. "He's not the one I want to be important to. You're my tree. My roots and my heart."

Not going to cry. Not going to cry. I swiped at my eyes.

He cupped my jaw in his hands. "I want a life. Not an afterlife."

With that, he leaned in and kissed me.

As I lost myself in his kiss, in his touch, my last coherent thought was that while I didn't know what tomorrow held, it didn't matter. I didn't need a plan.

I had my friends and the guy who loved me. Life was pretty damn fabulous.

I was pretty damn fabulous.

And the kiss ... well, let's just say that fabulous didn't even come close.

THE END
(a.k.a. Sophie's and Kai's Happily-Ever-After)

Acknowledgments

For the launch of *My Date From Hell*, I invited a bunch of readers to join the *Sassy Girl Swoony God Tourney*. In exchange for an ARC of the book, they took part in all kinds of crazy challenges ranging from making playlists for Sophie, to casting the film, and deciding where Kai had originally kidnapped our girl. They tweeted and blogged and were just so insanely supportive of both this trilogy and myself. Thank you so much, darling participants! Without you and your excitement for this story, I would have had a much harder road to tread.

In the end, one lucky reader won the grand prize of excellent swag and getting to be a character in the final book. Thank you Jennifer @ Boricuan Bookworms. You graciously allowed me to use your name and aspects of your personality to create my lovely tattooing goddess. Everyone please check out her blog and show her the love.

Enormous thanks to Professor CW Marshall for his help with the Ancient Greek in the love ritual. Any mistakes are my own.

Elissa, Siobhan, and Adam, what can I say? You all encouraged my madness and then went above and beyond to make the book better. Sophie and I both were lucky to have you!

Every once in a while, I remember to look up from my screen and when I do, I find a family that surpasses anything my wildest fantasies could ever have dreamed up.

My darling husband Loreto, you remain my best friend. You make me laugh, throw me impromptu kitchen dance parties, bake me muffins, and still give me butterflies in my stomach at the thought of your kisses. Plus you check to make sure I'm still breathing when I'm lost in fictional mancandy. Really, how could a girl ask for more?

Finally, though, it comes down to this - my beautiful daughter. At ten years old, you imperiously demanded a story that you were allowed to read. And then, for the next three books and two years, told me with unflinching honesty exactly what you thought of them. You are my joy and my delight, and my favorite reader girl in all the universes, real and otherwise. So this one, like all the rest to come, is for you.

You've been reading *My Life From Hell (The Blooming Goddess Trilogy Book Three)*.

Turn the page for an excerpt from:

SAM CRUZ'S INFALLIBLE GUIDE TO GETTING GIRLS

I. sam

Like other chica chasers of the grade twelve persuasion, I've got my preferred player strategy: hit 'em with a killer charm offensive, rock the pleasure palace, and everyone gets respected in the morning.

Though it's harder when pushing a giant broom, dressed in a blindingly turquoise T-shirt with *Come see stars at the Galaxy* written in gold like a shooting star on it, courtesy of my lame job at the movie theatre.

There's supposed to be this other dude, Todd, helping me but he's busy bragging to the concession guy about feeding string to some stray cat hanging around the parking garage. And since nothing says psycho like hurting animals, I decide it's not worth the potential carnage to try and get him to do his job. I can't wait to get "promoted" to front of house where at least I get to upgrade from janitorial bottom feeder, cleaning up random sticky liquids I can only pray are pop.

So when I hear my name called by a familiar, sexy voice from across the lobby, I shove the broom behind a giant cardboard movie ad and take a sec to re-rumple my dark hair in the "I don't even bother with it" way that is Kryptonite to females before I turn around with my most charming grin. Not ideal but the best I can do right now.

It's the super hot Cass, nineteen and naughty in her barely there miniskirt, from the perfume store across the mall. Come back for her fourth visit in as many days, which I figure means something good. My player strategy guiding rule number one (stay cool) is firmly in play and now it's time to jack it up to rule two so we can get to the excellence of rule three.

Cass tucks her jet-black hair behind her ear before holding out a small square of paper to me. "Smell."

I take it from her.

"What do you think?"

I shrug. "Eau de cardboard?"

"Funny boy." Cass holds up her wrist and wafts it under my nose. "How about now?" she asks, all flirty.

"You smell how happy feels," I tell her. Because she does.

I'm rewarded with a big smile.

"Is it your break time yet?" Cass looks hopeful.

I hate to disappoint her. "Sorry. Another half hour."

She pouts. "Could you switch? I reeaallly need some help jump starting my car."

I'm a sucker for a damsel in distress, so I grab my gray and black striped sweater to cover the hideous work shirt and follow her out of the theatre.

Cass leads me to her sweet sports car out in a deserted corner of the underground parking garage and unlocks her door with a click.

She notices my admiration for the wheels. "Daddy bribed me with this, thinking it would get me to behave," she laughs.

I'm betting he regrets having spent the cash.

"Okay. Let me pop your hood and see what's going on." I reach for the driver's side door but she stops me, directing me to the back seat instead.

Inside, Cass stretches back against the seat, propped on her elbows, and stares up at me through half-closed eyes. "It's not the hood I need popped."

No dead car battery? I smile. "You lying little minx."

She cocks an eyebrow at me.

"While I'm all about the blatant invitation, maybe we could move this somewhere less public? Away from the security camera?"

Cass pulls a condom package from her skirt pocket and flicks it at me. "Let them watch."

Looking at Cass lying there all "do me", I see she is the definition of "a hot mess." However, if that's why I'm about to get unexpectedly laid, then go "team crazy" and security cameras be damned.

Rule four, kids.

I'm in.

And out in about ten minutes. But I *am* in a car on my break, so cut me some slack.

"Short but sweet," Cass sighs happily, as we stand back up.

"I aim to please. Even on a tight schedule." I hand her a chocolate bar I snagged for her back at the theatre.

She takes it and with her other hand twines her fingers through mine. "What do you feel like doing, Sam?"

"I have to get back to work."

Cass wraps her arms around me and pulls me toward her. In a death grip. "Tonight, dummy. Where should we go on our date?"

Just like that, Cass morphs from rebel delight to buzzkill destructo, coiling herself around me like a metal snake as she spouts off about connections. Bad emotional ones; not good, blow-my-mind ones.

"We just had sex in your car."

"Yeah."

"And that means we go on a date *why?*"

She waves the chocolate bar at me. "You bought me candy."

Oh come on.

"That's not some Willy Wonka loophole to what was so obviously on the table." I give a good wrench and manage to fling myself backward, out of her hold.

Cass sends a furious glare my way. "You are such a dick."

While unfair and undeserved in this situation, I can't argue with the truth of it. Teenaged bros are dogs. We're walking, talking, idiots driven by sex and food. We bow before girls' much more complicated minds and don't get why they keep holding our nature against us.

But that argument won't get me anywhere. Believe me. I've tried. It's my fault. I need a better exit strategy because it's the rare gazelle who enjoys the bounce then throws you your pants with a "don't let the door hit you in the ass on the way out."

I try reason. "You faked a dead battery to trick me into coming out here so I would have sex with you."

"Well, it's not like you said 'no,'" she retorts.

"Because I'm male and breathing. If there were going to be other conditions on this offer you should have shown me the small print. Beforehand."

"If I'd done that, you would have freaked out."

And there you have it, boys and girls. The place where my rules, carefully constructed to ensure a mutual good time, fall to shit.

The fundamental problem between the sexes.

You girls keep screwing up the game plan with relationship crap.

I mean, I try and take precautions. I stay away from my female high school classmates. Those red flags of puberty induced insanity and jailbait awkwardness? Back away. Quickly.

But Cass is an entry-level college girl, high on freedom and experimentation. So you'd think she'd know better.

I throw Cass my most charming grin but it fails to remove her scowl. Her eyes narrow. She leans forward, arms out to grab onto some part of me, but I'm faster: the gold medalist of the morning-after dash.

I fly through the parking lot, trying not to pay too much attention to the stream of impressively foul names she's calling me, which echo off the walls.

It's a bummer but kind of a rush. Can I escape the garage without getting caught?

Some QB-type opens his car door, hears a particularly inventive phrase from Cass, and smirks at my predicament, throwing me a look like I'm some loser who can't handle himself.

Suck it, monkey. What happened to solidarity?

I round the corner to the lower level and slow down, pretty sure I'm safe. Feeling stoked, I strut across the cement because until she went postal it was a hot time. I'm still riding high off it when I trip over something that doesn't like being tripped over, because it attacks.

I check my ankle and find red scratch marks from a gray, collarless kitten, who hisses from a few feet away. It's the kind of furball you could stuff a stick up its butt and use as a mop, it's so fluffy.

Whatever. I've got to get back to work, so I step over her but she snags her claws on the hem of my jeans, refusing to let go, even when I try and shake her off. That's when I notice the string hanging out of her butt, killing her cute factor but marking her as Todd's furry victim.

Just because I'm a dog, doesn't mean I'm cruel to cats. Especially scared little ones.

Gingerly, I pick her up. She barely weighs anything. I gently flick her ear and am rewarded with a lazy bat of her paw before she snuggles into me and purrs. *Soft and cuddly, just like a girl*, I think fondly. Her claws come out again. Yeah. Definitely a trend.

Just then, Cass peels around the corner, gunning for me with her car. As I jump the kitten and myself out of the way to safety, an age-old question pops into my head:

Why the hell can't chicks be more like guys?

And what am I supposed to do with a cat?

About the Author

Tellulah Darling
noun

1) YA romantic comedy author because her first kiss sucked and she's compensating.
2) Alter ego of former screenwriter.
3) Sassy minx.

Writes about: where love meets comedy, flavored with pop culture. Awkwardness ensues.

Tellulah's Other Titles:
Sam Cruz's Infallible Guide to Getting Girls

The Blooming Goddess Trilogy:
My Ex From Hell
My Date From Hell
A Date of Godlike Proportions (short story)

**If you've enjoyed these books and want exclusive extras, then come be anointed with gifts:
http://tellulahdarling.com/let-me-anoint-you-with-gifts/

I love to hear from my readers! Hang out with me:
www.tellulahdarling.com
https://twitter.com/tellulahdarling
https://www.facebook.com/TellulahDarling

Sassy girls. Swoony boys. What could go wrong?